THE SIDELINED WIFE

More Than A Wife Series

JENNIFER PEEL

To all the women who have ever felt sidelined.

Take the field again.

*A special thanks to Kathryn Biel.
Your insight was invaluable*

CHAPTER ONE

HE HELD AN OPEN BOX FILLED WITH ODDS AND ENDS—HIS ALARM CLOCK, the paper weights that used to sit on his desk. He shifted the box to one hand while he reached into his pocket for our...I mean for *my* house key. There was no *ours* anymore. Well, maybe one thing, but I was claiming Cody mostly mine.

He barely met my eyes when he pressed the key into my hand and lingered. I knew that hand better than my own—soft but firm, a comfort once. I pulled away, but his grasp tightened.

"I'm sorry, Samantha."

My gray eyes bore into his tired brown eyes that now wore the mark of his age. Lines crinkled where there was once smooth skin. I used to see my future reflected in those brown pools; now all I saw was a fork in the road. This was where we parted.

I used more force this time and took the key and my hand back, along with my life. "Does it really matter?"

He shuffled the box in his hands, using both now to hold it. "I didn't mean for us to turn out this way."

"I think you mean you never meant to get caught."

His ears turned crimson. "I never wanted to hurt you."

I wanted to laugh in his face—I was done with tears—but I was too tired. "Goodbye, Neil." I reached around him to open the door.

"That's it, after nineteen years together?" His audacity was astounding.

1

"You should have asked yourself that when you decided to forget you *were* a married man." Some emotion crept in, but I held steady. I wasn't going to give him the satisfaction of knowing he could still hurt me.

"Sam…"

I shook my head. "Don't. Don't give me another excuse that will never explain or make up for the inexcusable." I'd heard them all already.

His head dropped and he muttered under his breath, "I'll always love you."

I mustered up some energy for that laugh when I opened the door and said not another word. I slammed the door behind him and took a deep breath. My eyes were begging for relief from the tears that stung them, but I refused to let them fall. He wasn't worth the stain on my cheek.

I turned around and took a hard look at the house we had built together; it already looked different. There were blank spaces on the mantle where once stood pictures of a happy family. Only pictures of our connecting link smiled back at me. The walls too bore empty spaces where Neil's artwork once hung. I saw an empty canvas waiting for me to make my own mark. I intended to.

The first things that were coming down were all the light-blocking curtains Neil preferred. This house—Cody's and my house—was going to be filled with light and laughter. Cody. I sighed. I missed that kid's laughter. With the divorce finally settled, I hoped it would come back. Now that he knew his home would continue to be with me, he wanted nothing to do with his father. Someday I would have to help change that, but not today.

I crept up the stairs to check on my progeny. He'd refused to come down when Neil arrived to collect the last of his belongings and drop off his key. I would have liked to have missed it too, but someone had to be the adult. I guess that was me.

At the top of the landing I surveyed the loft that used to act as Neil's office, and the bedroom and bathroom doors that outlined it. There were still indents in the gray carpet where Neil's desk and bookcases used to be. What was I going to do with all this space? Cody's vote was for us to knock all the walls down except for his bedroom and bathroom and make a massive theater room. Maybe if he wasn't leaving for college in three years.

Three years. My heart constricted. It did that every time I thought about my not so little boy leaving home. I'd bribed him to stay local— free laundry and food on the weekends for the duration. I mean, Northwestern was a good thirty minutes away, sometimes longer in Chicago traffic. And it was my alma mater, after all. He'd said he'd think about it. But he had his heart set on Notre Dame. Indiana wasn't horribly far, but I knew it would feel like a million miles for me.

I knocked on the surly teenager's door.

"Yeah." He obviously didn't want to be disturbed.

Too bad. I walked right in. Maybe not such a good idea. Teenage boys had this pungent smell to them no matter how much they bathed or how often I sprayed air freshener in his room. It was especially ripe now that football practice had started.

His room was covered in sports posters. I saw specks of carpet under the mounds of clean and dirty clothes on the floor. His dresser, desk, and bed were also covered in a collage of dirty dishes, wrappers, and empty plastic water bottles.

Cody was lying on his bed in the semi dark, some evening light creeping in from the closed blinds. He had grown four inches just this year and his feet dangled off his full-size bed. When did he start looking like a man? He was tossing a football in the air and catching it with ease each time.

"It's time to head over to Grandma and Grandpa's for Sunday dinner." I took shallow breaths to avoid a full whiff of his room.

He kept tossing the football.

"I know life sucks right now, but Grandma's potato salad will almost make up for it."

His lip twitched, if only barely.

"You have to come with me to protect me from Mimsy. Your handsomeness is my only hope."

Mimsy, previously known as Miriam before she had grandchildren, was my mom's mom, and divorce was a cardinal sin to her. Even knowing that my husband—I mean ex-husband, I needed to remember that—was having a baby with another woman. That was a fun piece of trivia to bring up at parties. Neil left me for a twenty-five-year-old waitress and, not only that, he believed her when she said she was on the pill. The man that only wanted one child, whose mind I could never change on the subject, would be a new father in several weeks.

Joke's on him, though. He was going to have fun getting up at all hours of the night now that he was in his mid-forties. And the crime rate was up, which meant he was busier than ever as a medical examiner. His little side project had announced she certainly had no intention of getting up. She needed her beauty rest, apparently.

Despite all this, Mimsy still felt the need to shout out whenever I was around that everyone should pray to Saint Anthony or Saint Jude for lost things or lost causes, as she now liked to call it. And then I always got a kiss on the cheek because that made it all better. Hopefully she wouldn't be sprinkling holy water on my head tonight to ward off evil spirits. It's happened, and I don't even want to know how she got the holy water.

But that wasn't as bad as when she called the priest over to bless my home and check for evil spirits. She didn't tell the poor man why he was coming before he made the house call with her and Ma. He thought he was coming over to talk about a generous donation for the new high school the church was building. He was disappointed on all fronts. No donation and no evil spirits. So maybe he was happy about the last part, Mimsy not so much. She was determined that Neil and I should work it out. She told me to look at Roxie, the extra-curricular activity, like a handmaiden for my husband. And that it would be okay for me to punish Neil for the rest of our marriage for what he did, as long as there was a marriage.

Maybe we shouldn't go to dinner.

That would only make it worse. The whole loud-mouthed Decker clan would come here if we didn't. And, like I said, I would be using Cody as a shield. Mimsy adored him and shoved cash at him whenever she saw him. I would have his college paid for in the next couple of years if she kept it up.

Cody decided to keep a hold of the football and look at me. "I call dibs on driving over."

"Deal." I cringed. I hated when he drove and he knew it. Another reason to hate Neil. I agreed to birth Cody if he taught him how to drive. I thought it was a fair trade. Who got stuck with both, though? Like I needed more torture in my life.

He sat up and ran his fingers through his thick, brown hair with golden highlights he inherited from me. Okay, so maybe my highlights were grayish in nature now, but no one could actually prove that, except my hair stylist. I begged her not to tell me the extent of it and just do what she had to do to make it look like I was still twenty-nine and holding steady. I was about ready to celebrate the eleventh anniversary of my twenty-ninth birthday. You do the math.

Cody's eyes, which looked like Neil's, were killing me. Loss and pain reflected in them. But despite all that, he was such a good-looking kid, if I do say so myself. Thankfully, he got my nose.

"I love you."

He mumbled something.

"What's that?" I cupped my hand around my ear. "I didn't quite hear you."

He stared at those big, bare feet of his. "I love you, too."

That's all that mattered, right there.

CHAPTER TWO

AFTER NO MAJOR INCIDENTS AND ONLY ONE MAJOR FREAK OUT WHEN CODY didn't slow down as fast as I thought he should have at a red light, we made it safely to my parents' home. The same home my parents had owned since I was ten years old. The two-story, yellow house with red shutters and door had had some makeovers through the years. I wasn't crazy about the bright colors now, but my mother had read that some famous actress painted her house the same colors, so my dad was stuck living in Ronald McDonald's house. He wasn't fond of us teasing him about it.

My brothers and their families were already there. Two *Decker and Sons Landscaping* trucks sat in the driveway advertising the family business most of us worked for. I was still irked about being left out of the business name. So maybe Decker and Sons and a Daughter Landscaping didn't roll off the tongue, but I made sure everyone got their paychecks and all the bills were paid on time. So what if I wasn't out in the elements all day long, whether it was in the pouring rain, blazing sun, or raging blizzard? I still played a vital role. And so did Avery, my sister-in-law. The name should really be Decker and Daughters and Sons Landscaping.

"Let's keep the roughhousing with your cousins down to a mild roar tonight," I threw out to Cody before we exited the car.

He ignored me and hopped out of the car, intent on finding Matt and James Jr., aka Jimmy, my brother James's sons. Matt was a junior this year, Jimmy a freshman, and Cody fell between them. Three good boys, but when they got together, something was sure to get broken. We had a running tally—everything from electronics to furniture. Those three reminded me of what it was like growing up with James, my older brother, and Peter, the youngest. Nothing was safe. Thankfully, as the only girl, I never had to share a room with the loveable imbeciles.

Cody was in the house before I even made it up the concrete walk that led to the covered porch with my triple chocolate mousse pie. Hanging ferns dotted the porch and pink impatiens lined the walkway. They didn't exactly match the house, but Ma always did things her way.

A wave of noise hit me once I reached the door. Not only were the cousins already at it, but my dad and brothers were heavily involved in a Cubs game, and from the loud cheering, something amazing just happened. The Cubs were only a warm-up to the Bears pre-season game that would come on later. The Decker men, all six of them to my mother's dismay, would wolf down their dinner so they could catch all the action. We may not go to church every Sunday, but the Deckers never missed a Bears game. I should have known Neil and I weren't meant to be when he told me he didn't like football. I wasn't a fanatic like my dad and brothers, but football was part of being a Decker. I thought maybe the sport would grow on Neil, but it never did, not even when our son started playing. Neil hardly made time to watch him play. Thank goodness for the goofballs I called my brothers and the best dad around that filled in. Though it wasn't a role that fill-ins really worked for. Cody always remembered the games his dad missed no matter who else came.

Those thoughts had me looking down at my pie, wishing for a fork and a corner all to myself where I could drown my sorrows in layers of chocolate mousse and ganache. The sounds of family should have made me feel better, but all I felt was more alone. Neil hadn't been to Sunday dinner in months, but this week it was official. I was single, and my siblings were happily married. My parents were married and mostly happy, maybe a tad combative from time to time, but at the end of the day we knew they loved each other, and come heaven or hell, they were staying together.

I breathed in and out while staring at all the photos that lined the hall back to the kitchen and family room area where everyone was gathered. Simpler and happier times stared back at me. Ma really needed to take down my wedding picture. I stared at my twenty-two-year-old self in a simple silk gown holding a ginormous cascading bouquet of white flowers. I had an all-white wedding. What a dumb idea. Neil looked ridiculous in a white suit. I was smiling up at him as if he held all the answers and the key to my happiness. A handsome, intelligent doctor smiled back at me. And he could be charming when he wanted to be. That quality faded over the years. His hair had too. He no longer had the thick, sandy mane. I smiled when I thought of his rather large receding hairline. Served him right.

My thoughts were interrupted by my mother. "Samantha Marie, are you here?"

She always used my middle name because all good Catholic girls, like my mother, Sarah, needed good Christian names. Samantha was not one of them, and technically neither was Marie, unless you were French, then it meant Mary. But my father loved the name Samantha, and Samantha Mary didn't sound as good, so that's how my name came to be. My mother was distraught about Cody's name, because unlike my brother, I didn't head straight for the Bible to pick it out. I appeased Ma by giving Cody the middle name of Joseph, which was my father's name and a solid Christian name. Now Cody would forever be Cody Joseph to my mother.

I took a deep breath. "I'm here, Ma." I headed straight into the fire.

Avery, James's wife—and one of my dearest friends, coworker, etc.—was in the kitchen with Ma putting the final touches on a variety of grilled meat with enough sides to fill a restaurant buffet. In between that they were smacking away the hands of the hungry teenage boys who were trying their best to get a taste before the food made it to the table. In the nearby family room, Dad and James were standing up watching the game; they must be the ones manning the grill, or semi-manning. Peter sat on the loveseat with Delanie, his wife, who couldn't have cared less about the game. But she cared about Peter; it was apparent from her gaze. They had an interesting love story, but I couldn't think about it at the moment. My heart couldn't stand the reminder. Tiny, feisty Mimsy sat on the recliner with her Cubs cap on her silver head of hair, cheering as loud as the men.

Ma spun around in her 1950's apron. "Oh, good, you brought the pie."

"I'm going to put it in the fridge."

She nodded, but before I could make it to the fridge, Ma patted my cheeks with her wet hands. "Smile, beautiful girl."

Smile? What was that? And at almost forty, girl was stretching it.

I mustered up a fake, close-lipped smile for the woman who gave me life.

She squinted her pale blue eyes, multiplying the wrinkles on her forehead. She still wore her long, gray hair pulled back in a ponytail most days. Her willowy figure was softer now, but I still saw the beautiful woman that raised us and did her best to keep us in line.

She patted my cheeks one more time for good measure. "You'll get there."

I let the cold of the refrigerator ward off any tears when I placed my pie on the middle shelf near what I assumed was the dessert Delanie brought. I wasn't exactly sure what it was. Maybe a cobbler or crisp? It was hard to tell, and it may have been burnt. Delanie was challenged when it came to baking or cooking of any sort. Peter would be kind and eat most of what she brought and do his best to pretend it was the best thing he had ever eaten. Avery and I would each have some to be supportive because we knew Ma didn't like her and we knew Delanie knew. But it wouldn't be pleasant. That's why I made an extra pie and kept it at home. Hopefully I would get some before Cody found it.

Avery was next. She got her hugs in while she stirred the Decker secret sauce that drenched any kind of meat we ever had. It was a barbecue sauce with a shot or two of whiskey, depending on the mood of the cook. It was a good thing it wasn't me today, or none of us would have been legally able to drive home. Avery looked at home in the kitchen, but didn't look like she ever ate a thing. Probably because she and my brother were that weird couple that thought running marathons was fun. And even though Avery was two years older than me, her blond hair and petite figure made me envious.

Then Peter went off and married Delanie, a red-headed, model-looking creature who was way younger than me. So not only was I now divorced, I also felt like the plain-Jane of the family. Divorce had a way of sucking the self-esteem right out of you. Did I mention my ex left me for a twenty-five-year-old? She was gorgeous too. I mean in the fake boobs, I-starve-myself sort of way, but I would be lying if I said she was ugly. She barely even showed that she was six months pregnant. Or was it seven? Regardless, I hated her.

Dad saved me from my complete self-loathing meltdown. He brought in some more grilled meat from the patio and finally noticed I was there. As soon as he set the platter on the counter he wrapped me up in his big, strong arms, made from working daily at Decker and Sons Landscaping. He wasn't only the owner and boss, he showed everyone how it was done and wasn't afraid to put in twelve-hour days. His beer belly said otherwise, but he was the hardest worker I'd ever known.

"Sammie." Dad squeezed the air out of me. He was the only person to call me Sammie, probably the only person I would allow. "How's my baby girl?"

I leaned into his shoulder and took a moment to answer. I wasn't sure how I was anymore. I think I was over the shell shock and denial stage. I'd probably moved into the I-hate-almost-everyone-and-everything phase, but I wasn't sure how to articulate that, so I went with, "Fine."

He kissed the top of my head. "Liar."

Before I could respond, Ma shooed him out of the newly updated kitchen with the stainless-steel appliances and granite countertops she'd been longing for. She didn't like her territory invaded by him. And you didn't mess with her when food was involved. It was probably one of the reasons Delanie stayed near Peter. Someday I hoped she would find comfort in our family, that Ma would realize Delanie was Peter's choice. Like I said, no time to think about the lovebirds today.

In the midst of the chaos, the doorbell rang. I was surprised I'd heard it above my loud-mouthed family.

"Samantha Marie, will you get that?" Ma was juggling plates and silverware.

Without a word, I quit tossing the salad I was working on and headed straight for the door. A surprise awaited on the other side of the heavy oak door. I swung it open expecting to see some kid in the neighborhood selling something or other for a fundraiser, but instead I was greeted with some mischievous blue eyes I hadn't seen in forever. Eyes that always spelled trouble. But the face and body were all wrong. Those pair of eyes belonged to Peter's scrawny best friend I used to babysit back in the day, not the tall, sun-kissed, well-built man that stood there holding a bouquet of daises.

"Reed?"

He flashed some seriously gleaming white teeth at me. "Samantha, you look surprised to see me." He sounded disappointed.

"You've grown up." That sounded ridiculous. Of course he had; he was thirty-four, the same age as Peter.

He laughed at me. "You might have heard. I have a big boy job now too and everything."

Something Cody and Peter mentioned to me played in my brain. I had a vague recollection of Cody saying something like the new coach knows you and Peter mentioning at the office that his friend had moved back. I had been in such a fog the last several months that sometimes things didn't register right away or at all.

"You're the new football coach," I stuttered. Now I remembered a letter coming home a couple of months ago mentioning Reed Cassidy would be the new head football coach, and something about Coach Gainer being let go for undisclosed reasons. It never occurred to me that it was *this* Reed Cassidy. Even when Cody said something, I didn't connect the dots. The Cassidys moved forever ago and I hadn't seen Reed in I don't know how many years. He might have been at my wedding with his parents. Maybe?

"Your kid has a great arm, by the way."

I shook my head, trying to let all this information sink in and reconcile that the man in front of me was the boy that annoyed me during my adolescent years.

"Thank you," I managed to get out before realizing I wasn't showing good manners. "Come in."

"I wondered if you were going to offer." His manly voice was throwing me off. It was nothing like the cracks and squeaks that used to frequently come out of his and Peter's mouths twenty years ago.

"Sorry, I didn't know we were expecting company."

"Peter invited me over when we met for lunch yesterday." He held out the flowers. "I brought these for Mrs. D."

I hadn't heard Ma called that in forever. "That's sweet of you. She'll love them." I was sure I was staring at him, but I couldn't get over that this was Reed Cassidy. I didn't want to think it because it almost seemed incestuous, but he'd done a good job growing up.

Cody passed by and caught a glimpse of his coach in the foyer with me. "Coach Cassidy, what are you doing here?" It was the happiest I'd heard him in a long while. He even smiled.

While Cody made his way to his coach, several other family members clued in we had a guest. They all herded over like sheep to greet him. That's when I made my escape. I did that a lot lately. Alone was better. Or at least emotionally safer.

CHAPTER THREE

IT DIDN'T TAKE LONG FOR THE LET'S-MAKE-THIS-UNCOMFORTABLE-FOR-Samantha show to begin once we sat down to eat at the table that was probably groaning from the weight of the food.

It all started with the seating arrangements. The Decker family table, which was specially made for our clan, sat in the dining room that had been added on to accommodate our numbers and the abnormally large table. The table could seat sixteen, though we were now only eleven, down from thirteen. The space to the right of me had been empty for months, and the chair across from me and next to Avery would forever remain empty, a tribute and reminder of the sweet nine-year-old angel with bouncing blond curls that used to sit there. Our sweet Hannah, daughter of Avery and James, was taken from us too early when she was hit by a car while she rode her bike to the park two years ago. I could still see the vacancy in Avery's eyes and the grief that lingered in James's countenance.

I wondered if my own reflection looked like Avery's and James's. For months now I felt as if a death occurred, my own, my family's. I wasn't sure what or who I was anymore.

Dad blessed our Sunday meal. He asked the angels to watch over Hannah, like he did every week, and keep her until we could all meet again. So each of our meals started with tears. With the way this one was going, it might end up with them too.

The rectangular table always had Ma and Dad at each end, my family and Peter and Delanie on one side, with James's family and

13

Mimsy on the other. Not sure why, but Reed ended up where Neil used to sit. I thought he would have sat by Peter; after all, they had been friends since boyhood.

Reed started the commotion with an innocent comment when I passed the potato salad to him.

"So how have you been, Samantha?"

"She's divorced," Mimsy answered for me while rubbing her rosary beads and crossing herself. She didn't stop there. She dipped her hands in her water glass and tried to flick some at me across the table while praying to Saint Anthony to help me find my way again.

"Mimsy, that's not even holy water," I complained, even though it was Cody that got hit in the face with the water.

Mimsy blew me a kiss before handing over her glass to Peter. "Can you bless this?" She also threw some cash at each great-grandson at the table.

Oh, help us.

Peter tugged on the collar of his polo shirt. "Mimsy, you know I'm not a priest anymore."

That set Ma off. It was never good to remind Ma that Peter left the priesthood for Delanie. In reality it wasn't for her; he was following his own heart. I always warned Ma that I wasn't sure entering the seminary was the right path for him. Peter loved God, but I always knew Peter would want to be a husband and a father. Meeting Delanie only made him see where his true desires lay.

Ma started making comments under her breath about Delanie's diamond stud nose ring and the vine tattoo down her arm that I found beautiful. Ma was old school and believed tattoos only desecrated your body. And did I mention Delanie wasn't sure she believed in God? None of the rest of us held that against her, but Ma couldn't understand how her sweet baby boy ended up with a heathen. Never one to let Ma intimidate her or make her feel less, Delanie grabbed Peter by the shirt and pulled him to her. I would label their kiss as the kind that probably would have been better saved for private. Peter sure seemed to enjoy it, running his hands through Delanie's hair. Cody and my nephews hooted and hollered like the teenagers they were.

Ma couldn't take it. She slammed her potato salad bowl so hard on the table that some egg and pickle landed on James. James took it in stride and laughed while wiping off his shirt. That got Peter and Delanie to pull apart, albeit with a too loud suctioning sound.

It was just another night at the Deckers.

I faced an entertained Reed, who couldn't have looked any happier. "To answer your question, that basically summed up how I am."

Reed's laughter filled the crowded room. His jovial tones had a few others joining in. Thankfully, Deckers loved to eat, and before long, people were shoving their faces full of the feast in front of us. Besides, the men had a game to watch, so there was no time for idle chitchat, which was fine by me.

Except, Reed had other ideas. He was politer than the Decker boys and men and took breaths between bites; he was full of conversation.

"I didn't realize you moved back here. I thought you were living in Chicago," he said to me.

I took a sip of ice water before responding. "We moved back to Clearfield a few years ago. I didn't want Cody going to middle school or high school in the city." And I was ready to build the home I had been dreaming of. The one we saved for and Neil made me wait for. He was adamant that we should pay cash for everything. It was a lot of cash to save, but I guess I should thank him now since I owned it outright.

"So tell us where you've been, Reed," Ma interrupted. She always had to be in the know.

Reed turned toward Ma. "After college I got a teaching and assistant coaching position in Wisconsin close to where my parents are now. But when the head coach position for the Panthers came up, I couldn't resist being back at my old alma mater."

I never went to Pomona High; it was built after I had graduated. Back in the day, it caused a lot of heartburn when our city went from one high school to two; now we had three. But I was proud to be the mom of a Panther. Matt and Jimmy attended James's and my old school. Technically they were rivals with Cody. Thankfully, Matt and Jimmy ran cross country, so there weren't any hard feelings between the cousins. They were happy to cheer each other on at their respective events.

"How are your parents?" Ma asked Reed.

"Good. Dad finally retired this year and they bought an RV to travel the country."

Ma gave Dad the eye that said, *See?* It was her dream to travel with Dad, but Dad wasn't done working. Dad grimaced before pretending like he hadn't seen her glare.

Ma let it drop for now, but I'm sure Dad would get an earful later. She still had some questions for Reed. "Are you dating anyone?"

Poor Reed.

He took it all in stride. "Not right now."

Ma got my attention. "What young women do we know at church that we could set him up with?"

I gave her a blank stare. I hadn't been to church since Easter and I wasn't up on all the single ladies. I'd had my own relationship issues to deal with.

Ma waved her hand at me like I was no use, but then a thought popped into her head and she was back to penetrating me with her all-knowing eyes. "We really need to come up with a list of single *older* men for you. You're going to be forty in two months, and you know what the odds are of you ever getting married after that? You're more likely to die in a plane crash."

I dropped my fork and it clanged against my plate. "Ma, could I at least be divorced for a few weeks before we talk about getting married again?" Not like I was ever planning on it. Dying in a plane crash sounded better.

The "D" word set Mimsy off again. Dad saved me and grabbed her glass before anybody else got sprayed with her unsanctified water. But Mimsy still had her two cents to add. "Whoever she marries now will be committing adultery since she's been married."

Snickers of muted laughter filled the room.

I really needed that triple chocolate mousse pie.

Everyone guffawed at my expense, well, everyone but Reed and my son. I could tell from Cody's stiff stance next to me that he didn't need to think of both his parents as adulterers, even though he knew what Mimsy said wasn't true.

While I touched my son's knee, Reed, in a very unexpected gesture, placed his hand on my bare knee under the table. "You'd be worth it."

He removed his hand as fast as he had placed it on me. Then he acted as if it never happened. Or maybe he was disgusted by how prickly my leg was. Shaving had gone way down on the priority list.

I wasn't sure how to feel about his touch. That man hand didn't belong to the boy I knew, and neither did his look. And why would he say something like that? What did he know? He was a kid.

CHAPTER FOUR

NIGHTS WERE THE WORST. MY MIND NOT ONLY RACED, BUT IT REPLAYED every gut-wrenching moment of the past eight months. From the second Neil confessed his supposed one-time indiscretion to the real truth. Or at least as far as I knew. I wasn't sure what was real anymore. He was gone, and all I knew was the king-size bed felt too big. Loneliness filled the room with the tray ceilings I had insisted on having.

I stared up at the ceiling fan spinning in a circle in the dark. It wasn't far from how I felt. I needed to get off that track and start to live again. I needed to do more than go through the motions like the fan above me. Cody needed to see that his mom was thriving, not just putting one foot in front of the other. So I had been sidelined, benched really. That sparked an idea.

I sat up and reached for my laptop on the nightstand. I was declaring my independence. Not like the divorce decree hadn't made that clear already, but it's different when it's by choice. I did choose the divorce, but there was no other choice. Neil's one-night stand turned into a full-blown relationship. He blamed it all on Roxie; she wouldn't let him be. She threatened and bribed him. He couldn't say no. Those were all excuses. I had believed his lies of it being a one-night stand. I even tried to work it out, and we sought counseling. The whole time he was still seeing her. I only found out about the pregnancy because I took his car one night. Over the car's Bluetooth I heard her on his mobile phone when I pulled into the garage. Their conversation came through loud and clear. I heard the distinct words, "I'm pregnant, Neil."

All the hurt and anger I already felt about his betrayal compounded and left me shattered. The man I had given my all to had decided I wasn't enough. That was the last night he ever spent in this house. Now he lived in an apartment near downtown Chicago. Roxie lived there too, though he still wouldn't admit it to me. I'm not sure why he bothered lying. I wondered if he was going to marry her. I asked him once out of masochistic stupidity. I had learned it was better to know the painful truth than live a lie. And I had a right to know because of Cody. He shook his head no, but he wouldn't look me in the eye.

I turned on my laptop and logged into the blog I had started several years ago chronicling the Higgins Family. When the blog came up, our last family photo taken a year ago on the shores of Lake Michigan stared back at me. I almost lost it, but I was done losing myself. I was going to rediscover Samantha Decker. Tonight, I was more than starting a new chapter. I was ending one book and starting another. I began to type as fast as my fingers and mind would allow.

I don't think people read family blogs anymore, but for those that do and that don't already know, there is a family here no more. At least, not the one that was portrayed in the pictures and posts. I didn't know I was lying when I wrote all those sappy lines about how amazing my life was and how blessed I was to have a husband that loved me even if he at times drove me mad. But it was all a lie, except for my entries about Cody. He's still the perfect kid and no one is changing my mind on that, not even him.

From now on it will only be the Cody and Samantha Show. It kind of has ring to it. I mean, who needs a husband, anyway? There's a lot less laundry and dishes now. And I can even blare my music in the morning when I get ready. So maybe I cuddle up to chocolate mousse pie at night, but there is no one to remind me how it causes heart disease or a few extra pounds. I always wanted dimples; I might as well get a few on my butt. It's not like anyone will see them, except maybe me. Maybe it wasn't the best idea, but wow, was it delicious. More delicious than stale morning breath, I'll tell you that. I don't miss that one bit.

You know what else I don't miss? I don't miss feeling alone in a relationship that was so one-sided. You ladies know what I'm talking about. We are the ones who scrimp and save to get by in those early years. We do all we can to make sure their dreams are realized. That the careers they longed for become realities. We bear the burdens of day-to-day life, from taking care of the children, to grocery shopping, cleaning, and making sure a nice meal awaits them. We don't get days off or even recognized for what a luxury it is for them to have a spouse at home holding down the fort. Some of us even have to work outside the home just to make ends meet at times, yet we still carry the weight of what makes a family function.

We are still the ones to get up all hours of the night with fussy infants or sick toddlers. We help with homework and shuttle children to and from school and a million activities. Somewhere in the middle of that we are running the errands our husbands never have the time for. Oh, and we're still supposed to look sexy while doing it all.

But what happens to those first wives, the first string, the ones who made their teams winners and held it all together, who came through with miraculous saves in the fourth quarter all for their spouse's glory and honor? The ones who never failed to score and make it all count? I'll tell you what happens. We get tired, and crow's feet start to appear. Our firm abs get stretchmarks from bearing their children, and it never seems to be the same no matter how many crunches you do. Our bathroom counters start being lined with anti-wrinkle and anti-aging cream, anything to turn back the clock on the bodies we've tried so hard to maintain for them even though we never had the time to put ourselves first.

They think we don't notice the little glances that linger longer on the younger women that pass by these men we've pledged our all to. The ones that we've let gracefully age, and even found their gray hair attractive and took pride in their laugh lines because those lines reminded us that we played a part in their happiness.

For all our effort and sacrifice, we get sidelined just when it starts getting really good. When that career he spent all his time on starts paying off and your children are older and don't need constant attention. That place where you think you can get back to the two of you and start living out your dreams of traveling and maybe even making love all night long like you used to when it was all new.

But before you know it, the second string is called in and you've been taken out of the game. You don't even know why, other than the new lineup is much younger and they think the moon and the sun rise in the pig's pants. The new string only sees a paycheck. They don't see the blood, sweat, and tears of the woman behind the man that got him there in the first place. They will never know what real love is, or what they destroyed. They may score some points, but they will never be champions, not of him or in life. But maybe someday, when gravity and time begin to make their appearance, they too will learn what it's like to live life on the sidelines.

For me, I'm choosing to live by my own game plan now. I'm more than someone's wife. I am me.

I wiped the tears away each time I read over it, thinking I should delete it. But some voice called deep inside and said I should tell the truth. That it would set me free. And it's not like anyone would ever read it. It felt like someone besides me clicked *Publish*.

I set my laptop aside and lay against my pillow. In the morning, I would probably take the whole site down. The Happy Higgins blog would be no more. I wasn't sure it was ever true. But from here on out, I was living the truth. Cody and I would be happy. We didn't need Neil for that. We never did.

CHAPTER FIVE

I WOKE UP WITH A PURPOSE. NOT EXACTLY SURE WHAT IT WAS YET, BUT IT was the best I'd felt in a long while. My first thought was, what does Samantha like to do? I thought that was a good start.

It was the last week of summer vacation and I didn't have to go into the office right away. Cody was riding to practice with a friend this morning even though that made me ill. Why was I letting another teenager drive my teenager? Something about having to learn to let go. What I really wanted to do was wrap my arms around him and keep him safe at home. That was a no-go with him.

The question still lingered. What did I like? What did I want to do? This shouldn't be such a hard question, but my life had revolved around all the things Neil liked to do. He was more of a quiet home-body that enjoyed things like searching out his ancestors and writing their histories. He thought I loved being involved, and for a while it was interesting, but I wanted to catch a Cubs game once in a while or take a dinner cruise down the river. I wanted to take Cody camping, but that was too much nature for Neil. He would have rather watched National Geographic. Sometimes he was too smart for our own good. The doctor wanted to know everything, but he forgot how to live in the process. I had too.

It had been a fight to get him to agree to let Cody play football. He found it barbaric. He'd had to do an autopsy on a kid that died on the field several years ago, so I could understand his concern, but Cody loved the sport. I did too. Watching him on the field filled me with great pride. Reed was right, Cody had an arm on him and he was a strategic thinker. He was on the varsity team this year, but not as starting quarterback like he was last year for the freshman team. He was disappointed, but the starting quarterback was a senior and he was good. Cody would have his day eventually.

So, I loved football. But what else? A silly memory popped in my head of me riding my bike with my brothers down to the lake in Michigan where we vacationed each summer while I was growing up. Reed popped in my head—he had been there too. Reed and Peter were inseparable when they were younger and Reed happened to spend a lot of time at our house. I had forgotten he went on vacation to the lake house with us. He and Peter were pests. The little fiends would take my bras and string them up outside. Once they rigged my room with those firecrackers that popped when you opened a door. They put them everywhere, including my dresser drawers. The worst thing, though, was when they put a load of dead fish in my bed. I almost killed them. Ma too. I think Reed was a bad influence on our saintly Peter. Not that he was completely to blame, but Peter only ever acted devious around Reed. I wondered now that they were adults if he would have the same influence. And what kind of influence would he be on the boys on his team?

It was weird to think that bratty kid was now teaching the rising generation. Reed mentioned he was the new Algebra II and Trigonometry teacher at the school. I admit I was shocked. Not sure why. I mean, I hadn't seen the kid in years and Peter obviously grew up. Why wouldn't I think that Reed would too? I must be getting old. Ugh! More bad news. Now I'm single and old. Worse, I'm becoming one of those women that look at people and go, "I remember when I babysat you; look how you grew up." And I was referring to him as a kid. I was going to turn into my mother. I loved Ma, but that wasn't going to do.

I took a deep breath and focused back on the things I liked to do. I think I left off at riding a bike and enjoying the outdoors. Maybe I would get a bike or go to the lake. Or both. Why limit myself? Too bad Cody had two-a-day practices until school started. Leaving town wasn't an option. Part of me wished we could leave town period, but the custody agreement said I had to stay in state until Cody graduated from high school. Not sure why. I had a feeling Neil wouldn't try and see Cody even though he was supposed to get him every other weekend. Neil said he wouldn't force Cody to come, and Cody was already refusing. But I wanted Neil to try. His blasé attitude only proved to Cody that he didn't care about him.

I shook my head. I couldn't even think about what I liked to do without my thoughts being interrupted by Neil. Neil was no longer in my equation. I needed to memorize this new formula as soon as possible.

The light was now creeping into my room through the cracks between the curtains. Which reminded me, I was going to go curtain shopping and get rid of the dark, light-reducing panels all over the home. In fact, I was starting now. I jumped out of bed and, with gusto, ripped down the charcoal gray panels that covered the large window in our room—I mean, my room. The neighbors behind me, if they were looking, probably thought I was crazy, standing there in my pajamas pulling down curtains, not even caring that they were ripping.

I stood there and soaked up the morning sun. I could do this. Samantha Decker would live. Not only live, but thrive. First, though, breakfast. I made Cody a protein packed breakfast sandwich and a berry blast protein shake before he left for practice. I don't know how people with several boys afforded their food bill. Keeping one boy fed cost a fortune. And he never seemed to be full, especially when he was burning so many calories during practice.

Cody seemed to be in a better mood as we sat together on the sectional in the family room and ate. Maybe like me, having the divorce finalized gave him permission to start moving on. The coffee table had taken the place of the dining room table. I think since Neil moved out, the smaller table was less depressing. It was one less reminder that we weren't a whole family anymore. This was Cody's and my thing.

"So you really knew Coach when he was a kid?" Cody spoke while inhaling his food. It was shocking. He didn't normally start conversations.

I grinned, like a real one, thinking about that scrawny kid and troublemaker. "Yep. He spent a lot of time at our house. He was kind of a brat."

Cody laughed. I missed that sound. And somehow it was deeper than I remembered. When did he grow up? And was that stubble above his lip?

"I'm going to tell him you said that." Cody wiped his mouth with his hand.

"You can also tell him that he owes me a new Bryan Adams poster and t-shirt." That punk and my brother had taken a red permanent marker to both and wrote *loser* across them. Ma made them clean the garage as punishment, but I never got them replaced. Bryan Adams was my first concert and I kind of had a crush on him.

Cody cocked his head and squinted his eyes. "Who is Bryan Adams?"

That pierced my soul. Not only did that mean I was old, but why had I never introduced my son to the gift of music that Bryan Adams was?

I shook my head. "He's some old guy that sings."

Cody shrugged and continued shoveling food into his mouth.

"Do you like Coach Cassidy?" It was so weird to call him that.

Cody smiled with his mouth full. "Yeah. He's way better than Coach Gainer. He even does the drills with us."

"Really?"

Cody nodded. "You should see how far he can throw a football."

"I remember going to some games where he and Peter played." Thinking back, Reed was good. I think he was a running back. Peter was a receiver. I was already in college by the time they were in high school, but I caught a few games when I came home for the weekend from Northwestern. I could have come home more, but didn't. I thought I was too grown-up. And once I started dating Neil, he filled my weekends. Not thinking about it.

"It's cool he went to high school at Pomona."

"I suppose it is. I'm glad you like him. You better get going, or you'll be late."

Cody looked at the time on his phone and scarfed down the remainder of his breakfast.

"Please no messing around in the car with Hershel, and text me when you get there so I know you're safe."

Cody rolled his eyes and stood up. "Okay."

"I mean it. You don't want me showing up at practice to look for you."

He gave me a look that said, *You wouldn't dare*, but he had no idea what a panicked mom was capable of. I had no problem showing up at practice to find out if he was alive.

"You don't want to test that out." I smiled.

"I'll text you." He hustled upstairs to grab his bag and hopefully brush his teeth. I wasn't sure why I still needed to remind him to do that. I hoped that meant he wasn't making out with girls yet. He said he wasn't, but he was cute, and I remember being fifteen.

With Cody out the door and a million prayers sent up that he would arrive safely at practice, I decided I might want to start living again by actually getting ready. And not the take-a-shower, throw-my-hair-up ready, but the take-my-time, act-like-I'm-still-a-woman kind.

Maybe I would even look at myself. For months now, I had done my best to avoid looking in the mirror. The woman I saw in there wasn't me. How could she be? I had done everything to foolproof my marriage, my life. I went to college and married a doctor. I volunteered at each one of Cody's schools. I did all the wife and mother things, from laundry to making balanced meals and chasing away monsters in the middle of the night. I hosted parties for Neil's associates. He hated that sort of thing, but knew it was good for his career. Thanks to me, he came off as socially adept, though he would have rather been poring over ancestry sites or reading encyclopedias or all those sci-fi novels he kept on his nightstand. The ones that started taking precedence over me at night.

I had done all the right things, or so I thought. I even did my best to keep up my appearance, hoping Neil would notice. He seemed to notice less and less as the years went by. I brushed it off as that's what happens when you get older, but some of my girlfriends the same age as me made it sound like sex had never been better for them in their marriages. Avery boasted that sex in her forties was amazing. When we talked about such things, and yes, women do talk about those things—a lot—I pretended it wasn't my brother she was sleeping with.

With all my friends having the time of their lives, it seemed, I jumped to the obvious assumption that there was something wrong with me. Then, to nail that point home, Neil altogether quit touching me. Later he said it was because he felt guilty about the affair and he was afraid he might transmit an STD to me. It was almost as if he wanted me to thank him for sparing me that. Somehow in his mind that made him heroic. Regardless, all I could think about was how undesirable I had become. Those high-priced creams and lotions hadn't done any good. That hour earlier I woke up every day to exercise hadn't mattered to anyone. I began to wonder if *I* mattered to anyone.

Had I even mattered to myself?

I stood in front of the bathroom counter, hands firmly gripping the marble. I looked to the left of me, at the desolate half of the double sink countertop. I hadn't even bothered to wipe out Neil's sink in months. A layer of dust lined the vessel sink, which looked like a free-standing bowl on top of the counter. They were exactly what I wanted when we built the house. I remembered the argument Neil and I had about them. He thought they were too trendy. That stinging feeling was back in my eyes. I took some deep breaths to stave off the tears. No more. I had promised myself last week when I walked out of the courthouse with my lawyer after the divorce hearing. It was the final time I would cry over him.

Before I could look in the mirror, I reached for Neil's unused hand towel and wiped out the layer of dust from his sink. I was done pretending that side didn't exist anymore. All of this was mine. I threw the dirty towel in the hamper inside the walk-in closet. I ignored how empty the closet felt now. Maybe I should go on a wild shopping spree. But that would require looking in a mirror when I tried on clothes.

Back at the counter, I gripped the marble tighter and painstakingly lifted my chin. At first I admired the dark wood that framed the oval mirror above my sink. I should probably dust that too. I was stalling. My eyes shifted to that reflective material they called a mirror. Maybe I should have showered first, or at least run a comb through my hair. I did run my fingers through my medium-length, brown hair with some of those, um, highlights, the fake kind that were masking the shiny gray kind that kept popping out in new places. My hair was soft and thick, with a natural curl. That was good. Right?

I pressed my lips together and leaned in closer to examine my creamy skin. Okay, it was pale. Normally this time of year it would have had a nice glow, but I had been holed up inside for months. My gray eyes were looking more on the blue side today. I still had long, thick eyelashes that hadn't seen mascara in months. What was the point when it would only be cried off? My skin wasn't hideous, I mean, at least I didn't look like a hag yet. So maybe there were the beginnings of crow's feet. And my skin wasn't as bright as it used to be. But no double chin. I was counting that as a win.

I ran my fingers down my neck and across my chest. I felt thinner than normal, if that made sense. I had recently gotten my appetite back. Watch out chocolate pie, I was coming for more of you later.

In a brave move, I removed all my clothing. Maybe it wasn't some courageous feat—I showered naked every day—but today I forced myself to look. Really look. I touched my arms and shoulders. I even ran my hands down my mostly toned legs and my gluteus maximus region that was never going to be firm again. At least no dimples yet. I would work on those later. I wasn't twenty-five, but I wasn't all that bad. Tears fell. Not for Neil, but for all the months I had been loathing myself. For the lingering effects I still felt.

I met my reflection one more time in all my natural glory. I would be okay. I repeated it over and over and over again. Maybe tomorrow I would believe it.

CHAPTER SIX

WITH ONE LAST SWIPE OF THE PINK SHEER LIP GLOSS THAT WAS PROBABLY expired, I answered my phone. Cody's name appeared, making me anxious. He'd only been gone an hour. Barely enough time for me to shower, shave my legs, and put on some makeup. Every minute I was looking less and less haggish.

"Hey, kiddo, what's up?" I tried to sound cool and collected. Inside I was imagining a concussion and someone using his phone to give me the terrible news.

"I forgot my extra water bottle and towel."

"Uh-huh. And I suppose you want me to bring these items to you."

"You're the best." He hung up.

It was a good thing I worked for my dad. My hours were flexible, and it's not like I had ever really needed to work except for when Neil was still in medical school. I supposed working was more important now. Not that I couldn't live off the alimony and child support, but I couldn't depend on that forever. Honestly, I should probably be looking for another job to support myself. My part time job doing the books was a nice supplement, but I would be in trouble if I had to live off it. Something to think about in the very near future. Kid first.

Every time I'd driven the last few days, I took a moment to laugh evilly in my head, or sometimes out loud if I was feeling particularly ticked. Which was pretty much all the time lately. For spite, I'd asked for Neil's luxury sedan in the divorce. He loved this car. It was the kind of car that said he'd made it. Meanwhile I had been stuck driving our old minivan. Neil hated the van. It wasn't my dream car either, but it was convenient to haul Cody and all his friends around, especially when they had gear with them. That car shouted domestic suburban bliss. That in and of itself was a good reason to let Neil inherit it. He shattered the illusion of domestic bliss I had constructed for our family. He deserved the car that propagated that lie. And I quite enjoyed the fine leather seats and sunroof of my new car. Not to mention the navigation system and fantastic sound system. Except I wasn't playing classical music over it like Neil used to, unless classic rock counted.

I was surprised Neil hadn't put up a fight to keep his car. But he had surprised me a lot over the last year. None of it good.

I pulled into the school parking lot and noticed there was still a lot of construction going on for the new addition. The added space was a long time coming and the reason school was starting two weeks late this year, the day after Labor Day. It caused a big brouhaha in the district. People were up in arms that school would run until mid-June this school year. I wasn't fond of it either, but I had been watching my life fall apart, so it was small in comparison. Honestly, school starting later this year worked for me. Having the divorce finalized before Cody started school was a good thing. We both needed that closure.

It was a steamy end-of-August morning. Mother Nature had teased us last week with a few fall-like days, so the humidity felt especially sticky. I hated Cody practicing out in this kind of weather, but Cody assured me they took plenty of water breaks. The team had water available, but Cody was particular about his water bottles. He had the kind that kept water cool, no matter the temperature outside. And I was glad he still felt like he could call me. Besides, it gave me a good excuse to check on him.

The humidity was doing no favors for my naturally wavy hair I hadn't really had time to do. All I got was some styling spray spritzed into it. It had taken me forever to unclog the spray bottle; I hadn't used it in months. Not like it did any good, the weather was making my hair look like I had gotten a perm.

I shuttled across the parking lot to the practice field situated well away from the school. With each step I felt my hair curling. I almost used Cody's towel to wipe off the sweat dripping down into my bra. He probably wouldn't have appreciated that. Even before I reached the field I could hear loud grunts and helmets colliding. Whistles blew and coaches raised their voices giving direction. I skirted the edge of the field near some bleachers. I didn't want to interrupt or embarrass Cody. I could see him on the far end of the field practicing with the offensive coordinator and the other two quarterbacks.

I wrestled with what to do. Stay out in the sauna until some kind of break was called? Or pass Cody's items off to one of the coaches on the sidelines? I zeroed in on Reed talking to a small group of assistants and coordinators. Oddly enough, when I focused on him he looked up and caught my eye. He tilted his head, probably wondering what I was doing there. It wasn't like parents were invited to practice. Or maybe he couldn't believe I would show my face in public after the show my family put on for him last night at my expense. Or perhaps he was remembering the forest on my knee where his hand had landed. I still thought his gesture was weird. I looked down at my longish legs that were smooth as a baby's butt today.

When I tipped my head up I was surprised to see Reed walking my way, grinning. He was looking grown-up in his tan shorts and polo shirt monogrammed with the school name and *Coach Cassidy* written under it. Despite that, all I could see was the boy with a mischievous glint in his blue eyes.

On a second glance, maybe that boy had grown up to look like...what? Thinking it made me giggle inside. I had to press my lips together so that laugh didn't escape, but the closer he got the harder it was to suppress. How did little Reed Cassidy grow up to look like one of those men that graced sports and celebrity magazines? I don't know why I found that so funny. By the time he got to me a snicker escaped.

"What's so funny?"

Should I tell him? "I just can't get over you coaching Cody's team." Not exactly what I was thinking, but true nonetheless.

His well-kept eyebrows knitted together. "I'm not a teenager anymore."

"I guess in my head you'll be forever fifteen."

He let out a heavy breath and focused on the towel and water bottle I was holding. "Do you need me to give those to Cody?" His smile was long gone.

It made me realize how rude I probably sounded. "I am so sorry. What I just said was ridiculous. I'm turning into my mother."

I noticed his eyes graze over me. "I wouldn't exactly say that." His smile was back.

I wasn't sure what to say to that, so I made things more awkward. "I'm sure I'll get over the fact I used to babysit you and see you as you know, what you are now."

This is what happens when you hide yourself away for months. I must have lost some brain cells along the way. Who was I and what was coming out of my mouth?

He stepped closer. His eyes were laughing at me. "And what am I now?"

I waved over his tall, lean body. He had at least five to six inches on me, which was weird because I used to be taller than him, but I maxed out at five-feet-eight.

I sputtered for words. "You know, a...grown-up person."

His laugh was loud and in my face.

As if the heat and humidity weren't bad enough, embarrassment coursed through me, making me feel like I had been swallowed by hell. I pushed Cody's towel and water bottle toward him. "If you could give these to my son, I would really appreciate it."

He wasn't taking them. He could hardly catch a breath he was laughing so hard.

I took matters into my own hands. I would give them to Cody myself. I needed to be anywhere except where I was. I headed for the field as fast as my strappy wedge sandals would take me.

It didn't take Reed long to come after me. "Hey, Sam."

I ignored him. The situation worsened when several of Cody's friends saw me and some of them said, "Hi, Mrs. Higgins."

It was like my kryptonite. My feet froze in the sweltering summer heat. Everyone told me not to change my last name because of Cody, but I could no longer be Samantha Higgins. She had been destroyed. But to everyone, that was who I was.

"Sam, are you okay?"

I met Reed's concerned eyes and made more of a fool of myself. "I'm Samantha Decker." My frame shook.

At first, confusion flooded his eyes and then a softening appeared. "I always liked that name. It suits you."

His words helped me snap out of my minor breakdown. A friendly scoff escaped. "You used to tease me about it." Peter and him taunted me about having a "boy" name.

"I plead my brain not being fully developed yet."

I shoved Cody's things toward him. "I need to go."

He partially took the towel and held it between us. "Sam, I'm sorry for whatever it is you're going through." He didn't sound at all like the boy I once knew.

It was then I realized how close we stood together and how weird it seemed. I let go of the towel, leaving it in his capable hands. "Thank you. And I'm sorry for…well, for…" I couldn't articulate a thing. What had happened to me? I had a degree in English. I sounded like I minored in stupidity.

I might have detected worry in his eyes, like maybe he should be calling someone for a mental health evaluation for me. It probably wasn't a bad idea.

I turned to flee the scene. I made it ten feet before Reed yelled out, "I'm sorry about your Bryan Adams poster and t-shirt."

I stopped and smiled, but couldn't face him. I felt too much like an idiot. Cody apparently had a big mouth.

"Bye, Sam."

"Bye," I softly murmured.

CHAPTER SEVEN

I WALKED UP THE WOODEN STEPS TO THE OFFICE, STILL SHAKEN ABOUT THE events that had taken place at the school. I took a deep breath, or several, and admired the beautiful wraparound deck my dad and brothers built last year around the double-wide that was our office, or as my brothers referred to it, headquarters. I guess that made it sound manlier. Our "headquarters" were located just outside Clearfield near a nursery and an apple orchard. We had a deal with the nursery for discounted materials and they had given us plenty of referral business. In exchange, we gave them free snow removal service in the winter.

I was glad only Avery was in the office when I arrived. She was really the one who ran the place. She did all the scheduling and most of the communicating with customers, unless they had unpaid invoices, then that was me. She also did all the landscape design work, as well as any company logos or materials. She had such a talent. She could transform any yard or business front.

James and Avery made a good team. His knowledge of plants, coupled with her gift, is what put us on the map. Their work had been showcased in several model homes and dozens of businesses, including large corporations in the Chicagoland area. They were the perfect couple, if there ever was such a thing. I would be jealous, but they deserved it. Not to say I hadn't wished for a relationship like theirs. The one where the husband couldn't keep his hands off his wife and she couldn't get enough of him even though they'd been together for over twenty years. Every time James would smack Avery's butt in the office, I would think, why doesn't Neil ever do that? Or why didn't he undress me with his eyes? Roxie popped into my head. I pushed the tramp back out. Mostly. How could I not compare myself with her? But it wasn't only her. I had lost my luster long before she entered the picture.

I shook my head and begged the tears to take a hike. I was Samantha Decker. Which reminded me of how ridiculous I'd sounded at the football field. I sighed and smoothed out my poly-cotton sundress before heading in.

Avery's gorgeous blonde head popped up from the front desk when I walked in to the jangle of the bell. "Wow. Look at you. What's the occasion?"

"What do you mean?" I shut the door to revel in the cool inside air.

She gave me that smile that said, *I think you need help.* Believe me, I knew.

"Oh, honey, did you look in the mirror?"

Wait. I hadn't told her about my mirror aversion, had I? I thought I kept that one close to the vest. She basically knew everything else about my pathetic existence, but that tidbit seemed better to keep private.

I nodded in response to her question.

"Did you notice anything?"

I wasn't sure where she was going with this. "I think I might have lost a few pounds, but don't worry, I plan on making those up." Not like losing a few pounds hurt me.

She laughed. "I was talking about how sexy you look today. I've always been jealous of your naturally curly hair. It has this 1980's pin-up-poster-girl vibe to it."

"What?" I ran my fingers through my unruly hair. "I haven't looked sexy in at least sixteen years."

She shook her head at me. "That's a negative. Maybe you haven't felt it, but whether you believe it or not, you're one hot mama."

"Did you fall and hit your head this morning when you went running?"

She laughed the daintiest, cutest laugh ever. "I don't think I'm the one with head issues here."

"Tell me about it." I related my recent mortifying tale to her.

She came around her desk and hugged me. She was so petite. I towered over her when I wore any sort of a heel.

For a tiny thing, she was strong and squeezed hard. "You're brave and beautiful, and you're going to get through this."

"You sound like those positive affirmation skits from *Saturday Night Live*."

"Well, gosh darn it, people do like you," she mocked the skit.

"I'm not so sure Reed Cassidy does anymore. Can you believe I called him a grown-up?"

She released me. "Serves him right. The snot snuck into the champagne at my wedding."

"I totally forgot about that. Ma was so mad. I think even Peter drank some." They couldn't have been older than thirteen or fourteen.

"I do have to say, though, he grew up to look mighty fine."

"Avery."

"What? I mean, it's not like I want to leave James for him. But don't tell me you haven't noticed that he kind of has it going on."

"I babysat him. If I thought like that I would be a pedophile."

Her dainty laugh turned into a very un-lady-like snort. "You're not even six years older than him. And it's not like you changed his diapers or anything, or did you?"

"No. I think he and Peter became friends in the fourth grade."

"Then you can totally admire his..."

"His what?"

"Oh, never mind. If you haven't noticed already, I can't help you. But seriously, check out his butt the next time you see him."

She got me to laugh. "Does James know you checked out his butt?"

"He was the one who pointed it out to me." She gave me a devious smile.

I headed for my office in the back, smiling at her attempts to make me feel better.

"Hey," she called out. "I read your blog post this morning. It was poignant and tragically beautiful."

I turned back to face her. "Oh. I forgot about that. I think I'm going to delete it."

"Don't. It's a good reminder."

"Of how much my life sucks?"

"Not at all. It's a reminder that even the best of us must go through the worst, but it only makes us better." She more than anyone knew that. Losing Hannah was the worst of the worst. How she still smiled and functioned made me admire her even more.

"Have I mentioned lately how glad I am that James was lucky enough to coerce you into marrying into our family?" The day James brought her home from the gym my senior year of high school was a game changing day for our family. James had some chasing to do, but he knew what he had in her and never gave up.

"If you hadn't been part of the package, I would have said no." She went back to work as if she hadn't made my day. She had no idea what her friendship had meant to me over the years, and especially this last year. She was a sister to me in the truest sense of the word.

I got settled at my desk and realized what a mess it had become. I used to be so organized you would hardly ever find a piece a paper on my desk. Now it was covered in invoices that needed to be filed, along with a few granola bar wrappers. That was changing, starting now. I was going back to the land of the living. Barely functioning wasn't cutting it. How could I expect Cody to move on if I didn't?

I took the first hour of my day and cleaned my entire office, including dusting. I didn't pause until I found the picture of Neil and me I had kept stashed in my top drawer. It was one from our honeymoon in London. After he told me about the affair, he'd talked about going there again. He knew I always wanted to go back. But I didn't want to go back under those circumstances. When he told me about Roxie, the thought of him touching me made me physically ill. Besides, he probably would have only done some family research. It wouldn't have been the romantic trip that our honeymoon had been. I stared at the young couple with stars in their eyes riding on top of a double decker bus. Who would have ever thought they would end up like this? Who would have ever thought that man would quit looking at me as if I was his one and only?

No crying. I steeled myself and tore the picture into pieces before tossing it in the wastebasket.

Going through this exercise reminded me of something our therapist said to Neil. He told Neil that he needed to learn to get out of his head. To look around and see, not only what he was missing, but to see what I had done for our family, for him. I didn't want to become a victim of my own head. I didn't want to miss out on life, especially Cody's life.

I took that moment to log into my computer and volunteer for the football booster club. I could help sell tickets and merchandise at the school before game days. I would also tell Dad that our business would sponsor an ad in the programs they handed out at each game. I would ask Avery if she could make an ad or maybe repurpose one we already used.

I sat back and stared at the screen. I could do this. Like everything else, I was going to keep saying it until I believed it.

CHAPTER EIGHT

THE THING ABOUT MARRYING SOMEONE IS THAT YOU CAN DIVORCE A MAN, but not his mother. At least not Neil's mother. I loved her as much as I did my own. Gelaire Higgins was and is pink fuzzy perfection. I wasn't sure how someone could be pink and fuzzy, but I'd had a pink fuzzy robe once upon a time, and she made me feel like that robe. Warm, cozy, safe, and loved. From the first moment I met her, I knew I would love her forever. She wrapped me in her arms that first meeting and told me we would be quick friends. She was right. I loved her before her son. She was one of the reasons I agreed to be Neil's wife. I mean, how could a woman like her not raise a good husband? She had. He used to be.

Gelaire lived in a Greystone townhome in one of the historic districts of Chicago. She was close to Lake Michigan and the cutest coffee shops around. A day with her meant sipping on tea and eating amazing peanut butter sugar cookies from the bakery in her neighborhood. It also meant taking her into the suburbs for groceries. She hadn't driven in a good ten years. Chicago traffic frightened her like it should any sane person, but the older she got, the less she could handle it. Her faculties were all intact and her sight was still good for being in her seventies, but she was smart enough to know she shouldn't drive anymore.

For the last ten years, I had been taking her to the store and spending my Tuesdays with her. It was like that book, but this was Tuesdays with Gelaire. Her other son, Anderson, and his wife, Nina, lived in Ohio. Neil was too wrapped up in himself and his career to take care of his mom, so that left me, and you don't know how glad I was about it. I looked forward to Tuesday every week.

Gelaire's home, which she had shared with Neil's father, who passed away from cardiac arrest before I ever entered the picture, was like walking into a museum. The historic Greystone held treasures from around the world—masks from Africa, wood carvings from South America, books from dozens of countries. Oh, the books. Gelaire owned a first edition of *Pride and Prejudice*. I admired it under its glass case every time I visited.

Neil's father, William, was a professor of fine arts, so their home was riddled with paintings and sculptures. Gelaire was an heiress of sorts. Not to a massive fortune, but one large enough to support their travels and penchant for collecting art. Gelaire's grandfather had owned large chunks of real estate in Chicago a long time ago, including the Greystone she lived in now. When he died, most of his assets were sold and divided among his remaining heirs, but the Greystone was promised to Gelaire and Gelaire alone. Her grandfather knew it was her favorite, and from the stories Gelaire had told of him, I think she was his favorite. Gelaire was the one to care for her grandfather in his old age, even spoon feeding him when it came to that.

Today was Tuesday, so I parked as usual on the street in front of the three-story Greystone with a turret. The first time I saw it, I thought it looked like an urban fairytale come to life. I imagined Neil as the prince. I was twenty; what did I know other than I was dating an attractive med student and his mother lived in one of the most expensive parts of town. I was naïve to think I had arrived. But I blamed Neil for allowing me to think that way and treating me like a princess. He was so romantic those first years, even though his coursework, residency, and fellowship were grueling. He always made time to call me or slip a red rose and a note under the windshield wiper of my car. The man could wax poetic, and he used names and terms I had to look up, like *mo chuisle*, which meant *my pulse*, or *buah hatiku* that translated into *fruit of my heart*. They all meant the same thing; he was crazy about me. And I for him.

I had to quit thinking like this. I had tortured myself enough trying to figure out where it all went wrong. And all that mattered was it went wrong. There was nothing I could do about it except move on.

I pulled myself together before I walked up the steps to the covered stone porch. I knocked on the black double doors before I unlocked them and let myself in.

"Gelaire, I'm here," I called out into the foyer.

Stepping into her home was like stepping into another time. A wooden spiral staircase greeted me on the left, and to the center was a round antique table with a crystal chandelier hanging above it. Neo-classic artwork filled the walls. Cody always snickered at the sculpture of the naked man that stood in the corner. One time I brought Mimsy here, and she had to touch it, and I mean *every* part. She informed us all it was anatomically correct. Then she made mention of how much she missed Grandpa. I'd never brought her back even though Gelaire found her to be hysterical.

Gelaire's light frame and lighter steps made it look like she was floating down the spiral staircase. The cream chiffon dress added to the illusion.

"Love, you're here." Her pure white hair capped her head like a halo. Her smile made her look more angelic.

I greeted her at the bottom of the staircase. We were about the same height, and when we embraced, she pressed her soft wrinkled cheek against mine. She smelled like lavender and all good things.

Her grip was tighter than normal. Moisture landed on my bare shoulder.

"Gelaire, it's okay." I knew it would be emotional the first time I saw her after the divorce was finalized.

"No. No. It's not. I knew the divorce needed to happen, but how I wish it wouldn't have."

"I'm still your daughter." I held on tighter.

"Forever."

I was so happy she felt that way too.

She kissed my cheek. "I'm not talking to Neil for at least a month. I'm very distraught over the whole situation. How could he give me another grandchild under these circumstances? The thought of that woman bearing a Higgins is detestable. My dear William must be roll-ing over in his grave."

"It's not the baby's fault," I gently reminded her.

She sighed. "You're right, but this is so wrong."

I nodded against her.

She leaned back. Her worried brown eyes met mine. "I'm sorry, love, you probably don't want to talk about my moronic son. I don't know what possessed him to ever let you go."

I had to bite the inside of my cheek so I didn't cry. "All you have to do is look at Roxie." There was no need to wonder. She was a bombshell with curves in all the right places.

"Do not speak her name in this house." She ran her delicate hand down my hair. "This is not about you, though I'm sure you feel like it is. This is all him. And unfortunately, he will come to see what a grave error he made. Deep down, I think he already knows. I fear for him once he admits it to himself."

I shrugged. "What's done is done. And he knew very well what he was doing."

Tears filled her eyes. "You're absolutely right. Let's go shopping. I'm going to buy you something pretty."

I grinned. "I don't think they sell pretty things at the market."

"That's why we must stop at the boutique first."

That was the thing about Gelaire. She shopped at boutiques and bought *pieces*, never *outfits*. I wasn't sure she had ever stepped foot in a mall. Don't get me wrong, she wasn't a snob and she never looked down on my blue-collar family. She just lived a very different lifestyle.

I think it was part of the attraction for me at first. It was fun to go to symphonies and lectures about European history. It was different than watching sports or going to obnoxious barbecues. I could honestly say I loved both, but Neil never could. He never enjoyed my family the way I enjoyed his. He began to complain about Sunday dinners and the constant sports on the TV at my parents' home. My brothers were too loud for his taste and he couldn't understand why no one wanted him to discuss his work at the dinner table. He dissected dead bodies and visited crime scenes for a living. That should have been his first clue. It didn't matter that he had found bizarre items like diamond bracelets in stomachs. That would have been okay to mention, but he would go into detail about the fluids and smell involved until we were all ready to toss our cookies.

I focused back on Gelaire. I had to quit thinking about her son. "You don't need to buy me anything."

"Of course I don't, that's what makes it so much fun. Besides, every single woman needs a fabulous little black number."

"I don't plan on dating anytime soon. Possibly ever."

She took my hands and stood back to look me over. "You are too gorgeous inside and out, love, to stay single forever."

"You might need an eye exam."

She squeezed my hands. "I know your confidence has been shaken, but some day you will see what a catch you are, and that age has only refined you. Mark my words, forty is amazing. If I could choose any age, I would choose my forties again."

"Really?"

She nodded. "Oh, yes. There is a confidence forty lends while not being cocky, and you're still sexy as hell at that age."

"Gelaire!"

"What? 'Hell' is a perfectly good noun."

I laughed, like in-my-gut laughed. She was always so proper. I had never heard her swear.

"It's good to hear you laugh again. Perhaps I will say 'hell' more often."

"I love you."

She pulled me to her once again. "And I you."

CHAPTER NINE

I DID COME HOME WITH A SEXY LITTLE BLACK THING OF A DRESS. NOT SURE where I was going to wear it to or why I let Gelaire talk me into getting it. Maybe because it was the first time in a long time I felt like a woman when I tried it on. And it was the first time since yesterday morning I looked at myself in the mirror for longer than two seconds. In fact, I stared at myself for a good five, pulling my hair up, sweeping it to the side to see what worked best with the dress. I stood on my tip toes, checking out every angle of the spaghetti-strap dress. Gelaire also insisted on buying me the most expensive Italian leather high heels that felt like butter. Gorgeous and comfortable was a win. I still wasn't sure when I would ever use them, except she did mention me escorting her to some concert in the fall. Normally that was Neil's job, but she wasn't fond of her son at the moment.

She was especially upset with his neglect of Cody. She begged me to bring him by before school started. Cody loved his grandmother, but he found her house boring. He didn't appreciate art or the classical music his grandmother adored. He very much took after my side. The world could thank me for another loud-mouthed Decker man, even if technically he was a Higgins. Cody had asked if he could change his last name too. Part of me wanted to say yes, but I knew how much that would hurt Gelaire. And someday I hoped he and his father would work things out like they should. And maybe someday I would be a better person and help them figure all that out. Today wasn't that day.

But today was a bizarre day. Avery called while I was making spin-ach manicotti for dinner. Cody was in the shower, where I prayed he was washing off the stink he brought home from practice. It wasn't bizarre that she called, but her yelling into the phone was unlike her, and her news was the most unexpected news I had ever received. I take that back. It was second on the list, but far more pleasant than the first.

"Sam, Sam, Sam, you are never going to believe this!"

"You sound too happy for there to be anything wrong, or is this so bad you're losing it?" Honestly, she never sounded like this before.

"I am kind of losing it, but it's good. So, so good."

"Did James finally figure out that dirty clothes go in the hamper?"

"Ugh, no. But you, my dearest, are famous!"

"What are you talking about?" I opened the refrigerator to grab some parmesan cheese.

"Your blog post."

"What about it?"

"AUTUMN MOONE POSTED IT ON HER WEBSITE!"

I stood frozen in front of the open refrigerator door staring blankly inside of it. "*Autumn Moone?* As in the author we secretly love, but hide her books and don't tell anyone we devour them, Autumn Moone?"

"The very one!"

"How? What?" I couldn't think.

"Go to her website. It's posted on her home page."

"Let me put you on speaker." I set my phone on the counter and clicked the speaker button before I clicked on my browser app. The refrigerator door was still wide open. "It's autumnmoone.com, right?" My hands were shaking.

"Yes, but you should get her new app. It sends you notifications when she's posted something new. By the way, a sneak peek of Hunter's new book is out."

Avery and I were shamelessly in love with Hunter Black, the pro-tagonist in Autumn Moone's only series. It's why we bought hardcovers of the books and hid them. Hunter Black covers weren't the same on an eBook. He was best held and admired and then kept hidden under my bed. That sounded creepy. But honestly, he was the only romance I'd had in months. There was something about his chiseled face and how in love he was with his best friend, Laine. She, of course, didn't know, and he kept having to watch her be with the wrong guy while he tried to be with other women who weren't meant for him. The angst and the drama were captivating. And Autumn Moone had this way of raising your pulse without being graphic or crude. That new book of hers, *A Black Night*, needed to come out stat. I would probably read the sneak peek a hundred times tonight. But first, Autumn Moone's post about me. How weird was that?

"Are you there yet?" Avery was growing impatient.

"Getting there. How good was the sneak peek?"

"Oh my gosh, it's running an ice cube over my chest good."

"Avery."

"What? James thinks it's because we made out in the kitchen before the boys caught us."

I laughed at her, jealous, but happy my brother was the kind of man that let his wife know he still loved her, in all ways. I would give props to my parents—they raised good men.

Autumn Moone's site finally loaded on my smartphone. I didn't have to scroll far to see her post, dated for today.

"I'm there."

A friend shared this blog post with me today. Never have I read anything that has touched me so deeply. I ache for this woman, but applaud her spirit. If only I could write the kind of emotion in my books that this woman conveyed, I think I could count myself a true writer. Here's to you, Sidelined Wife. Get back in the game of life and give 'em hell.

I wiped the tears out of my eyes and read her message one more time. "I can't believe it. I wonder who gave it to her?" I thought no one knew who she was. Could someone I know be her friend? Autumn Moone was a mysterious character. She used a pen name and had never been seen. She started off as an independent author, but her first book, *A Black Heart*, was so popular one of the powerhouse publishers picked it up. Her profile pictures on all her social media sites were of the moon in various phases.

"Who cares who she is, as long as she keeps Hunter Black books coming. But look at all the comments down below, and she added a link to your blog."

Scrolling down, I was barraged with over a hundred comments. Most all of them positive. Several women posted they'd had similar things happen to them and this was an inspiration to them. There were a few trolls who said I should get over my privileged self and quit whining. I ignored those and focused on all the other beautiful messages of hope and comradery.

"I can't believe this."

"Believe it, sister, your fifteen minutes of fame have arrived."

"It's probably more like one or two."

"Are you kidding me? Autumn Moone is the hottest author since J.K. Rowling. Her acknowledging your existence is huge. You should probably go check your blog. I bet you have a ton of new followers."

"No way."

"Check."

"You're bossy today."

She laughed. "That's what older sisters do."

I loved that we never used sister-in-law. "I'm checking." I logged into my blog's site. Avery was right. "I went from two hundred followers to seventeen hundred. That's crazy." I blinked several times, amazed.

"Did any of them comment on your site?"

I looked at the comments section. I had to approve any comments before they would appear on any given post. "Yes. Several. It's going to take me forever to go through these."

"Sounds like you have a good night ahead of you. See you tomorrow. That is, if you aren't too famous by then."

"Ha. Ha. Goodbye."

I hung up, shook my head a few times, and finally closed the refrigerator. I forgot to get the parmesan cheese out. I forgot about dinner. Cody was quick to remind me of that when he came downstairs, clean and smelling like Irish Spring.

Cody stood at the breakfast bar expecting food. "Are you okay, Mom?"

I stood mesmerized by my phone. "Yeah."

I couldn't tell him about the post. I didn't want him reading it. I had mentioned having sex in there, or the lack thereof. Nothing a teenage boy wanted to know about his parents. Obviously, he knew his dad had been having some. Cody would be a brother soon. We didn't know if the baby was a boy or girl. Neil and Roxie wanted to be surprised. I think it had more to do with the fact that it made it less real for Neil. He didn't want to be a father again. From the tiny bit I caught the night I found out about the pregnancy, I knew he was unhappy about it. In a jerk move, he asked if it was his, and he told her she ruined his life. A baby was a secret he couldn't keep very well. He begged me that night to forgive him. It was the first time he sounded truly sorry for the affair. I could see the fear in his eyes.

That night had been a turning point for me. I had been afraid too. Afraid what people would think about me if I got divorced. I was afraid that Cody would hate me. I was afraid of my future, emotionally and financially. I was afraid to live without Neil. But in that moment, I had clarity. My fear had been preventing me from really living. I would be no one's doormat.

I looked up from my phone into my son's eyes. "Do you want to go out to dinner? I want to celebrate."

He cocked his head, just like his father. "What are we celebrating?"

"Life."

CHAPTER TEN

I WAS DYING TO READ ALL THE COMMENTS ON MY BLOG AND ON AUTUMN Moone's page, but dinner with my kid first. I could read those posts anytime, and believe me, I would be devouring them along with that sneak peek after I went to bed. But I knew my time with Cody was precious, and I intended not to waste a moment with him. And hey, the kid was still willing to be seen in public with me, so I was counting that as a huge parenting win.

I let Cody choose, which meant we were going to Portillo's. It had been his favorite since he learned how to say "hot dog." I had to admit, they made the best burgers on the planet. And I had a few pounds I could gain, so I was ordering one of those. Fries, too.

The restaurant was always crowded, no matter the day. But I didn't mind waiting in line to order because they had fabulous old movie posters and memorabilia throughout the entire place.

It was all going great, my brooding teenager had his earbuds in, but at least he stood close to me and I felt better than I had in a long time. That is, until Reed walked in. I still felt like an idiot about our interaction yesterday. I didn't think he saw me, so I tried to camouflage myself between Cody and the wall. Which was a dumb plan. He was going to recognize Cody, regardless, and he did.

Reed walked straight up to Cody on the other side of the red rope that directed the line. "Cody, my man." Reed did what I could never do:

get Cody's attention right away. Reed put his hand up for a high five. Cody met it with a loud smack.

"Coach, what are you doing here?"

Reed peeked around Cody and grinned at me like he knew I was avoiding him. "Just grabbing dinner," he answered Cody.

Cody nodded his approval.

"How are you, Sam?" Reed apparently wasn't getting my *please move on* vibe.

"Good. Great, really." I stared forward, avoiding eye contact, making a bigger fool of myself.

"I'm glad to hear that."

I kept hugging the wall as we moved forward in the line.

Cody and Reed talked about the team and their first game the following weekend against the Spartans. I listened as Reed praised Cody.

"I'm impressed with the way you always find an open window, and your aim is spot on. I think we'll keep running the down the line drill. It seems to be helping."

"Yeah, it's helped me focus on my target," Cody agreed. "Do you think I might get some playing time in the game?"

I turned toward Reed, wanting to see his reaction and response to Cody's plea.

Reed looked torn. He pressed his lips together and thought. "You have a bright future, and someday you'll lead this team. We'll see how the game goes."

Cody's shoulders dropped, but he tried to act unaffected by the news by changing the subject. "Maybe we could run some more setup drills tomorrow. I want to improve my time getting back after the snap."

I was proud of Cody. I knew what a blow he had been handed.

"I'll let Coach Parsons know." Reed gave Cody a manly pat on the back. "You're doing great."

We were almost to the front of the line, so I figured our time with Reed would be coming to an end. But life was full of surprises for me that night.

Reed grinned at me. "Do you mind if I join you for dinner?"

I looked behind us at the long line. "You don't want to wait in line?"

Reed faked a stab to his chest. "I'm hurt you would think that. I just wanted to catch up with an old friend."

I narrowed my eyes at him. "Friends don't dump dead fish on your bed."

"You put dead fish in my mom's bed?" Cody bent over laughing as if that was the funniest thing he had ever heard.

Reed's reaction wasn't what I expected. I thought he would join Cody in his hysterical laugh, but instead I could see the muscles in his face tighten. And if I wasn't mistaken, I saw traces of regret in his eyes.

"I was hoping you had forgotten about that." He rubbed the back of his neck.

"That's not a smell you easily forget."

He went from rubbing his neck to running his fingers through his thick, dark hair. "Let me buy you dinner to make up for it."

I was taken aback by his offer. "That's not necessary. Besides it's my mom you really should apologize to. I think she washed my sheets ten times before she finally gave up and bought new ones."

Reed was undeterred. He pulled up the red rope and slid under it, taking his place in line by us. "I insist."

I was going to vehemently decline until I noticed the way Cody smiled and did that weird man-hand-clasp thing with Reed. Cody seemed at ease with him and happier when he was around. For the love of my son, I allowed Reed to stay, but under one condition.

"You're more than welcome to eat with us, but it's my treat." Maybe that would assuage some of the guilt I felt for basically emasculating him yesterday. But it only seemed to make him feel worse.

Reed let out this heavy sigh of what sounded a lot like disappointment. His blue eyes hit me. "I am more than capable of buying you dinner."

I had never noticed before, but he had pretty eyes. Why did I think that? I had more pressing matters. Did he take my offer as a slight? I wasn't sure how to respond, so I blathered like an idiot, which was apparently my new status quo around him. "I'm sure you are. I just thought, you know, since I said some stupid things to you yesterday, I could make up for it by buying you dinner."

Cody cringed upon hearing I said something stupid to his coach yesterday. Each crinkle in his brow said *please tell me it wasn't about me.*

Before Reed could respond, we were called up to order. He took matters into his own hands. He informed the kid taking orders we were all on one ticket and he was paying. His debit card was out, ready to go. Reed turned toward me. "Ladies first."

I hesitated. The whole scenario was weird to me.

"Don't be shy." Reed gave me a sly grin. It wasn't the same mischievous grin from his younger years. There was something different about it that I couldn't quite place. It was disconcerting. I ignored how off it made me feel and ordered.

While Cody ordered half the menu, I took the opportunity to give Reed an out.

"Are you sure I can't pay? Cody is serious about his food."

Reed didn't bat an eye at the growing total. "It's my pleasure."

"Thank you for the *grown-up* gesture," I teased, hoping he would take it the way I meant it. I thought maybe if we could laugh about my awkward behavior from the day before we could move on from it.

He didn't exactly laugh, but he smiled at me before he ordered.

Reed did laugh, though, when Cody grimaced at me. "Did you just call Coach a grown-up?"

"That's what she called me yesterday." Reed rubbed salt in my wound with a smile.

Cody shook his head at me. "Mom."

"I'm going to go get my drink and find a place to sit." The cashier set some cups on the counter, and I grabbed one to the tune of the two guys laughing at me. I might have been annoyed, but Cody's laughter filled me with hope. Hope would get us through the ugly gift life had handed us.

While I was dropping lemon wedges in my ice water near the beverage dispensers, Reed slid up next to me. "Cody's going to wait for the food and bring it to our table."

I nodded.

"Sam, please don't be mad at me."

His plea surprised me. "I'm not. I'm embarrassed."

"Hey." He rested his hand on my shoulder. My bare shoulder, I might add. His hand was warm and definitely grown-up.

I found myself looking into his eyes. Again, there was something different in them. I couldn't put my finger on it.

His hand stayed steady on my shoulder. "The last thing I want to do is embarrass you."

"You didn't do anything. It's all me. I'm sorry, I'm just having a hard time wrapping my head around you being, well, you know, older."

"I guess older is better than grown-up." His hand dropped. He started filling his and Cody's cup with ice.

My cheeks flushed. "I've done it again, haven't I?"

His mouth twitched. "Maybe we should start over." He set the ice-filled cups on the counter near my water. He held his hand out to me. "Hi, I'm Reed Cassidy. I think your son is on my football team."

I stared at his hand and maybe smiled.

"That's your cue to shake my hand."

I brought my hand up slowly and clasped his.

His hand enveloped mine and held firm. "And your name is?"

I took a breath and remembered my new name, my old name. "I'm Samantha Decker, Cody's mom."

He still kept my hand in his. "Do you like to be called Sam?"

"By my friends."

"Okay, Samantha, you tell me when I can call you Sam."

"You've always called me Sam."

"We've never met before, remember?"

I felt so foolish, standing there shaking his hand in the middle of the busy restaurant while people maneuvered around us to get straws and lids for their cups, but I also felt something else. Light. Was that a weird feeling?

"Okay. What should I call you?"

"Well, Samantha," he emphasized my name, "since we just met and I'm your son's coach and possibly teacher, we should probably go the formal route upfront. What do you think of Mr. Cassidy?"

My eyebrows raised. "I think you should try again."

He chuckled. "How does Reed sound?"

"Much better." I pulled my hand away. I swore I felt a tug, like he hesitated letting go. I must have been imagining things.

He went back to filling the cups of ice with soda. I noticed he got Cody's favorite. And he kept looking at me from the corner of his eye. "Since we just met, I think you are obligated to forget anything you think you may know or remember about me from twenty years ago until the present day."

I narrowed my eyes at him, not sure where all this was coming from. "I'm not sure that's possible. I still flinch every time I open a door, thinking a firecracker might go off."

"Hmm. That's odd." He placed lids on the cups. "I can't imagine why you have that condition."

"Yeah. It's almost as if someone—or someones—booby trapped my room on a regular basis."

"I'm sure whoever it was or wasn't only did or didn't do it to show how much they cared."

"Right." I took my drink and headed for an empty table toward the outskirts of the main area of the restaurant.

Reed followed. "Or maybe they did it because you got them grounded and they weren't allowed to watch their favorite TV show for a month."

"*The Simpsons* is so juvenile." I took a seat at a window table.

Reed sat down across from me. His face was a tad red. "I'm not saying that was the show or how I know this, but I think the perpetrators in question were juveniles at the time, so maybe you could forget it ever happened and that one of them had a Bart Simpson pillowcase."

I grinned. "I forgot about how much you loved him. Your impersonation of him was spot on."

Reed cleared his throat. "I don't know who you are talking about. And I hate to remind you of this again, but we just met."

"Yes, sorry." I took a sip of my water. "I have a question for you."

"Shoot."

"Do you frequently have dinner with random strangers?"

A smile played on his face. "This is a special circumstance."

"Uh-huh."

His grin grew.

"Thank you for dinner." I leaned forward. "And especially for making Cody laugh."

"I'm pretty sure he was laughing at you."

I sighed and sat back. "I'm sorry again about what I said. I'm not myself lately."

"You don't need to apologize. I know this has been a tough time for you and Cody."

"And how would you know that, stranger?"

"I mean, I'm guessing. But I should mention I know your brother, Peter, and he's concerned about you and Cody."

That piece of news shocked me. "Peter's discussing my family with you?"

"Did I say that?" He took a long drink of his soda and avoided my gaze.

"Peter has a good heart." I tried to put Reed at ease. Even though I would probably give Peter a hard time about it.

"He always has. He kept me out of a lot of trouble."

"And let me guess, you did your best to get him into some."

He smirked. "I'm going to plead the Fifth."

"That's probably a good idea, Reed Cassidy."

CHAPTER ELEVEN

WHAT A VERY ODD NIGHT IT HAD TURNED OUT TO BE. CODY CONFIRMED MY suspicions, and maybe one of my worst fears. There was a girl or two or three that liked him, and he reciprocated. Those girls stole my baby away during dinner, leaving me to converse with Reed. After the initial weirdness, it turned out to be pleasant. Not one trace came out of the annoying kid I used to know. My mouth behaved and didn't emasculate him again. And I may have taken Avery's advice and checked out his butt when he took the trash from the table to dispose of it. I could report that Avery, and apparently James, were right about it. It still felt somewhat wrong looking at him like that. The fact he was Cody's coach only added to the uneasiness of it. I had never checked out Cody's teachers before. But I had never been a single mom before either.

On that depressing note, I pulled out my laptop while propped up with pillows on my four-poster bed. I had been anxious to read more comments and that sneak peek. When I logged into my laptop, I was inundated with emails informing me I had new subscribers to my blog. There were so many, I couldn't count them. I was tempted to head to my blog first, but Hunter Black was calling to me. It was sad how in love I was with a fictional character.

I did make a note of how many more comments there were on the post about me on Autumn Moone's page before I dug into the sneak peek. It was mind boggling. So surreal. But not enough to deter me from getting my Hunter fix. I read and savored each morsel of heart-pounding goodness from the two-page excerpt. I couldn't believe it; Hunter and his best friend, Laine, were stranded at his family's mountain cabin, and it looked like things were going to finally come to a head with them. He was holding her near the fireplace to keep her warm. It was their only source of heat, well, that and each other. His lips hovered above hers, teasing them, but they never touched. She relaxed in his arms as if begging him to finally do what they both wanted. His mouth was ready to consume hers, I could feel it, and then that's where it ended.

"No!" I groaned. I'd been waiting for that kiss for two years.

Weird side note I would never admit to, but Reed reminded me of Hunter. They both had dark hair, stunning blue eyes, and a nice backside. I needed to get that out of my head. How was I going to picture myself now as Laine—or any of Hunter's other women—if I was picturing Reed as Hunter? That could get awkward. It'd be a whole other type of book, like *Naughty Babysitters* or *The Cougar and the Teacher.*

Reed had asked me tonight what I would think of him if this was the first time we had met. It wasn't an easy question, but I tried to be objective—and then I kept my answer to myself. Honestly, if it was our first meeting, I would have thought the school made a mistake hiring him. Not because he wasn't a good coach or teacher, which I really didn't know one way or the other for sure, but because he was quite pretty. With how the girls who stole my son away had snuck a peek at Reed, I had a feeling he would be the fantasy of many teenage girls, and probably a lot of the teachers at the high school.

When Reed pressed for an answer, all I offered was that he seemed capable and Cody liked him, so that was a plus in my book. I'm not sure that answer satisfied him, but at least he didn't look demoralized like he had yesterday and earlier in the evening.

The burning question on my mind tonight wasn't what I would have thought of Reed if we had just met, but did I know someone who knew the elusive Autumn Moone? Who gave her my blog? Was it a friend of a friend of a friend sort of thing? Did Autumn Moone live in the Chicagoland area? If she did, she should be best friends with Avery and me. We obviously had a lot in common. Or at least we all loved Hunter Black. Who knows, I could have walked by her in the market today when I took Gelaire shopping. Or maybe at the fancy boutique Gelaire took me to. Surely Autumn Moone could afford those kind of price tags. She sold millions of books. How I ever got on her radar was amazing to me.

But not as amazing as all the new followers on my blog and the comments.

After twenty-five years of marriage and three kids, my husband left us to pursue his dreams. I thought we were his dream. Now, while he's off exploring the world with his girlfriend, I'm working two jobs to make ends meet. He even missed our son's college graduation. We were high school sweethearts. I saw him through cancer treatments and job losses, only to be tossed to the side. Thanks for writing so eloquently how I'm feeling and for giving me courage to make it one more day.

I placed my hand over my heart. Wow. That was heartbreaking. And there were more.

I knew when his hours started getting longer at the office and his business trips became more frequent, something was wrong. But I kept thinking we'd had children together and I'd followed him around the country for his work, setting my career to the side to raise our children. Then he forgot his phone one day and she called. We had a nice little chat. She had no idea he was married. That didn't stop her from seeing my now ex-husband. They didn't last. Now he admits what a mistake it was. But I refuse to take him back. I'd rather be a sidelined wife than someone's afterthought or consolation prize. Hang in there, from one sidelined wife to another.

The Sidelined Wife? I scrolled through more comments to find that's what several people were referring to me as, just like Autumn Moone had. Not a title I ever thought I would have, but it was exactly how I felt. I wanted to respond individually to everyone that had commented, but it would have taken hours. I couldn't believe the response. I hated that we were all part of this club of cheated on and tossed aside wives.

I decided to write another post to thank everyone. I wasn't exactly sure what to say, so I went with a humorous approach.

Welcome to the Sidelined Wives Club. I'm not sure whether to congratulate you or give my condolences. Let's go with congratulations. We've all made it through hell and we're still alive; that's something to celebrate. And now we know we aren't alone.

We have each other in this sucktastic adventure. We should probably lay some ground rules for the club.

1. Absolutely no husbands. But bashing of said husbands is allowed, even welcomed.

2. If husband has moved on, bashing of new wife or girlfriend is allowed. For example: she has bad bangs, her taste in clothing is hideous, her eyebrows are too close together, her IQ is lower than her age. You get the idea.

3. Whining is allowed. Weeping and wailing is also permissible.

4. Sharing is caring. Be sure to share stories of triumph and survival tricks.

5. This is a safe space, although talk of doing anything illegal (i.e. anything that would put you in jail or make us testify against you) is frowned upon.

6. And never forget, you're not alone. You got this.

All joking aside, your words and stories have touched and inspired me, so thank you. I'm off now to see if there is any chocolate mousse pie left.

Yours Truly,
Sidelined Wife in Chief

I probably sounded ridiculous, but I clicked publish anyway. Like I said, it was the oddest night. I read the sneak peek one more time trying not to picture Reed. I did my best to picture the guy I usually pictured when I read about Hunter Black, the underwear model—I mean, the guy with the adorable puppy I started following on Instagram last year. That didn't help. It only made me see the resemblance between the puppy guy and Reed. If I started picturing Reed in his underwear, I was getting a lobotomy. He would be coaching my son, for crying out loud. Come to think of it, I had seen more of him than I'd ever wanted. Reed and Peter had streaked through the woods once and jumped into the lake during one of our vacations. Granted, they didn't know I was a witness. I had snuck off with Joel, the groundskeeper's son. I was seventeen and he was twenty. That seemed so risqué to me back then. Joel had taught me how to French kiss, and we were fine tuning our skills when Peter and Reed gave us a show. Joel laughed, while I wanted to throw up in my mouth. Thankfully, I only caught their backsides.

Now look at me, staring at Reed's butt. What had happened to my life?

CHAPTER TWELVE

The weird events from the day before followed me into the next day. I woke up to even more followers and comments. Not only that, but Autumn Moone linked my latest post to her website with the caption that she liked my style.

My rules for the Sidelined Wives Club were a hit, at least for most. Some haters and men didn't appreciate them, but I either ignored them or deleted their comments. It was much more fun to read women calling out their exes and their replacements. One woman even got creative and wrote a poem and added a picture of a buxom brunette.

Meet Susie. Susie is a floozy. I thought she was my friend, but that hit a dead end. But no need to worry, she left my ex in a hurry. Now Greg begs for me to take him back, but all I do is laugh. You see, the joke's on him, I got his money and a new honey. Life is swell with Miguel. So the moral of the story is, we are better off without the pigs. Don't you fret or sweat their loss. Go and live your life like a boss. And, P.S., it's his loss.

I laughed so hard I snorted there in the kitchen while making breakfast.

Cody came down stretching and yawning, but ready for practice. "What's so funny?"

I clicked out of my blog and set my phone down on the counter. "Just read something funny online." I wasn't sure Cody would appreciate my posts. I wasn't even sure he knew I had a blog. I followed him on

Instagram, which he hated even though he hardly ever posted anything. I guess there was this fear I would embarrass him on social media or perhaps catch him doing something he knew I would frown upon. That hadn't happened yet. *Yet.* I grew up with two brothers, so I knew it was inevitable.

Cody took a stool at the kitchen island and ran his fingers through his hair.

"We should probably get your hair cut this weekend before school starts." I started cracking the eggs I had been ignoring while reading comments.

He shrugged. "I was thinking about growing it out."

I stopped mid-crack and gave him a good look. "I thought you didn't like it longer because your curls came out."

He focused on the granite counter top. "Well, maybe I like it now."

"Okay. What's her name? Is it Rory from last night?" She was a super cute girl. The kind that made me nervous, with her tiny waist and chest that was bigger than mine. And she had the hair swishing thing down with her long, golden locks. I recognized it, because once upon a time I did the same thing.

Cody's head popped up with a disconcerting look. "I just want to try something new." He wasn't owning anything.

"It's okay if you like her." Not really, but I knew it was inevitable.

"We're just friends."

His declaration gave me no comfort. I could hear the hesitancy in his voice. "Well, I've always loved your curls."

Neil had the same ones when we met. I pushed that thought out and replaced it with my cute, chubby baby and his curls that I couldn't get enough of. I let Cody pretend he didn't hear his mom say she loved his hair while I finished cracking eggs for omelets. Then I did my best to pretend like everything was okay while I thought about getting a Latin lover named Miguel.

I was glad Hershel couldn't give Cody a ride today. Well, sort of. It meant allowing Cody to drive. I may have squealed a few times. He took corners way too fast. And morning traffic was no place for a fifteen-year-old. It certainly got my blood pumping. I would no longer be needing my cardio workout for the day.

Cody pulled into the school parking lot, and not a moment too soon. The omelet I had eaten for breakfast was debating on making a reappearance. Something else made my insides feel different, too. Reed was walking across the parking lot and waved at me. I was still feeling guilty for checking out his butt and seeing him as Hunter Black. I swore he gave me a grin like he knew it, too. How could he? I ignored him and focused back on Cody.

"Don't get a concussion, drink lots of water, don't look at porn, think good thoughts, and remember who loves you most. Me." This was what I basically said to him every time we parted. Someday soon I would be adding, don't make me a grandma.

And like he always did, he rolled his eyes. "Bye, Mom."

"I'm waiting for the 'I love you.'"

He mumbled, "I love you," before we both exited the vehicle.

It was then I noticed Reed hadn't kept walking toward the football field. He was now walking toward Cody. When he and Cody met, they high-fived and said a few words I couldn't hear. I walked around the car to the driver's side, while Reed headed my way. He was wearing another Coach Cassidy polo shirt and shorts that showed off his...Oh my gosh, I was doing it again. I was checking out his long, lean, muscular legs. I berated myself for being able to use so many adjectives to describe them.

"Samantha." He approached with his lips pressed together.

I opened my car door and paused. For some reason I was nervous. "Hello."

"That's better." He landed near me.

"What does that mean?"

"You blew off my wave a few minutes ago."

"Sorry." I shrugged my shoulders. Just like last night, I wasn't sure how to take him. "I didn't realize how sensitive you were about it."

He smiled. "Now you know."

"You've gotten touchy in your old age," I teased.

"Are we going to talk about my age again?"

"According to you, we only met yesterday. We've never discussed your age."

He chuckled. "Good point. Which means you don't know how old I am."

"And why does it seem to matter to you that I have a good approximation of your age?"

He swallowed hard. Any trace of a smile was wiped off his face.

"Are you okay?"

"Yes." He stepped close enough that I could smell his cologne. It was nice, like spicy dark chocolate.

I was disturbed I liked the way he smelled. I took a step back.

He erased my step and moved forward. "I want to be known for who I am now."

I let out a heavy sigh. "I can relate to that."

His smile was back. "Like I said, I've always liked Samantha Decker."

The way he said my name had me swallowing hard. "Seeing how we met yesterday, that's the only person you know," I stuttered.

"I should have specified the rules. I can remember my past."

"Whatever you say. I need to get to the office."

"I should get going too."

"Have a good day. Don't let anything happen to my baby."

"He probably wouldn't appreciate you saying that."

"Then don't tell him."

"I'll keep your secret."

"Thank you."

"You're welcome. I'll see you later." He turned to leave, but didn't quite make it. "Hey, I had a great time catching up last night. Maybe we could do it again." His smile was different than before. Almost sensual. That couldn't be.

I stared blankly at him, caught off guard by his invitation and smile. "Um... I'm sure you would have more fun catching up with Peter."

"I doubt that." His shoulders slumped before stalking off.

I stood staring after him. I wasn't checking out his butt. Okay, so maybe I noticed, but it was hard not to. Honestly, I was stunned and perplexed. It's not like we were really friends growing up. Sure, we had a nice time last night, but I didn't see us as the kind of friends that had dinner together. But once again, I think I demoralized him. I was going to do my best to stay away from the poor guy.

With swirling thoughts about my conversation with Reed going through my head on the way to work, another man interrupted my thoughts. It wasn't a welcome interruption, but I knew I had to take his call. Sharing a child necessitated it. I wasn't completely surprised he was calling. I had done the grown-up thing yesterday and emailed him a copy of Cody's football schedule with a note telling him he really needed to make the effort to attend at least the home games.

"Hello." I answered through the Bluetooth. The irony wasn't lost on me.

"Sam, it's Neil."

"Believe it or not, I know your number and voice."

"I wasn't trying to insult your intelligence. I was actually calling to check on you."

I shook my head. Did I hear him right? "Why?"

He cleared his throat. "I read your blog."

That was awkward. "Since when have you read our—my blog?"

"I'm the one who taught you HTML so you could set it up the way you wanted it."

That was true. It was hard sometimes to remember the good times. "I still don't understand why you're calling."

"Well, Roxie," he said her name with great unease, as he should have. I wasn't fond of him mentioning her and he knew it. "She mentioned something about an author, Autumn Moone, talking about you."

I laughed.

"What's so funny?"

"I didn't know Roxie could read."

His frustrated sigh came through loud and clear. "Petty doesn't work for you."

"I don't need you of all people lecturing me about my conduct."

"You're right. I apologize."

I didn't respond. He was right, it was petty, but I wouldn't admit it to him.

"Sam." He paused. "I want you to know that I never saw you the way you expressed in your blog. If anything, I felt unworthy of you. Your beauty only increased each passing year, while I settled into middle age."

All I heard were excuses. "Please stop. I can't take any more of your lies." I'd heard this one before. He said he'd needed to feel young again and desired. Blah, blah, blah. He never understood that I wanted the aged version.

"I'm not lying," he raised his voice. "Do you think I wanted our lives to turn out this way? I was willing to work on our marriage. You were the one that kicked me out."

"You're having a baby with another woman. That was your choice," I shouted.

Silence on his end.

"I'm not hashing this out with you again, but don't you dare blame me for this. I loved you, Neil, and gave you everything I had and sometimes more. *You* threw *me* away, not the other way around."

"I am sorry. I don't know what else I can say."

"Not a thing. Goodbye."

"Hold on." His pause was longer than before. "Do you think you could take down your blog post? You have to admit it's an embarrassment to me and Roxie. And you aren't one to air dirty laundry out in public."

All I could do was laugh, that tired, angry, maniacal laugh. "For a second, you had me fooled. I thought maybe you really were sorry, but like always, you only care about yourself. The answer is no, I won't be taking down that post. In fact, you can expect more. And if you were worried about being embarrassed, you should have thought about that before you decided to bed a girl that wondered why she was going to have contractors when she gave birth instead of contractions."

"Could you please forget about that? She misread a pamphlet. It was an honest mistake." He didn't believe a word he said. I could hear the grating nerves in his voice. Neil valued intelligence and decorum. Roxie had neither.

Maybe it was awful of me, but ever since Cody came home a few months ago and told me about what Roxie had said, I'd been laughing about it, as had everyone I told about it. Even Cody knew women had contractions. That was the last time Cody ever spent a weekend with his dad. I think he may have hated Roxie more than me. He came home early that weekend, vowing never to have anything to do with his dad or Roxie and begging me to get full custody. It was the first time Cody cried over the breakup. My heart broke in ways I never knew it could that day. I wasn't sure if or when those pieces would come back together.

"Neil, don't call me unless it has to do with Cody. Did you get the football schedule I sent you?"

"He doesn't want me there."

"He never will until you come. The more you stay away, the more he'll resent you."

"I'll see what I can do."

"We both know what that means. You're going to ruin the best thing you have going for you right now."

"It would seem that's what I'm best at." He hung up without another word.

At least he finally told the truth.

CHAPTER THIRTEEN

BY THE TIME I REACHED THE OFFICE, I WAS SHAKING AND CRYING. I SWORE I wouldn't cry over Neil anymore, but there was a part of me that desperately wanted him to acknowledge the pain he had caused me and Cody. I wanted him to truly understand what he had done. Deep in my heart, I knew he never would, but for a split second today I thought maybe he got it. Once again, though, he disappointed me. I needed to quit giving him that power.

I fanned my eyes and blew my nose, trying to get rid of the evidence of my breakdown. Judging by the trucks in the parking lot, I knew my brothers were there. It was one thing for Avery to see me in this state, but the men in my life liked to pretend I was handling it. They were fixers, and they knew this wasn't something they could make better. If only they knew that they were making it better. Sometimes all I needed was their arms, especially my dad's. And the way Peter and James took Cody under their wings meant more to me than they would ever know.

With most of the evidence of my tears gone, I headed in, taking deep breaths as I went. I was getting better, I reminded myself. I didn't even wince this morning when I looked in the mirror and got ready. That was progress. And Autumn Moone knew who I was, along with a bunch of other women I didn't know. Not to mention there was that sneak peek to read over and over again. Now I was sounding pathetic. But I was trying.

Avery's face lit up when I walked in, only to be doused when she took a second glance at me. She came running around the front desk. "What's wrong, honey?"

I apparently hadn't done a good job of hiding my episode. I should have touched up my makeup, but I hadn't carried any around in months. I figured, why bother? I couldn't even stand to look at me, so who else could? I found myself wrapped up in Avery's toned arms. It had been a frequent occurrence the past year, which made me feel guilty, considering her own loss.

I sank into her. "Neil called."

She swore in French under her breath and held me closer. She had spent a semester abroad in college and loved using her multi-lingual skills when she was angry. She always said it came in handy as a wife and mother. "He didn't ask for another chance again, did he?"

"No. He asked me to take down my blog."

"He read it?" There was a lot of glee in her voice.

"Supposedly Roxie is a fan of Autumn Moone too. I'll try not to let that affect my love for Ms. Moone." I sniffled.

James and Peter came walking in from the side door. I left the comfort of Avery's arms, but it was too late. I had been caught.

"What's happened now?" James approached, his overprotective brother jaw was tight. He could be a menacing creature if he wanted to be. He was tall and muscular. His jet-black hair with strands of gray gave off a shrewd look. In reality, he had a heart of gold and was mostly a teddy bear, unless you messed with his family.

"I'm fine." I smoothed out my white eyelet blouse.

James narrowed his gray eyes. Like I said, he was reluctant to know anything he couldn't fix.

Avery swatted her husband's arm. "Leave your sister alone. Neil called her about her blog."

"The one she wrote about her sex life?"

Peter's green eyes went wide and Avery rolled her pretty blue eyes.

"I didn't write about my sex life," I defended myself.

"What was all that crap, then, about you making love all night long? Hell, had I known you and Neil were having sex, I may have killed him."

"You're so immature. How do you think Cody got here?"

"We believe in virgin births."

Peter and Avery laughed at James.

James pulled me to him for a hug. "Maybe I'll kill him anyway."

See? He was a fixer.

I nodded against his chest. "Just don't tell me how or when. I don't want to have to testify against you."

"Don't worry. I have some friends that would be willing to bury a body for me, no questions asked."

Avery walked off. "You're all talk."

James gave me a good squeeze. "Just say the word and he's gone."

"I'll let you know." I pushed away from him. I wasn't fond of his cologne; it smelled like rubbing alcohol to me, unlike Reed's. Why had I thought that? Reed kept popping up in my mind at odd times the last couple of days.

"Are you okay?" Peter asked. He was a fixer too, but out of all the Decker men, he was the most sensitive.

I took a deep breath and let it out. "I'm just realizing I was married to the most selfish person on the planet."

Peter gave me a soft look. It suited his smooth, angular cheeks and light brown hair that shined like an angel's. He was a handsome kid. See me calling him a kid? Reed's emasculated cringe popped into my head. Reed really needed to quit doing that.

"I don't think he was always that way." Peter tried to see the best in everyone. "You wouldn't have married him if he was."

"Honestly, sometimes I wonder if I was blinded."

Peter stepped closer and rested his strong hand on my shoulder. "It was him that was blinded, by worldly pursuits." Sometimes his priest side came out.

"Is that a nice way of saying sex?"

"There you go with that word again," James shouted over by the coffee pot.

"You say it all the time."

"That's because I'm a man; it's what we think about ninety-five percent of the time. Baby sisters should be thinking about flowers and bunnies."

Avery and I both gave James an *are you serious* look.

"I hate to burst your bubble, honey, but Sam and I talk about sex all the time." That was true on occasion. Avery gave me an evil grin.

James about choked on his coffee. He grabbed some napkins to wipe his shirt where he dribbled coffee on it. "Did you tell her about—"

I put up my hand. "Don't say a word." I wasn't sure what he was going to say, but like him, I didn't want to discuss his sex life with him. With Avery it was one thing. And we never got detailed. It was more along the lines of what was going on with our bodies and frequency issues. For her, sometimes it was too frequent; for me and Neil, it had come to a screeching halt.

Avery was laughing hysterically while Peter was trying not to. I noticed his cheeks were a tinge pink.

Avery and James started in with each other about why Avery was talking to me about their sex life, but Peter flicked his head toward the side door. "Do you want to go for a walk? James and I have an hour before we have to get to the property on State Street."

I nodded and followed Peter out the door he kindly held open for me. The lovebirds were ramping up and their voices carried, even out the closed door.

"Those two." I shook my head.

Peter chuckled and followed me down the steps.

We walked past slats of stone and turf for their job today, heading toward the neighboring orchard. It was already warm at nine in the morning, but the humidity was down.

"How are you really, sis?" Peter shoved his hands in his shorts' pockets.

"I have my moments."

"Delanie really loved your post. She thought it was cool that Autumn Moone put it on her website."

"Does Delanie read Autumn Moone's books? I always pegged her as someone who read self-help and social causes books."

Peter shrugged. "She loves Autumn's books."

"Autumn? Are you acquainted with her books too?"

"There is nothing wrong with a man being interested in what his wife reads."

I couldn't help grinning. I nudged him with my shoulder. "You're a good guy. Delanie's a lucky girl." Neil would have never done such a thing for me. And I know James wouldn't be caught dead reading a romance novel.

"I'm the lucky one." Such love ran through his words for his bride of three years.

"She's great."

Peter stopped and kicked a rock on the gravel path we were on. "Do you think you could spend some time with Delanie? She's feeling out of place in our family."

That sent a pang through my heart. "Of course. I'm so sorry I've been too wrapped up in my own life to notice. Or to do anything about it. I know Ma hasn't been as kind as she should be." I felt terrible for not making more of an effort with her. The way she came into our family was unconventional, scandalous by Ma's estimation. Peter had just up and left the priesthood and eloped with Delanie. When he brought her home from Phoenix, we were all in shock.

"That's putting it mildly. Delanie doesn't want to come to Sunday dinners anymore."

"Tell her I want her there. I'll talk to Ma, and I'll be better about including Delanie in conversation. And now that I know she loves Autumn Moone books, I'll invite her to Avery's and my secret book club."

We should have anyway, but Avery and I both thought it wasn't her thing. Delanie was a content manager, or something like that, for an online publication. She didn't really like to talk about her work, which I thought was odd. But I had looked at the website and saw some published pieces about how fictionalized fantasy ruins relationships. We figured she agreed with the kind of articles that were published on the site. And I noticed that occasionally she wrote some of the articles. They were always raw and gritty. The topics dealt with poverty, censorship, the sexualization of children, etc. They were well written, and I tried to talk to her about them, but like I said, she did her best to avoid it. That didn't help with her relationship with Ma. Ma found her to be secretive. But Avery and I shouldn't have assumed she wouldn't want to join our Hunter Black fan club.

"You know that's not a secret, right? James knows all about you and Avery lusting over Hunter Black."

I giggled. "The fact that you know his name kills me."

"Happy wife, happy life. And don't you think I kind of resemble Hunter?" He held his chin in a model pose.

I took ahold of his muscular bicep and laughed more than I had in a long while. And no, I would not be picturing my baby brother as the object of my desire. Once my laughter died down, we began our slow walk again. "I can tell you're happy."

"You have no idea. I never knew life could be this good. I thought nothing could bring me more joy than dedicating my life to God, but I was wrong." He smiled down at me. "Does that sound terrible?"

"Not at all. You found your purpose. I'm happy for you." I tried to keep the envy out of my voice.

Peter placed his hand over mine on his arm. "Your day will come, sis."

"I had my day."

"And you will again."

"I don't know. I would hate to make anyone commit adultery on my behalf."

Peter's mouth twitched. "Mimsy means well. She values tradition."

"I value fidelity."

"As you should."

We walked in silence for a few steps. "You know, I ran into Reed last night. We ended up having dinner together."

"Really?" He didn't sound as surprised as I thought he would have.

"I think maybe he could use some of your attention."

"Is something wrong?"

"I don't think so. But I get the feeling that he's looking for connections. You know, his roots."

Peter tilted his head and scrunched his forehead. "Are you sure? That doesn't sound like Reed, and when I talked to him a couple of days ago, he seemed good."

"I'm not saying he's not. Maybe lonely is a better word. I mean, why else would he want to have dinner with me?"

A smile crept across Peter's face.

"What's that Cheshire grin for?"

"Did it ever occur to you that he likes you?"

"Sure, in that we-knew-each-other-way-back-when sort of way. And he's Cody's coach."

Peter's smile only grew.

"Am I missing something?"

"I think so."

"What?"

"I think I'm going to let you figure that out."

CHAPTER FOURTEEN

THE NEXT FEW DAYS WERE A FLURRY OF BACK-TO-SCHOOL SHOPPING, responding to comments on my blog, and thinking up new posts. My followers seemed to crave them. It was weird to have an audience. They liked it if I said, "I hope you all have a great day," but I tried to be more original.

I was trying to think up a gem of an idea while taking a really hard look in the mirror on Sunday morning. I'd gotten my butt back to the gym for a hip-hop class. Yeah, I said hip-hop. I thought since a long time ago in a galaxy far, far away I had been a cheerleader, I could do a dance-style exercise class. I wasn't sure what had happened to dance in the last twenty-plus years or so, but my body didn't bend, shake, or twist like the instructors or the cute twenty-something-year-olds in the class who all looked at me like I had been born during the dawn of civilization.

So I was sore, humiliated, and naked, looking at myself in my full-length mirror. That's when it struck me.

Now that I'm single, the big question on everyone's mind is, "When will I date again?" I'm not sure if or when that will ever happen, but this I know. Not only will I require a marriage certificate the next time someone sees me naked, but they must also sign an NDA. That's right, I want a written agreement that they will never discuss my naked body with another living soul, maybe not even me. Does anyone else feel this way?

I clicked publish.

What I wouldn't do to have that twenty-two-year-old body again. The one I was nervous about showing off on my wedding night. What was wrong with me? I should have put that body on parade. It's not like I had let myself go, but it wasn't the same. Twenty-year-olds didn't appreciate the bodies they were given. We should get those bodies when we're forty and have the good sense to know how amazing they really are.

I limped around all day Sunday. I was getting older, but I wasn't that old. Every part of my body ached. There would be no more hip-hop classes. I would have to try the walk and tone class, or maybe pull out my old exercise DVDs. Or I could just shove my face full of the Snickers apple salad I made to take to my parents' for dessert. I wasn't sure how it could be called a salad, considering there were candy bars in it, but I wasn't going to argue. And I was telling everyone I ate salad for dinner.

To my distress, Cody drove us over to my parents'. The Snickers salad almost had a mishap when Cody slammed on his brakes because he was following behind the person in front of us too closely and they made a sudden stop. I was thankful for the plastic wrap that acted like a seal, and that I didn't have bladder leakage issues yet. Teaching Cody how to drive was going to be the death of me or, perhaps, both of us.

By the time we arrived at my parents', I was already frazzled, and my loved ones didn't help. I was bombarded as soon as I walked in.

Ma was shaking her head at me before I could put the dessert in the fridge. "Samantha Marie." Her sigh was as heavy as the tray of raw meat she was handing over to Dad to barbecue.

"What's wrong?" I asked.

"Cody Joseph, join Matt and Jimmy outside," Ma instructed my son.

I thought for sure someone had died. Why else would Ma send Cody outside? And why was everyone else gathering around me? Even Dad, who was holding on to several pounds of steak. Mimsy was rubbing her rosary beads and silently praying. Oh, this wasn't good.

Cody saw the writing on the wall and didn't have to be told twice; he darted out of there.

To make matters more interesting, Reed showed up. Peter let him in before all the fun began. I didn't even know he was invited. Did he have a permanent invite now?

I began to really worry when Dad's face started to perspire, but then I noticed the evil grin on James's face and Avery trying to hold in a laugh.

Reed walked in bearing another bouquet of flowers, this time peach roses. I loved peach roses. He stopped dead in his tracks, though, when he noticed the powwow going on in the kitchen.

"Am I interrupting anything?"

Ma shook her head again and huffed and puffed. "You might as well know too, since apparently the whole world does." Ma laser focused her pale blue eyes on me.

I set the salad on the counter. "Ma, what's wrong?"

"Do you know what I read this afternoon?" She placed her hand over her heart.

"The *Reader's Digest*?" She loved that little magazine, and may very well be the only person that still had a paper version delivered.

"Besides that?"

"An obituary?" I guessed by her reaction.

"Well, I almost died after reading your...your...sexy talk."

James erupted in a laugh. The meat tray in Dad's hands faltered as he shuddered. And Mimsy began to pray out loud, asking for me to find my way. It didn't help that I caught a glimpse of the concern in Reed's eyes. I swore it looked like he might jump to my defense, the way he looked between Ma and me.

"I don't know what you're talking about, Ma."

"Of course you do. Everyone does. Even Bobbie Jean next door knows you've been writing all over the place about your sex life and how much you hate men and marriage."

If I wasn't so embarrassed that Reed was getting yet another front row seat to the "humiliate Samantha show," I might have been impressed that my parents' ninety-year-old neighbor was online.

Instead, I sighed. "Ma, I'm not writing about my sex life, per se, and I know not all marriages are bad." I looked at Delanie, who was glued to Peter's side, to prove my statement. They both gave me sympathetic grins. "But my marriage didn't turn out the way I thought it would, and I'm just being real. I think it's helpful."

"It's helpful to tell people that you're going to be naked and you need an NDA? What is that short for? Is it some type of code word for doing, you know, the deed?"

Avery's laugh found a way out, though she tried to hold it back.

Dad, without a word, turned around and ran for the patio door.

Mimsy's prayers got a little louder.

Reed's brow hit his hairline.

I walked over to Ma and took her hands. "Ma, an NDA is a non-disclosure agreement."

"What does that mean, and why do you need one? You shouldn't even be having sex. You're not married." She was beside herself.

And now I remembered why I'd had some issues with sex when I first got married. My entire life, I was told how bad sex was, and how horrible things would happen to me if I had it before I got married. Talk like that kind of does something to you. And it's not easy to flip a switch and go from "sex is bad" to "oh, sex is good." That's why I'd always told Cody that sex was beautiful, but it needed to be done with the right person at the right time. He doesn't appreciate those talks.

I looked around the room at everyone, and they all got the hint that I needed a private word with Ma. That was, everyone but Mimsy got the hint. It was probably good that Mimsy stayed. She needed to hear this too.

With everyone shuttled out to the backyard, I turned to the two women I loved but had complicated relationships with. They were good women with the best of intentions, but sometimes what they considered good for you wasn't right for you at all. I knew they loved me, but how they showed it wasn't always the way I needed it. They were byproducts of their generations and their own upbringings. They came from a work hard, stay in the lines, don't wear your emotions on your sleeve kind of stock. Both of them could be affectionate, but it was within their boundaries. And the world they lived in was black and white. The older I got, the more I realized life wasn't so cut and dry. There had been a lot of gray in my life, and lately a lot of red.

I dropped Ma's hand and took a deep breath. "Ma, Mimsy, I love you both, but this has to stop. I'm a grown woman and, honestly, my sex life is none of your business."

Ma grabbed her heart again like I'd stabbed her. Mimsy, on the other hand, bounced on the balls of her feet like she was excited about something. She was still rubbing her rosary beads, but at least the prayers had ceased.

"So you're saying you have a sex life?" Ma wasn't hearing me.

"I'm saying I need you to love and support me."

"But are you having sex?"

I held onto the counter for support. "Ma! I'm not having sex. Are you happy?"

"Yes." She breathed a sigh of relief.

"The point is that I'm trying to deal with my divorce." I gave Mimsy a cold stare. "Please don't start in on the evils of divorce." I turned back to Ma. "Ma, I'm trying to live again. To be the mom Cody deserves. I'm trying to learn what makes Samantha Decker tick and what she wants to do with the rest of her life. I'm scared and exhausted, but I'm doing the best I can right now. Those blog posts are helping me not get lost in my head. And yes, I may talk about sex and men from time to time. I'm almost forty years old. It's allowed. And it shouldn't be any surprise that I don't have a lot of love for the opposite sex right now. Neil did a lot of damage. I'm trying to repair that."

"Oh, my girl." Ma wrapped me up in her arms.

Mimsy joined in and tried to put her tiny, wrinkly arms around us. She made it about halfway. She was so short she was resting her hands on my butt. It was the only action it had seen in months.

I rested my head on Ma's shoulder.

"I love you, Samantha Marie."

"You're a good girl." Mimsy patted my butt. That wasn't awkward at all.

For a split second, I thought we were going to leave it at this beautiful moment, but I should have known better.

Ma kissed my cheek. "Just make sure to keep your NDAs to yourself. You can win a man's heart through his stomach, not his manhood."

That was something that should never be embroidered on a pillow or said again.

"Okay, Ma. Okay." What else could I say after that?

CHAPTER FIFTEEN

DINNER WASN'T QUITE AS EMBARRASSING, BUT IT DID PROVE INTERESTING. IT didn't help that Reed sat next to me again. In some ways, it felt less lonely having Neil's seat taken, but I wasn't sure how I felt about Reed filling it. Though he did talk a lot more than Neil had the past several years. Neil could frequently be found reading an article on his phone. A few times he had the gall to bring a book. Yep. He would pull it out once he was done eating. Reed, on the other hand, stayed engaged in all the table conversation. Including the one Delanie started.

"You really should think about expanding your reach as the Side-lined Wife."

It may have been the first time Delanie said anything out of the blue at the table. I think I was right, judging by the hush that fell over the table. If you could get the Decker clan to be quiet, that was saying something.

I turned from Reed, who had just been asking me for suggestions on where he could buy some window coverings for the little place he rented near the school, to face the gorgeous redhead a couple seats down from me. I swore she was wearing a bigger diamond nose ring than usual to irk Ma. And yeah, it was working, judging by the tsking noises Ma was making to my right.

"I'm not sure what you mean." I gave Delanie my full attention.

She smirked at Ma, like she was taking a stand, before she focused back on me. "For starters, you could rebrand your blog by changing the name to the Sidelined Wife. And you should set up a page under the same moniker on Facebook. I would also do Instagram and Twitter. I could even help with the cover concepts and your profile pictures. I have a friend who's a great photographer. And," she looked at Avery, "maybe you could help execute the cover designs."

Avery's face lit up. "I would love to."

This was the cue for some of those with a Y chromosome to flee the table. My dad invited his grandsons to join him in the backyard to toss the football around. I guess his sons and Reed were on their own. They didn't seem bothered by the topic because they all decided to stay. Ma wasn't thrilled; she waved her hands and said something about sex talk and NDAs while she cleared her plate and some of the serving dishes in front of her. That's when Reed acted the part of gentleman and helped Ma clear the table. Peter followed suit, but James stayed put. He was a good man, but he lacked being domestically helpful unless asked. Unless it had to do with lawn care or handyman stuff. He'd rather replace a garbage disposal than do the dishes. My dear grandmother, Mimsy, reached for some water like she was going to sprinkle some on me just in case, but Peter swiped the glass from her before she could. She walked out rubbing her rosary beads and muttering about the good old days when women knew their place.

With most everyone cleared out, Delanie scooted closer to me, and Avery leaned in, excited.

"I don't know. I'm sure this will all blow over soon," I said.

"I don't think so." Avery's blue eyes danced. "Did you see that Autumn Moone already linked your new post to her site? And she commented on how hilarious you are."

I hadn't seen that yet. "I messaged her through her contact page to thank her, but I haven't heard back from her."

"With a new book coming out, she's probably busy with edits. Or maybe her assistants haven't gone through the messages like they're supposed to." Delanie smiled with unease.

Avery and I both gave Delanie blank stares. Her engaging us in conversation was different all on its own, but the way she sounded so knowledgeable really threw me off.

Delanie swiped at some leftover crumbs on the table. "I mean, I'm guessing. I know how it is to be under a deadline."

"Well, maybe she doesn't think it's really me, or maybe she doesn't want to be bothered by mere mortals."

Avery and Delanie laughed.

James was tuned into his smartphone.

Avery batted at his phone. "Put that thing away and engage with real people."

James shoved his phone in his pocket with a grin. "So, what did I miss? What dresses you're all wearing to prom and what color you're going to paint your nails?"

I rolled my eyes at my big brother while Avery nudged him. "Very funny. Why don't you go help your Ma with the dishes like Peter and Reed, or go play with our sons."

He stood up. "I'm not wanted; I get it." He leaned down and kissed Avery on the head. She smacked his butt in return. James wagged his eyebrows. "Smack me like that again, honey, and I'll be hauling you up to my old room."

Avery didn't even blush anymore when James made comments like that. "Behave."

He gave her a wink and strode off.

Pangs of jealousy pricked my heart. I focused on Delanie, who wore a look like she understood how I was feeling. Her warm brown eyes spoke of an old soul. Much older than her twenty-eight years. Did I mention how gorgeous this girl was, with the perfect waterfall-curled red hair and creamy skin with freckles that looked strategically placed? Not a wrinkle or laugh line in sight.

Delanie rested her soft, feminine hand over mine on the table. "I know you feel like you're in unknown territory now. We've all been there. But your voice is helping women face the uncertainty, no matter what the circumstances are. You have the power to do a lot of good. Let us help you help others. And maybe we'll help ourselves in the process."

I felt like she wanted to tell us something. Was she facing uncertainty? Did she need help? I opened my mouth to speak, but Delanie removed her hand and gave a smart aleck grin.

"Besides, you're funny as hell. And," she lowered her voice, "it's nice to have your mom focus on something else she hates besides me."

I was going to have to help change that. Along with a lot of other things in my life. Maybe it was time to embrace the Sidelined Wife.

I did all the "mom" things before I went to bed that night. Cody started his sophomore year on Tuesday, and I wanted to get back into a good Sunday night routine. I wanted to purposely do things, not only get by. I whipped up batches of quick oats and placed them in the refrigerator for breakfast throughout the week. I even made sure he had balanced, protein-packed lunch and snack items he could easily grab each morning, so he would be properly fueled for practice. Cody wasn't happy about it, but I made him clean up his room and actually fold and hang up his clothes for smoother mornings. I knew it wouldn't last, but at least I was trying to give him habits he would thank me for later in his life. Maybe.

After saying my goodnights to Cody, I sank into bed and pulled out my laptop. It was all I had to snuggle up to at night now. Quite honestly, it was warmer than Neil had been the months leading up to our separation and divorce. And my followers were hilarious. There was a lawyer in the group that made up a mock NDA for me.

Section one started with, CONFIDENTIAL INFORMATION. *"Confidential Information" is defined as any information that I will personally see you maimed and silenced for if you share. It includes, but is not limited to, my weight, how many stretch marks there may or may not be, sagging skin in any or all locations, cellulite deposits...*

My phone rang, interrupting my belly laugh. I picked it up without even thinking, assuming it was Avery calling to discuss the NDA and more of our plans for the Sidelined Wife.

"Hello?" I was still giggling.

"You sound like you're in a good mood."

All gaiety ceased with the deep voice I wasn't expecting. "Reed?"

"Oh good, you recognized my voice." He sounded happy, but tentative.

"How did you get my number?"

"That's a good question."

"It's one that deserves an answer."

"You're absolutely right, which means I should first ask you if you are still available to sell gameday tickets at the school on Friday during lunch?"

"Since when does the head football coach organize that schedule?"

"I'm not; you should expect an email from Lisa Cardston, the booster president, in the next couple of days."

"I'm confused."

He took a deep breath and let it out in what sounded like timed intervals.

"Are you okay?" I asked.

"Never better."

"So why are you calling, and how did you get my number?" I was more than curious.

"I pulled your number off Cody's paperwork." Some guilt mixed into his words.

What Peter said last week played in my head, something about me missing something. He didn't think...? Did he? "Okay. Why?"

"We never got to finish our discussion about curtains versus blinds."

A tiny laugh escaped, making me forget I should probably question his judgement in using school information for a personal call. "I didn't realize how important that was to you."

"You have no idea."

"Do tell."

He had no problem obliging. "For starters, are curtains really manly? But, on the other hand, do I want to install blinds in a rental?"

"Those are deep and perplexing issues."

"I think you're making fun of me."

"I think you're right."

He chuckled on his end.

"Is that really why you called?"

He paused. "Honestly, I called to see how you are." His sincerity came through loud and clear.

"You did?"

"Yeah. You seemed upset when I arrived for dinner tonight."

One of those disgusted *ugh* sounds came out. "Could you please forget that whole conversation?" Ma had no decorum.

"I don't know. Sex and NDAs, that's an unusual conversation."

"I suppose it is." I smiled to myself.

"Samantha, I really am sorry for what you're going through. And just so you know, there's no reason for you to be embarrassed."

"Really? Does your grandma throw fake holy water on you, and does your mom feel the need to announce to your entire family and innocent guests the intimate details of your life?"

"I'm not sure I'm exactly innocent, unfortunately, I'm not even close. But no, both my grandmas have passed on and my mom doesn't announce anything publicly. But she calls me every day to ask when she can expect to finally be a grandma."

"Ma did the same thing after I got married. One of my wedding gifts from her was a bassinet."

"I think I remember that at your reception. Wasn't there a big pink bow on it?"

I guess he was there. I couldn't remember. "Yes. Ma was wishing for a granddaughter. We gave her three boys in a row."

"I heard about James's daughter. I'm so sorry."

I swallowed the golf ball of sadness down my throat. It always appeared whenever Hannah was mentioned. I loved that little girl. We used to have a once-a-month shopping and lunch date, just the two of us. I missed the way she said *Auntie Sam* and how she would cuddle into my side to watch girlie movies. Oh, how I wanted my own little girl.

"It puts life into perspective, that's for sure, along with making me more of a worrier. I would put a tracking device on Cody if I didn't think it was creepy."

"I'm sure he appreciates that."

"Not as much as he should."

"He really is a great kid. He's a natural-born leader, which isn't surprising considering who his mother is."

"Is that a compliment? Or are you saying I was bossy?"

"Definitely a compliment. But now thinking back, you were pretty bossy." I could hear the teasing in his voice.

"You know, if I'm forgetting your past, I think you owe me the same courtesy. And I wasn't bossy; I was in charge and trying to protect myself from your and Peter's antics."

"Antics? That's probably putting it nicely," he conceded.

"Agreed. At least one of you turned out nice."

"It's not very polite to talk about your brother that way."

I found myself smiling and laughing. "How about this? You forget how bossy I was, and I'll forget how you terrorized me."

"Deal."

"I should probably let you go. It's getting late."

"My mom gave me permission to stay up past my bedtime tonight."

I laughed again. "Now you're making fun of me."

"Never."

"Good night, Reed."

"Good night, Samantha."

"Reed," I blurted before he hung up.

"Yeah?"

"You can call me Sam."

CHAPTER SIXTEEN

WHY DID I STILL CRY ON THE FIRST DAY OF SCHOOL? YOU WOULD THINK I'D
be past it considering his age, but no. It was worse. Each year meant we
were getting closer to me not being present on the first day. And someday
there would be no more first days. Cody didn't appreciate the tears or
the awkwardly long hug at the door where his friend Hershel could see.
At least I was dressed with my hair and makeup done. Ma used to come
out in her bathrobe with curlers in her hair. I would at least give him
credit for not forcefully extricating himself from me. The kid had several
inches on me and he was a lot stronger. He could have easily gotten
out of my clutches, but he patted my back and kept saying things like,
"Mom, I really need to go." "I love you." "You're embarrassing me."

While wiping my tears away and getting ready to head into the
office, I got a text.

*Have a good day. This is Reed, by the way, in case you didn't add me to your
contacts yet.*

I hadn't. I figured Sunday night was a one-time deal.

Happy first day of school, I responded. I couldn't say enough how
weird it was to be talking to Reed like we were friends.

I've doubled up on coffee and I have the ibuprofen ready to go just in case.
Good luck.

Thank you.

I shrugged and threw my phone into my purse. So many unexpected things kept happening to me. At least Reed was pleasant.

Five minutes later, on my drive to the office, I received another text from him. My car read texts to me. I was sure it read this one wrong.

Hey, how would you like to help me shop for curtains? I decided to embrace my feminine side.

While funny, I wasn't sure what to make of it. And it wasn't like I could respond. I was a huge believer in no texting while driving. Ask Cody. I reminded him every time we got in the car that if I ever caught him texting and driving, I'd accompany him on every date he ever went on, as well as confiscate his phone.

Once I got to the office, I read the text to make sure my car wasn't playing tricks on me. What did I say? This was the kind of thing you asked your girlfriend or mom to do. Did he see me like a mother figure?

Another text popped up.

The students will be filing in soon, and I won't be able to teach if I'm worried that I'll buy the wrong length, or anger the home interior gods by mixing the wrong patterns. Don't even get me going on my curtain rod nightmares.

I probably looked like an idiot, giggling uncontrollably in my car. *Home interior gods?*

What? Do they prefer being called something else? Lifestyle gurus? Is that better?
Much.
So will you help me? I can't risk ticking off a guru.
I'm not sure I'm the right person, and I can't have your fate resting in my hands.
I'll take my chances.

I thought for a few more seconds. I needed to buy some myself anyway. And I'll admit, Reed entertained me. I could use some more of that in my life. *Okay.*

That sounded lackluster. We are talking curtains here. I need some enthusiasm.

Who was this guy? Certainly not the kid I used to know. I wasn't sure how to respond. I had never really gotten that excited over curtains. *Okay!*

That was better, but it still needs a little work. I've got to do some educating. I'll call you later to set up a time.

I didn't know what to say, so I let that be the final communication. In a daze, I walked into the office staring at my phone.

"More fan mail?" Avery interrupted my thoughts.

It took me a second to realize she had said something. "Huh?"

Avery tipped her pretty head to the side. "You all right?"

I threw my phone back in my purse. "Right as rain."

"I almost believe you. And if I'm not mistaken, you seem happy. I thought you would be a big pile of goo after sending Cody to school."

"I'm faking it until I make it." I gave her a semi-real grin.

"I know that routine."

"How did you do sending off the boys this morning?"

"Me? I threw a party. Your nephews aren't going to be happy until they knock down a wall or burn the house to the ground. I love those boys, but I miss my girl." Her voice cracked. "Next week it will be two years."

"I know." I met her at her desk where we embraced.

"She would have started middle school this year." Her tears landed on my shoulder. "When we went back-to-school shopping, I almost bought a pink backpack with hearts on it. Remember how much she loved hearts?"

"I do. I kept the notes she wrote me on the paper hearts she loved to cut out."

"I feel terrible for ever getting frustrated with her for leaving paper scraps everywhere. What I wouldn't give to have her paper fill the house."

I hugged her tighter. "She knew how loved she was."

"Why does life have to be so damn unfair?"

"That's a good question."

"I don't think this ache will ever go away."

"I don't know that it's meant to. How could it? Those creatures are a part of us."

"I don't think James understands that. Or he's better at hiding his grief than me."

"Men can joke all day long that they're glad they don't have to give birth, but if they really knew how amazing it was to give life, they would jump at the chance. We are connected to our children in a unique way. Not that men don't have value, well, at least some men, but I think deep down they know they are missing out on something wonderful."

"I'm not sure about that, given James's reaction in the delivery room, but I just wished he would talk about it more, or let me talk and not say anything. Sometimes all I need from him is to hold me."

"Have you told him?"

"I have, and sometimes he listens, but it only lasts for a day or so. Don't get me wrong. I love James. He's good man, but he's..."

"A man?"

She cried and laughed all at the same time. "You totally get me."

"I think that Y chromosome affects their brains. It takes whatever we say and translates it into a whole other language... or to whatever they want to hear."

"I think you're onto something, sister." She gently pulled away and wiped her eyes. I handed her a tissue from my purse. I always kept some handy.

"I'm here if you need to talk."

She nodded and took her seat back at her desk. "Oh, before I forget, speaking of dumb things your brother says, he thinks you and Reed were flirting Sunday night at dinner." She laughed and blew her nose at the same time, though I wasn't sure how that was possible.

I froze and tried not to make direct eye contact with her. "Why would he think such a ridiculous thing?"

Her shoulders twitched. "He said you looked cozy talking to each other, and he noticed Reed walked you out to your car."

"He was leaving at the same time," I stuttered.

"That's what I said. I mean, you babysat the kid."

"Exactly." Why was my voice high-pitched?

"I told James he was crazy, and you would likely date someone older than you who was more settled in life."

I rubbed the back of my neck. "Or not at all."

She gave me a big smile. "Oh, give it a while, hot mama. You'll have some irresistible debonair professor or something knocking on your door."

"Yeah, maybe."

"Not to say that Reed kid isn't a fine specimen, but he's totally not your type."

"Definitely not. I better get to work if we all want to get paid this week."

"Don't let me keep you. School fees were killer this year, and mama needs a new pair of shoes."

I waved and walked off, suddenly feeling deceitful. Why didn't I tell her that Reed called me, or that I agreed to go curtain shopping with him? I was going to have to cancel that. I didn't want anyone to get the wrong idea. I mean, Reed and me? What a preposterous idea.

CHAPTER SEVENTEEN

THE HIGH SCHOOL SMELLED LIKE TEEN SPIRIT. OR WAS THAT THE LUNCHES they tried to pass off as real food? One thing that penetrated the air was the perfume and cologne kids doused themselves in. While I appreciated the effort to hide body odor, my eyes burned when some of them came to purchase football tickets from me outside the lunch room Friday afternoon during their lunch period. I had yet to see my son in the noisy, smelly crowd. Not like he needed a ticket, but I hoped he would at least say hi. Some of his friends had. I had heard too many "Mrs. Higgins's" already, but I didn't have the heart or time to correct them. I had a steady stream of students wanting to purchase tickets since it was cheaper to buy them before the game.

I observed the interactions between the students and thanked my lucky stars that at least I wasn't a teen girl. In their eyes and posture, I could see the way they compared themselves and how uncomfortable they were. I wanted to hug them all and tell them it would be okay. But then, like a lightning strike, I realized it didn't change much as we got older. Maybe we were on different playgrounds, but our self-scrutinizing and comparing ourselves to others doesn't change with age. In fact, it may get worse. Especially with social media. I know I had played into it. Not that there wasn't something to be said for putting our best foot forward, but if we weren't able to ever admit life wasn't perfect or that it plain sucked from time to time, how could we ever get help and move on?

These last several days of communicating with women from all over the world made me realize how valuable honesty was. To know you aren't alone. I wanted to shout out to the girls hugging the brick wall or staring at their phone trying to be invisible that they weren't alone. But, instead, I found myself not alone.

Reed threw himself into the empty chair next to me. The other mom that was scheduled to help sell tickets had a sick child at home and couldn't make it. At first he didn't say anything. He went right to work taking cash and handing out tickets. Though he did give me an evil sort of grin.

I felt guilty and had hoped to avoid him. You see, I had been ignoring his texts for the last couple of days after I reneged on my curtain shopping promise. He hadn't let me forget. He sent me texts like, *Are you going to keep me hanging like the nonexistent curtains at my place? Do you know what one curtain panel said to the other? Me neither, because I don't have any.*

There were more, and each time, they gave me a good laugh and tempted me to respond, but if James thought there was something going on between us because we talked at dinner, what would everyone think if we were seen out in public together, alone? That was the last thing I needed.

You know what else I didn't need? To be attracted to the way he smelled. Even worse was the physiological response I had to him when our arms brushed each other. What was that? Did my heart rate increase, or was this the first sign of perimenopause? For as cold as they kept the school, I was feeling warm. It had to be out of embarrassment. It had nothing to do with the man I used to babysit, who was sitting next to me in a suit, ready for game day. So what if he looked nothing like that boy? He sure didn't smell like him.

I focused on my task at hand, only stopping to say hi to Cody, who looked reluctant to approach the ticket table. Okay, so he went to his coach's side and acknowledged my presence with a quick "hello." For Reed, he had fist bumps and smiles. Was he embarrassed I was wearing a jersey with his name and number on it? All the moms on the team had bought the official black Pomona Panthers jersey.

My sigh must have been too loud watching my son walk off. Did I mention he was with that girl, Rory, real name Aurora? She had come over earlier and introduced herself to me in her too short cheerleading outfit. "Hi, Mrs. Higgins. I love your son," she'd said.

I swore she clapped at the end like she had just finished a cheer. I had nothing against cheerleaders, being a former one myself, but she was too cute. And what did she know about love? I didn't like the way Cody's eyes filled with wonder when he saw her. The question was, what was he wondering about? What was under that uniform? How far he could or should go? I almost chased after him shouting about STDs and unintended pregnancies.

Reed chuckled next to me.

"Are you laughing at me?"

"Yep." He took money and handed a ticket to the next kid in line without missing a beat or saying anything else to me.

This went on until lunch was over and it was time for me to count the money and make sure it coincided with how many tickets were sold.

When the last kid scurried away down the locker-lined hall to get to class, I turned to Reed. "Thanks for your help. You should probably get to class."

He pressed his lips together and took a deep breath. "That sounded too motherly."

I had done it again. I shrugged. "Sorry, I can't help it." I started organizing and turning the money all the same way before I turned it in to the school cashier.

Reed started doing the same.

"I got this."

He glanced my way. "This is my planning period."

"Oh." I stayed focused on the piles of bills in front of us.

"How have you been?" There was a playful edge to his voice.

"Good." I sorted the money by denomination, pretending like I hadn't ignored him for the last few days.

"I'm glad to hear that." He was making his own piles of money.

"How are you?"

"Great. Looking forward to the game tonight."

"That must be exciting. Home opener and first game of the season."

"Yeah. I never thought I would get another one of those here."

"It must be gratifying to coach at your alma mater."

"It's an honor."

I nodded.

Silence fell upon us in the empty hall. We were surrounded by motivational posters and the lingering smell of lunch.

"Is your phone broken?" He casually tossed out there.

"No." My voice squeaked.

"So you're purposely ignoring me."

"I wouldn't exactly say that."

"What would you say?"

I turned and met his playful eyes. Were they always so blue? My head darted right back to the money.

"I've been busy with stuff, lots of stuff...Cody, work...and my sisters-in-law, they're really getting into this Sidelined Wife stuff." That was true. I had a photo shoot tomorrow, and Avery had been working with Delanie on designs for my new Facebook page and blog makeover. All that meant I had to go shopping. I'd taken Gelaire with me because she was the epitome of style and she too was excited about this new alter ego of mine. We'd found a great denim shirt and paired it with a black blazer. It was chic. Or at least that's what Gelaire said.

"Sounds jam-packed." His sarcastic tone came out loud and clear.

I decided to ignore it. "Yep."

"Well, I hope you can live with yourself, knowing that I forgot I didn't have window coverings and inadvertently flashed my neighbors yesterday morning."

I tried not to laugh, but I couldn't hold it in.

"You think it's funny?" He didn't sound upset at all. "Now, thanks to you, the senior citizen sisters that live behind me have become admirers. I got cookies and a dinner invite for this weekend."

"That sounds nice. You're welcome."

"I like older women, but not ones that could be my grandmother."

I dared a peek at him. "You like older women?"

He gave me a dazzling smile. "They're my favorite."

Counting money. Counting money. "Like, how old are we talking?" I tried to play that off as nonchalant as I could. I wasn't even sure why I was asking.

"My last girlfriend was ten years older than me."

"Wow!" Why did I react like that? If only I could kick myself under the table. I said the dumbest things around him.

He laughed good naturedly. "Why is that so surprising?"

I thought about what Avery said about my type. "I guess I'm old fashioned. You know, the man being older than the woman."

He flipped my hair, causing a weird sensation I couldn't exactly identify. "You *are* looking a little matronly."

"No need to get personal." I glared at him.

"I'm kidding, you don't look a day over fifty."

I elbowed him in the ribs.

"Ouch."

"Serves you right."

He leaned in too close. His scent excited me. I didn't know I could get that kind of excited still, especially around him. "Can I tell you a secret?"

Was he using intimate tones? No . . . I couldn't respond. The breath I was holding was keeping me hostage.

"Word on the street is that Cody's mom is a babe."

That held breath came out when my jaw dropped. "You're lying."

"I swear it on Mimsy's holy water."

I gave him a scrutinizing stare. "You know that stuff she uses isn't real."

"Be that as it may, Cody's friends think you're hot."

"Cody's never said anything." Waves of embarrassment were washing over me.

"Why would he? Do you think he likes the fact that his friends are checking you out? And believe me, they are. I heard a few of them talking about you when you showed up to practice last week."

"Are you putting me on?"

"I wouldn't lie to you."

I believed him. "We better finish counting this money."

"There you go, using those leadership skills again."

"I'd rather be bossy than annoying."

"I always enjoyed annoying you."

"Looks like some things never change."

"You don't know how true that is."

I tilted my head toward him. He was already staring at me with a penetrating gaze. What did that mean?

CHAPTER EIGHTEEN

ARE YOU COMING TONIGHT? I HATED TEXTING NEIL, BUT IT WAS FOR CODY. Cody wouldn't admit it, but I knew he wanted his dad there. He off-handedly had asked me this morning before he left for school if he was coming. I didn't have an answer for him.

While I waited for a response, I got all my game gear ready—a light jacket just in case, and a stadium seat. My butt was getting too old to sit on the bleachers all night. I also did something else, surprising the heck out of myself.

Good luck, I texted Reed. I wasn't sure if he would get the message since he was probably in the locker room with the team giving them a motivational speech or something. I wasn't sure why I even felt compelled to send it. Maybe guilt from ignoring his texts all week? Or maybe I couldn't quit thinking about our odd conversation at the school. The oddest thing being that a man had just jumped in and helped without even being asked. Come to think of it, he'd done that at my parents' house too. He was always the first one to help clean up. Neil never would have.

Thank you, Sam. Reed texted right back, unlike my ex-husband, whom I had texted three times already throughout the day with no response.

I did a quick check of my email before I headed to the game. My heart about stopped when I saw that I received a response from *the* Autumn Moone.

Dear Samantha,

First, let me apologize for my late response. My editors are breathing down my neck

Your thanks are not required. I feel as if I should thank you. Your insights and bravery have inspired me to be a better person and writer. I am a fan.

Keep writing those posts, and I will keep sharing them.

And I wish I could tell you if Laine and Hunter really get together in A Black Night, *but you'll have to read the book to find out.*

Back to editing.

All the Best,

Autumn

I laughed to myself. I knew it was a long shot, asking about Hunter and Laine. It was nice of her to respond. It probably wasn't really her. She more than likely had an assistant do it, but I would take it all the same.

Her site had even posted my little snippet from this morning about my new obsession, protein balls. Oats, honey, chocolate, and peanut butter with some flax seeds sprinkled in for good measure. Basically, they're a cookie in ball shape. But I could feel better about eating them because of the name. Which reminded me, it was time for some protein. I grabbed a ball out of the freezer and indulged in it while I hauled my gear to the car. I was too nervous to eat a real meal. I wasn't sure Cody would get any playing time, but I was nervous just in case.

It didn't help when Neil texted, *I don't think I'll be able to make it. Wish Cody luck for me.*

I shook my head in anger. *Do it yourself, coward.*

I threw my phone in my bag, doing my best not to cry. I shouldn't have been surprised. I ached for my son. He didn't deserve this.

I'm sorry, is all he texted back. He was the sorriest excuse for a human being. What had happened to him? Granted, he was never the most attentive father, but at least he used to try.

I had to get my head in the game for Cody. We had lived without Neil for months now and we had done okay. And we would do better.

I arrived at the school early. The stadium always filled up quickly and I wanted to get good seats for me and my family. Who needed Neil?

Unfortunately, Cody did. But not me. I'm not sure I ever needed him, but, oh, I used to want him.

I was able to snag the third row on the fifty-yard line. Sitting there by myself made me feel like a big arrow was pointing at me that said *divorcee*. The looks from some of our neighbors and couple of friends, like the Gephardts, didn't help. They gave me forced uncomfortable smiles and a wave, but didn't stop or utter a hello anymore. It was like somehow being divorced made me a pariah. For goodness sake, we used to barbecue on the weekends. Our sons even did a joint Harry Potter themed birthday party once when they were in middle school. It embarrassed Cody now to think of it.

I was never happier to see my parents and even Mimsy. She typically didn't come to games. As spry as she was in her eighties, walking up the stands and sitting on the bleachers wasn't easy on her little body. Dad carried the stadium chairs while Ma helped Mimsy make the short climb.

I made sure to mouth to Dad that he better be the one sitting by me. He chuckled before situating the stadium chairs and plopping down next to me. Ma didn't like his arrangement, so she moved her seat on the other side of me and moved Mimsy next to her. I eyed Mimsy's bottle of water. She better not think of throwing any of that on me.

Dad wrapped his arm around me and let out a meaningful sigh. I wondered if he and Ma had a blowup. They seemed to be ignoring each other.

I didn't directly address my suspicion. Instead, I reached my hand across and squeezed each of the matriarchs' hands. "Thanks for coming. How are you?"

"Eh." Ma shrugged.

Mimsy bounced in her seat like a toddler. "There was a catfight at the prison today."

Mimsy referred to the retirement community she lived in as *the prison*. She was still upset Dad and Ma moved her into it a few years ago after Grandpa died. It wasn't like she couldn't take care of herself, but she'd fallen once and lay injured for ten hours before we knew about it. Ma wanted her to live with them, but to Dad's relief, Mimsy refused.

They compromised on the lovely community she lived in now. I mean, I wouldn't mind living there. You got maid service, and all your meals were prepared. And who didn't love a rousing game of bingo every day?

"A catfight?" I questioned Mimsy.

Her aged blue eyes were all a-twinkle. "Ethel from two doors down was caught with her Depends down around her ankles with George from one floor up, who was seeing Polly from the building next door."

Did she say Depends? "Oh." As in *oh, I wished I hadn't asked*.

"Polly smacked her right in the face at lunch, knocking her dentures out."

"Mom, that's awful," Ma chimed in. Dad laughed, earning him narrowed eyes from Ma and an I-wish-you-dead look. Something was brewing that I probably didn't want to know about.

Mimsy swatted her daughter's arm. "It's the best thing that's happened since I've been there."

I leaned more into Dad, trying to forget about what Mimsy just said. Not sure that was possible. "How was your day, Dad?" I hadn't seen him all day, since I typically didn't go to the office on Fridays.

Dad cleared his throat. "I bought a boat."

Ma harrumphed next to me. I was pretty sure I knew the cause of their discord now.

"Really? What kind?"

Ma gave Dad a withering glance. "Yes, Joseph, why don't you tell her what you wasted our money on?" Ma said that loud enough to draw attention from the innocent bystanders in front of us who did their best to not openly stare back at us, but managed a peek.

Dad's free arm rubbed the back of his neck. "It's an ice boat."

"An ice boat?"

"Your idiot father thinks he needs to compete in some amateur ice boat competition in Wisconsin." Ma answered for Dad. "He saw it on some stupid sports channel. We could have gone to the motherland." Ma threw her hands up.

She meant Germany, where we descended from.

Dad stiffened and faced forward, not wanting to continue this conversation in public.

I hoped Ma followed suit. But Mimsy had to throw in her two cents. She took her daughter's hand. "Look at it this way, Sarah, he could die on the ice and then you can use his life insurance money to travel."

Dad's jaw dropped, but Ma's eyes filled with tears while she crossed herself. As angry as she got with Dad, I don't think she would know what to do without him. And more than anything since Hannah's death, Ma hated talking about anyone dying, except maybe Neil.

"Mom, don't talk like that." Ma was still crossing herself.

Mimsy shrugged. "I was just trying to see the bright side."

It was a wonder I wasn't in therapy.

Grateful didn't even describe how ecstatic I was to see the rest of my family arrive, minus Delanie.

Peter walked past me and kissed my cheek. "Delanie's sorry she couldn't make it. She's buried in work."

"They've really been putting her feet to the coals this week." She'd complained about it earlier this week when Avery and I had lunch with her to work on the Sidelined Wife stuff. Poor thing chowed down her salad, gave a few insights, and headed back home to work.

Peter's stance shifted while he ran his hands through his hair. "She has a big deadline this week."

"Some expose or something?" Delanie never did say at lunch.

"Yeah, something like that." He moved down past Mimsy, who already had Matt and Jimmy next to her. She was stuffing their hands full of cash. I wished she would have done that when I was growing up.

Avery and James sat directly behind me.

"No yelling in my ear," I warned James.

He rested his hands on my shoulders and gave me a gentle shake. "Don't count on it. I'm ready to see number eleven tear it up out there." Eleven was Cody's number.

"He probably won't get any playing time."

"Peter told Reed if he didn't, he was no longer invited to Sunday dinner."

I wasn't sure if I should believe James or not, especially since Avery laughed at him.

They looked content tonight, holding hands and wearing matching

Pomona High shirts. Jealousy crept in, but it was overcome by gratitude. Their support of Cody meant the world to me.

Avery leaned in and whispered in my ear, "Is Neil coming?"

I shook my head.

She patted my back, trying to console me.

James must have clued in. He started calling Neil names that had Ma crossing herself and Mimsy flicking water on him. I bowed my head. Not to pray, but to miss all the embarrassing glances everyone in the vicinity was giving us.

The game couldn't have begun any sooner. Who knew what else was going to come flying out of my family's mouth? The marching band came out and we all stood for the national anthem. Mimsy and Ma always got choked up during the song. My great-grandfather had served in World War II and died during the D-day invasion. A picture of him in uniform rested proudly on my parents' mantle.

Our team took the field to loud applause and cheers. I had a feeling my throat would be sore by the end of the night, especially if Cody got any playing time. Maybe if they were far enough ahead in the last quarter he would. James had it on good authority that the team we were playing—Buffalo Grove—wasn't a solid team. James was good to keep up on those types of things. So hopefully this would be an easy win for the Panthers, for both Cody's and Reed's sake. I felt nervous for both of them. Don't ask me why. Admittedly, Reed had taken up a lot of my thoughts today, remembering the way he smelled, his eyes.

"Go Cody," I yelled for no real reason other than I needed something to do besides think about his coach.

My family all laughed at my exuberance. If only they knew what was lurking in my brain. That was never going to happen, because I wasn't thinking about Reed anymore. Except I noticed how good he looked out there in his official Panther polo shirt and khakis. The headset made him look so official. There was an air of calm surrounding him. I already liked him better than the last coach, who would have been yelling at the kids even before they took the field for the first play. Then I noticed how he said something to Cody. I could tell by the way Cody stood up straighter it was good. I wondered what he said.

We lost the ceremonial coin toss. I wasn't even sure why they did that anymore. Everyone knew the real coin toss happened between the coaches and referees before the game. But I guess it gave the team captains something to do. So the Panthers would be kicking off to the Spartans. It was a great kick-off too. Our kicker was a phenomenal girl who was also a star soccer player. I loved that she was on the football team.

The first half of the game was uglier than I hoped it would be based on James's intel. The Spartans were playing dirty and hard. I watched Reed to see how he would handle it all. Again, he was calm and collected. I could see him trying to keep our guys focused, and it worked. By the end of the half, we were up 17–13. It was close, but we were edging them out.

Avery and I used halftime to hit the ladies' room, which was really an excuse to talk about my dad's purchase and my email from Autumn Moone. Avery was in a girlish tizzy over it, squeezing my arm and reading it several times on my phone.

She handed me back my phone. "You should see if she'll send us some signed copies. And maybe a large poster of Hunter Black."

"Where would you keep yours? I don't think James would appreciate it, but according to Peter, James is onto your obsession."

She waved her hand around in the air. "He has nothing to worry about. Besides, he still buys the *Sports Illustrated Swimsuit* issue every year. It would serve him right for me to put up a poster of Hunter Black above our bed. Ask for one of him shirtless."

I laughed at her. "I don't think we'll have any more correspondence."

"Come on, do it for me."

I shook my head. "Only because I love you and I want to see James's reaction to the poster."

She leaned into me and laughed evilly.

We brought candy and popcorn back for everyone and handed them out before the second half started. I still had hope Cody would get some playing time. I saw him throwing footballs on the sideline with the third-string quarterback, trying to keep his arm warm just in case.

Dad beamed at his grandson. "That kid is going places," he remarked.

"Hopefully close to home," I replied.

Dad wrapped his arm around me. I noticed when he reached across, he brushed Ma's shoulder first. She returned the gesture with a wry smile and a semi-glare. That was progress. I predicted by the end of the game she would be back to her normal rolling of the eyes, but holding his hand. The question would be if Dad would get to keep the boat.

Reed must have given one heck of a motivational speech in the locker room. The Panthers came back with a lot of roar. By fourth quarter, the score was 31–20. And guess who was sent in for the last few minutes of the game? When my baby's name was called by the announcer, I stood up clasping my hands together and holding them tight to my chest. So proud. So anxious for him. He looked taller as he jogged out to the huddle and called the play. Dad joined me. It made me feel all at once less alone and more alone, if that made any sense at all. Dads are amazing, but they don't fill the void left by a spouse, try as they may. Dad was doing his best, and I loved him more than he would ever know for it.

Suddenly, I realized how big some of the Spartans' linemen were. Those sumo wrestlers were going to squish my baby. I had to keep myself from hyperventilating, waiting for the ball to be snapped. Cody caught the snap fluidly, ran back, zeroed in on his running back, and threw a pretty spiral. The pass was completed but they only gained a few yards. The next down netted them maybe a yard—the receiver was pushed back by some of those sumo wrestlers.

Third down saw Cody having to run the ball himself since no one could get open. The Spartans defense was putting up a good fight. Thankfully, Cody ran out of bounds and wasn't tackled. On top of that, he netted them a first down. He carefully marched his team down the field toward the end zone, running down the clock and keeping possession of the ball. The defense was trying their best to stop them and get the ball back, but each time our offense answered.

I felt like I didn't breathe the entire time Cody was on that field. Thirteen yards from the end zone saw Cody taking a knee on the snap, letting the clock run down and ending the game. I knew Cody would be disappointed he didn't get the chance to throw a touchdown pass or score one by running it in. But his team won their home opener and he celebrated with enthusiasm, jumping up and down with his teammates on the field.

My eyes followed as Reed walked across the field to shake hands with the Spartans' coach. As soon as that obligation was taken care of, he was like a kid with a huge spring in his step, high-fiving and fist-bumping every player. I watched him give Cody a big bear hug. It tugged on my heartstrings.

I hadn't even noticed the major celebration going on around me. My dad, brothers, and nephews mimicked the team. Mimsy celebrated by handing more cash to Jimmy and Matt. I was handed a wad of bills with strict instructions that it was only for Cody, like I would steal from my son.

Soon the celebrating was over, and my family left. Peter was anxious to get home to Delanie. Matt and Jimmy had an early morning cross country meet, so James and Avery rushed them home. It was way past Mimsy's bedtime, and I got the feeling Dad wanted to talk to Ma privately. I noticed how he rested his hand on her lower back while she guided Mimsy down the bleachers.

The stands cleared. And that was that.

CHAPTER NINETEEN

THERE I WAS. ALONE.

The team had cleared the field and headed to the locker room. That was good news for me. It meant Cody should smell decent on the trip home.

I slipped into my lightweight nylon jacket, though it was still relatively warm and humid out. It brought me comfort, like a security blanket, even if it didn't match the shorts and jersey I was wearing.

I headed to the locker rooms with several other parents to wait for our children. Was everyone married? I hadn't noticed that before. And why was I feeling marginalized because I was single now? Maybe because I heard two of the moms up ahead whispering about me, but doing a terrible job of keeping their voices down.

"Did you know she's calling herself 'the Sidelined Wife' now?"

"Who does she think she is?"

One of the husbands looked back at me before also doing a terrible job of whispering to his wife. "I think she can hear you."

The women stopped and looked back at me, red faced.

I wanted to say something back to them. Something clever and witty that proved they didn't hurt my feelings or exacerbate my already vulnerable state. But all I could do was not give them the satisfaction of tears. Those would come in the privacy of my home.

They picked up their pace and mine slowed. I waited well outside of the locker room, staring at my phone, trying to be invisible like the teen girls earlier that day. Last year I would have been amongst the crowd, talking easily. What had happened?

I didn't comprehend a thing on my phone's screen. I was itching for the safety of my car, wishing for my old life back. But is that what I really wanted? The façade?

Boys, showered and dressed, started filing out of the locker room. Some went their own way, others into the congratulatory arms of their parents. With each emerging player, I looked to see if it was Cody. What was taking him so long? He finally came out wearing his winner's grin. He was joined by one of his teammates, Jayvin. They were laughing and talking.

"Cody." I waved, anxious to go, though I was the only one of two parents left now.

He ran my way and did exactly what I needed him to do. He threw his arms around me.

"Did you see me?" For a moment, he sounded like my little boy.

"You were amazing! Everyone thought so. They're sorry they all had to leave early, but they wanted me to tell you congratulations. And," I handed him the wad of cash I had stashed in my jacket pocket, "this is Mimsy's way of congratulating you."

He took the cash. "Awesome." He took a breath and lowered his voice and head. "Did Dad come?"

I thought my heart couldn't break any more, but it was like a meteorite hit and a crater was formed right in the center of it.

I shook my head. "I'm sorry, honey, no."

He shrugged. "It's no big deal."

"That's not true. It's okay to be disappointed."

He shook his head in defiance. I understood that. I had done the same thing many times.

"Jayvin was wondering if I could go to his house for a while. Some of us are getting together for pizza and video games to celebrate." His eyes begged me to let him go so he could forget that I was it. I knew he wasn't trying to slight me.

"Okay. Home by midnight, please. Or do I need to pick you up?"

"Jayvin's going to give me a ride." He turned to walk away.

"Cody?" Pleading was in my voice.

He immediately faced me.

"I love you." I knew that didn't make it better, but it was all I had to offer.

"Love you." He took off and never looked back.

The tears didn't wait. They filled my eyes. In a rush, I headed toward the stadium parking lot.

Not even my name being called was going to stop me.

"Sam," the familiar voice rang out.

Where had he come from? I didn't care. I kept my hurried pace to the car.

"Sam," the persistent voice neared.

I was wiping tears furiously as I walked.

"Sam," the voice was upon me and it came with a touch. Reed gently grabbed my arm. "Hey there, slow down."

I tried to turn my head away so he wouldn't see the emotion pouring out of me, but there was no hiding it.

His instinctual response was apparently to reach up to touch my tear stained cheek, but thankfully he stopped himself. What was he thinking? His blue eyes were big and flooded with curiosity and worry.

"What's wrong?"

I stepped away, making him let go, which was my plan. All I needed was this scene to play out in front of someone. Though it was innocent, after tonight, I felt like I had a mark on my head. Or that I had just became aware of it.

"I need to go." And that's what I did.

Did I mention Reed was persistent? He followed. "Sam, what happened?"

"Life." I kept my pace.

He had no problem keeping up. His legs were longer than mine and I'm sure he was in better shape. I was still sore from that stupid hip-hop class five days ago.

By the time I reached my car, I was a shaky, emotional wreck. Was I so naïve to think the Sidelined Wife stuff wouldn't get around to the people at Cody's school? Or did I just assume everyone would be happy for me? And then there was Neil. I was going to call him and let him have it. All of this was his fault. He divorced me, not Cody.

But before I could, I found myself in the most unexpected place. Reed wrapped his arms around me.

"Please tell me what's wrong." His chin rested on my head.

I stood stiff, in shock. But then he ran his hand down my back. His kindness and gentle touch made me lose it. I just needed someone in the moment. I sobbed into his chest until I realized he was back in his suit. I tried to pull away. "I'm sorry. I'm going to ruin your shirt and tie."

He pulled me closer. "I only care about what has you so upset."

"Why?" Why did he seem to care so much about me?

He thought for a moment and let out a slow, deep breath. "Let me take you to dinner, and we'll talk."

I jumped away from him. In a panic, I looked around, begging whatever saint I could that my meltdown and Reed's consoling wasn't on display. I didn't see anyone in the barren parking lot.

"Thank you, but we shouldn't."

He tilted his head. "Why not?"

"You're Cody's coach. Some things were said tonight. I don't want to give anybody the wrong impression. I really appreciate your offer and your kindness, but I better get home."

That answer didn't seem to satisfy him. He took my hand in his. "Who said what?"

"It's so embarrassing." More tears streamed down my cheeks.

"Did someone say something about us?"

Us? Why would he jump to that conclusion? I shook my head, confused. "No. Let's just say I'm a fool."

"Sam." He drew closer. "Please tell me what happened?"

I took a deep breath full of shudders before letting out my mortifying tale of the two women, and since I was on a roll and it felt good to let it out, I kept on going. "And to top it off, I feel like there is a flashing neon sign on my head that shouts, 'divorced woman, stay away!' Why?"

I just wanted to know why this was happening to me. I'd been wondering that for months. It was like the gift that kept on giving, but I wanted to give it back to the sender with a note telling them to go to the deepest place in hell.

Reed was more touchy-feely than expected. He went from holding my hand to hugging me again. I let him. This time I wrapped my arms around him. I needed a friend, and he would do. Besides, he smelled nice. And it was the most warmth I had felt in months. Peace settled into me.

"I know those women," he said as he rubbed my back. "They're jealous because their kids are, let's say, not Cody material. Had I been here when tryouts were held, their kids would have never made the team. Don't you dare let them make you feel inferior. You're a beautiful, intelligent, capable woman."

I snickered into his chest.

He leaned away and met my eyes. "What's so funny?"

"You called me beautiful."

His eyebrows knitted together. "Okay...?"

"You don't think it's funny that *you*, the boy that once teased me about playing connect the dots with the pimples on my face, just said that? I appreciate the gesture, but I don't need more lies."

He pressed his lips together, causing his jaw to twitch and then tighten. His gaze was penetrating. "I'm not that boy. But here's a news flash, even that boy knew you were beautiful."

I was taken aback by that revelation. But there was something else to address. How many times would I have to apologize to him? "I didn't mean to offend you again."

The warmth returned to his blue eyes. "You didn't. Let's go grab a late dinner."

"We shouldn't," I hedged.

"Sam, I just won my first game as head coach. I want to celebrate with you. And I don't think you want to be alone either. We'll go somewhere private if it will make you feel more comfortable."

Comfortable was something I hadn't been in months. And now I was anything but. Some sensor tingled in my brain, telling me that I had been naïve about a lot of things. But he was right. I didn't want to be alone. I gave him a weak nod.

CHAPTER TWENTY

WE SAT IN REED'S JEEP WITH THE TOP DOWN, EATING CHEESEBURGERS AND fries under the starry canvas in one of the forest preserves in Clearfield. Did I mention the forest preserve was closed? Reed took some back-access road he knew about. So to top it off I was breaking the law. I mean why not? I had already made a fool out of myself for the night, I might as well get arrested.

I looked out over the lake. The moon reflected in the ripples. The night had cooled off, making me glad I brought my jacket, though my legs were filled with goosebumps.

Reed was observant and slipped off his suit coat. "Take this."

"I would hate to drop any food on it."

"I'm already going to have to have it dry cleaned. Someone used it as a makeup wipe."

I gave him a small smile. "I don't wear that much makeup."

"It's one of the many qualities I like about you." He handed me the suit coat.

I draped the charcoal jacket over my legs. His lingering body heat felt good against my skin. In the awkward silence, I ate a fry and observed how clean his jeep was. I was surprised. Peter and he were slobs growing up.

"Thanks for dinner, by the way." I couldn't think of anything else to say, and he seemed nervous. Not sure why. Maybe he was worried about getting caught, though he assured me we wouldn't.

"You're welcome. I'm glad you finally agreed to go out with me."

I choked on my fry, coughing and spluttering.

He patted my back. "Are you okay?"

I was going to go with *no*. I held my chest and coughed one more time before taking a sip out of the bottle of water that came with my to-go meal. Once the coughing fit was over, I wasn't exactly sure what to say. Did he mean what I thought he meant? Or was it a general getting-together kind of a thing? My gaze stayed fixed on the lake while I tried to process.

"Will you look at me?"

That was an odd request. "What?" I didn't look at him.

He took the bottle of water out of my hands and placed it in the center console. "Sam, look at me."

I turned my head slowly, as if I was fighting against an unseen force. My plan was to do a quick glance, and that's what I did, but—

"Really look at me."

My eyes shifted downward. "I did." Why was he being so weird?

"No you didn't. And you haven't since I've been back."

My head whipped his way, our eyes locked. "I have no idea what you're talking about. Every time I see you, I look at you."

"You look for the boy you knew. He's not there."

"I know that."

"Do you?"

"I don't understand why this matters to you." Or did I just not want to admit it?

He was silent while I peered into his eyes doing my best to see what it was he wanted. A strange thing happened as I looked deeper. I saw something. Me. What was I doing in them?

Reed leaned in. His scent made me catch my breath.

"Sam...what if I told you that I was attracted to you?"

I shook my head. I must have had an aneurysm or a stroke. Out of body experience? Maybe a loss of hearing. Lots of weird noises escaped my mouth, not one of them a word. I finally managed to say, "No, you're not."

He wasn't amused. His jaw tightened, and he cleared his throat. "Obviously you're not ready to hear this."

If he wanted me to look at him, he succeeded. I couldn't not look at him. "Why?" was all I could think of to say.

"Why aren't you ready, or why am I attracted to you?"

"Sure," I breathed out.

His facial features softened with a smile. "This wasn't how I imagined us having this conversation."

"How did you picture it?"

"Well, first of all, I was going to take you curtain shopping and drag that out for as long as I could."

I returned his grin.

"That would have led to dinner. Throw some wine in there for good measure. And then I was going to lean across the table once we were both a little tipsy and tell you I've had a raging crush on you since I was thirteen. You would laugh and think I was joking. Then I would confess that I prayed to Saint Valentine to keep you single until I grew up. Damn fool, I'm still upset with him. He's really let me down over the years. And not just with you." Reed shook his head.

I sat still, in shock, trying to process what he was saying. And relating to him about Saint Valentine. I hated that guy and refused to ever ask for his help again. Reed wasn't the only person he had let down.

"Reed you're—"

"I'm what? Too young?"

"Well, yeah, kind of." At least for me. I had never dated anyone younger.

"You're thirty-nine and I'm thirty-four."

"I'm going to be forty next month."

"I'll be thirty-five in March. Who cares?" He loosened his purple tie, whipped it off, and threw it in the backseat like he was getting down to business.

I turned away from him and stared aimlessly up at the cloudless night sky. "This is crazy. I can't—"

"You can't what?"

"I can't date you."

He reached over and took my hand. It felt different this time. More than a friendly gesture. "Please look at me. Really look at me."

I faced him and took a deep breath. His smile, I noticed, had a smoldering quality to it. Wait. Had it been like that since he'd been back? He rubbed his thumb across my hand. Why wasn't I pulling it away?

"Sam," his voice was soft but deep, intimate. "If you hadn't known me as a kid, would my age really bother you?"

That was a good question. But it wasn't the only factor. "I don't know, but you're Cody's coach, and I haven't even thought about dating yet. I'm still a mess."

"A beautiful mess."

"Have you really liked me all this time?"

A sheepish smile played on his face. "This might be a good time to tell you it was Peter and me that let the air out of Neil's tires on the night he proposed to you."

"What?" I spat out.

"We overheard your mom talking about the big proposal and how he had asked your dad for your hand in marriage. Neither Peter nor I cared for the guy. Peter thought he was an uptight pansy, and I hated him because he was living out my teenage fantasy. I don't know why we thought letting the air out of his tires was going to stop him from proposing."

"I can't believe that was you guys! You ruined my proposal." Well, sort of. Neil could have asked me to marry him in a garbage truck and I would have said yes.

"What can I say? We were fifteen and stupid."

"I'll give you that." Neil was so nervous that night that he didn't even notice, and I was so wrapped up in him, I didn't either. But it didn't take long after we drove off to figure out something was wrong. Halfway up our street he got out, and when he realized what was wrong, he swore and kicked at the tires. But when he got back into the car, he looked at me, and it was like nothing else mattered to him. He pulled out the one carat princess-cut ring right then and there and asked me to be his bride. It was a fond memory, and one we laughed about for a long time. That was, until the laughter stopped and the ring came off.

"Did Peter know how you felt? Does he know now?"

"You're the first person I've ever told."

"I think both James and Peter are suspicious."

"It's hard when I'm around you to pretend I'm not attracted to you."

"I think you're mistaking attraction for something else." I mean, I found him to be physically attractive.

He leaned in closer. His vanilla-shake breath lingered in the air between us. There wasn't a lot of space, if truth be told. It wasn't bad at all.

"I think you're scared. I understand why you would be."

Scared didn't even cover it. "What do you even know about me?"

"I know you're witty as hell. I've been reading your blog posts."

I wasn't sure if I should be embarrassed or flattered. Probably some of both, but it wasn't like Ma hadn't embarrassed me enough about it in front of him.

He continued. "I know you're a fighter, a good mother, smart, generous. I remember you were always helping someone in your neighborhood, whether it was babysitting for free or watching their pets. You were the girl that always donated her birthday presents to the local women and children's shelter. I watched you more than you ever knew. And I only annoyed you because I couldn't think of any other way for you to pay attention to me."

I was truly at a loss for words.

He squeezed my hands. "Just promise me you'll think about it. About us?"

Us? I gulped.

CHAPTER TWENTY-ONE

REED WAS ALL I COULD THINK ABOUT. I GOT HOME IN THE NICK OF TIME—just before Cody arrived. Reed had dropped me off back at the school so I could get my car. I was worried I wouldn't make it home before midnight. How would I explain my absence to my son? "Hi, honey. By the way, I was parked with your coach in one of his old make-out spots"—a tidbit I'd found out on the drive home—"and, surprise, he wants to go out on a date with me. How was your night?"

I didn't see that conversation playing out too well. Even Reed knew it would be a complication if...if what? If we went out on a date? I couldn't even say it out loud.

I threw on some yoga pants and a t-shirt before jumping into bed just as I heard Cody walk in. I picked up my tablet and pretended to read something before Cody knocked on my door.

"Mom, I'm home."

"Come in." I found myself sounding like a nervous teenager who was afraid her parents might find out about what she had done that night.

Cody's eyes looked tired, and his shoulders were still slumped.

I patted a spot next to me on the bed.

He walked over and took a seat next to me even though he didn't seem keen on it. I would at least give Cody this, he tried to always show me that he loved me.

"How was your night?"

He shrugged. "Fine."

"Do you want to talk about your dad?"

He shook his head.

"You know it's okay to be angry."

"If he doesn't care about me, I don't care about him."

I took his hand. "You do care. You should care. This isn't about you. It's about me."

"I hate him." His hard brown eyes said he wasn't lying.

"I know, but don't let it tear you up inside. You can talk to me or Grandpa, James, or Peter. We're all here for you."

"I just want to go to bed."

I nodded. I knew not to push it with him. "Okay. Sleep tight."

He thundered toward my door, but he stopped before he exited and mumbled, "Love you."

"I love you more than you know."

I couldn't hope to sleep now. So many emotions coursed through me. I had half a mind to call Neil right then and let him have it. What was I waiting for? He needed to hear what I had to say. I grabbed my phone from the nightstand and dialed his number. It went straight to voice mail. I had forgotten he turned his phone off at night. A voice message would do for now. My anger needed an outlet.

"You should know that your son got to play in his first varsity game tonight, and you missed it. He noticed. You're breaking your son's heart. The sad part is I'm not even sure you care. You divorced me, not Cody. But I guess since you're having a new baby with your new whatever, we don't exist for you anymore. Go ahead and write us out of your life. Maybe I'll write someone else in. Someone that cares more about Cody than he does about himself. Someone Cody can look up to. Someone that's not you!"

I clicked end, not sure why I said all that. I really didn't think he cared anymore. Perhaps it bordered on childish, but you say stupid things when you're angry. Stupid things like letting another man in our lives. Did I really want to? I thought about being in Reed's arms. I didn't recognize it at the time, but it was more than nice. I missed that kind of affection. I'd been missing it for a long time. Well before Neil's affair came to light, those intimate type of touches disappeared. I was so blind. How did I not see that my marriage was in trouble?

How did I miss Reed's advances?

I gave myself a break there. I mean, who would have guessed? Okay, so my brothers saw it. That didn't help me feel any better, considering James was emotionally clueless at times and Peter had missed the signs for years despite being Reed's best friend growing up. And let's not forget I babysat him. I know Reed wished I could and would forget that.

If I could forget, how *would* I see him? Obviously, his attention flattered me. He was extremely good looking and, I suppose, charming in his own way. He was funny. I smiled and laughed around him more than usual. Other than that, I didn't really know a lot about him, other than Cody adored him, and he'd been nothing but kind to me. He let me cry it out on his suit. And he didn't try to fix anything; he just listened and held me.

I rubbed my face in my hands. Why was I even entertaining this? I couldn't. We couldn't. I shuddered at the thought of bringing him to my parents' place for Sunday dinner. Granted, he was already sitting next to me, but my brothers would tease me relentlessly, and Ma would probably ask him if he had seen my NDA. Or worse, she'd ask if were sleeping together. Oh my gosh, now I was going to have those thoughts in my head.

Remembering being in Reed's arms—or imagining more— reminded me of some of the reasons I had a mini breakdown tonight. Those women, and the way they treated me so different now. *Who does she think she is?* played in my head. I pulled out my laptop and logged into my blog. I was inundated with new comments about my protein ball post. Lots of people agreed with my assessment; some people wanted me to post my recipe. I obliged while Reed and that phrase played ping pong in my head.

When I was done sharing my glorified cookie recipe—and that's exactly what I called it—I started a new post titled, "Who does she think she is? Let me tell you."

Tonight at my son's football game, I was hit with the cold reality of what else divorce has stolen from me. It was as if going from Mrs. to Ms. changed who I was in everyone's eyes. I never realized what a difference that little "r" meant. Are people afraid divorce is contagious? Is that why they shy away from me? Or perhaps they wonder if it was my fault and what I did. Maybe they just don't know what to say, so they choose to ignore me. Surely they don't think I'm out to find the next Mr. and maybe it will be them or their spouse. Has anyone else noticed this behavior in others since their divorce? Does it get better? How do you handle it?

I wish the slights were the worst part of the evening. Just when I thought the night couldn't get any worse, when I felt as alone as I had ever felt, two women decided to pour vinegar into that gaping wound. This blog and the attention it has garnered apparently didn't sit well with them. I was privy to their mean-spirited conversation when one asked the other about this blog that has become one of my lifelines. The woman's words, "Who does she think she is?" rang loud and clear into the night. I wasn't sure if they meant for me to hear, but I did, and they know I did. For all I know, they will read this post.

So who do I think I am?

I'm the woman who would have sat alone tonight in the stands if it wasn't for my loving family. I'm the woman who could have used a friendly hello, but received nothing but a few strained smiles and a cold shoulder or two by people I had once considered friends. People I need now more than ever. I'm the woman who ached to turn to her spouse tonight to revel in our son's accomplishments, but knew that was forever lost to me.

I'm the woman who couldn't stand the sight of myself in the mirror for months and did all I could to avoid it. I have hated myself more than anyone could hate me. I'm the woman who gets up every day and puts on the mask of a brave face because there is someone I love more than myself and, at the very least, my son deserves that. I'm the woman you think you know so much about because you see my mask. I'm the woman who has judged others the same way and, now more than ever, feels ashamed of my behavior. I'm imperfect and, quite honestly, a mess, but I'm muddling through trying to figure it all out. I'm the woman that will keep falling and making mistakes.

I no longer get to have the title "wife," but I'm finding I'm more than that. I'm finding more about myself every day. Some things I like, some things need to change.

That's who I think I am.

I read over it a dozen times. It was bold, but all true. In my middle-of-the-night exhaustion, I threw caution to the wind and published it, knowing it would now go automatically to my Facebook page and Twitter account that Delanie had set up for me.

I needed to sleep if I wanted to look decent at all for the photo shoot. Maybe I should cancel. Give up this whole Sidelined Wife business. It obviously had ramifications I hadn't foreseen, and now I just added fuel to the fire. I should really quit doing things when I'm angry and confused.

Things to work on in the morning.

I drifted off into a restless sleep.

CHAPTER TWENTY-TWO

"OOOH. I LOVE THIS ONE." AVERY POINTED AT THE PICTURE ON DELANIE'S tablet of me leaning against the faded blue door looking sultry—or was that bored? I couldn't tell.

I had so many pictures taken of me yesterday that my cheek muscles still hurt. Not that I was smiling in all of them, but Delanie's friend, Roger, spent two hours shooting photo after photo of me in all sorts of poses and different locations around downtown Clearfield.

We had all come early for Sunday dinner so Delanie could show us the proofs of the photo shoot. It was decision time. I was all for not choosing. Though I was enjoying the autumn breeze on my parents' front porch. We were hiding outside so Ma and Mimsy didn't feel the need to get involved. And I didn't need another story about the soap opera taking place at the retirement community. I still couldn't shake the Depends around the ankle image in my mind. And the ice boat wasn't going anywhere, so Ma was still upset with Dad.

"Maybe I could be like Autumn Moone and my photo could be of a football field's sideline. That's clever." At least, I thought it was.

Delanie, who was between us on the porch swing, shook her head. "You already used your real name and you're writing about real life, so they need the real you. Autumn Moone only gets away with it because she started out unknown and her publisher made it part of their marketing plan."

"How do you know?" Avery asked.

Delanie pulled up the next batch of photos. "I think I read it some-where on a marketing blog."

"Huh. Well, it works for her." Avery was already eagerly scanning the new batch of photos.

This set was taken in front of a brick wall. In some I was leaning back, others had only one shoulder touching. In a few I was smiling, or was that smirking? There were serious, studious poses mixed in with playful candid shots of me rolling my eyes at the ridiculousness of it all or throwing my hands up. My favorite was the three of us laughing together. I think I had just tripped up some steps and Delanie and Avery had caught me.

"Let's use that one," I suggested, pointing at the photo of the three of us. It represented more of who I really was, and I hated being the only subject.

Avery and Delanie nixed that idea.

"By the way," Delanie said as she enlarged a photo she liked that had an artistic flair. I was standing in front of an old sign that read, *Crossroads.* How fitting. "I loved the new post. I hope those women read it and choke on their self-righteousness."

Avery agreed. "I feel terrible we left you alone after the game."

"Please don't. You guys have lives. I don't need to be babysat."

And someone *was* there to comfort me, though I didn't mention him or that fact he called me yesterday to ask if I would like to have a real dinner with him sometime this week. I said I would think about it, but probably not. He only laughed, not deterred at all.

"Besides," I continued. "What upset me most was Cody. He's hurt-ing and he won't talk about it. And all Neil can do is blame the divorce on me."

He'd had the audacity to call me back and inform me our family's situation was all my fault and I was turning Cody against him. We had some choice words before I hung up on him. I was glad the call had come after the photo shoot, or I would have looked like a splotchy, red, puffy-eyed mess.

Avery swore in French. I smiled at her. "Someday, you will have to tell me what those words mean and how to say them right."

"I'm happy to teach you some Spanish vulgarity too," Delanie offered. She'd volunteered in the inner-city schools in Phoenix where they had a high population of children from Mexico. It was where she met my brother.

"Perfect, the more the better."

We focused back on the pictures.

"Does my hair look too big? Do you think your friend could make me look twenty and svelte?"

"You look fantastic." Delanie nudged me.

I stared at my unruly curls, done movie-star style thanks to Avery. The denim shirt brought out the blue in my gray eyes.

While we hemmed and hawed over which picture to use, Reed pulled up. I knew he was coming, and I had been reminding myself not to act any different around him. I'd told him he better do the same.

He didn't listen. He came sauntering up with five bouquets of flowers. It looked like a multi-colored rosebush had exploded on him.

I ignored him, but my sisters-in-law didn't.

"Reed," Avery's voice was so cheery, "you're going to make Mom happy." Avery had always called Ma, Mom. Delanie, I think, tried not to call Ma anything, except for names in her head.

Reed approached while I tried to keep as focused as I could on the screen. I still caught his smirk from the corner of my eye.

"I realized how rude I'd been, only bringing one Decker woman flowers."

"Aren't you the sweetest thing." Avery jumped up to survey the roses. "James never brings me flowers unless it's my birthday or our anniversary."

Reed carefully handed her the lavender bouquet out of the mix. That was so sweet. I had mentioned something to him about my niece Hannah and how her favorite color was any shade of purple.

"These are gorgeous, thank you." Avery inhaled their scent.

"Delanie?" Reed held out three of the four remaining bouquets; he was holding back the peach bouquet with baby's breath. They were gorgeous. I figured he got them for Ma.

Delanie eyed him suspiciously. She was a smart one. Was she on to him?

"Yellow works for me." She went right back to work, laying the roses next to her where Avery had been sitting. Reed had failed to impress her. Probably because Peter was always bringing home thoughtful gifts, whether it was flowers or her favorite candy, sour cherry jelly beans. Once he even had me help pick out the perfect colored pencils to go with the adult coloring book he had purchased her.

Reed didn't seem fazed by Delanie's lack of enthusiasm. His sights landed on me instead. "How are you, Sam?"

I gave him my full attention, since ignoring him would have only drawn the kind of attention I was hoping to avoid. Like the kind he was bringing.

With a grin wider than Texas, he handed me the beautiful deluxe bouquet of peach roses. "I thought you would like these."

I wanted to shake my head at him or kick his exposed shin.

"Peach roses are your favorite," Avery commented.

"How did you know that?" Delanie interrogated him.

Reed didn't miss a beat. "She mentioned it last week when I gave Mrs. D some."

Those hadn't been as nice as the ones he was handing me.

"Thank you." I swiped them and turned back to the screen. He needed to go.

Unfortunately, he wasn't in a hurry. "What are you ladies doing out here?"

Avery's eyes lit up. "We're helping Sam choose a photo for her blog and social media sites. Maybe you can help. It would be good to get a male perspective.

That was a terrible idea. "We can just ask Peter or James later. I'm sure Reed wants to go in and hang out with the guys."

"I'm happy to help." The mischievous boyhood glint was back in his eyes. He walked behind us and looked over my shoulder, though he would have gotten a better view closer to Delanie. His cologne wafted in the autumn breeze, making me catch my breath.

Avery took her seat and laid both her and Delanie's flowers on her lap. "I love this one best, I think." Avery pointed again to the one of me in front of the blue door.

Delanie's vote was for the crossroads sign one.

I had no vote, except to be done.

Reed studied each picture carefully, asking Delanie to go back and forth a few times. "Wait. Go back to the one of her on the steps in front of the old church."

Delanie enlarged the picture in front of the old church house on Main Street. I was leaning forward with my arms resting on my legs, hands clasped together. I wore a hint of a smile.

"That's it," Delanie said. "It speaks to your vulnerability and strength. It's perfect."

"Yes," Avery agreed.

Both women turned back toward Reed. "Good eye," they echoed each other.

No one asked my opinion. But if I had to choose one, I guess it would work. I stared at the woman in the photo. She looked more confident than I felt.

Delanie stood up with her tablet. "I'm going to call Roger and let him know which one to touch up."

"Lots of touch-up," I called after her.

"I better go get these in water." Avery started toward the door with both bouquets.

I stood up. "I better do the same."

Reed met me around the porch swing. "Sam, do you think I could talk to you for a minute about the pancake breakfast the team is doing on Saturday?"

Avery didn't seem to find that out of the ordinary and left me there with him. I hadn't even volunteered to help with that particular fundraiser. And after the way I had been treated on Friday night, I wasn't sure I was going to go. My contribution for the season would be to sell tickets at the school and donate money.

But it was good Avery left; with only the two of us, I was able to let loose on him.

"What are you thinking, bringing everyone flowers?"

"I knew you had been a little down, so I thought flowers might cheer you up. But I didn't think you would appreciate it if I singled you out."

"You shouldn't be giving me flowers at all."

"I disagree. By the way, you looked gorgeous in those pictures. Do you think I could get a copy of a few?"

I wasn't sure if he was teasing or not. I sighed.

He smirked.

"We better go in."

"Not yet. I didn't ask you about the pancake breakfast. You don't want to make me a liar, do you?"

My look said he was pressing his luck.

He pressed it further by getting as close as he could, with only flowers between us. I was starting to see the man in him. He wore stubble well. And his eyes? Beautiful.

I took a small step back, not sure how to feel. Or perhaps I didn't want to feel at all.

His grin said he knew he was getting to me.

"Ask your question," I said, a little breathless.

"The restaurant wants to know if we want to use real butter or margarine. What do you think?"

"I think you need better excuses."

"Hey, that was good for on the fly."

"If you say so. Tell the restaurant you want the real deal. Butter."

He inched forward. "How do I get the real deal with you?"

That was a question I didn't have an answer for.

CHAPTER TWENTY-THREE

WHILE CODY WAS FINISHING UP HOMEWORK SUNDAY NIGHT AFTER RETURN-
ing from my parents', I went online. I hadn't logged in since Friday
night—technically, the wee hours of Saturday morning. Honestly, com-
menting and posting could be a full-time job. My Saturday had been
too busy attending my nephews' track meet and the photo shoot to even
think about getting online. I'd also wanted to do something fun with
Cody yesterday, so we headed to an indoor go-kart track for an evening
of fun.

The new status quo when I got online was a barrage of emails,
comments, shares, and likes. I already had twenty-five thousand people
like my Facebook page. It kind of blew my mind. Though, just like in
my real world, not everyone online liked me, but the majority of followers and comments were nothing but nice. Several people, mostly
women, shared their own stories about how divorce changed their social
circles. They even linked helpful articles, like "Coping with Divorce,"
"Life After Divorce," "How to Deal with the Loneliness." I bookmarked
each one of those links. I needed all the help I could get.

One woman, who professed to be a psychologist, commented that
it was common for friends that my husband and I had had as a couple
to be awkward around only me. She recommended that I move on and
find new friends. She said women may resent or fear me now that I'm
single. That made me feel so much better, because it wasn't bad enough
that my husband left me for a younger woman. Though the jerk still

claimed it was me that left him. For a doctor, he was an idiot. Avery taught me a new word for him, *le salaud*. I was going to love learning French.

While I was responding to my "friends," I received a text from Reed. *Would this be a good time to talk?*

I looked upstairs from the living room couch. Cody's door was shut. Then I looked at the beautiful bouquet in a vase on the coffee table in front of me. I thought about the way Reed's leg touched mine all during dinner, and how his hand purposely brushed mine when I handed him the salad dressing. So maybe there was a hint of a spark.

Do you need more advice on dairy products? I texted back.

This is much more important. Can I call you?

It should be a simple *yes* or *no* answer, but this was anything but simple. What did I say? I took a few minutes to think.

So is that a yes, you can't wait to talk to me? he texted again.

I laughed to myself. When did he get to be so charming? *Okay.*

My phone immediately buzzed.

"Hello," I whispered.

"Should I talk in hushed tones too?"

"If you want." I got up and walked into my room so Cody wouldn't hear me.

"Are you saying you want me to whisper in your ear?" He thought he was so funny and laughed at himself.

I couldn't help myself; I laughed too. "Did you need something?"

"Need? Hmm. Want? Yes."

"And what is it you want?"

"Two things. First, I want you to say yes to my dinner invitation. Second, I want your address."

"Can't you just get it off Cody's paperwork?"

"Well, I could, but that borders on being a stalker."

"I agree, so thank you for not going that route. Why do you want it?"

"I was thinking that the next time I gave you flowers, it would be cheaper if I had them delivered to you instead of buying some for your entire family."

"That would be more economical, but not necessary."

"It could be."

"When has anyone *needed* flowers?"

"We all do. They help rid the air of carbon dioxide and other toxins. And they feed honey bees. Where would the world be without honey?"

"It would be bleak and dreary, I suppose." I played along with the ridiculous conversation, grinning from ear to ear.

"Exactly. So what's your address?"

"I don't think bees feed off cut and delivered flowers." I wasn't giving in.

Neither was he. "Debatable, but think of the florist's job you could be saving."

"I'm always up for a good cause. I guess I'll start buying more flowers for myself. Thanks for bringing the plight of the florists to my attention."

"That did not go how I wanted it to go."

I laughed at him.

"Sam." His serious tone halted my laughter. "Have dinner with me."

I paused and paused some more. "Reed, it's so complicated."

"Because you may have been the older person in charge of me and Peter a few times a hundred years ago?"

I noticed how he refused to say *babysat.* "There's that, but you're Cody's coach. Think about what people would say if they knew we went on a date. I don't ever want anyone to question why Cody's on that team or anything he accomplishes on that field."

It was his turn to pause. His breathing patterns indicated he was deep in thought. "I don't want that either, but anyone that sees Cody's talent will know he's earned it."

"You know how people are. They don't usually look at things objectively. They'll see what they want to. Look at how those two women acted over my blog post. And apparently, since I'm single now, I will be resented and feared."

"By who?"

"Women."

"That's not true."

"I have it on good authority. And you should have seen the looks I got at the game Friday. If I went out on a date with you, those looks would morph into turned heads and whispers. Before you know it, they would be accusing me of sleeping with you so that Cody could get more playing time."

"Whoa. That escalated."

"You know it's true."

His sigh said I was right. "When does Cody graduate?"

"Too soon."

He thought for a moment. "It's dinner. We could keep that under wraps."

"You want to have a clandestine outing?" I cringed. Did I really just use that word?

"Maybe eventually, but I know how you feel about illicit interactions without legal binding documentation."

Did he just say that maybe he wanted to . . . you know? Moving on. "Are you mocking me?"

"Not at all. I just want to have dinner with you."

"And where would we go?"

"This is progress. I wanted to take you to this great hole-in-the-wall place in Chicago. They have amazing food and a live jazz band, but we'll save that for when you're comfortable being seen in public with me."

"You are getting way ahead of yourself, there. Dinner is a one-time thing."

"Frequently, dinners lead to more dinners, and other things."

I wasn't going to ask what those *other things* were. I was pretty sure I knew. "We could have an awful time together. Then we would always be uncomfortable around each other."

"I don't see that happening."

Based on our conversations, I didn't either but . . . "Reed, I'm a mess, trying to put my life back together right now. And what would people think? I baby—"

"Please don't say it," he interrupted.

I rubbed my forehead. "I'm sorry."

"You have nothing to apologize for. And Sam, I think you have it more together than you give yourself credit for."

"I feel like I'm fumbling through life right now."

"Perfect. On the field, I hate fumbles, but off the field, I'm your guy. We can fumble together."

"You're not going to take no for an answer, are you?"

"I'm only asking for a chance. Go out with me once, and if you like it, we can do it again. And maybe again after that."

My bedroom felt like it was spinning. My breathing shallowed. However, in the midst of my mild panic attack, I pictured Reed with Cody at my parents' house earlier tonight. They had high-fived their way through the first half of the Bears game, laughing and joking as they went. During some of the commercial breaks, they went out and tossed the football. I wanted to know what they were talking about in the backyard, but I knew if I interrupted, Cody would have clammed up. But Cody smiled and laughed, so that's all that mattered to me.

Reed made me smile and laugh, too. It was only one dinner.

"Okay," I breathed out, "but no one can know. I won't do that to Cody right now."

"You have my word. Now, what's your address?"

CHAPTER TWENTY-FOUR

I HAD A DATE FOR SATURDAY. IN FIVE DAYS. ONE-HUNDRED-AND-TWENTY-plus hours away.

That didn't seem far enough away.

I wasn't even sure it was going to happen. How was I going to explain my absence to Cody Saturday night without lying? Keeping it on the down-low was one thing, but I refused to lie, especially to my son. He already had one parent that was good at that. I didn't even know where we would go. Reed said he had a plan and would let me know. Was I even ready to date again?

I went to my people while I got ready for the day Monday morning.

How do you know when you're ready to date again? Asking for a friend, I posted on my Facebook page. That's where most people responded, it seemed, and quickly too. I had forty comments in the time it took me to put on my makeup. The comments were all over the place.

Tell your friend that the fact she's asking this question may mean she's ready.

Was that true? But I wasn't sure that pertained to me since I was asked out and already accepted before I posed this question.

Girl, just stay away. Stay away.

That was probably good advice.

Tell your friend to date for money this time. Love is highly overrated.

This was not a bad thought.

Do you have anyone in mind? I have an older brother.

No way was I being set up with or dating anyone I met online.

Have you thought about what you want and don't want in a mate? Are you excited about it? Are you over your ex?

Those were good questions to ask myself.

I knew I didn't want a cheater, but who did? What else did I want? I wanted the little things that had been missing from my marriage for a long time. Kisses when parting and greeting each other. A hand to hold. Someone who not only listened to me, but actively wanted to know how my day was. I wanted someone to go on bike rides and pick apples with. What I wouldn't give to cuddle on the couch with someone and watch an old movie and eat popcorn. I wanted someone who would love Cody and put us first in his life.

Was I excited about dating? Not necessarily. But was I excited about going out with Reed? If I was honest, the answer was yes. I enjoyed being with him and I was flattered he liked me, even if it was weird. And I had a sneaking suspicion that we would have fun.

Was I over Neil? I didn't want him anymore, at least not who he had become. I hadn't in a long time. His injury severed that connection. But the wound had not healed. He had left his mark. And there were still times I ached for the man I'd married almost eighteen years ago. Did that mean I wasn't ready?

I grabbed my phone off the charger to throw in my bag before going out to make Cody breakfast. I had two texts.

The first one was from Avery. *Are you really thinking about dating?*

Yes. I was honest.

Next up was Reed. *Tell your friend to get ready. She's going to have a great time this weekend.*

Do you follow me on Facebook? I had no idea who was and wasn't. I gave up looking at the notifications after the first couple of thousand people.

Of course. I need to know what type of legal documentation I may require in the future. And I've always wanted a good protein ball recipe.

Now you're lying.

Only about the protein balls.

I need to finish getting ready. Have a good day.

You too. I'll call you tonight, just let me know when you're available to talk.

Why are you calling?

I like talking to you. And how else will I know how your day was?
Oh.
Is that okay?
I thought for a moment. *Yes.*
I look forward to it.
Me too, I thought.

I arrived at the office with Avery's favorite orange scones from a bakery we frequented, and purple gift bag full of paper hearts I had cut out last night while I couldn't sleep. My mind was preoccupied. With mostly Reed. Did this make me a cougar? Not thinking about it.

This was a tough week for our family, especially James and Avery's family. Tomorrow it would be two years since our beautiful Hannah had been taken from us. I knew Avery and James would go to her grave tomorrow. I think they went more than we knew. I made the hearts so Avery could spread them on her grave. She had the prettiest little headstone made of white marble, inscribed in gold. It fit Hannah, golden and pure.

I set the bag of hearts and the scones on her desk without a word. I could tell by her blurry eyes and rosy cheeks she was doing her best to hold it together. And I knew she would know what the hearts were for. She had been unnecessarily apologetic about only wanting James and their boys with her tomorrow at the grave. We all understood.

Avery gave me a weak smile.

I tried to return it with a reassuring one, but I knew nothing could take away the ache her mother heart felt.

In her show of bravery, she grabbed my hand before I could walk away. "I want to show you something." She let go of my hand and clicked on a few folders. Up popped a gorgeous banner.

I knelt next to her chair to get an up-close look. I touched the screen and ran my hand over the title, The Sidelined Wife, done in a bold, curvy font. A lighted football field subtly played in the background. She added a subtitle that read, *Getting Back in the Game.*

"It's gorgeous. You're so talented."

"You really love it?"

"So much." I ran my fingers across the screen again.

"Let's put it up on your site. And the new photo. I know Delanie sent it to you."

I had been avoiding that. I liked the blank space where my photo was supposed to go. "How about the banner only?"

"No deal. You look beautiful."

"You're a liar, but fine."

She rolled her eyes at me before logging into my various sites and uploading the banner in different sizes for the different platforms. "Now send me the picture. I'll upload it for you."

I obeyed and pulled out my phone. Within seconds it was in her inbox. And before I knew it, my face was plastered on my Facebook page, blog, Instagram, and Twitter. I felt more self-conscious than ever.

"So," Avery was still clicking on things, "are you really thinking about dating again?"

I stood up and rubbed my neck. "I'm thinking about it. I mean, that's natural, right?"

"I think it's a great idea. You know, our neighbor, Gary, is single. He's attractive; nice, too. I think you met him last year at our Halloween party."

Avery loved Halloween and threw a Halloween bash every year for adults only.

"Maybe. I can't place him." I was married last year, so it's not like single men were on my radar. Neil hadn't come to the party with me. He said he was researching a case he was working on with the police department, which wasn't unusual, but they had become more frequent. I was so naïve.

"Do you want me to set you up?"

I tensed. "No. No."

She laughed at me. "Do you have someone in mind?"

Thankfully, the office phone rang and she had to answer it. I didn't want to lie to her, but I couldn't tell her about Reed. I would have dinner with him once, and someday we would laugh about how silly it had been. And maybe in ten years I would tell my family, and they could all laugh too.

I rushed to my office and shut the door as if I could hide from my own thoughts. Wouldn't that be nice if I could?

CHAPTER TWENTY-FIVE

"THERE'S SOMETHING DIFFERENT ABOUT YOU, LOVE." GELAIRE EYED ME from across the table.

We were near her home, grabbing lunch at a cozy little café that made the best grilled cheese and vegetable sandwiches before I took her to the market. It was Wednesday, a day later than normal. Tuesday I'd stayed in the office since Avery was out all day celebrating the life of her daughter and mourning her death. I'd shed my share of tears, too.

For a second, I thought about the conversation I'd had last night with Reed about Hannah. He was a great listener. He laughed with me at the silly and sweet things Hannah did, like painting James's toe nails. That little girl had her daddy wrapped around her finger. Neil would have just zoned out after a while. He acted as though after Hannah's funeral was over, I should have been over it. But he had never put in a lot of effort to be a good uncle. Which was unfortunate, because I loved being an aunt. And Hannah, being my only niece, held a special place in my heart.

I tucked some of my curls behind my ear and responded to Gelaire's comment. "I'm trying out this new styling spray for my hair that's supposed to add sheen and keep away the frizz."

She grinned. "Your hair looks lovely as always, but that's not what I was referring to."

I took a sip of my ice water. "I'm wearing makeup again."

"It's more than physical. You seem...happy."

"I'm getting there, depending on the moment."

"Are you seeing someone?"

I set my glass down. Heat flooded my cheeks. "Why would you jump to that conclusion?"

Gelaire's green eyes sparkled with a hint a mischief. "My son," she was still saying his name with some derision, "mentioned you left him a message about replacing him. I told him I would gladly help you."

She always knew how to get me to smile. "I appreciate that, but I made that call in anger. It wasn't my finest moment."

"He deserved it. You have him worried, you know."

"What about?"

"That he'll soon be a distant memory."

"Honestly, I wish that could happen, but Cody will connect us forever." I shrugged. "Well, maybe."

Her eyes narrowed. "What do you mean?"

I felt like I was tattling. "Neil still hasn't seen Cody. It's been weeks now. They haven't even talked."

Outrage filled her features. Red blotches of anger popped up on her cheeks while her fists balled. "I will be having words with my son. Again."

"You don't need to do that."

"I most certainly do. I didn't raise him to be this kind of man. His father most certainly didn't." She took some deep breaths to try and calm herself. "How's Cody handling it?"

"Not well. He's keeping it bottled up inside. He says he hates his dad, but it's only because he loves him so much." Tears stung my eyes.

Gelaire reached for my hand. "I will right this. Why don't you bring Cody over to spend the weekend with me? He needs to know that the Higgins side loves him."

I wasn't sure how Cody would feel about that. He loved his grandma, but she wasn't into the kind of things Cody was. And the naked statue in her foyer, while funny to him, kind of freaked him out. But it would free me up for Saturday night. Though I wouldn't put Cody up like some sacrificial lamb so I could go out with his coach.

"Please?" Gelaire begged when I didn't answer right away.

"I'll talk to Cody, but promise you won't spring Neil on him without asking Cody first, if that's your plan."

She squeezed my hand. "I give you my word. I only want my grandson to know he means the world to me. Maybe I can take him to a Cubs game or something."

"You hate baseball."

"Cody loves it, so I'll love it."

Knowing her, she would get the box seats where they would be waited on hand and foot. "He would love that."

"Then it's settled. Do you think he would like box seats?"

What did I tell you? "Who wouldn't?"

"Would you like to come too, love?"

"Uh, I think it would be good if only the two of you went." That was true. Really, it was.

"I think you're right. We will have a grand time."

The fact that she said *grand* made that questionable. Cody wasn't used to *grand* times.

Saturday I found myself driving a reluctant Cody into the city. He was tired from the late night at the away game and getting up early to serve pancakes at the fundraiser this morning. It didn't help that he was cranky with me for setting up the visit with his grandma, and he hadn't gotten any playing time last night. The game was a nail biter, and the Panthers only won by a field goal. Neil was a no-show again. That made Cody going to see Gelaire even more important. He needed those family connections, whether he saw the value in them or not. Someday he would be grateful. I hoped.

"You have to be at least a little excited about the game tonight." I glanced at my son slouched in the passenger seat. I wasn't brave enough to let him drive in downtown Chicago yet. Not sure I ever would be.

He stared out the window and shrugged.

"Come on, box seats. And you know Grandma will want to buy you a new jersey and probably anything they're selling there."

"I'm missing a party at Rory's tonight."

More reasons for me to be happy he was going to be at his grand-ma's. "There will be other parties. And if you want you can have her over to watch a movie or something next weekend." You better believe I would be out there the entire time.

"Maybe."

"Cody, this is a good thing."

"Her house smells weird and she listens to old music."

"It smells like lavender, which is nice. And if you ask, she would probably turn off the music or let you choose. She loves and misses you."

"Is Dad going to be there?" I heard both the hope and resentment in his voice.

"I don't know. How would you feel if he was?"

His only answer was to shrug and throw in his earbuds.

I reached over and patted his leg and shouted, "I love you."

I saw a hint of a smile.

The rest of our drive was quiet. It gave me too much time to worry about my date. I hadn't gone to the pancake breakfast this morning because I feared people would be able to tell by the look on my face that I had a date with the coach.

And, last night at the game, something weird happened. A few of the other moms crowded around me like we were back in high school. They linked arms with me and everything. To top it off, they still had perky cheerleader voices. And get this. Their names were Kerry, Karen, and Katrina. It was very Stepford-wife-ish. They invited me to their book club and asked if maybe I could post about it on my blog and Facebook page. They said it could be, like, a "thing" I do. Then they went on to give me false flattery about how funny I was and how they loved my posts. I felt like they wanted to assimilate me. More like use me. It was nicer than the mean moms who'd slighted me last week. Last night they made sure to give me those fake who-do-you-think-you-are smiles.

I didn't even recognize my life anymore. I used to be one of those moms that played in the background. I helped out whenever I could, but I was never in charge of anything. I had friends, but never a large circle. My closest friends were always family, especially Avery.

But now I had this large following and people that were vying for my attention in both positive and negative ways. Did I mention I had a date with my son's coach? I didn't even know what I was going to wear, other than something casual, per Reed's instructions. I kept thinking I might back out. But then I would think about my phone conversations with Reed during the week and how much he was looking forward to it.

I also had some creepy messages to deal with from random men on Facebook after I'd put up my new picture. One guy offered to be my love slave. What? Ew. I had been doing a lot of blocking people this week.

But one perk was that Autumn Moone was going to have her publisher send me and my sisters-in-law advanced copies of *A Black Night* in November. A full *month* before it released in December. Avery and I might have squealed over it. Delanie acted mildly excited about it, as in she mentioned that it was nice I had asked for a copy for each of us. I still wished I knew who sent Autumn Moone that original post. I felt like it was too gutsy to ask Autumn. She obviously valued her anonymity. I couldn't say I blamed her.

Saturday traffic wasn't horrible, and before I knew it, I was dropping off my son at Gelaire's Greystone. By the look on Cody's face, you would have thought I was dropping him off at prison. His grimace said, *shoot me now.*

"It's only one night, and maybe if you're lucky you'll meet someone famous tonight sitting in the box seats with you."

His face scrunched the way it always did when he wasn't buying what I was trying to sell.

"If you smile and pretend like you enjoy your time, I may be willing to bribe you with that new video game you've been wanting."

His lip twitched. "The deluxe version?"

"For that, your grandma better think that you love every second of being with her."

"Will you pick me up early tomorrow?"

"Does that mean we have a deal?" I held out my hand for him to shake on it.

He was quick to take it. He'd been wanting that game for several weeks now. I'd been saving it for a moment like this. I had learned a few tricks over the years, and I was not above bribing him.

"I love you. I'll miss you." I held his hand tight. "Be a good boy," I teased.

He rolled his eyes.

"Oh, and don't let grandma drink at the game. She might start talking about your grandpa—probably about things you don't need or want to know."

Cody's eyebrows shot up to his tousled hair.

"I'm sure she'll be fine."

The question was, would I?

CHAPTER TWENTY-SIX

WHAT WAS I DOING? WHAT WAS I DOING? HAVING A PANIC ATTACK, THAT'S what.

I hadn't had a first date in almost twenty years. And twenty years ago, if someone told me I would be going out with Reed Cassidy, I would have died of laughter—after asking them if they were high. The worst part was I couldn't even ask anybody for advice. I mean, what did *casual* really mean? Like, shorts and a t-shirt, or jeans? I texted Reed and he said yes, but added that I might want to bring a jacket. So yes to shorts or yes to jeans? Shorts meant making sure my legs were extra smooth. But was that showing off too much leg? Not like he would be touching them. Or would he? Was he going to touch me? What did he expect?

Almost everything I owned was strewn across my bed. I had tried on at least ten outfits and hated every one. I felt like vomiting. How was I going to eat? I don't remember feeling this way before dates. Excited, sure, but this was more like terror.

I ended up in some tan shorts, a white t-shirt topped with a jean jacket, and some canvas shoes. My hair had a mind of its own. Curls were everywhere. I even poked my eye with my mascara wand.

Maybe this is a bad idea, I texted once my eye quit watering from being jabbed.

I'll be there in twenty minutes. He wasn't giving me an out.

Remember, just text me when you get here and don't pull up if you see anyone.

Do you see how ridiculous this was? I was suddenly back in high school trying to sneak around with Mark Stein, the resident bad boy. That lasted all of one time when I learned the hard way his reputation was deserved. First and only time I ever used pepper spray. Oh my gosh, I didn't even have any of that stuff. But Reed wouldn't try anything, would he? I mean, they do background checks on teachers. Not to say that's ever stopped anything from happening, judging by the news reports about teachers being arrested. So, basically, I should stay home in my bubble.

Relax, Sam. We're going to have a great time. Reed texted back.

I took a deep breath and tried to apply the rest of my makeup without injuring myself. It was only dinner, I kept trying to comfort myself. And this was Reed. We would laugh about it someday. Yes. Those were good thoughts.

I think I peed five times in that twenty minutes out of nerves. I must have applied deodorant three times. I stared in the mirror for a good ten. Which brought my attention to a crime against humanity.

I pulled out my phone and posted on my Facebook page, *I think there should be a law of nature that states pimples and wrinkles are not allowed to exist on the same face. Can I get an amen?*

Before I got any *amens* a text came.

I'm here.

Oh, crap. I grabbed my bag and chest. My heart was working overtime. I stepped onto the porch and turned to lock the door behind me, taking a deep breath and a moment to gather my courage. When I turned around, there Reed was, sitting in his jeep in front of my house in the late afternoon sun.

I looked out over our good-sized front lawn. It needed to be mowed. That was always Neil's job. It was the one domestic thing he was good at and didn't complain about. Which surprised me because it was outdoorsy, but I think he liked the hour of uninterrupted listening to one of his podcasts on genealogy or the anatomy of birds. *Stop thinking about him, Sam. He's gone.*

Reed smiled at me through the passenger side window. I found myself smiling back and found some courage to proceed. He looked good in shades with his baseball cap on backwards. My brothers wore that look a lot growing up. I think Reed had too. I hurried down the porch steps to his jeep, not because I was excited, but nervous about prying eyes.

I jumped in, shut the door, and let out the breath I'd been holding.

Reed rested his hand on my leg. That answered the touching question. I tried not to tense.

"You look great. Are you ready to have some fun?"

I half nodded and looked in his backseat. It was filled with a cooler, blankets, and camping chairs. "Where are we going?"

He wagged his eyebrows. "Indiana."

"You're taking me across the state line?"

"Don't worry, I'll bring you back." He removed his hand from my leg and we took off.

"Why Indiana?"

"You said you wanted it to be private. I know a great secluded camping spot near the dunes on Lake Michigan."

"Camping?" I was ready to start panicking. Again.

"We're not spending the night. What kind of guy do you think I am?" He teased.

"A guy."

He chuckled. "You got me there. But relax. We won't be doing anything that requires your legal documents tonight."

"I'm nervous," I admitted to him.

"I know. I am too."

My head tilted, surprised. "Why are you nervous?"

"Because you're the first woman I ever had feelings for. I knew they would never be reciprocated, but now here you are, looking more beautiful than you did twenty years ago."

My cheeks warmed. "That can't possibly be true."

"I didn't think it was possible either, but you exceeded my expectations." He turned out of my neighborhood.

"You look better than you did twenty years ago too," I teased, trying to add some levity back to the conversation. Honestly, I wasn't sure how to respond. It had been a long time since I had received such a compliment.

It worked, judging by his laugh. "Well, I would hope so. Fourteen, fifteen wasn't a good look for me."

"I enjoyed the voice cracks."

"Hey now," he used his manliest, deepest voice. "You don't know how mortifying that was, especially around you."

"I'm sorry for laughing at you."

"You don't sound very sorry."

"Need I remind you that you booby trapped my bedroom? And there is still the matter of the dead fish. Oh, and my Bryan Adams poster and t-shirt."

"Speaking of Bryan Adams..." Reed pushed some button on his fancy touch screen stereo, and the "Summer of '69" filled his jeep. It was one of my favorite Bryan Adams' songs.

"Wow."

"Nice sound system, right?"

"It is, but I was thinking how sweet it is that you remembered."

He did a quick glance my way while maneuvering through the crowded I-94 tollway. "I think you would be surprised how much I remember about you."

"I think you're right." It was getting warm in the car. "But tell me about you. I know you've been coaching and you lived in Wisconsin for a while. But what else? Where did you go to school? Peter said something about a mentoring thing."

"I went to Purdue."

"You were a Boilermaker?" I laughed.

"Don't knock the name." He grinned. "I played for them for three seasons before I blew my knee out."

"Ouch. I'm sorry."

He shrugged. "It wasn't like I was headed for the NFL. Looking back, it was probably a good thing. I was more focused on academics after that."

"Did you always know you wanted to be a coach and a teacher?"

"Coach, yes. Teacher took some convincing. I honestly wasn't sure that's the route I wanted to go until I did my internship. But once you help a child no one else has been able to, it changes you."

"And them."

He grinned. "I love that part of my job."

"So what was the mentoring project you started?"

Even though he was driving, I could see his eyes light up. "I worked in a lower income district in Milwaukee. They didn't have half the resources the district here has, but it was a good district. Great kids. Unfortunately, a lot of them come from broken homes or homes where academics aren't a priority. Surviving was the name of the game. Kids that come from homes like that are less likely to graduate from high school, and the odds of them going to college are even less."

He checked his blind spot and changed lanes before continuing. "The head coach and I decided we weren't doing our jobs right if all we did was get them through. We needed to show them what they could do. What the possibilities were. But that meant getting their parents involved too. So we reached out to local and community leaders in business and government. We were able to coordinate workshops to help the students' parents attain more job skills. Some of them hardly even knew how to turn on a computer, much less use one."

"Really?"

He nodded. "You'd be surprised by the number. I know I was. But it was gratifying to see some of those parents placed in better jobs. And I loved watching our mentors work with the students. Even better was seeing a few of them head off to college."

"It must have been hard for you to leave all that."

"It was a tough decision, but to be the head coach at my alma mater was too hard to pass up. And it's been great to reconnect with Peter. And some other people." He grinned my way.

I skipped over that part. "Had you guys not kept in touch?"

"On and off. I knew he had entered the priesthood. He called me after he and Delanie got married. Surprised the hell out of me."

"You weren't the only one. Ma still hasn't forgiven him."

"She doesn't seem to like Delanie very much."

"Which is a shame. She's great, and they're good together. I've tried to talk to her about it, but you've probably noticed that Ma does what Ma wants. And everyone does what Ma wants."

"Even you?"

"Pretty much all my life. But there are some things she doesn't know about."

His eyebrows raised. "Like what?"

"Things you don't need to know either."

"Those must be some stories. You're blushing."

"Pay attention to the road." I tried to sound lighthearted and not motherly.

He turned his gaze back to the road. "I like paying attention to you."

"So I've noticed."

"Are you okay with that?"

I tilted my head. "You know, it's not half bad."

His laughter filled the jeep along with Bryan Adams. And it wasn't bad at all.

CHAPTER TWENTY-SEVEN

AN HOUR AND A HALF LATER I FOUND MYSELF IN A LITTLE PIECE OF HEAVEN. The drive through the state park was breathtaking. So much foliage, and the fall colors were starting to peek through. My head kept turning, trying to get it all in.

"I can't believe I've never been here before."

"I'm surprised too."

"My, uh..."

Reed rested his hand on my knee. "You can say his name."

I took a breath and let it out. "Neil wasn't much for this kind of thing."

"But you are?"

"I love it. Looks like a great place for a bike ride."

"Had I known you loved to bike, I could have put my bike rack on and we could have brought bikes up. They have some great biking trails around here."

"I haven't had a bike in years, but I'm going to change that."

"If you want help shopping for one, let me know."

"I will." I kept my focus outside. It was easier that way. Reed was quite honestly scaring me. The boy I knew was fading away and being replaced with not only a man, but what appeared to be a good one. I wasn't sure how to process that.

We passed several other campers on our way. Some in RVs, some doing it the old-fashioned way in tents. Reed pulled into a secluded camping spot, just like he had promised.

Once he put the jeep in park, Reed turned my way. "You have time, right? Cody's staying with his grandma tonight?"

"Yeah," I was reluctant to say.

"Do you want to hit one of the trails first and take a walk? I know it's more than just dinner, but we still have plenty of daylight." He moved his shades up to rest on his ball cap. His eyes were asking me to seriously consider this change of plans. Or was this his plan all along?

I tucked some hair behind my ear and tried to decipher the ping-pong match in my head. Yes or no? Good idea or bad? The game was evenly matched. Agreeing meant elongating the date. Saying no meant hurting his feelings and perhaps missing out on what could be a great time.

"There's a beautiful waterfall I want to show you," he sweetened the deal. "And fires are better lit in the dark. Don't you agree?"

Did he lean in closer? Yes, he did. I could see the violet specks in his gorgeous blue eyes. I lost my head and nodded my agreement.

"Great, it's settled then. I'll come around and get your door. Hang tight."

I needed to hyperventilate, but didn't have time. The car ride was perfect. Safe, even. Now that we were here, the date felt real.

Before I knew it, he was opening my door and holding out his hand.

I stared at his hand, unsure.

He reached in and took mine with a sultry smile. "I know it's been a while for you, but this is how we do things now." He gave my hand a gentle tug and out I came. Without letting go of my hand, he reached in and grabbed his fleece jacket. "Just in case your jean jacket isn't enough to keep you warm."

The weather was beautiful now—in the low seventies, high-sixties, I would guess—but I knew that wouldn't last long, especially being this close to Lake Michigan.

"Good call. Thank you."

He shut the door, locked the jeep, and looked down at our clasped hands. "Is this okay?"

I took a second to think, but was finding it difficult. "Honestly, I don't know. This is all new for me. And it's you."

"It is me." He drew me closer. "I don't want to push you or make you feel uncomfortable."

My heart skipped a beat. "I am uncomfortable, but it's not because of you."

He ran his calloused thumb across my hand. More of the boy was slipping away. I realized I wanted to hold on to that part of him; if I saw only the man drawing me in with his eyes and body, I knew I would have decisions to make. I would have to feel again.

Vulnerability scared me more than anything. My heart knew, though, that you could never have total intimacy without it. That's what my marriage had lacked for years—honest and complete intimacy. Far more potent than sex or physical touch, an intimate, emotional connection made every aspect of a relationship better, or worse when it was absent.

But this was only a date. A one-time thing.

"What can I do to help you feel more comfortable?"

I took a moment to really look at him. I was amazed by his thoughtfulness. "Uncomfortable isn't necessarily a bad thing. Maybe it's time I get out of my comfort zone."

If that's even what I had been in. Whatever zone it was, I wanted out of it. I wanted to feel anything but the pain and loneliness that had enveloped me for months.

"I'm happy to help you out." He pulled me along. "Just remember, we're here to have a good time."

That made me feel better. He obviously wasn't looking for anything serious. Like I said, we would probably look back on this one day and have a good laugh. A *remember when we went on that date?* His future wife would look at me and think, *you went out with her? She's old.* Though he did like older women, so maybe she'd think I was young. My brothers would tease me and we would move on. Hopefully by then I would be moved on from my current state of being. I might even be happily married myself. Obviously, I was thinking *way* into the future.

Our clasped hands swayed between us as we walked the dirt path, breathing in the end of summer air. The smell of barbecue and campfire tickled my nose.

"Do you come here often?" I asked.

"It's been a long time."

"Was this another one of your make-out spots?"

With a playful grin, he took his ball cap off and did his best to place it on my head. He didn't account for my thick, unruly curls, but he managed to make it stay. "You're the first woman I've brought up here."

I looked around at the beauty that surrounded us. "It's gorgeous. Thank you. I needed to get away."

"The best is yet to come." He picked up the pace and took me along for the ride.

I heard it before I saw it. The sound of rushing water played in the background. Reed deftly maneuvered us off the trail and led us through the grass and brush to a small, worn path that led to the river and water-fall. The falls expanded the width of the river, and what it lacked in height, it made up in beauty with breath-taking rock formations.

"Let's go sit on the bank." Reed's voice was filled with a childlike excitement.

I followed him. He seemed to know exactly where he wanted to land. It was the perfect spot. It was as if the two flat rocks were placed there for our use. Reed helped me sit down before joining me. The rock was warm from catching the sun's rays, which now landed on me.

I took Reed's hat off, closed my eyes, and breathed in the peace of the river and the sound of the falls. Nature was breathing life into me.

"This is heaven."

"Yes, it is."

I opened my eyes to find Reed staring at me. Suddenly, I felt shy. That was a feeling long dormant. I pulled my knees up to my chest and looked out over the expanse of the river. A fish jumped out to catch his dinner.

"Did I make you uncomfortable?"

I rested my head on my arms and looked his way. The sun illuminated his handsome features, adding more sparkle to his eyes. "It's been a long time since someone has found me beautiful."

He grasped one of my curls and ran his fingers down it. "I doubt that. They just weren't brave enough to tell you. It took me twenty years.

Granted, you were married most of that time, or dating idiots like Ben Averill." His grinned turned wicked.

I nudged him with my shoulder. "He was a nice guy, until he broke up with me."

He pressed his lips together as if he was debating on what to say next. "Peter and I caught him kissing Mandy Olson."

I sat up. "What?" Ben told me he hated Mandy Olson.

"Peter may have punched him. And I threatened to tell everyone that he—you know, maybe I'll keep that to myself since I'm in the presence of a lady."

That piqued my interest, but I didn't press him. And I could guess.

"Anyway, we made him promise to break up with you."

"Peter never said anything."

"The guy was a loser. We didn't want you to get hurt."

"That seems to be my lot in life. Cheaters." The waterfall became my focus again.

"Hey." He rubbed my arm.

I met his concerned eyes.

"Your ex is a special kind of stupid. But let's change the subject. We're here to have fun. And I have the most amazing dinner and dessert planned." He stood up and reached his hand out. This time I took it without hesitating.

"You're a fast learner," he teased. "Before you know it, you'll be grabbing my hand first tonight." He pulled me up.

"You think so?"

He gave my hand a squeeze. "I hope so."

As the sun sank down below the horizon, I found myself next to Reed in a camp chair, eating the most delectable foil dinner of garlic shrimp and potatoes, and listening to the cricket's chirp and the fire crackle. The glow of the fire warmed me, as did the man next to me. He couldn't have been more thoughtful. Foil packets with apple crisp sat baking in the coals, only proving what an exceptional human Reed was. I loved apple crisp. The sweet smell of the apples and cinnamon in the air only added to the ambiance. And although I thought I would be too nervous to eat, I found I was more than comfortable and hungry.

Using my fork, I pointed at the food on my paper plate. "You weren't lying. This is amazing. Thank you."

"I'm happy you're enjoying it. I wasn't sure if you liked seafood."

"Love it."

"Duly noted." He took a bite of his own food, chewed, and swallowed. "What other things do you love?"

"Food-wise?"

"Food, wine, movies, sports—please say football. Men preferences?"

I laughed. "Definitely love football. Men are questionable, unless I'm related to them and even then, Peter and James push it."

His laughter filled the chilly night air. "We will see what we can do about your aversion to the opposite sex."

"That's a tough job."

"I know. I've been reading your blog. Do you really think all men are evil and must die?"

"You took that out of context. I said, 'must be destroyed,' not 'die.'"

"I'm pretty sure I read it exactly the way you intended it."

"You know, my rules state no men allowed."

"It says no husbands, so I qualify."

"Come to think of it, you would make a good wife for someone."

He fluttered his eyes. "These hairy legs don't look great in heels, but I did get an A in home economics."

"Let me guess. You wanted to meet pretty girls."

"That's still my objective in life."

"Hmm. I bet."

"Judging by the woman sitting next to me, I do okay in that department."

I leaned over and nudged him with my shoulder. That's how the rest of our night went. Playful conversation, good food, and laughter, lots of laughter. Best night in a long time. So good, we lost track of time and didn't leave until well after midnight. Then Reed made it more adventurous—we drove home with the top down on his jeep, the heater blowing on me all the way home, the wind whipping through my hair. The twinkle-filled night sky made up for the chilly air.

I almost felt like a teenager again. Especially when the moment came. You know the one. The door scene. He insisted on walking me to the door even though I thought he should leave me and take off. I didn't want anyone to see us together. But since it was two in the morning by the time we arrived, he thought the gentlemanly thing to do was make sure no one was lurking in the bushes or my house. I assured him I had a great alarm system, but he wasn't taking no for an answer.

He walked around to get my door. Hand holding was part of the package again. And maybe there was a tingle there when he took it. And maybe I was a little too tired and not thinking straight, because I found myself staring up at him and wanting to run my hand across his stubbled cheek. Not only that, I longed to get lost in his eyes. Eyes that no longer held a mischievous boy's glint, but the look of a man who yearned.

"Thank you," I whispered into the still night.

"Let's get you inside." He was using hushed tones too.

I followed his lead, paying attention to the way his thumb brushed my hand and how close he walked next to me. The smell of campfire and his cologne made me feel some other things. Was that desire? It had been so long.

We walked up the porch steps, slow and deliberate, taking cover under the porch, landing at the door.

I looked down at our hands. He didn't seem in a hurry to let go. I lifted my head to meet his gaze. "I had great time."

"Me too." He drew closer and took my other hand. The space between us began to evaporate. What was he doing? He leaned in, his breath was warm. His lips, oh, his lips were—

A stupid, girlish giggle escaped me.

His head popped up in shock, maybe embarrassment.

I knew I felt both. I sighed. "I feel like I say this a lot to you, but I'm sorry."

In my defense, though, I wasn't expecting a goodnight kiss, and I never imagined *us* kissing.

He dropped one of my hands and inched back. Consternation flashed in his eyes. "Sam, I'm not a child."

"I know."

The yearning was back in his eyes, erasing the frustration from the seconds before. "Close your eyes."

My eyes did the opposite and widened.

His smile said he wasn't deterred. He edged forward, running his hand through my wind-blown hair. "Close your eyes, Sam."

As if hypnotized by the sound of his sultry voice, my eyes fell shut. With my eyes closed, my other senses were heightened. The finger he ran down my cheek left a trail of sparks in its wake. His lips took over where his finger left off. He blazed a path of soft kisses leading to the corner of my mouth. I held my breath in anticipation. He let it brew and stir while he hovered near my lips, teasing me with his warm breath. There was a passion and an angst I had never experienced before.

His hands went to work cupping my face. My own hands landed on his chest and instantly liked what they felt. They, of their own accord, moved over his defined chest. And before I knew it, Reed brushed my lips with his, testing the waters. After one more gentle caress, he pressed his lips against mine. My hands glided up his chest and around his neck. His tongue invited my lips to part, giving me a taste of what he had to offer. It was sweet and sensual. And over too soon.

When he backed away, my eyes fluttered open. The kiss ended so abruptly, I wondered if maybe I had done something wrong. Or maybe I was horribly out of practice and he hadn't reveled in it the way I had.

My eyes locked with his under the light of my porch. In front of me stood a man that left me wanting.

His penetrating gaze, his stance, they all said one thing—*see me*.

I saw.

CHAPTER TWENTY-EIGHT

I WAS TOO OLD TO BE UP THIS EARLY RELIVING EVERY MOMENT, TOUCH, AND kiss with Reed. The kiss. Oh, the kiss. I don't remember first kisses being that good.

Except, I didn't think it was that good for Reed. After he kissed me and stared at me for a few seconds, he saw me to my door and made sure the premises were secure before saying goodbye, but that was it. No, *I'll call you later*, or *wow Sam, that was amazing, it lived up to all my teenage fantasies about you.*

Okay, so maybe I didn't expect him to say that. And maybe I hadn't fantasized about him, but that kiss was fantasy worthy. Like, relive over and over again. I had been doing just that for the past hour after a restless few hours of sleep.

The sun was barely up, but my room was bright since I hadn't replaced the curtains. I should get on that so I didn't have any "flasher" moments like Reed. He never did tell me if he'd had dinner at his admirers' yet. Perhaps he would never tell me because this was a one-and-done like I imagined it would be. So why was I suddenly disappointed by that? Had I offended him one too many times? Yes, the giggling before the kiss was lame, but I responded appropriately after that. Maybe my breath was wretched. The shrimp was tossed with garlic, but he had eaten it too, and I quite enjoyed the way he tasted. I could still taste him now.

This was so ridiculous. I was a mother of a teenager. I shouldn't be thinking like this. It was a date. I survived it, even enjoyed it. It's over. Period.

I held my stomach trying to stave off the flutters I felt there when I thought of Reed. I had already checked my phone, even though it was early, to see if he had texted.

I threw off my covers and stared down at my frumpy flannel mom pajamas with polka dots, and sighed. I was no longer the wannabe hot babe in silk nighties. Not like I would wear sexy pajamas even if I owned some. I had a teenage son in the house. But maybe that's why Neil looked elsewhere.

Reed probably instinctively knew I was the kind of woman who valued comfort and warmth over pretending to be nighttime eye candy. I used to figure, flannel came off as easy as silk, and it was less embarrassing for my son to see me in it. Cody would hate for me to ever mention it, but he was afraid of the dark for the longest time, and many nights he ended up sleeping on our floor until he was about nine years old. I would wake up and there he would be, curled up with a blanket by my bedside. I missed those days.

Reed's teenage fantasy had grown up to be a middle-aged, flannel-wearing, hair-dying, divorced mom. Now that he'd figured that out, we could all move on.

That's exactly what I was doing. I traded in my frumpy pajamas for another sexy outfit—oversized t-shirt and yoga pants. It went perfectly with my twenty-year-old workout video from back in the day. Who didn't love a little Tae Bo? No one had ever toned my butt and thighs like Billy Blanks. And bonus, it was in the privacy—or semi privacy, still needed to get curtains—of my own home. No little hard bodies running around reminding me why I was single at almost forty.

I kicked, punched, and squatted until I was drenched in sweat. Maybe I wore flannel to bed, but at least I knew there was a somewhat toned body underneath all the layers. That's what counted. At least that's what I told myself.

By mid-morning, I was ready and dressed to face the new day. Cody was ready too; he kept texting me the SOS emoji. I guessed that was his way of saying *come and get me*. He'd made it longer than I thought he would. I supposed that meant I would be buying another mind-numbing video game for him. I hoped he had some fun and was still talking to me.

During my drive into the city, I did my best to not think about anything that had happened in the last eighteen hours. I hoped the person I was not thinking about wasn't coming to Sunday dinner. I wasn't ready to laugh about it yet. Unfortunately, I kept thinking about how much I would have loved a repeat of what went down on the porch.

All these thoughts, or non-thoughts, had me mentally and emotionally unprepared to face what was lurking for me at Gelaire's.

When I pulled in behind the shiny, new red Camaro in front of Gelaire's Greystone, it never even occurred to me that Gelaire had another visitor. And there was nothing in my history with Neil that would have ever given the slightest hint he'd purchase a sports car. He watched National Geographic, for goodness sakes, and his idea of fun was looking at gravestones online. His car—my car that I drove now—screamed expensive, but in that boring-dad-bod sort of way.

Worse was how I found out that the car was Neil's. There I was, looking forward to seeing my kid, minding my own business. And *she* appeared. When I exited my car, she opened the door of the Camaro on the passenger side. No one was in the driver's side.

I froze on the busy street and watched her toss her long blonde hair before leaning against the sleek new car. It still had a dealer tag on it. She wore a sports bra and tight exercise pants that showed off her tiny bare baby bump and toned body. There was no way she was due in October or November. I'm sure I looked that big in my first trimester. I bet she didn't even have swollen ankles. Something swelled in me worse than any amount of water retention had. Would this hate ever fade?

She causally looked at her cell phone as if she didn't have a worry in the world, not knowing or probably even caring that she had destroyed mine and my son's life. I wanted to lash out at her. But I knew it wouldn't do me any good. This hate I held only hurt me. I refused to let myself give her any more power over me. She had taken enough; she would not have my dignity. I could, at the very least, keep that.

I steadied myself and took a breath, knowing Neil must be inside with our son. All at once, I wanted to run in and save Cody if needed, then run the other way to save myself from facing Neil. But Cody would always win, always.

When my wedges hit the sidewalk, two things happened. The bimbo was alerted to my presence and she gave me the loveliest of snide grins while appraising my boyfriend jeans and t-shirt. I gave her no satisfaction of a response one way or the other; we both knew she had won, so what was the point of engaging her? Instead, I focused on the house, only to see Neil walking out. But not my Neil. This Neil had dyed his graying sandy hair a deep brown. And please tell me those weren't hair plugs where his receding hairline used to be. Was he wearing skinny jeans? I didn't even like it when Cody wore them.

Neil obviously wasn't prepared to see me either. Even from a distance, I could see the crimson flood his face. He looked between his past and future. Past is where his focus landed.

"Sam, I didn't know you would be here already." His eyes were pleading with me not to judge him for his desperate attempt to look like he belonged in a boy band.

I didn't know what to say. I stood stunned by his change, inside and out. Who was this man standing in front of me running his fingers through his hair, trying his best not to touch the grafted in parts? Certainly not the man I had pledged my heart and soul to almost two decades ago. That man would have laughed at the man standing in front of me. The brown hair did not suit him. It made him look pale and unnatural.

My mouth may not have worked, but my feet did. I headed for the door he recently exited.

Neil met me head on, not letting me pass. "How are you, Sam? You look good." He kept his stilted voice down.

I couldn't say the same for him, or acknowledge him, but Roxie could and did.

"Baby, we need to go. I'm going to be late for Pilates."

I hated her even more for being able to do Pilates while pregnant, and for calling him baby. He hated cutesy names like that. Perhaps the man standing in front of me didn't. I didn't know this man.

"I'll be right there," he snapped.

"Don't let me keep you." I sidestepped him.

He gently grabbed my arm. "Sam."

I looked at his hand touching my bare skin. It didn't belong there. I felt nothing but my skin crawl from his touch. I pulled away.

His eyes pooled with regret.

"Neil," Roxie yelled.

Neil shook his head and walked away at her command. I didn't get a second glance.

Internally, I shook my head too. Is this what he really wanted? Someone to change him? I didn't bother to watch him drive away. I had already done that. I refused to do it again or let it affect me like it had that day. I wished I could say that he didn't affect me at all. But that would have been a lie.

Cody didn't divulge too much information about Neil's brief visit on our drive home, other than to say, "It was all right. He might come to my game this weekend."

I let it lie, knowing Gelaire would tell me more about it on Tuesday. And I didn't want to push Cody. He'd been through enough.

"At least tell me how the game was."

Cody leaned his head against the window with one ear bud in, giving the illusion he was willing to converse. "It was all right. The Cubs won."

"Tell me something I don't know." It was all over the news that the Cubs had won.

"The food was good."

"Okay." I grinned. "How was grandma?"

His mouth twitched. "She sings, 'Take Me Out to the Ballgame' too loud."

"Oh really?"

"And she talks to everyone."

"So you had a good time with her?"

"It was okay. You still owe me."

"I have the download code for you ready at home."

He sat up straight, a real smile on his face. "You're the best."

He didn't always think so, but I would take what I could get.

While Cody indulged in his new video game, I was reminded of how old I was and took a nap on the couch. It was an uninterrupted nap, since no one called. Not that I was expecting a call or that one even needed to happen. And after seeing Neil today, I was reminded of the fickleness of men and how easily their affections change. It was good no one called.

Even better, no one came to Sunday dinner. Or so I thought. The seat next to me was screaming *you're alone*. It screamed louder when Reed showed up late.

He walked in carrying a bouquet of flowers as always, sunflowers this time around. He kissed Ma on the cheek. "Sorry, I'm late, Mrs. D. I got caught up at the gym."

She stood and returned a kiss on his cheek while taking the flowers. "Thank you, these are gorgeous. You're becoming my favorite." She glared at her own husband and sons who never thought to bring her flowers. "I'll go put them in some water. You sit down and fill your plate."

I looked up expecting him to sit next to me. He acknowledged me with hardly a glance before taking a seat next to Peter.

No one but me seemed to take notice that he'd switched spots. Was the kiss truly that awful? Had I done something? I wasn't expecting some lasting relationship out of the deal, but I enjoyed his company. And until that moment, I hadn't truly realized how he had taken the sting of loneliness away from me at the family table. The biting sting was back, and as piercing as ever.

The world kept turning for everyone else. For me, I stared down at the ribs and salad on my plate, not at all hungry. My mind raced with why Reed had slighted me. We'd seemed to have such a great time together yesterday. So I giggled once, but I thought I responded appropriately afterward. I didn't know why this was bothering me so much. Perhaps because I felt like I was never enough. I didn't look like a supermodel when I was pregnant, not even when I wasn't. I couldn't do Pilates. If I tried, I would probably end up in the emergency room. I wasn't flirty and fun or extraordinarily talented at anything. I realized what a bore I was.

My stomach started churning. Without a word I got up, to go where, I didn't know. No one noticed, except Ma when we crossed paths in the kitchen while she was arranging her flowers in a vase.

"Are you all right, Samantha Marie?"

I nodded. "I'm not hungry."

Her eyes narrowed and her nose did this weird scrunching-flaring thing like it always did when she was trying to determine if we were telling the truth or not. Then she felt my forehead and cheeks.

"Ma, I'm fine."

"Why don't you go lay down in the guest bedroom?"

"I was thinking maybe I would go home. Do you think you or Dad could bring Cody home later?" I didn't want to interrupt dinner or draw attention to myself.

"Are you upset because you saw Neil today?"

I had told Delanie and Avery about my encounter with him while we set the table; I guess Ma overheard. I shook my head.

She rested her hand on my cheek. "You are loved; don't you ever forget that."

My eyes began to water. "I'm going to go."

Ma did exactly what I needed. She hugged me and let me go without a fuss. I rushed out the front door and barely heard Ma tell everyone I wasn't feeling well. That about summed up my life for the year.

CHAPTER TWENTY-NINE

For an hour, I lay in my bed contemplating my life. And not just the surface things or the weekend's events, but the whole of it. The good, the bad, and the ugly. I turned to my blog for comfort and snuggled under my covers on my bed, already in those frumpy pajamas as I waited for my son to come home. For some reason, I gained strength when I let my feelings out in words. It was like drawing poison out.

The self-loathing reached new heights today due to some unforeseen circumstances this weekend. One being running into my ex-husband, who apparently wants to start a middle-aged boy band by the way he looks, and his gorgeous, half-naked, pregnant girlfriend. The other event, let's just say, reminded me why my ex now lives with a woman that will probably pop his baby out in the morning, hit the gym that afternoon, and be back in her skinny jeans before dinner.

These unfortunate events had me thinking about everything that I'm not and why I'm on the sidelines instead of in the game. But then it hit me that if it wasn't for the people on the sidelines, there would never be any game. The coach, who some might consider the most important person in any game or team, does her work from the sidelines. She directs the game and calls the plays. She's always strategizing and looking ahead. She helps others believe in themselves and keep things in perspective. She knows there is no room for ego.

For example, if my ex would have come to me and said, "I'm thinking about a new look; what do you think of this?" and held up a picture of a man twenty-five years his junior in pants that probably had him singing soprano, I would have laughed. But then I would have told him that while he wasn't a fashionista, I always appreciated that he didn't dress like a slob. I also would have told him he really should learn to iron his own pants and shirts. I don't even want to think about all the time I wasted ironing his clothes for work. But I digress.

My point is that perhaps my work on the sidelines was far more important than any play in the game. I would have kept him from looking like a classic mid-life crisis wrapped up in a whole bunch of ludicrous. So maybe he didn't think I was an all-star on the field, but I kept a lot of stupid plays from being made, aka hair plugs. And once in a while, I had a genius plan, like when I convinced my ex we should invest in Netflix ten years ago. I bet he used his half of that money to buy his alter-ego sports car. At the very least, I kept things in perspective.

Ladies, I wear frumpy flannel to bed. I gained weight while I was pregnant and loved every minute of it because I knew what I was creating was far more important than getting back into my tight jeans. Not that sometimes I don't miss that firm butt. I may not be sexy or give the kind of kisses that keep men begging for more, but I can keep a clean and organized house, make well-balanced meals, and budget. I can help with homework, even the complicated math equations. And when called upon, I can throw a lovely dinner party. I even know how to fold fancy napkins. Inconsequential things, I know. But you and I need not let anyone make us feel like what we do on the sidelines is menial. It's important work. It's not for the faint of heart or those who think more of themselves than others.

And don't worry about getting back in the game, because there will always be another yahoo who wants to sideline you or ignore you because you aren't a supermodel or because you laugh at inappropriate times. Guess what? You don't need them to validate you. You never did. Now go eat a cookie—I mean, protein ball. (See earlier post for recipe and thank me later.) And don't forget to thank your lucky stars that you no longer have to clean up their pee on your toilet seat and that you get to sleep in a snore-free zone.

Sidelined Wife in Chief and Loving It. (Or at least trying to.)

I threw off my covers and did what I did best: I made lunches and breakfasts for the week and even organized my pantry while I waited for Cody to come home. I also ate a protein ball or two. After all, I didn't have dinner. In the midst of it all, I answered texts from Avery and Delanie asking if I was all right. I was sure trying to be.

Cody walked in a little before nine, all smiles. I figured it was because the Bears had won. I had listened to the end of the game on the radio while I indulged in domestication.

He headed straight for the fridge like he hadn't eaten a thing in hours and grabbed a couple of cheese sticks. "Hey, Mom"

"How was your night?"

"Awesome. Coach brought me home and he let me drive his jeep."

"What?" I looked up from the grocery list I was making on the breakfast bar. "Why didn't Grandma or Grandpa bring you home?"

"Coach offered since he was coming this way and Grandma scares me when she drives and Grandpa was tired."

Ma was a terrible driver; she was always pointing at things like sale signs when she drove and paying attention to anything instead of the road.

"Oh, well, that was nice of him."

Cody, instead of pulling apart the cheese stick, just took a big bite of it. "Yeah," he said through a full mouth. "He wanted me to tell you he hopes you feel better and you should expect a call from him about selling tickets at the school." Cody grimaced. "You won't embarrass me at school, will you?"

After that question, I had no time to wonder why Reed needed to call me about tickets or why he needed to call me at all. Or why he would, considering he ignored me today, and how stupid he must think I am after last night. I had other things to worry about.

"When have I ever embarrassed you?"

He leaned on one leg, just like his dad. "Rory thinks you don't like her."

"Why?"

"She said you ignored her when she tried to talk to you when you were selling tickets."

"I didn't ignore her. She said she loved you. How was I supposed to respond to that?"

Cody's face burned red and his eyes looked anywhere but at me. "She didn't mean it like you think."

My eyebrow raised. "How did she mean it?"

"That's just the way girls talk."

"Uh-huh. Do you love her?" I hated even saying the words.

"No."

Oh, thank goodness. I believed him, I think. "She caught me off guard. The next time she comes to talk to me, I'll say, 'my son doesn't love you.'"

His head whipped my way and was met with my evil grin.

"You know you're not funny."

"Whatever, your lip is begging to smile. But don't worry, I'll be totally cool around her."

His face scrunched. "Don't use words like cool."

"What about gnarly, tubular, dynamite? Do those work for you?"

He rolled his eyes. "I'm going to play one game and then go to bed."

"Okay, I love you my Cody Bear. Remember when I used to call you that? I could mention that to Rory."

He walked past me shaking his head, not bothering to respond to my idle threats.

I finished my list and stayed up with him until he headed off to bed. While he played, I enjoyed reading the responses to my post from earlier.

Yes! Yes! And yes!

My ex decided to have every inch of hair on his body waxed after we split up. He developed a terrible rash, which turned into an infection. His new girlfriend was really into home remedies, so she ran him an oatmeal bath and didn't tell him. He has a rare oatmeal allergy. Too bad she called 911. I was still the beneficiary on his life insurance policy. At least I got to enjoy the pictures his little barely legal girlfriend posted online.

I giggled to myself. These women were hilarious.

I crawled into bed feeling much better than I thought I would about my day. Then my phone rang. I wasn't keen on answering Reed's call. I knew we would have to see each other from time to time, but I wasn't ready to laugh over our date yet. And as much as I knew I wasn't that woman who turned heads and made men lose their minds and other body parts, I would be lying if I didn't acknowledge that part of me wished I was. I truly was coming to terms with being on the sideline, but there was always that little part of you that wondered if you could be the star on the field. I debated too long and he hung up. That worked out well. Or so I thought.

Sam, please call me. We need to talk.

What did we possibly have to talk about? He could email me about tickets, or I'm sure Lisa, who was in charge of them, would.

He didn't even give me time to call before my phone rang again.

This had better be really important. "Hello?"

"I'm sorry," were the first words out of his mouth.

"For what?" I found myself annoyed with him.

"About today."

"What about it?" Still annoyed. And maybe hurt, if I was being honest with myself.

"Sam." He paused. "I couldn't do it today."

"Do what?"

"Pretend." He inhaled and exhaled. "After last night, I couldn't sit next to you, hell, even talk to you, and not give away how attracted I am to you."

I leaned back into my pillows. "Oh."

"How could you call me a yahoo on your blog and tell everyone I ignored you?"

"I didn't," I blurted, flustered he read the post.

"You were talking about somebody else?"

"I was speaking in general terms."

"Right. I suppose you were speaking generally that you laugh at inappropriate times, like when someone tries to kiss you, too."

I sank lower in my covers, as if that would hide my embarrassment over the situation. "I told you I was sorry."

"There's no reason for you to be."

"So...it wasn't awful for you?" I couldn't believe I was asking him that. It's not something I would have done twenty years ago.

He didn't hide the smile in his voice well. "It was all right."

"Thanks." I rolled my eyes even though he couldn't see me.

"I'd like to do it again, if that means anything to you."

"We shouldn't."

"Why? We're two consenting adults. And you seemed to have a good time last night. I particularly enjoyed the gasp that escaped from you when my lips left your beautiful mouth."

Holy Saint Raphael, my pulse raised along with my body temperature like I had dialed one of those call-for-a-good-time numbers. Did those even exist anymore now that we had the internet? No one had talked to me like that in a long time, maybe ever.

"Um..." All I could think about was the feel of his lips and how he tasted.

"Sam, I want to take you out again. I'll even sit next to you at Sunday dinner and do my best to keep my hands and eyes off you so you don't feel ignored. I should have called you before dinner so we could discuss how we would handle things, but I didn't want you to think I was being pushy. And when I saw you tonight, all I could think of was *how can I get her alone*. I knew sitting next to you wasn't a good idea. But when you left, it took everything I had not to go after you."

As far as apologies went, it was a good one. "I wasn't really sick."

"I had feeling. I'm sorry if you left because of me."

"It was just one of those days."

"From the sounds of your blog, it was a rough one. I didn't mean to add to it. By the way, your kiss made me want more. And I bet you make flannel look good."

I bit my lip as if I wasn't the only one in the room. "You really should quit reading my blog posts."

"No way. It's free, unlimited access into your beautiful head. And your followers are entertaining."

"Yeah, they are."

"Sam," he paused, "you may think you're ordinary, and maybe that's what makes you so likable, but you're anything but. Don't you see how people respond to you? It's anything but typical."

"I'm just me, trying to figure me out."

"Do you want some company on that journey?"

"And what would we do? We can't keep sneaking away to Indiana."

"Don't worry, I have some ideas."

"Like what?"

"For starters, when and where do you grocery shop?"

CHAPTER THIRTY

I HAD NEVER BEEN ON A DATE TO THE GROCERY STORE. THAT IS, IF YOU could call this a date. We were showing up a few minutes apart, Monday night, in separate vehicles. Reed's objective was for us to run into each other but act as if it was happenstance. How did this become my life? And why did I agree to this? Probably because I liked him, he made me smile, and I really did need groceries. And never had anyone gone to such lengths to see me.

I chose Jewel, my favorite grocery store and the one farthest away from my house in Clearfield, so I hoped we wouldn't see anyone we knew. I was also going later than normal, which made me feel some guilt knowing Cody was home alone, but I knew he enjoyed the freedom. Besides, he was the reason I needed to grocery shop so often.

Grocery store dating also meant wearing something besides yoga pants and a t-shirt. I decided on a dark pair of jeans because they made me look thin, and a form-fitting, burgundy sweater with leather flats. I felt like it fell nicely between I-couldn't-care-less-what-I-look-like and I'm-trying-way-too-hard.

The plan was for me to show up first, which I did, but that didn't stop me from looking around the half-full parking lot to see if he was there. I admit I was looking forward to seeing him.

I started in the produce section with my cart and list. My heart was pounding more than normal in anticipation. It made it hard to focus on getting the perfect Honeycrisp apples Cody and I were both fond of. I must have picked up ten and not looked at one of them. I tried not to look around too much as I wanted to act nonchalant, but I felt like I was failing miserably.

Then it happened. I was placing the perfectly shaped apple in the appropriate green produce bag when Reed walked behind me and, in passing, said, "Fancy meeting you here."

I smiled before I turned to meet him, but he had already passed and was looking at the bananas not too far away. He gave me a sly grin from across the way. I finished picking out my apples and moved on to tomatoes.

"Excuse me, ma'am." Reed had moved on to grapes. He held up two bags. "Green or red grapes?"

I barely paused. "Red."

"Those are my favorite, too." His grin was now more seductive. I should mention it looked like he upped his grocery shopping wardrobe too. He wore some nice jeans and a blue button-up that enhanced his eyes.

I went from tomatoes to pears. One of my favorite snacks was dehydrated pears, and my dehydrator at home was prepped and ready to go.

Reed was getting bolder as we went. He pulled his cart next to mine and waited for the woman next to us to pass by. "Does your preference for red grapes mean you prefer red wine?" His tone was hushed and he didn't look at me.

"Yes." I focused on the pears.

"Good to know." He moved on.

We played that game all through the produce section. It wasn't a bad way to shop.

I moved on to the bakery while he hit the floral section. I got a series of texts. He had taken pictures of several different bouquets.

Which one do you like best?

I scrolled through my phone while I waited for the bakery to slice the multi-grain bread that was a fan favorite at our house. *You don't need to buy me flowers.*

There you go being selfish again. Think of the bees and florists.

I laughed out loud to the stares of my fellow shoppers and bakery workers. I focused back on my phone. *You choose.* They were all lovely.

If I must. Meet me in greeting cards in five minutes.

Okay. I found his request to be odd, but I was rolling with it.

I took the five minutes to load up on milk. Cody could easily drink a gallon every two days. I also got eggs and cheese while I was at it, all before making my way to the greeting cards. I thought maybe he needed help picking one out, but I was learning not to underestimate this man. And yes, I saw him as a man.

Reed was standing at the end of the aisle thumbing through a magazine from the rack across from the cards. He was the only shopper there. He glanced up as I neared, but went back to his *People* magazine. I had to stop myself from laughing at the scene. Or smiling at the beautiful bouquet of red lilies, orange roses, and greenery. It was the one I loved the most out of all the pictures he had sent me.

"You should check out the *Thinking of You* section." He continued to thumb through the magazine.

I did as directed. I swore I felt his eyes on me. I scanned the section and midway down found a pink envelope with my name on it. I gingerly reached for it, feeling like we were doing something wrong, but excited to see what it said. I opened the unsealed envelope and pulled out the vintage card with a little girl kissing a little boy on the cheek. I peeked a glance at Reed. His eyes were on me, all of me; his head flick said to continue.

My pulse raced as I opened the card and began to read what he wrote.

1. You look gorgeous tonight.

2. I'm going to hit the frozen food section next to cool off.

3. You're going to have to give this card back to me so I can pay for it.

4. I forgot to tell you last night that I don't pee on the toilet seat and I always put the seat down.

5. I only snore when I'm sick. You can't hold that against me.

6. I think your kid is great, but he takes corners way too fast.

7. I want to kiss you again.

8. As soon as possible.

9. Like right now.

10. Go out with me this weekend so I can.

I was going to have to join him in the frozen foods section. I looked up and met his gaze with a smile on my face and a heart that was beating wildly out of control. My stomach was also doing something it hadn't done in forever, flip-flopping with that new-infatuation sensation. I didn't even know I could feel this way again. I nodded my acceptance of seeing him again without even thinking about any of the logistics of it. All I could think about was being in his arms.

His probing eyes said he knew he got to me. Did he ever. Grocery shopping would never be the same again.

I wore a permanent grin for the next few days, and it didn't go unnoticed.

Gelaire certainly detected something while we ate lunch together on Tuesday. "Something you want to share, love?"

I pushed around the harvest salad I'd ordered. My appetite was gone, but it was in that good my-stomach-was-full-of-butterflies sort of way. Suddenly I was twenty again.

"No. Why?"

"I thought you would be upset after your run-in with Neil, but you seem—" She tossed her head from side to side, studying me. "I can't quite put my finger on it."

I shrugged, trying to brush off any hint there was anything different in my life. I had been on two dates, with one lined up. I wasn't sure that was life changing, and I couldn't tell anyone anyway. I focused on her son.

"I was at first, but he's changed so much. I don't even recognize him anymore."

Gelaire's brown eyes pooled with tears. "You're moving on."

I reached for her delicate hand across the table. "I'm trying and I have my moments, but I'll never move on from you."

She patted the top of my hand. "I want you to be happy, and I know it's the best thing for you, but my son is so unhappy. I can see it in his eyes. I observed him while he tried to talk to Cody Sunday, and he's miserable. He must have asked Cody how you were a dozen times during their strained conversation. And I'm abhorred by his appearance."

I shook my head. "I don't know what has possessed him."

"I do. It's that vile woman. She wouldn't even come in with him, not like she was welcome, but she's not even trying to be a part of his life. She only wants him in hers. And it is a ridiculous life, unbefitting for a Higgins." She steadied herself and dried her eyes. "I'm sorry to keep bringing him up in front of you. Tell me how your life is going. You look fabulous."

I ran my fingers through my curls. "Not sure I feel that way, but thank you. I'm just busy doing the mom thing and work."

"What about your Sidelined Wife project?"

"It's going well. I've actually had a few marketing firms approach me about doing some merchandising. I'm not sure what to think about it."

Gelaire's left brow raised. "Well, that is certainly interesting and something to think about. I know you've talked about maybe the need to find a different career path. Perhaps this is it."

I hadn't even thought of it in that way. "Hmm. I don't know if having the Sidelined Wife plastered on t-shirts and mugs is really a career."

"You need to look at the bigger picture, love. Those are only the beginning. Have you thought about writing one of those motivational books? You could use your inspiring blog posts."

"I don't know how inspiring they are, and I can't imagine people wanting to read an entire book of them. And really, who am I?" Not to quote the mean-girl moms. "Some people think I'm a bitter divorcee who has nothing better to do with her time than bash her ex."

Though I rarely talked about him. Not to say he was happy about my Sunday post. Apparently he didn't appreciate me telling the world about his boy-band persona and that he peed on the toilet seat. At least that's what his angry text had indicated. I texted back that I didn't like him sleeping around when we were married. I never heard back.

She waved her hand. "There will always be naysayers. Don't let them get to you. You, through your humor and insights, are helping women cope with their own situations. It's marvelous, just like you." She reached over and tapped my nose. "Think about this, love."

I sat back, letting her advice jostle around in my mind, seeing if anything took hold. It was a left-field idea for me, but... what if?

CHAPTER THIRTY-ONE

"Mmm. Mmm. Mmm." Avery fanned herself after unrolling a rather large poster of Hunter Black, sent courtesy of Autumn Moone's publisher, along with an entire box full of goodies. Several signed books, bookmarks, and pens with Hunter Black's pretty face and gorgeous body plastered all over them filled the package. This particular poster had him shirtless and in tight jeans.

So perhaps it was juvenile and maybe even tasteless, but his smooth, sun-kissed chest was worth ogling. To say we were in heaven was an understatement. We didn't even care that James and Peter walked in with Dad after a long day of working out in the warm fall day. Dad took one look at the front desk covered in every woman's fantasy and hightailed it to his office. I think he mumbled something about having to get home for dinner.

James stood with his eyebrow arched and a mix of irritation and playfulness etched on his face. He cleared his throat. "Yo, *Mrs*. Decker," he sounded like a knock-off Rocky Balboa. "Why are you looking at that crap when you've got this?" He flexed his t-shirt covered biceps.

Peter and I both laughed at him.

I would give it to him, he was in shape. Not like Hunter Black shape, or you know, that guy I was going out with on Saturday. Two more days until I would probably find myself wrapped up in muscular arms. From all of Reed's texts and calls, I knew that wasn't all. The thought of his lips covering mine had me feeling like we should crank up the air conditioner. How old was I again?

Avery looked up from all the eye candy and grinned at her husband. "You know I love you."

"Prove it." He gave her a seductive grin that should have been saved for a private moment between the two.

"Please don't." Peter approached us at the front desk. He was shaking his head at us. "Where did you get all this stuff?"

"Good question." James took matters into his own hands and wrapped his arms around Avery from behind and planted a kiss on her cheek.

"Autumn Moone's publisher sent it to me."

"Why here?" James's tone said he was wishing I had received it somewhere his wife wasn't.

"It dawned on me that Autumn Moone could be a man, so when *she* asked for my address, so *she* could have *her* publisher send me a box full of swag, I gave the office address just in case."

"She's not a man." Peter's face tinged pink while picking up one of the signed books and thumbing through it.

We all gave him a strange glance, but James was the one to speak. "I'm disturbed you know that brother."

"It's not that he does, it's *how* does he know," Avery interjected.

Peter shrugged and set the book down on the desk. "You can tell by the way she writes."

James snorted. "Tell me you aren't reading this crap."

"I think it's sweet that he reads it with Delanie," I said.

Avery elbowed James and caught him in the gut. "Be nice to your brother and maybe learn a few things from him."

"Ouch, woman. Don't expect me to get all metro-male and read this junk with you. The only feminine side I have is you."

"Metro-male?" Avery and I said together.

"We heard that phrase on the radio the other day." James looked to Peter to confirm. "It's men that carry hand bags and get facials and manicures. Not real men."

I ignored the older, dumber brother and focused on the younger, smarter one. I touched his arm. "Don't listen to James. I would love it if a man read Hunter Black books to me."

"Is that right?" James asked. "Do you have someone in mind?"

"Sure." I pointed at the poster of Hunter Black, thankful I was quick on my feet with a reply that was true, though not entirely accurate. Not to say that I would ask Reed to do something like that at this stage in the game, but I could imagine him doing it, and I was sure I would enjoy it.

"He's too young and pretty for you," James scoffed.

"What's that supposed to mean?" I gave James the evil eye.

James gave me that stupid grin he'd been giving me since I was old enough to remember. The one that said he still enjoyed tormenting me. "What, are you a cougar now?"

Avery elbowed her husband again. "Of course she's not. But a little eye candy never hurt anyone."

Yeah, of course I wasn't. I would never date anyone younger than me. That was my story and I wasn't mentioning it. To anyone. Like ever.

"You know, Hunter Black kind of looks like Reed." A sly smile played on Peter's face. "Don't you think, sis?"

I casually took another peek at the poster. "I suppose."

"He kind of does." James took a closer look before addressing me. "So, does this mean you have the hots for Reed?" He wagged his eyebrows.

"Don't tease your sister," Avery poked her husband.

I pointed to my office with a strained smile. "I need to print the invoices that should go out tomorrow morning." It was a lame excuse to leave, but it was true so I ran with it. I tried to keep my voice and footsteps steady as I fled the scene.

Good thing there was nothing serious going on between Reed and myself. How could I ever tell my family if there was?

"Are you sure you measured right?" I asked Reed.

"We could always go to my place to make sure." He inched closer to me on the picnic blanket.

"I don't have time, and—"

"And what?" He leaned in and brushed my lips. He had been doing that any chance he could since I found him two hours ago, per the map he made for me. He'd texted it to me this morning. I couldn't believe how fun and romantic he was. He had set up the perfect picnic, complete with tiny sandwiches cut into hearts, at a secluded spot in the Half Day Forest Preserve. He promised we would curtain shop too, so I didn't have to lie to Cody about where I was.

So there we sat with his laptop using a personal hotspot, searching for curtains online. I had already ordered some, but now we were choosing some "manly" curtains for his rental. He was partial to the navy blue set on the screen.

I took a second to think about how to answer him. I closed my eyes and enjoyed the feel of the sun in the cool breeze. Fall was definitely in the air, but I was warm in my light sweater as I sat next to Reed, sharing his body heat.

"I'm not sure I'm ready to go to your place." I opened my eyes to see what his reaction would be.

He reached up and tucked an errant curl behind my ear. "I would never do anything you weren't comfortable or ready for."

I nodded. "I believe you."

"Good." He leaned in again, but this time his lips pressed hard against mine and begged mine to part. He moved the laptop off his lap without missing a beat and moved in closer. His strong hand ran through my hair and pulled my head closer to his.

I easily fell into his kiss. My lips parted and I drank him in. I could taste the chocolate strawberries we had eaten earlier. They were better the second time around. He deepened the kiss and groaned. I had missed this kind of affection. And someone to kiss my neck. He deliberately lingered on each spot of my neck he kissed. His warm breath against my skin combined with his soft lips made me gasp.

He chuckled before lifting his head and meeting my eyes. "I like that I'll always know when I've pleased you."

"Are you teasing me?" I had forgotten about my little gasps. It had been a long time since I'd had anything or anyone to cause such a response.

He shook his head. "I've never been more serious."

I placed both of my hands on his stubbled cheeks and gazed into his blue-as-the-sky eyes. "This is so surreal to me."

"Not to me."

My head tilted. "Not even a little?"

"No. For me, this is a *finally*, and I'm going to enjoy every minute of it, while it lasts."

"I can't believe you've liked me since you were thirteen."

"Believe it." He pecked my lips before reaching up and taking my hands from his cheeks, holding them capably in his own.

"You haven't said anything to my brothers, have you?"

"And ruin our clandestine meetings? No." He grinned.

"Would you please forget I used that word?"

He shook his head in that slow seductive way he was a pro at. "I like that word."

"I bet you do." I was sure it was a favorite for most men.

"Did your brothers say something to you?"

"Not directly, but Peter keeps hinting like he might know something."

"I'll keep sitting by him during Sunday dinners."

I paused, thinking how to best say, "Not that I don't want you there, but maybe you shouldn't come."

He let go of one of my hands and slapped his hand across his heart. "That hurts, Sam."

I let go of my inhibitions and kissed him first this time.

His grin said he liked that I made the first move.

"I'm only trying to be cautious. I don't want to rock Cody's world more than it has been. Or have my family freak out."

"I like spending my Sundays with your family. I especially like getting to know Cody better."

I was going to keep kissing him if he kept talking like that. "That means a lot to me. To him."

"He's going to come through this okay. He's got an amazing mother."

"I hope so."

"I know so."

I sighed with contentment. "I better go. Thank you for the beautiful afternoon."

He rested his forehead against mine. "I wish you could stay, but I understand. So where should we clandestine next?"

A small laugh escaped me. "How about I come up with a plan and let you know." I figured I should take a turn.

"I like that. I like that a lot, Samantha Decker."

I found that I like him a lot, too.

CHAPTER THIRTY-TWO

M<small>Y MIND MULLED OVER WHAT WE COULD DO TOGETHER THE FOLLOWING</small> Saturday. Reed was already requesting that we grocery shop again on Monday. He proposed it be a weekly activity, which meant I would see him Mondays, Fridays, Saturdays, and Sundays. We couldn't do more than acknowledge each other at the football games and Sunday dinners. But there was something comforting to his presence all the same. He made me feel less alone, wanted, even. That gaping hole left by Neil didn't seem unfillable now. It wasn't just Reed, though. It was me. I was finding myself among the ruin.

I wanted the date I was planning with Reed to reflect me. The me I had forgotten for so long. I wanted to be the sweet girl he remembered from forever ago and the woman he saw now. Because he saw me the way I wanted to see me. In his eyes, I was witty and capable, strong but soft, and beautiful. It was as if he didn't see the emerging crow's feet or the gray strand or two that were peeking through—my hair appointment was later this week to remedy the annoying matter. Granted, he didn't know I had cellulite on my upper thighs, but I had a feeling he wouldn't hold it against me, even if he did know. I should probably mention it to him, just in case. I hadn't reached dimple level yet, but let's be real, someday it would happen. I was trying to delay it with the help of Billy Blanks, but gravity was not my friend.

Reed was a good reminder that I needed more fun in my life. It had been an aspect of my life long absent. And he was correct, we had no idea how long this would last, and we should enjoy it. I was sure he would move on someday soon. It was inevitable. Avery was right, I would probably end up with some professor, or maybe alone. I was becoming more okay with the latter prospect. The more I liked myself, the easier that thought became. Don't get me wrong, I was loving the affection and someone to talk to. Not that I hadn't had people to talk to before, but when there was a romantic aspect to your relationship, it added something to conversations. There was a connection there that couldn't be duplicated in familial or platonic relationships.

On Monday, while we grocery shopped near but far from each other, we conversed on the phone. I wanted his opinion on a proposal that had come my way earlier in the day from a woman who had found my blog and was apparently a fan.

"What was the name of the organization again?" he asked.

"Clearfield Women's League."

"You're a woman, that makes sense."

I clammed up and moved out of the way of the man perusing the cereal near me. I focused on the pancake mix while the guy took his sweet time. Reed disappeared for a minute. What a weird game of cat and mouse we were playing. Once the man left, I spoke again about my dilemma.

"That's about as far as I'm qualified. They want me to speak about empowering women and girls. I have no idea what I would say, and I haven't spoken in front of a group since my sophomore speech class in high school. And if I remember correctly, I felt like puking before each assigned speech. I'm pretty sure I might follow through with that now."

Reed reappeared and paused on the opposite side of the cereal aisle from me. Even from afar, I could see his come-kiss-me grin. He had no idea how much I wanted to. I had these urges to make up for lost time. It was a lot of time to make up for, I'll tell you.

"Do it, Sam. You'll be great."

"You don't know that."

"I do; you just need to. That's what you do every time you fire off one of your silver-tongued posts. What did you say this morning? 'Don't wait to be taken out of the game. March right off the field, fire the coach, and start making your own calls.'"

I grabbed a box of some sugar-filled cereal Cody loved while holding the phone to my ear and trying not to grin too much. "Something like that."

I had been lamenting this morning on my blog that I hadn't taken more control of the situation earlier because I was too afraid to admit the truth. Deep down, I knew Neil was being unfaithful before he ever told me. I was too afraid to believe it. But I was learning that it was better to deal with the unpleasant truth than to live a lie. I would have saved myself a lot of heartache in the long run had I dealt with it up front, on my terms, not his. It would have made me the victor instead of the victim.

"You're that woman. The only difference is, instead of a keyboard, you have to use that beautiful mouth of yours that I wish was tangled up with mine right now."

My blushing self was going to have to head over to the frozen food section. I gave him a quick grin from across the way. "I would be amenable to that."

"Don't tempt me."

I turned my cart around to walk the other way because I was just as tempted.

"That side is as tempting as the front."

Definitely in need of the frozen food aisle. I smiled into my phone. "Are you going to do it?"

"Kiss you? Or speak at the Women's League luncheon?"

"Both."

"Yes to the kissing, but not tonight. Maybe to speaking."

"We need to start shopping in Michigan where no one knows us." I could hear his cart following behind me.

"I don't think I could justify a several-hours-long grocery trip to Cody. Saturday isn't that far away."

"Says you. By the way, what do you have planned?"

"I have two ideas in mind, depending on the weather and how much time we'll have. I was thinking we could go apple picking or bike riding. But I would have to get a bike this week, and I'm not sure I'll have the time."

"Why don't we go pick apples, and afterward we can hit a bike shop— out of town, of course. Then next weekend we'll take that bike ride. I wouldn't mind crossing the state line with you again."

"Isn't that homecoming weekend?"

"Hell, you're right. This is the downside to clandestining."

"Is that a word?" I laughed into my phone.

"It is now. You know, you could come with me to chaperone the dance if you were willing to date me out in the open." His tone was testing the waters.

I paused. "We can't do that to Cody." Especially for something that more than likely wouldn't last.

"Yeah, you're right." He didn't sound convinced. "I guess we will figure out some other ways to see each other that week."

"I'd like that."

"Me too. Now meet me in the candy aisle."

"Craving something sweet?"

"I'm craving something."

"And what's that?" I knew I was rusty at this dating thing, but I was proud of the flirty comeback.

"Head to the candy aisle and you'll find out."

I went one direction and he went the other. I was the first one to arrive, and it didn't take long to find what I was searching for. I stood, at a loss for words, staring at where the prices were listed on the shelves of several different types of candy. Little white notes with red ink were placed near the prices. The first one I noticed was *I "mint" to tell you how much I like you.*

Reed appeared with his cart. He was slyly looking at the chips opposite the candy.

"I like you too," I whispered in my phone.

"I had a feeling."

Next was the Milky Way candy bars. *Nothing could be better than you and me under the Milky Way.*

"When did you do all this?"

"I can't reveal my secrets."

I was perfectly okay with that.

My eyes fell on the Hot Tamales. *Whether you believe it or not, you are hot.* I laughed and put my phone away. I wanted to enjoy this unhindered, and for some reason my phone was a distraction.

Being with you is better than PayDay.

I can't wait until our lips are tangled up like a Twizzler.

Your kisses are sweeter than Hershey's.

I love when my Butterfingers run through your hair.

I took each card as I went, intent on keeping them, smiling and trying not to giggle to myself. I could only imagine what I looked like to our fellow shoppers. But I honestly didn't care what they thought. This was one of the most thoughtful things ever done for me. I found myself saying that each time we were together.

As indifferently as possible, I glanced his way and mouthed, "Thank you."

"My pleasure," he mouthed back. In his eyes I could see that it was.

In my heart I felt it.

CHAPTER THIRTY-THREE

"Wow, sis, you've outdone yourself with this pie." James talked with his mouth half-full. "You need to get this recipe, honey." He held his fork out with a nice-sized bite of pie on it for Avery. They were sharing a piece. Weirdos were training for another marathon and watching their empty calorie intake.

Avery took the bite and a dreamy sigh escaped her. "Oh my gosh, I might need a piece of my own."

"Are these apples from Baker's Orchard?" Ma asked. That was the orchard near the office.

"No."

Not sure why, but Ma gave me a shrewd look as if she knew how I had, or should I say, who I had acquired the apples with. "Grocery store?"

My eyes hit my plate. "No." Why did it matter?

"Where, Samantha Marie?"

Was I in trouble? All eyes were suddenly on me. Everyone was still sitting around the table since the Bears were playing on Monday night. The timing was awful.

"Weatherby Orchards." I quickly shoved a bite of pie in my mouth, hoping to deter any more questions.

I swore I could feel Reed's glance from down the table. The same Reed who helped pick the apples and kept me warm on the chilly fall day yesterday, with hot chocolate and other means. Means I was beginning to crave.

I felt sixteen again, wishing I was alone with him right now. I could still feel his warm breath against my neck and the shivers it caused. But that had nothing on the way his lips felt on mine. We spent so long getting lost in each other at the orchard, we didn't have time to buy a bike. I didn't regret it one bit. I would do it all over again, from watching Reed from below on the ladder—what a sight it was—to the way he kept pulling me behind the trees to kiss me thoroughly. We are talking pushing me up against the trees, messing up my hair, making me think of things I shouldn't be kind of kissing. I needed to stop thinking about it now or I was going to have to excuse myself from the table to throw some ice cubes down my sweater.

But all that had nothing on the easy, no-pressure conversation. He was happy to listen to me gush about Cody and blather on about how stressed I was about my upcoming speech at the Women's League luncheon. He didn't even mind when I talked about how hurt and angry I was that Neil had yet to show up to one of Cody's games. Their team was still undefeated, and Cody threw for his first touchdown Friday night. The kid was still on cloud nine. Reed had just listened.

And I loved listening to him talk about his students and players. I could tell he genuinely cared for them. So much so, he went to school every morning early to tutor those that needed extra help. There was never a silent moment between us, except when we were speaking a language that required no verbalization, unless you count those gasps I couldn't help but letting out. I think Reed was now making it his mission to make sure I did that often. I wouldn't complain about it at all.

"Weatherby Orchards? Why so far?" Ma's suspicion brought me back to the present. Too bad, I was enjoying reliving yesterday. Unfortunately, her suspicious tone had the added effect of making everyone at the table, except my son and nephews, look my way with scrutinizing gazes. Reed joined in. He had to, or it would have looked suspect, though I swore his lip twitched.

Thankfully, I had an excuse ready to go. This probably wasn't good. If Cody ever found out, how could I ever tell him not to sneak around? Or worse, what if he already was and he was so good at it that he hadn't been caught yet? *Yet* was the operative word. I would find out eventually.

I hoped. I was at least thankful Cody knew I had gone to pick apples. It was hard to miss the baskets of them on our island.

I gave Ma my best smile. "They have Granny Smith apples, which make the best pies, in my opinion."

"I won't argue with that." Dad took another large bite of pie.

I hoped it would end with that, but where there was Mimsy, there would always be a show. She eyed her glass of water before her cataract eyes hit me. "Samantha Marie, you're blushing. Perhaps you decided to partake of some forbidden fruit while picking mankind's downfall."

Did she really just say that? By the snickers around the table I would say yes, yes she did.

A deep sigh escaped while I tried not to roll my eyes at my grandmother. "Mimsy, there is no evidence that Adam and Eve ate an apple. For all we know, that was symbolic."

"And what was it symbolic for? Sex, I tell you." She was itching to get her hands on her glass of water.

Her great grandsons ran out of the room with their pie, laughing as they went.

"Are you having sex?" Ma was now in a panic. Her fork dropped and clanged against her plate. "You promised me you weren't." She was practically on the verge of tears.

How did we get here? It was apple pie, for crying out loud. All eyes were on me, except Reed. He was shoveling pie in his mouth at record speeds. And James had a hard time focusing because his body was shaking so hard trying to hold in his laugh. My sisters-in-law gave me we-are-so-sorry smiles, but better you than us.

Dad surprised me and tried to come to my rescue. "Sarah, lay off her, she's a grown woman; we can't tell her what to do." I knew he meant that, but in his father eyes, I could see he was hoping I wasn't *partaking*, as Mimsy called it.

I gave him a thank-you smile.

Ma did not like that at all. She conjured up the worst evil eye in the history of vile looks. The temperature in the room dropped to Siberian Tundra levels. "Joseph, so help me, I'll sell your ice boat on eBay."

That was an idle threat. I didn't think Ma knew how to do that. I still had to help her order things on Amazon.

"We're having a house built!" blessed, wonderful Peter shouted.

Every head whipped his and Delanie's way. It was the first time ever I saw Delanie look irritated with her husband. She had obviously wanted to keep that a secret by the look of her scarlet tinged cheeks and clenched fists. Peter kissed her head as if to say sorry. I mouthed my thanks to the pair. I felt horrible and grateful all at once. At least no one at the table considered purchasing a home a sin.

Scratch that. I should have realized if apple picking was cause for concern, so was building a house, at least where Ma was concerned. While the rest of us were bombarding them with normal questions like where, when, who's the builder, and why didn't you say anything before, Ma studied the pair. I could see her blood pressure rising. It was almost enough for me to falsely admit I was having sex to protect Delanie from the wrath building up in Ma.

"Ma, I'll help you with the dishes." I stood and picked up my plate with a half-eaten piece of pie on it, hoping she would follow me. I figured it was better not to blurt out that I was breaking my mother's top commandment, especially since the man I was secretly dating was sitting at the table. He may wonder if I was dating other men and why I wasn't sleeping with him. Not like he had asked me to or that we had ever discussed any sort of relationship status. A fact I was grateful for, I might add. It was one of the reasons I liked dating Reed, he seemed to be in it only for fun. He wasn't putting any pressure on me, nor I on him. We never discussed our future or what it was we were doing together. We just had a great time no matter what it was we were doing, even if it was talking on the phone. He was exactly what I needed.

Ma wasn't falling for it. She didn't even acknowledge me. I sat right back down, bracing for the cyclone that was about ready to blow. The final straw came when Peter reluctantly admitted where they were moving.

He reached under the table, I assume to hold Delanie's hand. At first I found it odd, but it made more sense when he said, "Bridgefield Estates."

A hush fell over the table. Everyone but Mimsy seemed to know where that was. I knew because it wasn't all that far from my house.

I frequently drove by the gated community with the gorgeous houses on my way home from the office. The question on everyone's mind was...well, Ma went ahead and voiced it.

"I knew it. I knew it." Ma's penetrating glare at Delanie blew the vile look she had given Dad moments earlier out of the water. "I just knew you were into something illegal. How else could you afford to live in such a community?" Ma held onto the table like it was all that was keeping her from going ballistic.

No one else thought Delanie was into anything illegal; Peter would have never married her if she had been. But we *were* all wondering how they could afford to build a house in a community where, according to the signs outside of Bridgefield Estates, the starting price was $750,000. We all basically knew how much money we each made, except for Delanie. We assumed, or I had, that it couldn't be much since they'd been living in a small apartment ever since they moved here. And there was nothing in Delanie's appearance or clothing to suggest she was rolling in dough—she always had a vintage boho look going for her. Nothing expensive. Maybe those diamond studs in her nose were the real thing. I assumed cubic zirconia.

If we thought Ma was mad, she had nothing on Peter. He rose slowly and deliberately, like an ominous figure, and threw his napkin on the table. His green eyes bore into Ma's.

"I've had enough of you disrespecting my wife."

With those words, Delanie stood and took her husband's hand and leaned into him. Her face was beaming up at him with pride and love. Her diamond nose ring seemed to sparkle brighter.

Peter let go of her hand and securely wrapped his arm around her waist. "Delanie is the best person I know, and until you recognize that and apologize to her, we won't be coming back."

Peter demanded with his eyes that Ma do exactly that. Immediately, if not sooner.

Never had a more stubborn woman lived, except the woman who'd given her birth, who was taking pictures with her smartphone. I told Ma we shouldn't have given Mimsy that.

I couldn't help but catch Reed's eye to see what he thought of it all.

It was a good thing we weren't serious. He would have bailed on me. Was this part of the reason Neil left me?

Reed pressed his lips together with brows raised. I could tell he didn't want to linger too long on me, but his eyes said we would talk later.

We all focused on Ma to see what she was going to do. She, too, stood. "I did not teach my children to talk to me this way." So much for her doing the right thing. "And I know when people are keeping secrets, so be careful, son, about which side you choose."

Families shouldn't have sides.

The table erupted. Dad was now up, telling Ma to apologize, which didn't go over well at all. Mimsy was snapping pictures of this Kodak moment. I prayed she didn't know how to get on any social media sites. Oh, have mercy if she did. James and Avery were also trying to talk some sense into Ma, who now had marched out of the room in tears muttering how ungrateful we all were.

Peter and Delanie walked out hand in hand without another word to any of us. I couldn't blame them. To be honest, it was a long time coming, but there had never been a rift in our family. Deckers were loud and obnoxious, but we stuck together through thick and thin. I prayed Ma came to her senses. This was not worth losing family over. We had already lost too many.

All that was left at the table was Reed, Mimsy, and me. Reed smiled at me before Mimsy added to the joy of the day.

"Samantha Marie, you never did say whether you were having sex or not."

Reed chuckled under his breath.

I stabbed my pie with my fork. "No, Mimsy, I never did."

CHAPTER THIRTY-FOUR

"Have you talked to Delanie or Peter?"

I curled into one of the decorative pillows on my sectional, taking a breather before I went to bed. "Neither will answer their phone," I lamented to Avery.

"We tried over here too."

"I feel awful. I should have said more tonight, or a long time ago." I had tried, but Ma was dismissive.

"Poor Delanie came into the family right before we hit our low points."

"I know. I've been so wrapped up in my own head that I didn't pay attention to her like I should have. And I should have been more forceful with Ma when I talked to her a few weeks ago."

"You know that wouldn't have gone over well."

"You're right. I just don't understand what she has against her. It wasn't like she made Peter leave the priesthood. And I don't think he broke any vows before he decided to leave."

Avery paused. "I agree with you, but...don't you find it odd that they are building such an expensive home?"

"Yes," I admitted. "Maybe Delanie makes more money than we assumed, or maybe her parents are wealthy."

We had only met them once. Cat and Ron were both psychologists. They lived a very free kind of lifestyle. So much so that Delanie called them by their first names. They didn't want to be defined by any label.

They even combined their last names to create Monfort. I couldn't remember what two names they'd meshed together. Though Delanie never said anything, I believed her parents embarrassed her.

They certainly didn't blend well with my parents. The one get-together we all had a couple of years ago was filled with awkward silence. And I was pretty sure that Delanie's parents feared for her emotional well-being now that she was a Decker. Especially when Ma had a fit when Peter informed us they, too, were thinking of combining their last names and becoming either the Deckmons or the Mondecks. I'm not going to lie, I thought that was weird. Ma flat-out said it would break her heart and she wouldn't hear of it. To make peace, Delanie remained a Decker. She was probably regretting that now.

"I guess they could be," Avery didn't sound convinced.

"What's wrong?" Avery wasn't sounding like herself.

"James is upset."

"About what happened tonight?"

She inhaled and exhaled. "He's got this complex. He gets in these moods where he feels like he should be a better provider, that he should have gone to college like you and Peter."

"James?" I never knew those kinds of things bothered him. He was lovable, but always acted self-assured. I called it arrogant when we were younger.

"Tonight only drove that point home."

"You guys have a nice house and he's happy doing what he does. A lot of people can't say that. And hey, if it makes him feel better, you can tell him that neither Peter nor I use our degrees."

Not to say Peter hadn't used his master's in theology once upon a time. But not once had I used my degree in English, unless you counted editing my blogs and Cody's school papers.

"He would say your house is nicer and you both have something to fall back on."

"I would counter that his house comes with a gorgeous wife, and if he's worried, he should go back to school. But you know Dad's going to leave him the business. That is, if he ever retires. Honestly, if anyone has to worry, it's me. Alimony won't last forever, and if I think about it too much it kind of makes me feel like vomiting knowing I'm still dependent on Neil."

"Delanie and Gelaire are right, you could take the Sidelined Wife and run with it. How many companies have contacted you now to be sponsors on your site or offered to market products related to it? And you have how many followers now?"

The answer was a lot. More than I ever thought or dreamed possible. "Isn't it weird?"

"Completely, but it's also amazing. Take the bull by the horns and run with it. Delanie seemed to know who was reputable to work with."

"I'm beginning to think there is so much we don't know about her. I'm going to redouble my efforts to get to know her better."

"Me too. I'll invite her to have lunch with us this week and you guys can help me plan my Halloween extravaganza. By the way, Gary, our neighbor, remembers you from last year and is interested."

Uh. That could be a problem. "You talked to him?"

"Maybe." She giggled.

"Avery, I don't want to be set up."

"Think of it as exploration."

I was already doing that, and I was more than happy with it. I laughed at her. "Call it what you want, but I'm happy with the way things are right now."

"I was going to mention you do seem happier. Anything happen? Did Neil rip his boy band pants in public or something?"

Another laugh erupted at the thought. "That I wouldn't know. Our only communication is when he tells me he's going to disappoint our son and how sorry he is about it."

"He's going to regret that someday."

"I just hope once he does, it isn't too late. Cody won't admit it, but he needs his dad. At the very least, he needs to know his dad cares and he's trying. But if Neil can't figure this out, Cody will never admit it to him."

Speaking of Cody, he surprised me and appeared in his pajama pants, running his fingers through his hair.

"Avery, can I call you later or talk to you tomorrow?"

"Sure. Everything okay?"

I studied Cody. "I think so."

"Call me if you need anything."

I knew she meant that. I hung up and, for a moment, I saw the little boy I once knew in Cody's brown eyes. "Everything okay, bud?"

He shuffled his bare feet around, unsure. "Can I ask you something?"

My heart thumped and jumped. "Anything." I patted the seat next to me.

He didn't hesitate and landed next to me.

I ruffled his hair. It was getting longer and the curl I loved was more prominent. "What's going on?"

He leaned forward and rested his hands on his knees, making my heart go into overdrive. This couldn't be good if he wouldn't look at me.

"So, I was thinking about going to the homecoming dance since I'm on the team and all."

That made sense. "Yeah, you should."

He lifted his head and turned my way. "I, um, want to ask Rory if, you know, she wants to go with me."

"Oh." My heart may have stopped. "It's kind of short notice, don't you think? The dance is in six days."

"Yeah, I know. But I know she's not going with anyone."

"You do?"

"Her friend, Jasmine, told me."

"I suppose she mentioned Rory wants you to ask her."

His crooked grin made an appearance. "Yeah."

Not sure if it was because my baby was growing up or if I wasn't ready for all this, but I had to hold back the tears. I took a deep, brave mom breath. "You should probably ask her tomorrow."

He nodded. "I want to do something fun to ask her."

"Do you need some ideas?"

He nodded more vigorously.

"I can help with that."

I wasn't sure I had ever seen him look more relieved or happy. Stab a knife in my heart. He was growing up, and I knew that meant some-day I wouldn't be the most important woman in his life. I wasn't ready to relinquish that title. But I did what any good mother would.

"Let me go upstairs to get some poster board and markers. While I'm doing that, google some cute sayings we can work with." I had a few in mind based on Reed's candy notes, but I wanted Cody to own this.

Cody's smile said he liked the plan.

While I walked away, I heard the faintest, "Love you, Mom."

"I love you, too." I was not quiet about it.

You have to keep an eye on Cody for me at the homecoming dance.

The offer for you to come with me is still on the table.

I was tempted, in light of the darling poster we made with some of Cody's favorite candy we had on hand, Reese's Peanut Butter Cups. The black poster had them plastered between the words written in white, *Rory, I can't Reese's-ist asking you to homecoming.* Cody was so proud of it.

Tempting.

I can work with that.

I snuggled into my bed under my thick covers, trying to avoid telling him no again. I couldn't do that to Cody right now. *I'm not ready for him to date.*

How do you think Cody would feel about his mom dating?

So much for avoiding uncomfortable topics. *I don't know. And after everything he's been through with his dad, I'm afraid to ask.*

You'll have to have that conversation with him at some point.

Or I'll become a nun. That would make my mom happy.

That wouldn't deter me.

Could he ever make me smile. *Don't worry, I don't think a habit would look good on me.*

I disagree, but I do prefer you in more form-fitting clothes.

I was thinking the same thing about you.

You're making me blush, Samantha Decker.

I don't know why, but I liked when he called me by my full name. Maybe it was a good reminder that I was Samantha Decker. And I was learning to kind of like her.

By the way, I'm sorry for the crazy Decker show today.

You should be. You were partaking of forbidden fruit and I missed it. Were you meeting other men at the orchard this weekend?

Yes. For that whole five minutes you left me to use the restroom.

I knew it.

You may want to rethink coming to my parents' place. It's like the insane asylum now.

All families are crazy. Besides, I have the best view at dinner.

I'm worried about Peter and Delanie.

I'll talk to Peter. Don't worry. It will all work out.

How was it that he always made me feel like it really would be okay? *I hope so.*

Tell me what your plans are for the week. I need to know what I'm working with.

Pretty much the same as always, except I imagine I will be helping Cody get ready for homecoming. I'm still selling tickets Friday at the school. And I have to get ready for that speech you convinced me to do. I'm treating myself to a pedicure to make myself feel better about it.

Pedicure? When?

I'm not sure yet. Maybe Thursday, if I have time.

Make time Thursday evening and I'll come with you after practice is over.

I don't have time to go two hours away to get a pedicure.

You don't need to. I have a plan.

You always do.

I do what I have to do to clandestine with you.

That rhymed.

I have more where that came from.

I had no doubt that he did. My yawning was becoming uncontrollable. It was already eleven. *I better go. Goodnight.*

Goodnight, beautiful.

I held the phone to my chest, believing he meant every word.

CHAPTER THIRTY-FIVE

WHY IS IT WHEN YOU FEEL LIKE YOU ARE GETTING ONE PART OF YOUR LIFE SETTLED, or at least in the managed-chaos stage, that colossal chaos comes your way? I'm partially blaming you all for my current dilemma. Apparently, there are people that think I may know a thing or two since so many of you follow me. If you are under that impression as well, please let me apologize. I'm not sure where they got their information.

But now I'll be making my first public appearance. I'm supposed to string words together that sound intelligent and insightful. I've never ranked myself high on either scale. To top it off, my son is going on his first date this weekend. And not just any date, but a homecoming date. I'm gulping down my heart as I type.

I don't know about you other single, divorced moms, but now I worry even more about being enough. Am I enough to show my son how to be a man? A better man than the one I chose for him?

Does he know that there is nothing more "manly" than showing his emotions or admitting when he's made a mistake and then trying to do better? Does he know the influence he has to empower the future girls and women in his life? Have I empowered him? Will he know what it means to be a partner when I feel like I'm just learning that lesson now? Does he know that sometimes the strongest thing he can do is be gentle? Or that saying no to his own desires in place of another person's shows strength beyond compare? Will he be brave enough in the tough moments to do the right thing? I know the man I trusted to be strong in the moments that truly counted wasn't.

My hope is that my son sees what a destructive force selfishness is and chooses a better way. I hope that I will choose better. And I'm not talking about a man, though

I do have a working list on the must-haves for the next husband, assuming there will be a next one. I'll share that list in a later post, but spine-tingling kisses is a must.

As always, carry on, and don't forget the important job we do on the sidelines. I especially love the support you all lend to each other and me on every thread. If you have any tips for how to make it through your son dating, or a good, stiff drink recommendation, send them my way. Just kidding. I should probably remain sober for this. So any non-alcoholic advice would be terrific.

Yours Truly,
Sidelined Wife in Chief

P.S. Return to Sender *was riveting. I give it two thumbs up. Next up on the book club front is* Midnight Promises. *I'll be sending out more info and the These Chicks Read Lit book club questions in my newsletter if you want to participate via Skype.*

Yes, I had a newsletter. That was Delanie's idea. And the Stepford Wives—aka These Chicks Read Lit—had assimilated me. The first book club had been last week, and I admit I enjoyed myself, even if we weren't reading Hunter Black books. I even posted pictures on my blog and Facebook page of all my new artificial friends, who might turn into the real thing as long as they didn't want to start braiding my hair or having sleepovers. I was afraid that was a possibility for some of them.

Did I mention one of the mean moms was a member? Her name was Clarice, as in *Silence of the Lambs*, though I pegged her more as the serial killer, not the heroine. Her beady-eyed stares all night bothered me. And every time someone mentioned they loved my blog, she made *ugh* sort of sounds that she tried to pass off as clearing her throat. I was so proud of myself when I finally handed her a cough drop halfway through our discussion. She begrudgingly had to take it, but I could tell with every fiber of her being she wanted to shove it down my throat.

Good times.

I clicked publish on my post and checked the time. I probably shouldn't be writing posts at work, but that was one of the perks when you worked for family. Delanie was meeting Avery and me for lunch at the office to help Avery plan her Halloween party, even though she had it mostly planned already. This was more of an excuse to let Delanie know we loved her.

Delanie offered to bring the food. I hoped she wasn't making it. I loved her and wanted to do what we could to mend the gaping hole Ma created and was adding to every day by refusing to apologize. It had been four days now. At least Peter and Delanie weren't cutting off ties with everyone, but I couldn't imagine Sunday dinner without them. I hated that our numbers were shrinking. Well, Reed had filled a spot, but how long would that last?

Speaking of Reed, my phone buzzed. I looked down and saw this message.

I want to know if your spine tingles when I kiss you, and how does that feel? My spine has never tingled.

My Reed grin came out.

First, I'm disappointed your spine doesn't tingle when we kiss. And second, aren't you supposed to be educating the next generation right now instead of reading my blog?

Just like I should be working. I had to get our third quarter tax payment transferred to the state. How were we already well into October? That meant a baby would be born soon. I forced that thought out of my head. Reed helped me out.

If you weren't such a lady and I wasn't doing my best to be a gentleman to you, I would tell you some things that . . . never mind, just know I look forward to each and every touch. And by the way, it's my planning period.

I hoped no one walked into my office. Not only was my spine tingling, but I felt the mother of all hot flashes—the good kind, not the menopausal kind.

That's right. I forgot.

You never did answer my original question.

I bit my lip. *I would have thought the gasps would have answered that question for you.*

I do enjoy those. It's a shame I won't be able to hear any in the near future.

That is a shame. Really it was. There was no time this week for us to sneak away. The last time we had seen each other was Monday to grocery shop, and as fun as that was, it left something to be desired. Namely, him.

Are we still on for pedicures this evening?

If you're sure.

I still couldn't believe he wanted to get one. I wasn't entirely sure how we were going to pull it off together, but he said he had it handled. He hadn't failed us yet. Although a woman had recognized me in the grocery store Monday, thankfully, Reed noticed and was able to scurry away unseen by the eager fan.

That was weird for me, by the way. She told me her whole life story there in the international food aisle, including how all three of her husbands had left her. One left her for a man, so she didn't feel too bad about that one, but her last one left her for a much older woman. She was salty about it. So much so, she spray-painted his car and was arrested. I hoped she read the rules of the Sidelined Wives club: no talking about any illegal activity that would make us testify against you. I confess, I faked a phone call from Cody to get away from her. She frightened me.

I wouldn't miss it. See you soon, gorgeous, Reed texted back.

I look forward to it.

And did I ever. I wasn't sure I ever had this much fun dating when I was younger. Maybe it was the whole secret aspect. More than likely it was Reed. He was the epitome of fun. When we were younger, I considered his carefree attitude annoying. It's amazing what twenty years could do for your perspective.

Lingering thoughts of Reed were interrupted by the sound of Delanie's and Avery's voices. I clicked out of my texting app and slid my phone into the pocket of my jeans before heading out to the front of the office to have lunch with my sisters. We would eat at Avery's desk since we didn't have a break room—there was only a small area in the back with a refrigerator and a microwave on a stand. Nothing fancy. The guys usually ate at the site they were working at. Once in a while they came to the office when James had a lunch date with Avery or if Peter was sneaking home to be with Delanie.

Delanie and Avery were already seated with a large paper bag from the local Thai restaurant on the desk. Relief filled me. No home-cooked Delanie meals. Delanie sat stiff and pensive opposite Avery. Even so, she looked gorgeous in her brown cable-knit sweater, her hair draped to the side. No wonder Peter was sneaking off any chance he could.

I was determined for Delanie to feel welcome in our family. I headed straight for her, pulled her up even though it was awkward, and hugged her like I would Cody. The feel-how-much-I-love-you-never-let-go type. It took her a moment to reciprocate, but she relaxed and squeezed back. With it came tears. Avery came around and joined us, wrapping her tiny arms around us. She was shorter than both of us, but stronger. Her toned arms were boa-constrictor-level tight.

My own tears started to fall. "Delanie, if we haven't said it before, we are so happy you married our brother."

Avery considered Peter to be every bit her brother. She had watched him grow up since he was in middle school.

"I am too, but how can so much happiness bring so much misery?"

"Mom will come around." Avery tried to sound sure.

"I'm not sure, and it's making my husband miserable. Family is everything to him."

"And we're all still here," I tried to comfort Delanie.

She shook her head and took a step back from us, breaking up the group hug. "There's more to it." She pressed her lips together as if she had said too much.

Avery and I both glanced at each other before taking a closer look at our uncomfortable sister. Avery was bolder than me. "What are you talking about, honey?"

Delanie wiped the tears off her smooth, creamy cheek as if she was trying to get rid of any evidence of them. I had been there. More than I wanted to admit.

"I never imagined my life like this."

Worry rose in my chest. Was she rethinking Peter because of our family? That would devastate him.

Avery and I leaned in, waiting for her to elaborate.

Delanie took a breath and looked up to the popcorn ceiling. "I never planned on getting married or settling down."

Oh, this was bad. We leaned in closer.

Delanie's eye filled with more tears. "Then I met Peter, a priest of all things." She laughed to herself. "I never believed in God, but I thought if there was one, I was sure I would go to hell for the way I felt about him.

From the moment Peter and I met, I couldn't stop thinking about him. We tried to stay away from each other, but it proved impossible. Like a moth to the flame, I found myself finding any excuse to be around him. I even attended mass; anything to see him. He tried harder to resist me."

Peter had never shared any of their history, so Delanie had our rapt attention. I felt butterflies in my stomach as if she was telling us a tale of forbidden love.

"Peter even asked to be reassigned to another diocese. I thought I would never see him again, so I told him I loved him. I fell in love with a man I had never touched, yet he had touched me so deeply with his kind heart and smile. He was passionate about helping the poor. He loved the kids we worked with. Kids," she whispered, like she was being haunted by a ghost.

Avery and I looked to each other with a knowing glance. Delanie's earlier comment was beginning to make more sense.

Delanie stared off into the distance. "I've never met a man who wanted kids more. Ironic, considering he once vowed to be celibate. Then he married me. Someone who believed there were too many children in the world that needed care. No need to add another. Except now there is nothing I want more than to give him, us, a child. And I can't. We've tried and tried."

I reached out and took her slender hand, which was covered in a phoenix-shaped henna tattoo. "I wish you would have said something. I'm so sorry." I had wondered if they would have kids, but that was a private decision. Ma hadn't even hounded them about it. I think she hoped they would break up. But as far as I could tell, that was a wasted hope that Ma needed to get over as soon as possible. Delanie and Peter loved each other. Anyone could see that.

Avery took Delanie's other hand. "What can we do?"

Delanie shrugged. "I don't know. Not even the doctors know what to do. Everything appears to be working fine, except it isn't. And it's not like—" She shook her head in a panic.

We didn't press, but we were both curious.

Delanie composed herself and continued. "Peter says it doesn't matter to him whether we have children or not, but he's been talking more about adoption. Though in his eyes, I see how much he wants one of his own. How devastated he is with every negative pregnancy test."

"Men," Avery laughed. "They have this thing about wanting to spread their seed around."

Delanie and I laughed with her. It was better than crying.

And I had a feeling we had all cried more than we ever wanted to share.

But that day, we shared part of ourselves, some of the most vulnerable, messy parts of our lives that we did our best to keep hidden. We never did talk about the new house or the Halloween party, but none of those seemed important in light of the secret pain our new sister had been carrying.

It was a reminder to never judge a book by the pretty cover we all put on display. We each carried burdens only known to us. We each needed relief and a shoulder to cry on, even if it was digitally. Sometimes we needed help to write the next chapter in our book or the strength from another to burn the one we were working on and start again. Avery had done that for me. The women that followed me on online were helping too. And now we would help Delanie however we could, even if we could only lend an ear. We'd shake some sense into Ma too, if possible.

I only hoped one day that Cody found a woman that loved him so fiercely.

But not until I was dead.

CHAPTER THIRTY-SIX

AFTER THE DAY I'D HAD CRYING WITH MY SISTERS, FINISHING MY SPEECH, sending in quarterly reports, making dinner, ordering a corsage for Rory, and responding to comments on my latest post, I was more than looking forward to the pedicure and time with Reed. He texted me earlier and told me to arrive ten minutes earlier than him and to keep my cell phone out.

I was seen to a chair right away after picking out the deep red polish for my toes. I couldn't wait to get my tired feet into the jetted bath of warm water.

Except there was a problem. The tech was not the usual cute little woman I was expecting. Instead I found myself staring at an attractive man with overly blond hair and too tanned skin. His aqua eyes were flashing a brilliant smile at me and asking me what kind of pedicure I wanted. I wanted the one where he wasn't touching me. Not like I had anything against men touching me, but I didn't want to pay them to touch me.

"So what will it be?" Nail tech man asked in his bedroom voice. Oh goodness, was this one of those places that was a front for a brothel? Did they have back rooms? Was that what he was asking?

I stared long and hard at the menu he had handed me when I sat in the chair. I carefully read each item on their "menu." Were these code words? If I said, *I'll take the margarita pedicure*, would I suddenly find myself whisked off to one of their back rooms? And then would he be like, *welcome to Margaritaville* and strip off that tight tee he was wearing along with his asset-enhancing jeans?

"Just a regular pedicure, thank you," I stuttered out, not able to even look at the guy. I handed him the card and swore he brushed my hand on purpose. This was not going to do. How could I relax now?

Before I knew it, Tony, I think he said his name was, had his hands on me. Like I needed help rolling up my pants or putting my feet in water. I looked at all the cute little ladies in the place not busy with any customers. Why couldn't they help me? How rude would it be for me to ask for a new tech?

To make matters more interesting, I received a text.

I'm here. Pretend like you don't know me when I walk in.

If ever I wanted to blow our cover, this was it. I wanted Reed to take the chair right next to me and hold my hand. I placed the phone in my lap and, unfortunately, caught the stare of Tony.

"Is the water temperature good for you?"

I nodded.

"Good. I'll be right back." He winked, like an honest-to-goodness, couldn't-be-mistaken-for-an-eye-twitch wink.

In the moment he was gone, I tried to enjoy the feel of the water swirling around my feet. That lasted all about ten seconds. Reed and Tony walked back at the same time. My hopes soared that perhaps Tony just ran the water. Yes, yes. I liked that thought. My cute woman should arrive any moment to massage my feet and calves. That was a lovely thought that went down like the Great Chicago Fire of 1871. Tony took his stool back at my feet, but not before sizing up Reed. Why do all attractive men do that to each other?

I knew I was supposed to pretend like I didn't know Reed, but it was hard to miss his eyebrows shooting up to the ceiling and his double take of Tony.

From the corner of my eye I could see Reed being seated two chairs down from me by the cute looking grandma woman. I wanted to trade, though I doubted Reed wanted a man touching him.

My phone buzzed. *Who's the Don Juan getting ready to rub you with oil? Tony.*

You're on a first name basis?

It's a requirement before someone touches me.

I hope you didn't give him your NDA.

I giggled too loudly.

"I'm sorry, did that tickle?" Tony was taking my right foot out of the water.

I set my phone down. "No."

"So what do you do?"

Ugh. He wanted to talk.

"I'm a bookkeeper."

Did he glance at my empty ring finger?

Reed answered for me. *He just checked for a ring.*

I grinned down at my phone before texting, *How was your day?*

Fine until now.

I heard Reed ask his tech what a margarita pedicure was. I was curious, but she better not invite him to the back room. She mentioned something about a tequila scrub. I didn't catch it all because Tony's hands were all over my calf. I'm not going to lie, it felt divine. If only he wouldn't talk.

"I just moved here from California."

That explained the tan.

"That's nice."

It's not nice, Sam. He's touching you more than I ever have.

I cleared my throat so I wouldn't laugh again. *Are you jealous?*

No.

Of course he wasn't. We were only having fun. But something like disappointment bounced around in my head. I had to remind myself I liked our arrangement.

"Are you from around here?" Tony ran his hand up my leg.

I had to think for a second about what to say. My phone was buzzing like crazy, not helping me formulate a response. I finally just looked at it. *Tell him no*, repeatedly appeared on my screen.

"No." I gave Tony a strained smile.

"Just in town visiting?" His hands worked their magic on my feet, rubbing all the right places, almost making me forget how uncomfortable this all was.

Reed began coughing loudly to my left.

His cute little woman asked him if he wanted some water.

"No, thank you," he responded.

I took his nonverbal cue. "I'm here visiting an old friend." That was a completely true statement.

I picked up my phone when Reed texted again.

Nicely done. This guy has sleazeball written all over him.

He's just doing his job.

Right, while he's undressing you with his eyes.

Relax.

I will once he stops groping you. At least pretend you aren't enjoying it.

I caught a peek of the little lady rubbing the tequila scrub into Reed's foot. *It looks like you should be enjoying yourself.*

She's old enough to be my grandmother.

You like older women.

"Ooh," I jumped. Tony had hit a sore spot. The kind that hurt, but felt good when it was rubbed.

I detected movement from Reed. His tech asked if everything was okay.

"Yes," Reed growled.

Tony, on the other hand gave me a grin. "You have a knot in your foot. Don't worry, I'll work it out."

Did you by chance look at my speech? I had emailed him a copy of it this afternoon once I was finished.

Is this guy making you uncomfortable? He didn't answer my question.

I tried to sneak a look at Tony; I didn't want to make direct eye contact. He looked to be enjoying himself more than any other tech I'd ever had. *Kind of, but I think it has more to do with the fact that you're here, watching.*

I would rather be the one touching you.

Do you rub feet?

Very well.

Is that an offer?

Yes. By the way, your speech was brilliant.

Really?

I loved the line where you said, 'No one will ever truly be empowered until we can see each other and work together as equals. For no one is truly empowered until we all are.' Very insightful.

I just made that up.

Reed chuckled to my left.

Just kidding, I texted again.

I did feel that way—my only hope was to live it and breathe it. Teach it to my son. Help the women in my life feel like they could overcome anything, even teach my own mother, if necessary. If Ma only knew the heartache Delanie was going through. But Delanie swore us to secrecy. She didn't want to be looked at as the infertile couple. I could understand that.

My thoughts were interrupted by Reed's tech, who was complimenting him on how smooth his feet were and how impressed she was with his trimmed toenails.

I guess my secrets are out now.

I like a man that takes care of his feet.

Is that one of your husband requirements, along with spine-tingling kisses?

It is now.

What else?

You'll have to keep reading my blog.

Tony was done with my right leg and reaching for my left foot and leg. I had almost forgotten about him for a second. It was easy to get caught up in Reed. That all ended, though, with the woman seated next to me.

"OMG. Are you the Sidelined Wife?"

I didn't think women my age should say *OMG.* And I didn't particularly like being recognized, especially because that meant that my date with Reed was all but over, unless I wanted to be overtly rude. It was tempting.

I fired off a quick, *Sorry,* before I faced the woman that would proudly call herself a trophy wife. You know the type. Huge, sparkling wedding ring, all the right designer brand-name clothes. Her long, auburn hair was impeccably draped to the side. Tony was now wishing he was with her and not me, by the way his tongue was wagging. It wasn't surprising. I was the sidelined wife, after all.

"I'm Samantha." I reached over to shake the woman's hand.

"Belinda." She did that shake where she hardly gripped my hand. "It's so nice to meet you. My girlfriends and I were just talking about you at the country club. We were all like, have you read the Sidelined Wife? She's hilarious, but maybe a little bitter—no offense."

"None taken."

"And I was like, she looks so pretty online, but I bet she was Photoshopped, because really, if she looked that good, her husband wouldn't have left her." She took a deeper look at me after insulting me. She shrugged. "I guess I was wrong. No Photoshop." She was awfully disappointed.

I couldn't help but turn to Reed to see if he had heard. Even though he was looking at his phone, I knew he had. His face was blotched in red and his jaw was tighter than Belinda's botoxed forehead.

I wasn't sure how to respond to this woman.

My phone buzzed and Reed had a suggestion too crude for me to repeat.

Belinda didn't seem to care that I hadn't responded or that she marginalized every woman that had ever been cheated on by callously blaming it on looks. "If you're local, you really should join the country club, there's a lot of single men—"

Tony's head popped up at the mention of me being local. Great, now I was going to get caught in a lie.

"Thank you, but I'm not interested." I tried to skirt over the issue and decided I would go ahead and be rude. I texted Reed. *Can you believe this woman?*

Belinda didn't get the hint. "Of course you are. You know those looks won't last forever. If you want to snag another man, you better get on it." She sounded like my mother, but worse, which I didn't know was possible when it came to this subject.

I'd had enough. I turned toward beaming Belinda. "I appreciate your offer, but if and when I ever decide to remarry, it will be to a man that is more concerned about who I am as a person and not how I look."

Her mouth fell open in disbelief. "Honey, men fall in love with their eyes, not their hearts."

"You haven't met the right men then."

"You can believe your fairytale." She turned in a huff.

I looked down at Tony, who was painting my nails at a furious pace, hoping to help Belinda, I'm sure. Why wasn't I surprised?

Don't believe her, Sam.

I stared at Reed's message. I didn't want to believe her, but sometimes I wondered.

CHAPTER THIRTY-SEVEN

OUR PEDICURE DATE WAS NOT THE FUN OR RELAXING EVENT I'D HOPED IT
would be. The worst part was that we wouldn't be able to see each other
for a while, at least not alone. Suddenly, life and the Sidelined Wife took
over. I wasn't sure how to feel about it.

First up was homecoming. It, too, did not go as planned. The Panthers lost their first game by one measly point. It was hard fought. Cody
didn't get to play at all. And Neil was another no-show. The season was
going to be over soon, and I had zero hopes of him making it to a game.
His excuse this time was a false labor scare. I knew the due date was
close. To be honest, it had me reliving a lot of bad memories. I'd wanted
more children more than anything. It had caused a lot of discord in our
marriage.

Cody wasn't the easiest of babies; he was colicky. Once we got that
sorted out, he was a party animal at night. I felt like I didn't sleep for
two years. They were rough times, but I loved it, if that made sense. His
smile in the middle of the night always made up for it. Neil was not left
with the same impression. I think he was jealous of the time I had to
give Cody; Neil's baby was his career.

For years I ached for another child. Neil would never budge. And
now here he was, having what I always wanted. Avery was right, life was
so damn unfair.

After the game Friday, I wanted to comfort Reed. Wrap my arms
around him and tell them they would get them next time, but I barely got

to wave at him before I walked off with a dejected Cody. It was a somber scene after the game. I saw a few tears in the boys' eyes. Nothing to be ashamed of.

Saturday I spent all day helping Cody get ready for his big first date. I ended up having to hem his pants, and at the last minute, he decided he hated the tie we picked out earlier in the week, so we made a trip to the nearby department store to get the perfect pink tie to match Rory's dress, which I prayed covered up more than it showed.

Yeah, that was a pipe dream. The *Teen Vogue* princess showed up in a dress that left nothing to the imagination, and my son had never grinned so wide. I was going to need a valium. I almost wished we bought a corsage that had to be pinned on and Cody would have stuck her and ruined the pink Tinkerbell dress. Instead, I snapped pictures of Cody slipping the wrist corsage on. I had to pin on his boutonniere, because little Miss Thing's fake nails were ridiculously long. I kept imagining her scratching my son with those and then I had some violent thoughts. I would be checking Cody's back when he returned, and if I saw one claw mark, there would be hell to pay.

Rory was older than Cody and had a license already. She drove a Miata. Thankfully there wasn't a lot of room in those babies, but I also knew it didn't take a lot and, well, you could get inventive in the heat of the moment. I couldn't do this. I sent up a prayer to Saint Jude to rescue me and my son. My son, who looked so happy and like he'd hit the jackpot.

I embarrassed him and hugged him extra-long before they walked out the door together hand in hand.

I watched my son open her car door. She stood on her tip toes and kissed him on the cheek. He touched his cheek and helped her in. At least I had raised a gentleman. Tears welled up in my eyes. This was all so new, and I was alone. I hated Neil even more in that moment. I was supposed to have someone to turn to and tell me it would all be okay. That this was normal, the natural progression of things. There was nothing natural about watching your baby take his first steps into a world where you were no longer needed.

I can do this, I chanted to myself. I'd been alone in this parenting thing most of our marriage anyway.

With the last tear wiped away, the doorbell rang. Did Cody forget his house key? Or maybe I got lucky and he decided he'd rather stay home with his mom on a Saturday night. So, I was living in a fantasy world.

I opened the door and came face to face with a vase full of multicolored roses, red, pink, purple, yellow, peach, white, all mixed together.

"I have a delivery for Samantha Decker," the man holding the bouquet informed me. "I'm going to need you to sign for them."

I took the man's pen and scribbled my name on some electronic device before he handed me the *large* bouquet with a card sticking out. I had a feeling I knew who they were from, but I couldn't think of why he would send me flowers; my birthday wasn't for another nine days.

I walked the flowers back to the kitchen, set them on the island, and eagerly grabbed the card. The tiny card read, *I wanted to get you a corsage, but I didn't know what color dress you would have worn tonight had we been able to go together. I chose every color they had to cover my bases. I'll be missing you in my arms tonight.*

I pressed the card to my chest. I looked down at the sweater and jeans I was wearing, wishing I was dressed up for a night with Reed.

I grabbed my phone. *The flowers are beautiful. Thank you. I would have worn a little black dress.*

Promise me you'll wear it for me someday. He responded right away.

I promise.

I'll keep an eye on Cody for you.

Thank you.

You got this, Sam.

It was exactly what I needed to hear.

I took the flowers to my room and hid the card in my top drawer with all the sexy underwear I had no use for except to hide all the little notes and cards from Reed. I knew if Cody, for whatever reason, ever looked in there, he would close it right back up and never look past the silk, lacy panties and bras.

I spent the rest of the night polishing my speech and checking the time, anxiously waiting for Cody to return. I had entered a new phase in my life. Those phases seemed to be coming in a tidal wave. I hoped I didn't drown.

Sunday did me no favors. It, too, didn't turn out like I'd hoped. Reed wasn't feeling well and couldn't make it to dinner. Maybe it was a good thing. The mood at the table was somber, our party of twelve was down to nine. Delanie and Peter's empty chairs were glaring reminders of the divide present in our family. Even our rambunctious teenagers were subdued. Everyone seemed to be looking into their plates of pot roast and mashed potatoes. Except Ma, whose red eyes were daring anyone to tell her this was all her fault. She knew darn well it was.

I reached over and took Ma's hand. "Ma, please. This isn't right."

She steeled her already stiff stance. "I never told them they weren't welcome here."

"Delanie never felt welcome."

"That's not my fault." She pulled her hand away.

I looked down the table at Dad, who shook his head at me as if to say *drop it*. But how could I? The holidays were coming up, and this wasn't what being a Decker was all about.

"Ma," emotion crept in to my voice, "we have lost too much in this family already. I can't stand the thought of another person missing at this table."

Ma's eyes blurred with tears. Hope rose in my chest, but fell when she stood up and threw her napkin in her chair without a word.

A collective sigh filled the dining room.

Mimsy threw cash at the boys. Even I got a ten-dollar bill out of it, like that would make it all better.

The only good thing to come out of the night was that I got to see where Reed lived. Ma insisted we take a plate to him since he was sick. I called Peter for his address, since it would look suspicious if I texted Reed. I offered to bring Peter and Delanie a plate too, but he declined. I hated this.

I had Cody run the plate up to Reed's cute front door. Reed was renting a darling, older brick rambler. It had a yellow door and black shutters. Wrought iron railing lined the brick steps to the door. The yard was small, but well kept. I noticed the navy-blue curtains he'd picked out hung in the front window.

I hoped he was feeling better; he sounded miserable when I talked to him earlier. I had been thinking about a way to do something for him. Ma, unbeknownst to her, helped. She probably would have had an aneurysm if she knew we'd been seeing each other. She was hoping to set him up with Penelope Gifford, a nice younger woman that had recently returned home from modeling in Italy. Reed had acted mildly interested. It made me wonder how much time we had left.

I caught a glimpse of Reed. Even from my car, I could tell he didn't feel well. His hair was going in all different directions and he was in pajama pants, no shirt. I'm just going to say a word I never thought I would say unless I was talking about my fictional boyfriend, Hunter Black. *Yum.* So I said it and I felt ridiculous for it. I rubbed my face. I was a mother, I repeated to myself.

Reed waved at me and I waved back, trying not to think about how good my hands would feel on his taut, defined chest. It was a far cry from the undefined bald chest I remembered from his adolescent days. I rolled down my window a tad to let some cold air in.

Cody jumped back into the car. "Coach said 'thank you.'"

"How's he doing?"

Cody shrugged. "I don't know. He sounded bad." He had inherited the Decker men's unobservant gene.

It turned out Reed was in bad shape, like walking pneumonia bad. So bad, we missed our grocery shopping date and I snuck soup over to him and left it on his front porch. He didn't want me to get sick and I didn't want us to get caught, but when I dropped off the chicken noodle soup, I couldn't help but want to go in.

I missed him, and I wasn't sure how to feel about it.

CHAPTER THIRTY-EIGHT

THUNDEROUS APPLAUSE RANG IN MY EARS. I LOOKED OVER THE CROWD OF women who had each been seated at their respective round tables eating lunch. Those same women were now on their feet, clapping for me. Reed suggested I end with the line he loved so much about none of us truly being empowered until we all were. From the looks of it, it had an effect.

My heart was pounding wildly. I wasn't expecting such a response. I only spoke from the heart about my journey and where I hoped to go. I used football as an analogy for how we can empower women and girls. I talked about the teamwork it required and how if we as adult women stopped comparing ourselves, how much better equipped we would make the next generation of women. I talked about the need to persevere, even if the odds were against us and it looked like we might lose. The great thing about life, though, was there was plenty of over-time; we just couldn't give up. These were all things I needed to hear more than anyone.

I had posted the speech on my blog that morning and had gotten the same response, minus the standing ovation. Though a few people sent standing ovation gifs. Others sent some not-so-nice ones. The more followers I got, the more detractors that came with it. I was called, among other things, a flaming feminist, bitter, ugly, and with Halloween around the corner, someone wished a house to fall on me.

There was enough love for me, though, that I had met with Delanie, a Chicago-based marketing group, and agent to talk about "selling me" earlier in the week. That sounded awful and frightening, because it was. It was also exciting and intriguing.

These people were talking about getting me on talk shows and shopping around for a publisher. The agent even threw out reality TV. I shut that down immediately. I had enough reality in my life. I didn't need some camera crew following me around documenting it. Besides, I was boring. He wouldn't let it drop. He was thinking of doing like a Bachelorette type show where I chose to get back in the game and choose my next husband. Never in a million years was that going to happen. Marriage wasn't meant to be mocked. I didn't care that Kevin, my wannabe agent, was throwing around six-figure numbers at me.

I didn't even have time to see Reed, and I already knew I liked him.

In all the chaos, and with his illness, I wasn't going to get to really see him until James and Avery's Halloween party that Saturday night, two days before my birthday. Even then, we wouldn't be able to connect in the way I would have liked. The way he kept texting me about how he planned to make me gasp, I was ready.

I probably shouldn't have been thinking about all that while I was standing in front of strangers taking in their applause. I should have been thinking about my exit strategy. What was I supposed to say and do?

Thankfully Delanie and Avery were in the audience. I looked to them. Delanie was trying to mouth something to me. She was a smart girl. Like, I-really-wanted-to-know-what-she-did-for-a-living smart. You should have seen the way she handled the agent and marketing firm. I was beginning to think that online publication she worked for paid her some serious bucks, and she was worth every penny. She was savvy and showed them who was boss right down to telling them if we used them, we wanted full control and say over anything that had the Sidelined Wife's name attached to it. She even named an entertainment lawyer we would be bringing to our next meeting. When I'd asked her how she knew one, she brushed it off.

I finally figured out what Delanie was mouthing: *Tell them where to look for you online and thank them for hosting you.*

Oh yeah, I think she mentioned that beforehand when I almost puked from nerves. I stood up tall at the podium with the Clearfield's

Women League sign adorning it. I took a deep breath. "Thank you so much. I'm overwhelmed. If you want to hear more from me, please follow me online. You can find me at theSidelinedWife.com or on Facebook. Thank you."

I did my best to gracefully exit the stage. I shook the president of the league's hand on my way off the raised platform. She was a lovely lady, from what I could tell.

I walked to the table where Avery, Delanie, and the leaders of the league were all gathered. My sisters greeted me with open arms. I drew from their strength and sent a prayer of thanks up for not wetting my pants, tripping, vomiting, mispronouncing words, or in general embarrassing myself. But, honestly, what had I gotten myself into?

I wondered that exact same thing when I showed up to Avery and James's annual Halloween party across town in my Little Red Riding Hood costume a few days later. It was a mix of sweet and sexy, with a full-length red satin cape, and a corseted dress that fell a couple of inches above my knee. I wore white stockings to my knees with heels.

It wasn't really anything I would want my mother to see me in. Which was why I dropped Cody off at my parents' place to stay the night with Jimmy and Matt before I dressed up like a very grown-up Red Riding Hood. Also, James and Avery's parties sometimes got a little wild. That's what happens when you throw alcohol into the mix. Nothing we needed our children to see. Or the parents. Or so I thought.

I had asked Avery if she wanted me to come early and help, but she repeatedly told me she had it covered. She specifically told me to show up at 6:30 that night. I did as she instructed, with my basket full of wolf-shaped cookies I'd made earlier in the day. I was being one of those over-achievers. It wouldn't last. But every Little Red Riding Hood needed a wolf, and mine tasted yummy.

When I showed up, there was a hardly a car in their middle-of-the-middle-class neighborhood, and none but mine in front of their house. So maybe Avery wanted me to be there early to help after all, I thought. It made sense; the party normally started at 7:00.

I almost felt like skipping up the stone paver walk. Not sure where that urge came from. Maybe because I knew I would see Reed, or perhaps I kind of liked the way I was looking tonight. Even my hair did what I wanted it to. Sexy curls outlined my face. It looked great with the hood.

I shook my head at their door with a sign that read, *Sorry, We're Dead.* That was James's idea. He loved that sign and couldn't wait to put it out every year. Avery would promptly replace it the day after Halloween next week with a fall harvest wreath.

I tapped on the door before turning the knob to let myself in, like I normally did.

For a split second, the front room and foyer were dark. The next second, it was all lit up and several people jumped up and shouted, "Surprise! Happy Birthday!"

I was so startled I dropped my basket of cookies. It took me a second to process what had happened and focus in on the familiar faces. Avery caught my eye first, beaming, knowing she had pulled off this little ruse of hers. She was coming my way with open arms. Before I could hug her, I caught a glimpse of Reed. Was he wearing a wolf mask? I had told him what I was coming as tonight. I didn't have time to worry about it. I was being bombarded with throngs of family and old friends I hadn't seen in a while

Avery wrapped her tiny arms around me. She was the cutest Alice in Wonderland to James's Mad Hatter costume. "Happy birthday! Are you surprised?"

I reciprocated the hug. "That is an understatement. How long have you been planning this?"

She released me and grinned. "Forever. You only turn forty once."

Forty? I was still coming to terms with that number. While everyone was saying the forties are the new twenties, my body was saying, *You wish.*

"Thank you. I think." I grinned.

Up next were my brothers. I got a big bear hug from each. Peter was dressed up as Fred Flintstone. I assumed that meant Delanie was dressed up as Wilma with her red hair; it would have been perfect. But

I didn't see her right off. That made sense when Peter backed away and made room for my parents. I noticed the hard stare he gave Ma before he walked off. They still weren't talking.

I thought for a second Ma was going to say something to him, but instead she turned her sights on me . . . or should I say, my costume. She shook her head and pressed her lips together. Neither she nor Dad were dressed up, unless shocked was a costume.

"Samantha Marie, what is this you're wearing?" Ma waved her hand up and down. "You're going to give everyone the impression that you are spreading your NDAs around!"

Oh, why couldn't she forget about that? "It's nice to see you too, Ma."

Dad stepped in and wrapped his arms around me and whispered in my ear, "Happy birthday, baby girl. You look too good."

"Thanks, Dad." I hugged him for a few seconds longer, enjoying the safety of his arms and trying to avoid Ma for as long as possible.

Dad stepped away, giving Ma a clear shot of me. She was about to lay into me again, until . . .

"Happy birthday, Sam." Reed, my savior, showed up, and he was definitely wearing a wolf head. He was opening a can of worms I wasn't ready for.

"Hi." I did my best not to grimace at his costume. His smile made it hard to be upset with him.

He turned toward my parents. "I'm sorry, am I interrupting any-thing? I just wanted to wish Samantha a happy birthday."

Ma patted his arm. "You are such a nice boy. Had I known you were going to be here, I would have invited Penelope. I've been telling her all about you. You really should come to church and meet her."

Reed rubbed the back of his neck. "I'll think about it."

"I better go say hi to everyone else." I made a quick escape while jealous tinges tried to take root. I tried to fight them off with logical thoughts. For example, Penelope was young and a model, of course Reed should want to meet her. And we had made no commitments to each other, so he was free to date whomever he wanted. Not sure any of those thoughts helped, but the barrage of people greeting me helped me to at least focus on something else.

There were so many people I hadn't seen in years. I had a feeling my newfound semi-fame played a role in their attendance. People like the Pollards, who I hadn't seen since my wedding, were there and hugging me like we were the best of friends. Or the Brownings, who made mention how much they loved my blog and wondered if I would mention their tire store in exchange for a free rotation. Not sure what to say, so I moved on. And there were a lot of people to move on to. Eventually I got to Delanie, who was indeed Wilma Flintstone and wow, was I envious of her twenty-something body. No wonder Peter was holding on tight.

She kissed my cheek. "You look gorgeous tonight."

"Not as gorgeous as you."

She waved me off. "This was Peter's idea."

"Guilty," Peter admitted while he ogled his wife.

Delanie leaned in toward me. "Did you and Reed coordinate costumes?"

"No," I immediately shot that idea down. "It's a weird coincidence."

"Yeah." She nodded.

"He said he was a German Shepherd," Peter interjected.

"Oh. I can see that." No, I didn't. Who dressed up like a German Shepherd?

"Uh-huh." Delanie wasn't buying it.

"I'm going to get a drink," I interrupted. "Does anyone want one?"

"It's your party, sis, let me get you something," Peter offered.

"You married a keeper, Delanie."

"I know." She pecked Peter's lips.

"I'll take anything from the non-alcoholic table. Thank you." I couldn't stand the thought of Ma scolding me for drinking dressed as I was, plus I had to drive myself home. No more designated Neil.

I wanted to talk to Delanie more, but Avery and James's neighbor, Gary, the one Avery had been trying to set me up with, decided to engage me in conversation.

"I'm not sure if you remember me, but I'm Gary Wright. I live next door." The distinguished man with traces of gray in his chestnut hair, a spark in his emerald eyes, held out his hand.

I took a closer look and had to admit he was handsome, but I couldn't place him. Maybe it was the *This is my Halloween Costume* shirt that was throwing me for a loop. It reminded me of Neil. He was the last person I wanted to be reminded of tonight. He'd found adult Halloween parties juvenile. Maybe they were, but they were fun.

I took his hand. "I'm sorry, I don't remember you, but it's nice to meet you again. I'm Samantha."

"The birthday girl." He let go of my hand after his firm shake.

"Girl is stretching it, but yes, in a couple of days." I had kind of been dreading it. And now look, I got to celebrate it early.

His baritone laugh filled the crowded room. "Well, you look good to me." His ears turned bright red.

Delanie's eyebrows raised.

Yes, that was awkward. "Thanks." My voice was hitting some high notes.

Might as well add a dash more of awkward. Reed joined us in his "dog" costume.

"Sounds like this is where the party is." He held out his hand to Gary. "I'm Reed, longtime friend of the guest of honor."

Gary studied the fur face atop Reed's head. "Gary, new acquaintance of the birthday girl."

Both men turned to me and smiled as if they expected me to say something.

I said the dumbest thing I could. "I heard it might snow tonight." Wow. Sam for the win. The really ridiculous part was that I hadn't heard that; it was fifty degrees outside. It had been a warmer than usual fall day.

"Really?" Gary seemed intrigued and pulled out his phone to check his weather app. Exactly what Neil would have done.

Reed, on the other hand, knew I had no idea what I was talking about. The biggest smirk filled his face. "I hope you don't catch a cold, Little Red Riding Hood."

"Thank you for your concern. Excuse me, I'm going to see if I can help Avery in the kitchen."

"Me too." Delanie followed.

Peter noticed and walked into the kitchen with us. He handed me some punch and Delanie a glass of white wine. I almost begged her to swap. But who knew what would come out of my mouth if I added alcohol into the mix?

"Thank you," I said as I took the punch.

"You okay?" Peter asked.

"Looks like Sam has a few admirers tonight," Delanie answered for me.

"Ooh, is Gary one?" Avery jumped in with her hands full of wrapped wieners on a tray.

"Yes, and Reed is the other."

I choked on my punch.

"No way." Avery laughed. "She babysat him."

"From the looks of it, I don't think he would mind if she took care of him again," Delanie commented.

Peter didn't look surprised at all.

Avery was still shaking her head. "That's crazy talk. I heard he was going to ask out Penelope, the model girl from church."

Jealousy pricked my nerves again.

"Hmm." Delanie stared at me. "What do you think?"

"I'm sure they would make a lovely couple." I set my drink down on the kitchen counter before reaching for the tray Avery was holding. "Let me help you."

"It's your party, I got it," Avery tried to protest.

"Please, let me help." I wasn't taking no for an answer. I took the tray and headed for their dining room where there was a huge spread, including a large sheet cake with, *Happy Birthday, Samantha,* written out in red icing.

Avery laughed at my side. "What a riot, you and Reed. Funny, though, how your costumes match."

"Peter said he was a German Shepherd."

"That makes sense."

No, it didn't. None of this was making a lot of sense to me.

"Thanks, by the way." I set the tray down near the condiments on the table. "You didn't have to do this."

"It was my pleasure. You needed to ring in forty with a bang." She shimmied up close to me. "So what do you think of Gary? Handsome, huh?"

"Yeah." I nodded.

"He's a loan officer for a local bank. He's been divorced and has two younger girls that he gets every other weekend and a couple of times during the week. Cutest things ever."

I hadn't thought about dating someone with children. Blending a family. I supposed I should have. There were a lot of things I should have thought about. Not that I was against it; I wasn't. But what would Cody think? And I would have to think about someone else's ex. Maybe I wasn't ready for all this. Then there was Reed. From the sounds of it, our fun could be coming to an end.

"Sounds nice." I grabbed a cheese cube from off the table and popped it in my mouth.

She waved her hand in front of my face. "Are you okay? You seem lost in thought."

"I think I just need some fresh air. This is kind of overwhelming for me." She had no idea how true that was.

"You deserve it." She gave me a tight Avery hug.

I slipped out the back door, well, sort of. At least five people wished me happy birthday before I could make my escape. I took a deep, cleansing breath once I hit the night air and closed the sliding glass door behind me. It was a little chilly in my getup, but no snow was in the air. I retreated down the deck steps and headed for the koi pond they had in their beautifully landscaped backyard. In the summer it was more glorious, with a variety of blooming flowers. Even now it was beautiful, but most importantly, peaceful.

I took a seat on the small stone bench near the edge of the pond. The cape was hardly any source of warmth, but I pulled it around me. I thought back to last year when I found my solace out here during the Halloween party. Same place, different reason. Or was it different? Maybe it was a new set of issues, but it all stemmed from my marriage falling apart. Last year I was in denial. This year there was no denying it.

I think part of me wished I could be like the koi fish that had retreated to the bottom of the pond, invisible. I had done my best for months to make myself as scarce as possible, even from myself. Now that I was emerging, there were growing pains. More lessons to be learned. Pain that had to be dealt with.

"Hey, there."

My time alone had come to an end. My focus stayed on the dark pool of water. "What are you doing out here?"

"This is where you are."

"You shouldn't have come out here. My family is already suspicious."

"Would it be so bad if they knew?"

I swiveled on the bench to face him. He looked ridiculous. "Nice costume, by the way."

His lip twitched, forming a half smile. "I couldn't resist once you told me what you were coming as. You're stunning, by the way, but you're avoiding the question."

It was a good question, and one he deserved an answer to.

He stepped closer. "I'm not asking you for a commitment."

Right. I knew that. It's not like I should be thinking along those lines anyway. "I have to talk to Cody first."

His eyes dared me . . . or was that pleaded with me? I couldn't tell in the dark.

"But will you?"

I wasn't sure.

CHAPTER THIRTY-NINE

THE PARTY WAS NOT THE LIGHTHEARTED EVENT I'D IMAGINED IT WOULD BE. I did best my best once I came in out of the cold to be engaging and, most importantly, grateful to Avery and Delanie for putting it all together.

Avery was exhausted from playing hostess, and Delanie and Peter had a mini blowup with Ma at the party when I opened my gift from them—it was a full-size cutout of Hunter Black. I was staring at him right now, shirtless and smiling back at me. Ma thought it was highly inappropriate and voiced her loud opinion. Peter wasn't having it. He told Ma he was tired of her criticism of all of us. That did not go over well. She left in tears.

Then there was Reed, for my birthday he had bought me the same Bryan Adam's poster and shirt he ruined all those years ago. I'd wanted to kiss him right there in front of everyone for it. And find out how he found them. They had to cost a pretty penny. But I'd had to play it cool even though I loved it more than Hunter Black. I would find a special place for both the poster and the cutout.

To top it off, Gary was giving all the signals that he would like to ask me out on a date, but I knew I would say no. He reminded me too much of Neil. I didn't care that Ma gave him her seal of approval, except that it was in front of Reed. Reed acted unaffected. I wasn't sure what to make of it, or if I was just making something out of nothing, or was that nothing out of something? But a weird tension hung in the air between Reed and me. I didn't like it, and I wanted to fix it.

It all had me in no mood for the caller in the middle of the night. I'd barely climbed into bed when Neil's name popped up on my phone's screen. Was this one of those middle-of-the-night drunk dials you hear about in songs? It seemed unlikely, since I'd never seen Neil drunk. I didn't answer the first couple of times he called, but by the third time, I figured I'd better. Actually, I panicked that there might be something wrong with Gelaire. Why else would he call me so late?

"Hello?"

"Sam, sorry it's so late."

"Is there something wrong with your mom?"

"No." He paused.

"Why are you calling?"

Then I heard it, the unmistakable sound of an infant's cry.

"Shhh," Neil tried to soothe the baby in hushed, tender tones.

My eyes flooded with tears. I hated myself for it. "I suppose congratulations are in order."

"Sam, I'm so sorry."

"Why are you calling me?"

"Because, you don't know how sorry I am. I didn't know until the last few months, until the last few hours. Sam, this should have all been with you."

I squeezed my eyes shut. "Stop, stop, stop. I can't do this with you."

"Please let me get this out. You were right, I was selfish."

"Great. Do you feel better now?" I knew I didn't.

"No," he cried. "I miss you, Sam. We should have had another baby together. I'm sorry we never did."

I thought of all of the games he'd missed over the years, and anger took over my sadness. "Why? So you could ignore more of our children?"

"That's going to change. I want Cody to know his sister, to know me."

He had a girl. Tears streamed down my face.

"Neil, you can't do this to me anymore."

"If I could take it all back, I would."

"You made your choice."

"I was a fool."

"I won't disagree with you. Goodnight."

"I love you, Sam."

I hung up. I couldn't take it. Why did he have to call? Why did he have to be with someone else to figure out he should have been with his wife all along?

The bed felt incredibly empty all of a sudden. I needed someone desperately right now. Reed kept popping into my mind. But could I just call him in the middle of the night? Especially now since there was this weirdness between us.

My mind wouldn't let it go. Fine. I'd text him. If he answered I would take it as a sign.

Can I come over?

Why did I text that? I meant to say, can you talk?

I didn't have time to worry about how stupid I was; he texted right back, *Yes, please.*

I didn't think. I threw on my slippers and fled the house and thoughts of Neil and his daughter. Tears poured down my face as I sped down the deserted roads to Reed's. He had to be wondering why I was coming over. Or maybe he thought he knew and I was going to disappoint him. I wouldn't blame him for thinking what he was probably thinking. I knew what I would think if he had texted me in the middle of the night. Oh, gosh. What had I gotten myself into? Thoughts of turning around screamed in my head, but thoughts of being alone shoved those other thoughts right out.

Before I knew it, I was sitting in front of Reed's house. Not a soul in sight on the sleepy street; even the lampposts were out. I looked down at my frumpy plaid flannel pajamas in pink. I was a sight with that ugly cry-face on top of my outfit. Crap, I wasn't even wearing a bra. Good thing my shirt was loose, and I was never well endowed. I should have probably left, but Reed had already seen me. He was standing at his front door waiting for me.

I turned off my car and took another breath. I was committed now to this half-cocked emotional reaction. I made my way to Reed, who was also in pajamas. They were even flannel, at least the black bottoms were. He was hiding his glorious chest behind a white t-shirt. Not going to lie, I was disappointed by that.

I stopped a few feet short of him and his door. The sight of him had the tears reappearing.

"Will you hold me?" Did that sound pathetic? I didn't really care.

Without a word he stretched out his arms. I flew into them. He embraced me before shutting his door with his foot.

I cried into his chest. He didn't utter a word. He only stroked my hair while holding me tight. We stood like that, minute upon minute, until every shudder, tear, and sniffle was done. Reed gave me a good squeeze once it was all out of me. "Can I hold you on the couch, or do you want to stay here?"

I laughed into him. "The couch sounds great."

In a fluid move, he took my hand and led me through his entryway to the small living room on the left. He flipped on a light as we went.

"You might want to keep that off. I don't want to scare you any more than I probably already have."

He chuckled and pulled me along. "I was right, you make flannel look good."

His large brown leather sofa that had some serious puffiness to it filled the small room along with his fifty-inch TV. Such a bachelor pad. The only feminine touch were the navy curtains. He sat down on the couch first and pulled me right onto his lap. I curled into him and rested my head on his chest. His heartbeat was strong and steady, like him.

"Do you want to talk?"

I snuggled in closer. "Neil called me. He's a new dad."

Reed ran his fingers down my arm, again, not saying a word.

"He was crying. He never cried once when we were married. He wished the baby was ours."

Reed's hand froze in place, mid stroke. "And what do you wish for?"

"For a long time, I wished for a little girl with him and another little boy. I wished for a lot of things." I kept the tears at bay.

"You could still have those things."

I spat out a laugh. "I'm forty. I don't even know if those parts of my body still work. And before I know it, Cody will be in college."

"What do *you* want, Sam?"

I thought for a second. "I'm trying to figure that out."

"Do you still want Neil?" He tensed.

"No." I knew that for sure.

Reed relaxed and kissed the top of my head. "What about Gary?"

I wrinkled my nose. "Too much like Neil."

Silence hung between us for a moment.

"I'm sorry I woke you up in the middle of the night and cried all over your shirt again."

"I put it on especially for you."

"Oh."

"You sound disappointed."

Oops. I bit my lip. "I was kind of hoping you would be shirtless like the time we brought you dinner," I admitted.

"You liked what you saw?" He sounded as happy as could be.

"Yes." My cheeks were burning. I don't remember being this forward.

He took a deep breath in and let it out slowly. "If we're being honest, I put my shirt on because I wasn't sure why you were coming over. But let's just say I was hoping the shirt would come back off."

I stopped breathing. I had a feeling he might think that. The only sound was the beat of his heart. It was louder and more frequent now. "Reed." His name came out as a breath.

"But... I know you're not ready for that step, and as much as I want to pick you up and take you to my bed, I wouldn't do anything to jeopardize what we have."

What was it that we had? Thoughts of ... well, thoughts of us being together were tempting. And he had no idea how good it felt that he wanted me. It had been a long time, but I wasn't sure I was that woman. I needed commitment, and not because of my mother. I knew how intimate that act was, and for me, love must be there, the all-encompassing kind.

"Waking up in your arms sounds lovely, but you're right, I'm not ready. And could you imagine Sunday dinner? I have a feeling if I ever had sex without being married, some radar would go off to alert my mother. Mimsy, too."

He ran his fingers through my hair. "I would hate to be the cause of that wrath, and I don't think I would fare well in that scenario either."

"Not at all." I laughed.

Reed didn't laugh with me. Instead, he tilted my chin up and leaned back so we could see each other. In his eyes, I saw myself again.

He brushed my lips before letting out a deep breath. "You are tempting."

"Next time I'll show up with bad breath."

"If only that would help. But, Sam...I want there to be a next time. I'm tired of sneaking around. Football season is almost over. I would like to date you out in the open."

Was I ready for that? Now my heart was pounding. "I don't know how Cody would feel about it..."

"I don't think you're giving him enough credit. Have you even broached the subject with him?"

A thousand thoughts ran through my head while I peered into Reed's beautiful blue eyes. Eyes that were waiting for an answer. "How would his teammates treat him if they knew?"

"It might be a little weird at first and he might get razzed some, but they're good kids. Cody is well liked and respected. It would blow over."

I bit my lip and thought some more.

Reed ran the back of his hand down my cheek. "Sam, we can't keep going on like this. You're getting to be too well known; it's bound to come out, one way or the other. And as fun as sneaking around with you is, it's not really my style."

There was a lot of truth to what he was saying. I leaned back against him and closed my eyes. "I'll talk to Cody."

CHAPTER FORTY

"How are you holding up, love?" Gelaire asked over the phone.

I stared down at my pajamas. It was noon, so that's how I was. Granted, I didn't get home until four in the morning. Reed's arms were hard to leave. We hardly said a word, barely even kissed. He just held on and I soaked it in. I knew what I had to face today, and I needed what he had to offer.

Cody would find out he was a brother and that I had been dating his coach. I was going to see how the whole baby thing went before I sprung the latter on him. Maybe Reed was right. I wasn't giving him enough credit. Cody did adore Reed. But if Cody knew, my family would know. And I'd heard Avery last night. She thought it was a joke.

I let out a deep sigh into the phone. Gelaire responded with one of her own.

"I'm okay. What else can I be?"

"I would say you have room for a gamut of violent thoughts and emotions."

"I'm tired of feeling that way."

"Love, I'm so sorry. Neil is sorry."

"What good does it do now?"

"Unfortunately, it is too late for the two of you, but I hope for my son and my grandson's sake, and...," she hesitated, "for Farrah's sake, his remorse will be meaningful. That he will be the father I know he can be."

Gelaire had mentioned the baby's name earlier too. Come to think of it, Roxie reminded me of a young Farrah Fawcett. It was a fitting name for her daughter. And though Gelaire was unhappy about how the child entered the world, she was thrilled to have a granddaughter. She tried to not let that come through for my sake, but she'd wanted another grandchild forever. Neil's older brother and wife had decided parenting wasn't for them, and Neil pretty much had too, so she never thought this day would come. She had already been to the hospital.

"I hope so too." I meant that for Cody's sake.

"You are queen among women, love. Never forget that."

"I love you. I should probably go. I need to get ready for the day and get Cody. He needs to know."

"Do you think Neil could tell him?" Her voice shook.

"Does he want to call him?"

"He was hoping to come over."

My heart stopped at the thought of having to see him today. "Why didn't he call me?"

"He feared he upset you last night, rightly so. It is unfair of him to tell you of his feelings now." He must have told his mother what he said.

"Agreed."

"But don't you think this should come from Neil?"

I did, but seeing him today was not on my to-do list. I rubbed my face with my free hand. "When did he want to come over?"

"This evening. I was going to go back to the hospital to stay with the baby while he's gone."

"Where's...you know...?" I couldn't say her name.

"I'm doing my best to be positive, but that woman is positively unfit to be a mother. My son will have his hands full. I fear I may have to step in and help during the day. You know I'm not a religious woman, but pray for me, love."

"I can do that."

"Can Neil come by?"

I closed my eyes and soaked in the afternoon sun filtering into my bedroom, hoping to find some strength in it. "I suppose he should.

Please don't let him disappoint Cody again. I don't want to tell him his dad is coming only for him not to."

"He'll be there."

For my son's sake, I hoped she was right.

That changed my plans for the day. I would have to cancel Sunday dinner with my family and Reed. A twinge of guilt panged me; I was kind of glad for the excuse—dinner wasn't the same without Peter and Delanie. Though I would miss seeing Reed.

Now, though, my focus had to be Cody and getting him through this day. I wished for a hand to hold to help get me through.

6:00 p.m. He should be here. I knew it, he wasn't going to show and there my son was sitting on the living room couch doing his best to act unaffected. But he was fidgeting and staring aimlessly at his phone. I wanted to brace him for the news he was about to receive, but it would be best coming from his father.

I continued to pace the kitchen, pretending like I was doing something useful like checking the empty oven and opening the refrigerator half-a-dozen times.

When the doorbell rang, I jumped. I turned to Cody; he was stiff with wide eyes.

"I'll get it," I offered.

Cody nodded his appreciation.

Have I mentioned how it sucked to be the adult sometimes?

For the love of my son, I straightened my black rayon blouse. I was dressed nicer than normal, with newly acquired thigh-slimming jeans and some leopard print shoes. I don't know why, but leopard print shoes said you were ready to roar. I didn't feel like that at all, but I was faking it.

I gave Cody a quick this-is-going-to-be-alright smile before I opened the door. A wave of cold wind rushed in. It was enough to ruffle Neil's hair plugs. I maintained my composure and didn't laugh.

"Come in," I said in a rush.

He didn't hesitate until he stepped inside. He looked so out of place here now. At least he wasn't wearing skinny jeans and some of the dye had faded out of his hair. But he didn't belong here.

He looked around as if he hadn't ever lived here. "I like the new curtains," he stammered, staring at the tall windows that stood on either side of the fireplace.

I doubted that. They were cream and ruffled. "Thanks."

We both focused on Cody, who was now standing in the living room. The gas fireplace illuminated him from behind. I looked between the two. For Cody, I had a warm smile; for Neil, I had a warning.

"Don't blow this," I whispered. It was then I realized he held two cards in his hands, red from the cold.

The shimmering envelope had my name on it. Neil handed it to me. "I know it's a day early, but happy birthday."

"You shouldn't have." I took the card, but only because I wanted to set a good example for my son.

"There are a lot of things I shouldn't have done; this isn't one of them."

"I'll leave you two alone." I didn't need any more confessions from Neil. I passed by Cody and gave his hand a quick squeeze on my way to the family room.

His eyes said, *don't go too far.* I had no intentions of doing so.

I sat on the sectional, holding my breath and sending up prayers to heaven. In my heart, I knew this needed to happen, but it didn't make it any less difficult. It didn't help when I opened the card. *Thinking of You on Your Birthday.* I refrained from scoffing. His written message inside was worse. It started out like a Cher song, *If I could turn back time, I wouldn't miss a single moment with you. Happy birthday. All my love, Neil.*

It was going in the fire as soon as Cody went to bed.

I tuned into the uncomfortable conversation in the living room.

"How have you been, son?"

Cody didn't respond verbally, but I imagined him shrugging.

"I'm sorry I've missed your games. I'm probably not going to make any of them this year because, well, I have some news for you. But I promise next year I'll make every one."

"Right." Cody wasn't buying it.

"I know you have no good reason to believe me, but I'm going to change that."

Cody was silent.

"Son," Neil paused and paused some more, "your sister was born last night."

I desperately wanted to see Cody's reaction, but I would have had to go into the kitchen, and that would have been obvious.

"She resembles you, same chin and eye shape."

So she looked like Neil.

"I want you to meet her."

Cody still said nothing. That worried me more than anything.

"Maybe this coming weekend you could come stay with us." Neil's nerves were coming through.

Cody was quick to respond this time. "I don't want to stay at your place."

"Understandable." Neil thought for a moment. "Would you stay with your grandma? I can bring Farrah, your sister, there. We could spend our time together there."

"I can't. My girlfriend is having a party."

His *what*!? When did Rory become his girlfriend? Last I heard, the homecoming date was awesome and he kissed her goodnight, but there was never any talk of steady dating. My heart couldn't take all this.

"You have a girlfriend? What's her name?"

"Rory."

"That's nice."

It wasn't nice. And what did Neil know? He wasn't the one dealing with it.

"Well, what about the following weekend?"

Cody took his time to answer. "Maybe."

"All right, I'll call you this week."

"Yeah," Cody didn't sound like he was buying it. I couldn't blame him.

Neil tried to make some more small talk, but Cody wasn't having it. Neil finally said, "I better get back to the hospital. Take care of yourself and your mom."

It was as if I could see Cody glare when he responded, "I'll do a better job than you ever did." Anger wrapped around every word, and if I wasn't mistaken, I heard his voice crack as if he was holding back tears.

I was ready to rush in with my tear-filled eyes, but I let him own his emotions. His father needed to see them and feel them. Cody needed to feel them.

"I know you will, son."

I couldn't take it anymore. I stood and walked into the kitchen. There I saw two men face-to-face, one standing proud, the other dwindling in his son's shadow.

Neil handed Cody a blue envelope. "I know this doesn't make up for anything, but maybe you can put it toward the car you've been saving for. I'll call you." He tried to drive that point home.

Cody took the card but said nothing.

Neil knew he could do no more. He gave me a wave and walked out looking like he had lost a few inches. His stature had certainly been lost in our son's eyes.

We let Neil see himself out.

I paused in the kitchen, waiting for a cue from Cody on how to proceed. I got one all right, and it brought me both joy and heartache. He hurried to me in the kitchen and put his arms around me.

I held my man-child—who stood taller than me—like I once had long ago to keep him safe from the monsters he was afraid of under the bed. Unfortunately, this time there was nothing pretend about the situation. And I would have to help him see that his father wasn't a monster. Along the way, I would have to learn that too.

There were some other lessons in store for me.

"Mom, I'm glad you're not with anybody."

CHAPTER FORTY-ONE

"I'M SORRY, I COULDN'T TELL HIM AFTER THAT."

Like a teenager, I was sitting on the floor of my closet having whispered phone conversations with a man I was secretly dating and would be for the foreseeable future, as long as he was still okay with it. Was that wrong? Was I lying to my son now?

Reed was awfully quiet for longer than was comfortable. "It's understandable."

"He's been through a lot."

"You both have."

"I really am sorry."

"Don't be. Cody comes first, I get that."

"We can still grocery shop tomorrow. It's what I've always wanted for my birthday."

"It's probably not a good idea for us to go out in public anymore."

I leaned back against the wall in my closet. "You're probably right."

"I'm beat. I'm going to head to bed."

"I guess that's what happens when emotional women show up at your doorstep in the middle of the night." I tried to add some humor and longevity to the conversation. I didn't want to end on this note.

Reed wasn't taking the bait. "Goodnight, Sam."

"Goodnight." I stared at my phone after we hung up. Loss filled me. What was I going to do? I felt like I had moved into the space between the rock and the hard place. No matter which way I went, I felt like I would hurt someone I cared about.

Reed was right, though, Cody came first. Maybe in a couple of months Cody would feel different. So maybe Reed and I couldn't see each other as often, but we could still see each other. It's not like anything had really changed, except it felt like there had been a major paradigm shift. I couldn't understand it. If we were only having fun, why did it matter if it was private or public?

I took to my blog. My feelings needed an outlet, even if I couldn't express exactly what I was going through.

Tomorrow I turn the big 4-0. I smell a mid-life crisis the size of the Sears Tower coming on. Okay, it will probably be more like me going crazy and throwing in some towels with my jeans when I wash them. I know, I live on the wild side over here. I should probably invest in more lint rollers. Besides that, I will probably down half the chocolate pudding cake I plan to make myself. Which brings me to some life lessons I've learned during this supposed first half of my life:

1. Don't buy jeans that you think you will fit into. You never will.

2. Don't wear those jeans. Just because you can zip them up with the help of a crane doesn't mean they fit. UTI's are not fun, sisters.

3. If something feels wrong, it is. Don't run from it. If you do, it will run right over you when you least expect it. Face it head on. It won't take the pain away, but there is power in choice. Choosing to go through the obstacle rather than being forced lends you amazing strength and a sense of control.

4. Act. If you don't, someone else will, and you won't like it. Guaranteed.

5. Leave the dishes until morning. The world will not come to an end. I promise. I didn't used to believe it, but I've tried it a few times and I've never died. There's always tomorrow, though.

6. Lick the spoon.

7. Raw cookie dough is worth risking salmonella poisoning. You only live once, might as well enjoy it.

8. Cereal can replace any meal.

9. Frozen food will not kill your family, at least not while you are feeding it to them.

10. Fat weighs less than muscle. I'll let you proceed with that information how you best see fit.

11. Don't let the number on the scale rule your mood. P.S. remind me of this daily.

12. The next step is always the most important step you will ever take.

13. You can always take a step back if you need to.

14. Send thank-you notes.

15. It's okay if you don't know everything.

16. Don't be afraid to ask for help.

17. You don't find your soul mate, you make them.

18. Don't take what's not yours, especially someone's spouse.

19. It's okay to burn bridges.

20. Look back to learn, but don't dwell.

And maybe life is like a box of chocolates and you never know what you're going to get. But don't be afraid to spit that crappy filled piece of chocolate right out of your mouth. Try every piece in the box until you get the right one. And once you get the right one, a new box will come along, and you'll have to start over. That's life. It's a series of starting over and over.

Here's to forty.

Sidelined Wife in Chief

Reed was one of those pieces of chocolate I wasn't too sure about, but once I was brave enough to taste it, I liked it. A lot. But now I wondered if I had soured in his mouth. Or perhaps I wasn't exactly the filling he was looking for. I knew things would eventually end, but I wasn't ready. I enjoyed our friendship and rendezvous. I thought he had too. Some part of me maybe even thought there could be more someday.

I never thought I would start forty this way: divorced, single parent, in some weird relationship with a guy I once babysat, and more confused than ever about life.

My birthday was going to be a low-key affair owing to the big party on Saturday. It started with a text from Reed wishing me a happy birthday, but even from his text I could tell something was off. There were no teases about what he would like to be doing to me or plans for seeing each other. It was just, *Happy birthday, Sam. Have a great day.* My fans on Facebook were more personal than that. I got smiley faces and hearts from them. Even all caps from some. And wishes for the best year ever.

I decided to take my own advice and acted instead of waiting to be acted upon. I didn't want to lose Reed's presence in my life.

Thank you. Cody might stay with his grandma next weekend. If he does, I would like to make you dinner at my place. I could wear that black dress.

I waited for his reply while I made Cody breakfast. Reed was taking longer than normal to reply. Maybe I should have called.

The oatmeal was done and in bowls by the time I got his response.

It's a date.

Maybe not as enthusiastic as usual, but I would take it.

Can't wait.

Me either.

That was better.

So maybe all would be right in the world, at least for the day.

My birthday had a surprise after all. Delanie called me mid-afternoon while I was at work.

"Are you sitting down?"

"Yes, but now I feel like I should stand up in case I need to get help."

"You might want a paper bag to breathe into. You're going to be on TV."

It felt like a vessel in my brain popped. No words would form for several seconds. "What?"

"Kevin called. He wants you as a client, bad. He's booked you a gig, free of charge."

"I don't do gigs."

"You do now."

"No. No."

"You haven't even heard what it is."

"You said 'TV.' Enough said. The camera adds like fifty pounds and highlights your wrinkles."

She laughed. "You don't have wrinkles and you're thin. You have nothing to worry about."

"I know, because I'm not doing it."

"You can't pass this up."

"What is 'this'?"

"Have you ever watched *Weekend Musings* on channel ten?"

"A few times, but it's been awhile."

"Well, brush up on it, because they want you to come on and make your 'protein balls' and chat with them. No big deal."

"This is huge, like the-Cub's-winning-the-World-Series huge."

"I understand why you may feel like that, but these local weekend morning shows don't have huge ratings. Think of it like dipping your toe into the pool to see if you want to dive in."

"This is insane."

"It's mini-insane." Delanie was quick with a comeback.

"Then I'll only have a mini heart attack."

"Does this mean you'll do it?"

"I didn't say that."

"I'll be there with you. I'll make sure they give us a list of questions they might ask."

"They do that?" I drummed my fingers on the desk.

"These types of shows are more scripted than you think."

"Huh. That's disappointing."

"The exposure would be good, and it would really add some legitimacy to your brand."

"I can't believe I have a brand."

"Well, you do, and like any living thing, it has to be fed."

"What if it eats me up whole?" That was a real question and one I'd been thinking about lately.

"That will only happen if you let it. I'll come with you. Avery can come too."

"I'm going to have to think about it. Like forever."

"You have until tomorrow morning. They had a cancellation so they are scrambling to fill it and need to know sooner rather than later."

"No pressure there."

She laughed. "I'll call you later to talk you into it."

I was going to need a lot more than a pep talk. A lobotomy was coming to mind.

CHAPTER FORTY-TWO

Sending you happy vibes.

Can't wait to see you on Weekend Musings.

What time is it again?

Can I stream it online?

My followers had been posting sweet notes to my Facebook page.

I'd lost my head and agreed to do the show. More like Avery and Delanie made me do it. They hounded me until I said yes. Honestly though, it wasn't the scariest thing I had to do today.

Cody was spending the night at Gelaire's with his dad and sister. That was still hard for me to say. Cody had a sister, and it wasn't my daughter. My dad was dropping him off for me since I had to be at the news studio way too early for a Saturday—or any day. Apparently, I had to have makeup done and meet the hosts beforehand. Delanie had been prepping me all week. I kept running through my head *have an opinion, but not an ego; be funny; don't give one-word answers*. It's hard to be funny when you're trying to be, and one-word answers are so easy.

After I embarrassed myself on TV, then it would be time to get ready for Reed. I hadn't really seen him since the night I went to his place. I caught glimpses of him at both football games that had been played in the interim. I had a feeling he might be bummed tonight. They had won last week, the final game of the regular season, but last night they lost their first playoff game, knocking them out. The season was over. It was a great season, even if they didn't make it to the championship. Reed should be proud of his first season as head coach.

I'd called him late last night to see if he needed consoling. It was a short conversation, like most of them had been for the past two weeks. I almost wondered if he still wanted to come over.

I rushed around getting ready. Gelaire had helped me pick out a red trumpet blouse, black pants that really made me look womanly, and paired them with those fabulous shoes she had bought me earlier to go with the little black number I was planning to wear tonight. Maybe? Were Reed and I over? I hoped not. Or were we ever anything?

While I brushed my teeth, my phone buzzed on the counter; I had been monitoring the time with it.

Good luck this morning. I can't wait to see you tonight.

I let out a sigh of relief. So maybe I was worrying for nothing. Reed's text especially meant a lot since the sun wasn't even up and he had to be exhausted from the game the night before.

Thank you. Me too. Bring your appetite. I was making red wine stew. Now that we were into November, winter was knocking on the door, and it was soup and stew kind of weather. We already had a couple inches of snow.

For you or the food? Reed was back.

I'd missed his playful banter.

Both.

I'll be ravenous. Get ready.

Oh, I would be. I'd missed him.

I headed up to Cody's room before I left. This was a huge weekend for him. I don't think he would admit it, but part of him was excited to be a big brother. When he was little, he used to ask for a little brother or sister for Christmas. Each year, I begged Neil to change his mind. Once he'd said fine, but it wasn't his first choice. I couldn't bring a baby into the world under those circumstances. Maybe I should have. Neil, from all accounts, was the ever-doting father this go-around. I tried not to dwell on it.

I sat on the edge of Cody's bed. His room was as messy and pungent as ever. Maybe with football season over the air fresheners might start to make a dent again. I brushed his hair. I was loving the curl.

"Hey, sleepyhead."

One eye opened and he gave me an if-you-weren't-my-mother-I-would-kill-you look.

"I'm leaving to go make a fool of myself on TV. We may have to change our names and move after this."

He rolled his one eye. He'd already told me earlier this week not to say anything about him on TV.

"This is serious."

He mumbled something unintelligible. He seemed to try to know as little as possible about the Sidelined Wife stuff. I wasn't sure if it was because it embarrassed him or because he was truly a Decker man and he liked to live in oblivion.

I kissed his head. "Have fun this weekend. Give your dad a chance."

Those words were hard to say. But watching my family fall apart only made it hit home how important family was. We had to heal the rifts when we could. If Neil was willing to try, Cody needed to let him and participate. As much as it hurt, I had to help Cody see that. I was sure if things went well this weekend, I would have to share Cody more than I was used to or wanted to.

Some more moans and groans escaped Cody. I think there was an okay somewhere in there.

I kissed his head once more. "Grandpa will be here in a few hours. Don't forget your bag. And if anything happens, I'm a phone call away. I can be to you in thirty minutes if I have to be."

He nodded, rolled over, and hid his face with his blanket. I suppose that was his way of dismissing me.

I felt like throwing up on the drive downtown with Avery and Delanie, and it wasn't because Avery drove like she was an Indy 500 racer. My mind was going blank. I couldn't remember my name or how to make protein balls. Samantha. Yes. Yes. I could work with that.

I listened to Delanie and Avery chat in the front seat about Thanksgiving and how Delanie and Peter would be going to New York. I thought Delanie's parents lived in Oregon. I didn't ask, though, because opening my mouth was only giving the vomit an invitation to come spewing out. I wondered if Ma knew they'd be away. Holidays were a big deal to her. And Avery and James were headed to Iowa to be with

Avery's family. My heart constricted, thinking that technically—and by law—Neil could have Cody for Thanksgiving this year. I couldn't take all these thoughts as I sped toward my utter embarrassment.

I prayed silently to every saint I could think of—except Valentine—for help. That guy had been no use whatsoever.

I was in a daze while I was herded around the studio set and behind the scenes. Was this real? Why did everything seem shiny, even the people? Maybe all the lights? I felt like I should invest in teeth whitener strips. The hosts, Marla and Manny, nicknamed M&M, especially gleamed. Marla was a former model that still looked like the catwalk would love her with her luscious dark tresses and goddess cheekbones. Manny was what my followers would call Latin-lover material. He had caramel skin, beautiful brown eyes, and a voice that could talk you into anything. I only met them briefly; they said they wanted to save it for the show, whatever that meant.

You know what made it even worse? They had a studio audience. How did I not remember that there would be people there to laugh in my face?

Avery and Delanie were having the time of their lives, chatting it up and eating the food provided for the crew and guests. Who could eat at a time like this? I was never eating again.

I sat, dazed, in a makeup chair while the makeup artist, Liv, did her best to clog my pores with massive doses of what felt like shellac for my face. Liv even offered fake eyelashes. No thanks.

I was the second guest. M&M were interviewing the cast of a local playhouse first, talking about their upcoming holiday schedule and performances. All the actors looked so good sitting on the immaculate white couches. They sounded good too, charming and funny. And they sang, like bring-the-house-down kind of singing.

I shook my head, watching the monitor in the green room I was in. "I can't do this."

Avery and Delanie both laughed like this was some kind of joke. "Of course you can," they both said.

Avery must have clued in to the sheer terror in my eyes. She took my hands. "You are going to be amazing. Just pretend like you're talking to friends or typing on your laptop. You talk to strangers every day."

"They don't see me, though, and I have a delete button on my laptop. There is no taking anything back here."

Delanie stepped in. "The reason they asked you on is because they like your candidness and honesty. If you say something off the cuff, they'll love it."

"Let out the breath you're holding," Avery suggested. "You got this."

Whether I did or not, it was my turn. I had a production assistant coming to march me to my death. This called for some macabre music. Avery and Delanie each gave me a squeeze and I was off like a lamb to the slaughter.

Before I knew it, I was in the wings listening to people talk about someone I wasn't sure I knew.

"We have a special treat this morning, a homegrown celebrity that is taking social media by storm. That's right, we have the Sidelined Wife in the house. If you haven't heard of her yet, you will. She's known for her quick wit, and advice on everything from sex, fashion, and how to make your toilets sparkle."

Did they really need to bring that up? Ma was going to flip about the mention of sex.

"She's here today to delight us with her wisdom and to show us how to make her famous glorified cookies—I mean, 'protein balls.'" Marla and Manny laughed together before standing up to greet me.

The assistant had to push me out there.

Don't fall, don't fall, smile, make eye contact, don't fall.

Like a bizarre dream, I walked out onto the set, which was a lot cooler in person. It looked like someone from HGTV had designed the set. It was stylish, homey, but with a dose of class. White furniture with wicker baskets and rustic vases filled the space.

Applause rang in my ears as I approached the shiny hosts with outstretched arms. Oh, we were hugging. That wasn't awkward at all. But it wasn't bad—Manny smelled like crisp citrus. It was nice. Not Reed nice, but nice. Was Reed watching? I'd given him the time. I couldn't think about it. *Focus, Sam.*

"Welcome, welcome." Marla waved to the chair near the couch where they sat. "Have a seat."

Sitting was good; my legs felt like jelly. At least I hadn't fallen. "Thank you for having me." I smiled. Or did I? My face felt frozen.

Manny was closest to me and leaned in, blinding me with his gleaming smile. "Tell us a little bit about yourself."

I said the first thing that popped into my head. "Well, I just turned forty, I'm a divorced, single mom, but I do get to host my book club this month, so you could say I'm living the dream." That sounded so dumb. Why was everyone laughing?

"What did we tell you? Isn't she great?" Marla addressed the audience.

"The big question on our minds is, do you know who Autumn Moone is? She's really who we have to thank for bringing us you." Manny patted my knee. Was that allowed?

"I don't think she knew the kind of crazy she was unleashing on the world when she posted my blog, but I would love to thank her in real life. And find out if Laine and Hunter will finally be getting together."

"Don't we all wish we knew that?" Marla fanned herself. "What do you predict?"

"I think they'll come together, but will get torn apart by the end."

"Ooh, good theory, and it means more Hunter Black books," Marla purred.

"I'll buy every one." I smiled.

We chatted some more on the couch before they wheeled in a kitchen, or at least a kitchen counter. Did I mention how bizarre this was? Before I knew it, I was in an apron plastered with Marla and Manny's faces on it, standing there getting ready to make protein balls.

All the ingredients were laid out and premeasured. I was told just to mix and explain. They even had some premade protein balls under the counter for Manny to pull out when I was done making a few as a demonstration.

While I dumped the oats and scraped the peanut butter into the mixing bowl in front of me, they continued to talk to me.

"You know, I have a bone to pick with you," Manny teased. "My girlfriend asked me to sign one of your NDAs."

Laughter filled the studio.

"I have several printed out, ready to go," Marla jumped in. "Women needed something like this a long time ago."

"Not according to my mom. Hi, Ma." I waved. That was going to cost me.

More laughter.

"Speaking of dating, what advice do you have?" Marla asked.

"Proceed with extreme caution," rolled off my tongue. "And try dating yourself. It might be the best time you ever had. That goodnight kiss is a little awkward, though."

Why was everything I said so funny to these people? Laughter pealed through the studio.

"I guess that means a second marriage is off the table for you?" Manny asked.

I tossed my head from side to side. "I wouldn't say that. But when I see women jumping from one marriage to another, I'm like, honey, you just got your one-way ticket out of hell—oops, can I say hell?"

"Well, you just did." Marla slapped my arm playfully.

"Anyway, I just think, enjoy the clean toilet for a while."

Manny leaned back. "Hey, now."

"You know it's true." Marla gave her co-host a wink.

"Let's get back to the protein balls," Manny suggested.

You could never go wrong with a protein ball. That was going to be my new motto.

CHAPTER FORTY-THREE

GIDDY. I FELT POSITIVELY GIDDY. I SURVIVED THE INTERVIEW, MY HOUSE smelled heavenly, like red wine stew and the homemade rolls I had thrown in the oven a few minutes ago. Cody was surviving per Gelaire. She said it was tense between him and Neil, but Cody lingered wherever baby Farrah was. I took that as a good sign. Not only that, in moments my spine would be tingling. I planned to pull Reed in the house and kiss him thoroughly. I hadn't realized how much I'd missed him.

I was flitting around my kitchen like Doris Day, checking on the last-minute details of our candlelit dinner that was way overdue. I had set everything up at the breakfast bar. For some reason, I still couldn't do the formal dining room. The candles flickered to the tune of Frank Sinatra on the surround sound. The wine was chilling and the glasses sparkled, waiting to be filled. I stirred the stew one more time and turned on the oven light to check on the rolls before the doorbell rang.

I hustled out of the Marla and Manny apron I was given today before I left the studio. I smoothed my little black dress and checked to make sure I put on deodorant and that my armpits were still smooth. A lot of skin was showing. I had to moisturize the heck out of myself this afternoon. Don't even get me going on the hair removal. When I deemed myself passable, I headed for the door in my heels, clicking against the hardwood floors. All in a rush to see Reed.

I swung the door open and before I said a word, I looked to the left and right to make sure he wasn't seen. I didn't even see his jeep. He must have parked far away. Good plan.

I pulled him in by his red tie and shut the door before wrapping my arms around his neck. I let my lips say hello.

Reed didn't reciprocate the way I thought he would. It took him several seconds to wrap his cold hands around me. His lips were hesitant. No tingling spine moves.

I pulled my head back. I was eye level with him in my heels. "Hi."

He pressed his lips together. His blue eyes studied me. "Hi."

"I'm glad you could make it. I missed you."

"I missed you too," he replied, but it sounded against his will.

I took his hand. "I hope you're hungry." I pulled him toward the kitchen.

He didn't respond, but followed me.

"Did you see my interview?" I continued to drag him along.

"Yeah," he sounded off. What was going on with him? He was probably bummed about the season being over.

I led him to a stool and sat him down hoping to kiss him again, but his tightened jaw was flinching in addition to his stiff posture.

I stood for a second, not sure what to say or do. "Is everything okay? Did you think I was awful?" Delanie and Avery had called it fantastic, though I wouldn't go that far.

He looked me over and I couldn't tell if he liked what he saw. I'd hoped by this point he would have told me how much he loved the barely-there dress and that I'd be needing to fix my hair.

My heart raced. "Reed?"

"You were great."

I tilted my head. "You don't sound so sure."

"It gave me a lot to think about."

"Are you going to give up cookies for protein balls?"

He didn't even crack a smile. "Sam." He took my hand, but not as a romantic gesture. It felt more out of necessity than want. "Did you mean what you said today in the interview?"

"The part about protein balls lasting for up to a month in the freezer?"

"Could you stop it with the protein balls?"

I stepped back. I had never heard him upset before. "Okay. What part?"

"The part where you dismissed relationships. Is that how you really feel?"

"You mean about marriage and dating?"

"Yes. Is that not something you want?"

I braved edging closer. "Reed, we date."

He let out the heaviest of breaths. "We don't date, Sam. You squeeze me in when it's convenient for you, all secretly. All on your terms."

Where was this coming from? My feet shifted. "I thought you understood my circumstances and that you were okay with the way things are."

"I'm sorry if I gave you that impression. I told you sneaking around wasn't my style."

"You know how Cody feels about it. I can't change that."

He shook his head. "You don't know how Cody really feels about it because you won't talk to him. And you don't want to."

"I was going to."

"Sam." He pulled me closer. "You were relieved when you didn't have to. You used Cody as an excuse."

My first instinct was to deny what he was saying, but the truth rang in my head. He was right. "I still don't get why that bothers you. You've never indicated you wanted a serious relationship with me. You even talked about dating Penelope."

"I only said that to your mom to keep playing your game."

"I'm not playing games with you."

"Maybe that's the wrong word, and maybe I've been playing games too, all in hopes that you would come around and let me in."

Confusion continued to swirl in my head. "What do you mean 'let you in'? I've been open and honest with you from the beginning."

A softness washed over his features. "You've done your best to keep me at arm's length. And I don't blame you. I probably should have waited to ask you out. I knew you were hurting, rightfully so. I thought if I played it cool, with no pressure, you might open yourself up to the possibility of a real relationship. But every time I tried to talk about it or tell you how I really felt, you would change the subject or say something funny to brush over it."

"I didn't—"

Reed placed his finger on my lips. "Think about it, Sam."

I thought back to all the times we were together and suddenly, as if a light went on, I saw them in a whole new way. He was right. I ran my fingers through my hair, taking shallow breaths.

"I think today on that show is the most honest you've been. You don't want to date, and you certainly don't want to get married." He wrapped his arms around my waist and peered into my eyes. "I do, though. I want those things. I see myself having those things with you."

It was as if a wave of ice cold water hit me, tossing me every which way. I wasn't sure what was up or down. "You want to marry me?" I stuttered.

"I'd like to explore that possibility someday, but I can't until you're willing to move on and let yourself be vulnerable again. I'm through sneaking around and pretending this is all for fun. Don't get me wrong, it is the most fun I've ever had and I don't regret a second of our time together. But I can't keep doing this. I can't keep falling in love with someone who has no intention of loving me back."

"I . . ." What did I say? My heart was pounding so hard I could feel it in my head. I could barely hear over the blood rushing through my ears. "I care about you. I don't want us to end."

He pressed his lips to my forehead. "You didn't let us begin." He pulled away and stood up.

"You're leaving?" My voiced cracked.

"I think it's for the best."

"So that's it?"

He shook his head. "If and when you're ever ready, call me. I'm not going anywhere. I've waited a long time for you. I can wait some more . . . but not forever."

I stood staring at him, dumbfounded, tears pricking my eyes.

"Goodbye, Sam."

He left. He just left. It was like watching Neil leave me all over again.

The timer went off for the rolls, giving me a heart attack. With tears streaming down my cheeks, I took them out of the oven and threw them on the counter. The sound of metal against the granite reverberated through the kitchen. I looked at the melting candles and flickering lights, trying desperately to think of all the reasons he was wrong and how unfair this was of him. I was over Neil and my divorce. I was only trying to protect my son. I hadn't known how deep Reed's feelings ran. Or did I?

I looked at the breakfast bar, set for dinner. It was glaring proof; Reed was right. I couldn't even face eating in my dining room because Neil's ghost still haunted it. And maybe I was trying to protect Cody, but it was my heart that I shielded more than anything.

But in trying to protect my heart, did I forfeit what it had truly wanted all along?

CHAPTER FORTY-FOUR

I SHOULD HAVE BEEN BASKING IN THE GLOW OF MORE OFFERS THAN I COULD count, of TV interviews, book deals, and sponsorships. Instead, I felt like I was wandering around in the dark, all while reality hit me.

I wasn't as whole as I thought I was. Sure, I knew I was a mess, but I truly believed I was over Neil. But not wanting to be with someone and being over them are two starkly different things. That realization had me hating Neil more.

I hurt someone I truly cared about, albeit unintentionally, but he was hurt. I saw it in his eyes. And worse, I knew how it felt to love someone that didn't love you back. Neil could profess that he still loved me all he wanted to, but his actions spoke the truth. Just like my actions spelled out to Reed where he stood.

The worst part was I didn't know how to fix it or if I could. Was I damaged beyond repair? All I knew was when Reed left, he took something. Something I missed. Him.

Not only did he disappear from my life, but from every Decker, even Peter. It hadn't gone unnoticed.

Peter stopped by my office the Monday before Thanksgiving. He and Delanie were leaving the following day for New York. I was probably more depressed than I had ever been, but like always, I was trying to hide my emotions. It was a horrible habit and had cost me dearly. But I didn't even know where to begin.

Not only had Reed walked out of my life—or more like I'd pushed him—but Peter, Delanie, and Ma were still on the outs. It was causing marital discord between my parents. More and more when I was at my parents', Dad was disappearing into their garage to tinker on the boat Ma hated. And Ma was digging in her heels, unwilling to even talk to Peter or Delanie until they apologized. Peter and Delanie, like the rest of us, weren't sure what they had done, and Ma couldn't articulate it. To top it off, it was the first time I would ever be spending Thanksgiving without Cody. I saved the advanced copy of *A Black Night* to help get me through, though I wasn't sure it would help. Reading a romance was probably the last thing I needed, seeing I was incapable of having one of my own.

I was beginning to wonder if August Moone had some supernatural abilities beyond being unknown. She sent a card with the book that read, *Embrace the night, learn what the darkness has to teach. You can never appreciate the light until you do. Then once the light comes, it will warm you and illuminate your path in ways you never dreamed of.*

It was like she knew what I was grappling with. Maybe I should have been creeped out by it, but I took solace in her words. Though I had no idea how to embrace the night. I was afraid of the dark.

Peter peeked his handsome head into my office. Like all of us, some of the light was dimmed in his eyes. He was team Delanie one hundred percent, as he should have been, but family was important to Peter and he hated the separation between him and Ma. He had been a mama's boy growing up. And James and I always suspected Peter was Ma's favorite.

"Hey, sis. Can I talk to you?"

"Sure." I turned away from my monitor. I was tired of updating vendor accounts anyway.

He shut my door and took the only other seat in the office, in front of my desk. He looked worn, with red cheeks from working out in the cold. They were finishing up a job for the city park, winterizing and redoing the mulch before the big snow came. He rubbed his cold, dry hands together and blew into them.

"You look like a lumberjack in your flannel shirt."

He gave me a small smile. "Delanie finds it sexy."

I knew someone else that liked flannel, but I didn't mention it. "That's true love, there."

"Speaking of love." He leaned forward. "Do you want tell me what's going on between you and Reed?" Peter's knowing eyes weren't going to let me off the hook.

I took a deep breath and let it out. "I can honestly say, nothing."

"Let me rephrase. What happened between you?"

My eyes betrayed me; they pooled with tears.

Peter handed me a tissue from the box that sat on my desk.

I took it and dabbed the corner of my eyes. "We were secretly dating, or at least I thought we were."

He tilted his head. "Either you were or you weren't."

"I thought we were, but what I was really doing was hurting him." Moisture continued to accumulate and run down my cheeks.

He handed me another tissue. "It looks like he wasn't the only one hurt. What happened?"

I wrung the tissue in my hands. "I didn't realize—or I wouldn't admit it to myself—that he wanted more than I could give, more than I was ready for. I'm damaged goods, and I really suck at relationships."

Peter shook his head. "That's not true. You are a great friend, sister, mother, daughter, and you were a good wife."

"Then why did Neil leave? And now Reed?" I begged to know.

Peter's eyes said he wished he had an answer. "Have you ever asked Neil?"

"He thinks I made him leave."

"What about Reed?"

"He says he's willing to wait until I figure things out. He thinks I'm still hung up on Neil and closed off."

Peter leaned back. "Is he right?"

My fists balled up. "I don't love Neil."

Peter reached across and placed his cold hand on top of my clenched one. His eyes were trying to reach me and understand my pain.

"You were married for a long time. That kind of love just doesn't go away, even when a betrayal so deep has occurred. Maybe you've been hiding from the love to lessen the pain. That's a natural reaction."

"How could I still love him after everything he did to me?"

"Because you're human, Sam. Loving him doesn't make you less of a person, nor does it mean you should be together. But you have to go through the pain."

"I feel like that's all I've done," I cried.

He squeezed my hand. "You have to forgive him, for yourself."

"How do I do that?" I desperately wanted to know.

"We think that time heals wounds, and maybe it helps, but I've found that we must actively be doing."

"Doing what?"

"All that we do requires action, faith, love, forgiveness. Even letting go and receiving love."

I wiped my eyes. "It might be too late for Reed. He said he wouldn't wait forever."

"Sam, if we all waited to be whole to give or receive love, we would live in a very dark world indeed. We're all broken. Some more than others, and some less than they think." He gave me a little wink.

"I bet you were a good priest."

He sat back. "I hope I'm a better husband."

"I think you do okay there." I gave him a small grin. "Thank you. I guess I have some work to do."

"You're not the only one."

Was he talking about himself or someone else?

CHAPTER FORTY-FIVE

I SAT CROSS-LEGGED ON MY BED LATE THAT NIGHT. MY HAND SHOOK AS I dialed Neil's number. I tried to take Peter's advice. I had to feel the pain, and the only way I could think of was to get the whole truth, the why of it all. Maybe if I knew, I could deal with it, as painful as it would probably be.

His phone rang a couple of times. Perhaps I should have waited until morning, but I figured he had a newborn, he would be up. According to Gelaire, the bundle of joy had her days and nights mixed up. Cody had attested to that and her set of lungs.

I almost hung up.

"Sam, is Cody okay?"

"Uh, yeah." His query caught me off guard. "Why wouldn't he be?"

"I can't think of why else you would call."

"I hope I didn't wake you." I stalled to tell him the reason.

"I've got a long night ahead of me."

"I bet."

"What's wrong, Samantha?"

I guess he still knew me. I breathed in deep to not only draw some courage, but to stave off the tears. "Where did it go wrong for you?"

He paused. "Where's this coming from?"

"I need to know why you left me."

"You told me to leave."

"That's not what I mean. You left me long before you moved out. What changed for you?"

"Sam, does it really matter? It doesn't excuse what I did."

"It won't change our circumstance now, but it does matter."

I could almost see him pinch the bridge of his nose. Maybe take off his reading glasses and rub his eyes. He had probably been reading.

"You changed, Sam. You went from being my wife to Cody's mother. I admit I was jealous, and it's why I never wanted another baby."

"You never said anything." Though I had my suspicions.

"Listen to how that sounds."

"I was trying to be a good mom and wife."

"And you were, but there were times I thought you loved Cody more than me."

I did a quick internal evaluation. Was that true? "I loved you differently, not unequally."

"I'm beginning to see that now. I'm sorry you bore the brunt of parenting. I realize now, had I helped you more, you wouldn't have had to give so much of your time to Cody. Not to say that you wouldn't have, but it could have been something we shared instead of a source of contention."

I sat back, stunned. "I would have liked that."

"Me too. I wish for it more now than you'll ever know." I knew from talking to Gelaire that he was the primary caregiver and was probably going to have to hire a nanny while he worked. Perspective. It does something to you.

"Why didn't you just talk to me?"

"I guess I didn't know how to articulate what I needed."

"Did Roxie give you what you were missing?" It was like asking him to shove the knife in farther, but I had to know.

He thought and thought some more. "For a while, but it wasn't what I really needed or even wanted."

"Was she the only one?" That question had nagged me, but I had been too afraid to ask.

"Do you really want to know?"

Direct blow to the heart. Don't cry, I begged myself, but then I remembered I had to feel it. All of it. "I guess that's my answer," I cried. "How many?"

"Sam, let's not do this."

"I have to know. I can't move on until I do."

"What if I don't want you to? What if we tried again? I'd go to counseling, whatever you want. We could have a baby."

"Stop, Neil. Please stop. Tell me how many and when."

"Two, besides Roxie," he whispered, ashamed. "Halloween last year and the other while I was seeing Roxie."

"Does she know?"

"She doesn't care."

"Anything else?"

"I knew I changed in your eyes, too. That I became the kind of husband I didn't want to be. I didn't know what to do about it. I obviously went about it in the wrong way. You deserved better. You may not believe it, but I'm sorry."

"I don't, but maybe I will someday."

"I hope to prove it to you."

"Just be a good dad to our son. To your daughter."

"I'm determined to."

"Goodnight."

"Maybe I could call you for parenting advice?" he got in before I could hang up.

I almost laughed. "I don't think so."

"It was worth a shot."

"Goodnight." I hung up right away this time. I grabbed a pillow from Neil's old side of the bed and grieved into it. Racking sobs. I don't know if it helped or if I was any closer to getting over him, but I'd taken a step. The most important one, the next one.

~*~

Peter became my confidant and counselor. He was a trained professional, after all. We took long, cold walks during work when we could, even in the snow. He was the only person who knew about Reed. I wasn't keeping it a secret anymore because I felt like I had to, but because Reed had disappeared. I had texted him on Thanksgiving in an effort to reach out. It was a simple, *Happy Thanksgiving. I hope you're enjoying your trip.*

He was supposed to go home to Wisconsin to be with his family and serve dinner at the high school he used to teach at. They did a dinner there for kids with no family or place to go. He was a good man. Even if he was ignoring me. I knew he was alive because Cody mentioned talking to him in the hall last week at school—after Thanksgiving break.

I pulled my hood on and shoved my gloved hands in my coat pockets. Flurries flitted in the cold December air. "How's Delanie? Is she recovered from her cold yet?" She had gotten sick on their trip to New York.

"She's better. Thanks for the soup and dinners every night last week."

"You're welcome. I have no life."

"Whatever, Sidelined Wife."

"Such a fitting title for me." I was thankful for my followers. They had gotten me through my sucktastic first holiday without my kid. I ended up running a contest of the best holiday breakup where we all voted for the winner.

The lucky—or unlucky—woman received a gift certificate to her local spa. The poor dear who won had been with her boyfriend for five years and she thought they were getting engaged. She found the ring of her dreams in his nightstand drawer. She told her mom and sisters and they frantically prepared with manicures and the perfect outfit. She and her boyfriend showed up at her parents' place for Christmas dinner and, no kidding, when he was down on one knee asking for her hand in front of her entire family, the police raided the home and arrested him for counterfeiting. The ring was paid for with counterfeit bills.

She deserved more than a spa day, especially since she was interrogated for hours to rule her out as a suspect too, but that's all I could afford for now. I did have some lucrative contracts lined up, though. I was about ready to sign a deal for a cookbook with a dash of my wisdom sprinkled throughout. Not sure how wise I was. I was trying, this time harder.

"I thought you liked the sidelines?" Peter laughed.

"I do."

"Maybe you'll find someone who likes them as much as you."

I shrugged.

"You still haven't heard from Reed?"

"No." I kicked a rock on the path. "Maybe that's good. I've taken your advice. I'm painting my room and making it my own, trying to stay busy, but not so busy I'm ignoring my feelings." I found painting to be therapeutic. You could cry and paint at the same time.

"Are you still writing in your journal?"

Peter had suggested I get a journal since writing my blog had been helpful. He thought a private journal where I could write intimate details and pains I'd rather keep discreet would be beneficial. I think he was right. Anger subsided quicker once it was out on paper. It even let me feel the good times with Neil, which was harder than the worst times. Those pages had many tear stains, but in those moments, I could see peeks of light at the end of what seemed like a very dark and lonely tunnel.

Autumn Moone was right, I had to learn from the darkness. And oh, what a book she had written. *A Black Night* was her crowning achievement so far. The chemistry was amazing and ice-cube-down-my-shirt worthy. Laine and Hunter came together and it was magical. Unfortunately, I was right. They were torn apart at the end by Hunter's mother, who, oddly, kind of reminded me of Ma. I didn't guess that she would be the means, but I was furious with her. I mean, why did she have to bring up Laine's past? There were hints of a child. Very intriguing. I couldn't wait until the next book.

"I've filled several pages, brother. I'll probably burn it someday."

"That's not a bad idea."

I kept my focus on my feet and the gravel path. "Are Reed and me a bad idea?" I wasn't even sure why I was asking. From all the signs, he wasn't waiting.

"You care about him?"

"Very much. He probably doesn't think so, but I felt like I could talk to him about anything. I was more myself around him than with any man I'd ever been with. Maybe I wasn't as open as he would have liked me to be, but I was me. Or at least all of me I could be at the time. That should count for something, right?"

Peter's breath played in the cold air. "I think so. And as weird as it is to think about you dating Reed, I think you deserve each other. He's a good guy, despite what I consider his recent failings."

My head popped up. "What are those?"

"He gave up way too quickly. You deserve better than that."

"Thanks, little brother." I nudged him. "I think if you hurry, you can still have *lunch* with your wife."

The red in his cheeks wasn't from the cold. But no one needed to tell him twice. He sprinted to his truck.

Maybe someday I would have a man run home for me. And maybe next time I would be ready for it.

CHAPTER FORTY-SIX

I KNEW I WOULD REGRET NOT GOING TO THE GROCERY STORE EARLIER, BUT life had been chaotic with Christmas shopping, signing contracts, attending to my blog, work, getting Cody through finals, the list could go on and on.

That's why I was shopping the Saturday before Christmas along with everyone else in Chicagoland. It didn't help that the weather forecasted ten inches of snow tomorrow. People were stocking up. They all knew ten inches could easily turn into twenty with lake effect snow. At least my Christmas shopping was done. I had done most of it online. I even had most of the presents wrapped.

It was our first Christmas as a family of two. We were starting our own traditions, like we planned to go to the movies Christmas Day instead of watching Neil's favorite holiday movie, *It's a Wonderful Life*, at home. Though we would still have Christmas Eve tea with Gelaire and, yes, Neil and his daughter, possibly baby mama too. We had to be parents to Cody, despite our feelings for each other, or should I say my feelings for Neil. Christmas Eve night we would eat dinner at my parents' before heading to mass. My Christmas wish was that Ma would make amends with Peter and Delanie so we could all be together. I wasn't holding my breath.

What I was doing was making my way through the maze of people in the store. I had to squeeze between two other shoppers to get to the oranges. I always made orange rolls for Christmas Eve dinner, and I needed the zest and juice from several oranges to make them just right.

While I was picking out the perfect citrus, I heard my name. The voice made my insides swish and my heart swell. My head popped up to see the man that belonged to the voice. He stood across from me near the apples.

This wasn't our grocery store; I was back to using the closest one to me, but he looked as good here as he had in *ours*. He was wearing a stocking cap and a tentative smile. It went well with his stubble and bright blue eyes.

"Sam, how are you?"

I swallowed down my heart. I held up my bag of oranges for some reason. I always did stupid things around him. "Busy, but good."

It was true. I wasn't completely healed, but I was on the road to recovery. I was inching my way through the dark; sometimes I even felt like I moved a few feet. "How are you?" I remembered to ask.

His tentative smile showed signs of smoldering. "Better now."

Another shopper was giving me the look and huffing like I needed to move on. She probably wanted oranges too.

I was torn. I wanted to stay right where I was and talk to Reed, but it wasn't the time. And for all I knew, he had moved on. I hadn't heard a peep from him in weeks. "I hope you have a Merry Christmas." I placed the bag full of oranges in my cart and moved out of the way.

"You too." He didn't follow me or say another word.

I don't know why I expected him to. Disappointment filled me, but there was nothing I could do about it in the middle of the crowded store. I would go home and vent to my journal, or maybe paint my bathroom. Home improvement projects were becoming my favorite form of therapy.

Ten minutes later, while deciding whether I should buy premade eggnog or make my own, all while trying to not think about Reed, my phone buzzed. I picked it up expecting a text from Cody to pick him up some type of snack he wanted—it was a regular occurrence.

It wasn't Cody.

Go to the greeting card aisle. Look in the For Her section.

Suddenly all the organs in my body reacted. My heart raced, my stomach felt like someone was using it for a slip and slide. I was shaking even though I was warm in my turtleneck sweater and jeans. Despite my out of control body, I hustled over to the greeting cards, looking for Reed as I went. Was he still here?

I looked at each sign detailing the different types of cards until I spotted *For Her.* There were a few people perusing cards. A couple were giggling to themselves as they read, in my way. This was no laughing matter to me. I needed to find my card.

I left my cart to one side and pushed my way between the two women. "I'm so sorry, excuse me."

I wasn't really that sorry, not even when their faces scrunched in that *wow, she's rude* sort of way. I was being totally rude, but if they knew what hung in the balance, they would surely understand. Not like I was taking the time to explain it to them. I was on a mission.

I scanned the cards. They had ones for birthdays, thinking of you, just because. Oh. There it was. A bright red envelope with my name on it in Reed's chicken scratch. I took several shallow breaths before I snatched it.

As soon as I opened the envelope and pulled out the card, everyone around me melted away. All that existed for me were my thoughts and the card in my shaking hand. I hardly bothered with the front, it said something about meeting under the mistletoe. I took that as a good sign. I would love to meet Reed under the kiss-inducing plant. But right now, I needed to know if he had a message for me. When I opened the card my heart soared. His scribble filled the whole left side.

1. I'm sorry.

2. I was a fool.

3. Please forgive me.

4. You look more beautiful than ever.

5. I want to kiss you.

6. Right now.

7. I'm going to have to head to the frozen food aisle, thinking about how much I want to kiss you.

8. I love you.

9. I'm going to need you to give me this card back so I can pay for it.

10. Did I mention I am in the frozen food aisle?

My eyes were so blurry after the *I love you,* I could hardly read the rest. I chased my heart to the frozen food section, not caring that I left my cart in the card aisle.

I wasn't exactly sure how I made it to the frozen food section or how many people I may have pushed out of the way, but before I knew it, I was there. He was there.

He was loitering with no cart, just waiting. Waiting for me. His grin said *come kiss me.* All right.

Holding his card, I met him halfway. Without thinking or caring who might see, I dropped the card, threw myself into his arms, and wrapped my arms around his neck. He leaned in and our lips collided. For a second he acted surprised and paused, but when I didn't pull away, he parted my lips. Yep, we were French kissing in front of the frozen French fries. My tingly spine was back, and he tasted better than I remembered.

We pulled apart when we heard a child comment to his dad, "Ooh gross, they're kissing." The dad wasn't too impressed with us either. "Grow up." He scowled on his way by.

Maybe not my finest moment, but I didn't care.

Reed ignored the grumpy man. He brushed my cheek with his hand. "You kissed me in public."

"I did."

"You know what that means?"

"I think we better talk to Cody."

"We?"

"We." I smiled.

"I like we."

"Me too. But, Reed," I took a deep breath, "I'm still broken. I don't know where this will go."

With his thumb, he caught the tear in the corner of my eye before it had a chance to fall. "Sam, I'm so sorry."

"What are you sorry for?"

"I asked you once if you wanted company on your journey. Somewhere along the way I forgot it was *your* journey. I got in a rush to make it to the finish line, so I ran when I should have been walking beside you. Showing you how a real man acts when he loves you. Instead, I acted like the boy I wanted you to forget."

Tears ran down my cheeks. "You know, thinking back, I liked that boy...when he wasn't booby trapping my room."

The back of his hand glided down my cheek. "That boy liked you, but not as much as the man in front of you loves you."

I swallowed hard. "I can't say that back right now, but I'm working on it." I had to be honest, even if it meant losing him.

"I don't expect you to. I'm not expecting anything from you."

"Are you sure? I don't want to hurt you."

"He sounds sure to me, lady." A gruff voice interrupted. "Do you think you could move out of the way?"

Reed and I turned toward the surly bald man who looked like he needed a cigar in his mouth and a gangster suit on.

"We're sorry." Reed pulled me to the side so the man could load up on fries.

The man gave us a half smile. "Mazel tov. Now go get a room or something."

I laughed and grinned up at Reed. "Does 'or something' work for you?"

"I'll take whatever you have to offer. But just know, someday I plan on signing that NDA."

CHAPTER FORTY-SEVEN

We were dashing through the snow, but in Reed's jeep, not a one-horse open sleigh. The weatherman was partially right—we got a foot of snow, but a day later than predicted. It did add something to the Christmas Eve holiday, but it made driving downtown a pain. Thankfully, Reed's jeep had four-wheel drive.

I turned back to talk to Cody, but took a moment to stare at him first. I thought back to a couple of days ago when I'd shown up at our house with Reed carrying in our groceries. Cody's brown eyes went from happy to see his coach to confused as to why he was at our house and why he'd walked in through our garage door. I think some terror showed up when Reed asked to speak to him. Maybe he thought he was in trouble at school. They sat down on the living room couch together. I sat on the coffee table so we were all close. Cody looked between Reed and me, not sure what to make of it.

I started off. "I know this has been a rough year for us and a lot of things have changed. But not all change is a bad thing." I smiled at Reed.

Reed took that as his cue. "Cody, I care about you and your mother."

Cody tilted his head.

Reed reached for my hand.

Cody's eyes bulged.

"I'd like your permission to date her."

I held my breath, waiting to see what my son would say.

Reed, on the other hand, took Cody's hand. Neil had never done that, at least not since Cody was small.

"Cody, I can only imagine how hard it might be to see your mom date, but I promise you, I'll take good care of her and you, if you'll let me."

Tears filled my eyes.

Cody looked down at his and Reed's hands. I could tell he thought it was weird, but his lip twitched, then a full-blown smiled appeared. "You guys aren't going to embarrass me, are you?"

"We might," Reed answered. "But we'll do our best to keep it to a minimum."

Cody nodded, but he gave Reed a I-mean-business-stare. "Don't hurt my mom."

"You have my word."

And that was that. They ended up playing video games while I made lunch. One of the best days ever.

I focused back on the here and now. It was a good thing to do. I smiled at my son sitting in the backseat. "You look sharp."

He flicked some lint off his black dress pants. "Do we have to stay long?"

"Define 'long.'"

"Ugh."

"I'm with you," Reed agreed with Cody.

For a brief second, I rested my hand on Reed's leg. I wasn't sure how much affection to show Reed in front of Cody yet. Cody had given his stamp of approval, and if I'd been reading him right the last couple of days, he liked the idea of Reed and me. But I still wanted to tread carefully. This was new for all of us.

"I didn't make you come," I said to Reed. Though I was happy he was. Gelaire was downright tickled I was bringing him to Christmas tea.

"You made me," Cody complained.

Reed chuckled before taking my hand. He couldn't hold it long because of the snow and slick roads, but if felt good all the same. He felt good. The last couple of days had been perfect. We spent the days playing board games with Cody and making and eating lots of food. Nights after Cody went to bed were spent wrapped up in his arms, sipping wine in front of my fireplace. We weren't just sipping wine, but whether we were or not, I was still tasting it and gasping. Lots of gasping.

Honestly, I worried less about having Reed with us at Gelaire's than I did at my parents'. I hadn't told them yet. I thought telling them in person would be better. My siblings all knew. Avery screamed in my ear over the phone over it. James roared like a cougar, teasing me because I was older than Reed. Our night was sure to be fun, or was it we were sure to be made fun of? I was going with both. Reed made everything fun. Even shoveling snow. He helped Cody and me clear our sidewalks and driveway this morning, but it turned into a snowball fight. It was good to see Cody smile and laugh through his frozen cheeks. We consumed a gallon of hot chocolate afterward.

Now here we were, getting ready to announce our coupledom to my ex and his family, my family. Well, Gelaire. Roxie would never be part of my family. Farrah I would have affection for because she was my son's sister. Though I wasn't ready to hold her. I was still mourning that she wasn't mine. And that was okay. I wasn't wallowing, just working through it; ask my journal.

We parked in front of Gelaire's Greystone. I was disappointed not to see Neil's car. Not because I wanted to see him, but for Cody's sake. He had been making an effort, and I'd hoped that would continue.

Reed came around and got my door while Cody headed in. Snow swirled in the air. The storm was heavier closer to the lake. He leaned in and pressed his lips hard against mine. "Are you ready for this?"

"I think so. Are you?"

"Oh, yeah. I've been waiting for this moment since I was fifteen and watched that loser marry you."

I kissed him. "Be nice."

"I plan on being very nice . . . to you."

"How nice?"

"So nice, I might make it on Santa's naughty list."

I pushed against his chest and giggled. "Stop it."

He brushed my lips. "For now."

I took a deep breath. "Let's do this."

He grabbed my hand and helped me out, taking the bag of gifts I had for Gelaire and the ones I made Cody buy for his dad and sister. On the way in, Reed shielded me with his coat, doing his best to keep the snow off me. Even with the frigid temperatures and flakes of white, I felt warm. Warmer and lighter than I had in a long while.

When we entered Gelaire's home, I was surprised to see Neil already there holding a baby wrapped in a pink fleece blanket in his arms. How did he get here? Cody stood near him, smiling at the precious bundle with blond wisps of hair.

My heart hiccupped, but then I looked between the two men who were in a serious showdown of stares. It struck me how different they were. Neil would have never agreed to come with me under the circumstances. He never shoveled the snow or had a snowball fight with his son. Reed always thought of others, and Neil, for most of our time together, thought of himself. Maybe the infant in his arms would change that; that would be good for him. But I was finding I didn't have to let how he behaved affect me. I had a choice, like Peter said. And I had to actively choose how to feel about each situation. Today, I was choosing to be happy with Reed by my side.

Gelaire came sweeping down her spiral staircase in a red velvet gown that screamed style and Christmas. Christmas in a castle, that is.

"Did we underdress?" Reed whispered in my ear.

I shook my head. I would explain later—this was just Gelaire.

"Love, you made it. I was worried with the weather."

I took Reed's free hand. "We had a good driver."

"Handsome too, I see."

I looked up into Reed's smiling eyes. "Yes, he is."

Gelaire approached and held out her hand. "Gelaire Higgins, mother-in-law to the sweet thing you hold."

Reed set down the bag of gifts and shook her hand. "It's a pleasure to meet you. Sam speaks highly of you."

Gelaire kissed my cheek. "Merry Christmas, love." She turned her sights to Cody. "Come kiss your grandmother."

Cody did his best to smile on his walk over. He had to lean down now to kiss her cheek.

"I do believe there are some gifts waiting for you under the tree. Shall we retire to the sitting room?"

I couldn't wait to see her tree. She never decorated it the same, but it was always worthy of a Christmas card or storefront window.

The awkward moment came when we realized we would have to converse with Neil. I took the lead.

"Neil, I don't know if you remember Reed. He was a friend of Peter's growing up. Now he's Cody's coach." I wanted to add in that he was mine too, but I figured that was obvious by the way he was glued to my side.

Neil continued to look him over with a raised eyebrow. Not only were they dissimilar in disposition, but in looks as well. Despite Neil's attempts to look younger, the over ten-year difference was apparent. Reed had a youthful glow and was lean and muscular. He was the kind of guy that if you saw him walking down the street, you would take a second, third, and fourth look. You might even track him down and get his number. Neil, on the other hand, was handsome in that professional stature sort of way. The hair plugs hadn't helped. I was happy to see him back in khakis and a button-up. It was much more him.

I appreciated Reed extending his hand. "It's nice to see you again," he lied. But it was a good lie. "Cody is a great kid and fantastic player. He's going to be my starting quarterback next year." Reed smiled at Cody.

Cody's face exploded with a burst of happiness. Reed just gave him— and me—the best gift ever. Nothing was better than seeing my son happy.

Neil shifted his daughter so that he could reciprocate, though it was obvious he didn't want to. His eyes were filled with contempt for Reed. "Cody is a great kid. I look forward to his games next year." He shook Reed's hand.

He better mean what he said and show up.

That exchange was pretty much how the afternoon went. Reed was pleasant and attentive to both Cody and me, even Gelaire. He cleared the dishes after tea, which was just a fancy name for lunch. He also helped pick up the torn wrapping paper. Neil attended to Farrah and watched. I hoped he was taking lengthy notes. I hoped Cody did too.

Reed was the kind of man I wanted Cody to be like when he grew up. That thought settled into my soul. And with that, some of the darkness dissipated. Some of the hold Neil still had on my heart vanished.

We had survived our first family event. Now, for dinner, we were on to the insane asylum...I mean, my parents'. Cody was more animated on our drive there, talking to Reed about the team and his plans for conditioning in the off season. Cody also liked my parents' place more because that meant Matt and Jimmy would be there, and he knew he would leave with a wad of cash from Mimsy. While he loved Gelaire, he left her house with cardigans and Shakespeare's full collection. Those were going to get a lot of use on his floor. At least Neil got him something he really wanted—the latest and greatest smartphone.

The roads were terrible. It was slow going, but I didn't mind one bit. I liked the cozy feel of the three of us in Reed's car. There was something right about it all. That lovely feeling all ended when we pulled up to my parents' place. It was now dark out, and the snow was tapering off. I loved snowflakes at night. On Christmas Eve, there was something magical about it. Or was it the man who was holding my hand?

"Cody," I stopped him before he hopped out. "Your grandparents don't know about Reed yet, so mum's the word until we get in there."

Cody's eyes lit up with mischief, just like someone else I knew when he was fifteen. "This is going to be fun." He exited, laughing.

Reed laughed too.

"That's not the word I would use," I grumbled.

"What word would you use?"

"Nothing my mother would approve of."

"Would she approve of this?" His warm lips landed on mine. They lingered for a bit before his tongue anxiously parted my lips, making me wish we could stay a little longer. My hands decided we should anyway and delighted themselves by running through Reed's hair. He groaned and kissed me deeper, only to pull away too soon.

He let out a deep breath of content. "We're not leaving if we keep doing that."

"Okay."

"Don't tempt me."

"Are you sure?" I grinned playfully.

"No, but I want your parents to approve of me, so we better go."

"If we must. Let me apologize right now for anything my family may say."

"I'm kind of looking forward to it."

"You know they're going to ask you if we're sleeping together."

He wagged his eyebrows. "How do you think they'll react when I tell them we've slept together twice now?"

My mouth dropped open. "That lie will cost you."

"I'm not lying. You've fallen asleep in my arms the last two nights."

And it had been amazing, but not as amazing as my parents would take it. "We should probably keep that to ourselves."

"Now we're back to sneaking around?" he teased.

"Only if you want me to keep falling asleep in your arms."

"My lips are sealed." He pretended to zip them up. "Repeat tonight?"

"If we survive dinner and mass, I'm all yours."

"I guess Santa finally got my letter."

"You asked Santa for me?"

"Every year." He pecked my lips.

The moment of truth arrived. We walked in hand in hand, holding a bag full of gifts that had tags from Samantha, Cody, and Reed, in addition to the oranges I needed to make my rolls.

Reed gave my hand a little squeeze before we headed back into the fire.

"Samantha Marie, is that you?" Ma called out.

"Yes, and Reed too."

We paused, waiting.

Ma walked out of the kitchen and stared down the hall to the foyer. She laser-focused on our clasped hands. "Joseph! Joseph! Come here." That urgent call had the whole family coming, minus Delanie and Peter. My heart ached, knowing they weren't here. But I didn't have time to dwell on it, being a target for the firing squad.

The entire motley crew stared at us. Some were shaking with laughter, aka James and Avery. Matt and Jimmy were looking at Cody to see what he thought about it.

Mimsy bounced on the balls of her feet shaking her head. "Adultery." She left, no doubt to get some water. I should have seen that one coming.

Ma edged closer, wiping her hands on her apron. "What do we have here, Samantha Marie?"

Dad followed behind her, waiting to see how she was going to react before he did.

I stepped forward with Reed, squeezing the life out of his hand. "Someone who makes me very happy."

Ma gave Reed an appraising look, her eyes narrowed, lips pursed together. She eventually nodded. "See that you keep it that way, Reed Cassidy."

"Yes, Mrs. D."

"I need help in the kitchen, Samantha Marie." She turned without another word.

"I'm coming." I stood on my tiptoes and kissed Reed's cheek. "I think that's what we call a Christmas miracle," I whispered.

It wasn't the only miracle of the night.

Reed and I sat behind my parents and Mimsy during mass. Their stares throughout dinner had become too much. I think they hardly ate for all their staring. And I needed to keep an eye on Mimsy. There was holy water in our presence, so there was no telling what she would do. Cody sat on the other side of Reed. I didn't mind. I was happy he was comfortable there. Avery, James, and their boys sat behind us.

While we listened to the organist play a beautiful rendition of *Adeste Fideles*, Delanie and Peter walked in to my surprise. We slid down our pew to make room for them. Ma turned around and locked eyes with her son, but she said nothing.

Peter sighed and took Delanie's hand. Delanie looked uncomfortable as she looked around at all the people and the ornamentally decorated church with stained-glass windows and low lighting. The only light source was the flickering candles on the old golden carved candle sticks. To me it was cozy and welcoming. But for Delanie, I swore I saw a hint of fear in her eyes. I wondered why. It was a question for another day.

I took Peter's free hand, emotion flooding me. "I'm so happy you came," I whispered.

Peter squeezed my hand before acknowledging Reed. "I'm glad to see you finally took my advice."

This was news to me. I leaned into Reed. "When did Peter talk to you?"

"A few days ago."

"And what did he say?"

Reed kissed my head and whispered in my ear, "That I was a jerk and James knows people who will dispose of dead bodies."

I laughed a little too loud.

"They're probably talking about sex," Mimsy said way too loud to Ma. "Have you seen his butt?"

Wow. Just wow.

Stares multiplied our way. I swore the organ quieted.

Ma whipped around. "Have you given him your NDA, Samantha Marie?"

If I could have slinked under the pew or vanished, I would have. Everyone was now looking at us. The organ music all but ceased. Cody actually did slide down and moved away from us. If only I could have.

Ma's eyes demanded an answer while Dad shook his head, probably wishing he drank more at dinner.

"No, Ma."

She huffed out a breath. "Keep it that way."

But as embarrassing as that all was, that's when the miracle happened. Ma turned to Delanie and Peter. "We're having dessert after. I made your favorite, cinnamon pie." It wasn't what most of us considered an apology, but it was the best we could hope for from Ma.

Peter rested his hand on Ma's. "We'll be there."

I caught the tears in Ma's eyes before she turned around.

"Forgiveness is an action," Peter whispered in my ear.

And Reed whispered in my other, "About that NDA."

EPILOGUE

Six Months Later

"WE'RE GOING TO BE LATE FOR OUR RESERVATIONS."

Reed pulled me into the grocery store. We looked too nice to be shopping—me in my little black number and him in his black suit and tie. He looked divine. That new CrossFit regimen he and Cody were doing together this summer was really paying off. I was reaping the rewards.

"I promise we won't be late."

"The dinner cruise leaves at 7:00," I reminded him.

Reed looked at his watch. "We have plenty of time. I'll drive fast."

We hustled in out of the warm summer evening.

"This humidity is going to ruin my hair."

He stopped to tug on one of my curls. "You look gorgeous."

"You always say that."

"I mean it every time." He pulled on my hand. "We need to hurry."

"Okay."

His behavior was puzzling. He'd been acting nervous ever since he picked me up and had some secret conversation with Cody while I finished getting ready. I thought maybe he was giving Cody the talk about what it means to be a responsible man before Cody's date with Tia—we had moved on from Rory—but Reed's leg bounced the whole drive over. And he changed the radio station ten times in the five-minute drive, making me think it might be something else. I prayed it wasn't the kind

281

of news that was going to ruin my night, like *surprise, honey, you're going to be a grandma.* Reed would have told me that already, right?

"Did Cody say anything to you?" Now I was nervous.

He grinned. "He's not having sex, if that's what you're worried about." He knew me so well.

I kissed him. "Oh, thank goodness."

He went back to pulling me along.

"What did you say you needed again?"

"I didn't." He smiled back at me.

"You don't need to get snacks. They have appetizers and drinks available when we board." He and Cody were obsessed with snacks.

"I'm not getting snacks." He laughed, picking up his pace once we entered the store.

"These heels aren't made for running."

He slowed his pace. Barely. "Sorry."

When we hit the produce section I stopped. "Do you hear that?"

He came to a halt. "Hear what?"

"The music. Do they normally play music?" I didn't remember that being a thing.

A devilish grin appeared on his angelic kiss-me face. "I've never noticed."

I listened harder. "Is that "(Everything I Do) I Do It For You?" It was my favorite Bryan Adams' song ever from one of my favorite movies, *Robin Hood: Prince of Thieves.*

Reed looked up to the ceiling like that would help him hear better. "What are the odds that they're playing your favorite song?"

That was odd. "We need to watch the movie again."

He rolled his eyes. "I've seen that movie more than I ever wanted to and discussed Kevin Costner's butt more than any man should."

"We don't know if that was his butt." That was the great debate back in the nineties. Did Kevin Costner use a body double, or was it him?

"We could google it," Reed suggested.

"No."

He laughed at me. "I know, it would ruin the movie for you if you found out he used a double."

"It really would."

"Can we move on now, honey, or talk about my butt instead? Or better yet, yours?" He gave my backside a glance. "It looks good tonight, by the way."

I smacked his arm. "Let's go get whatever it is that's so important to you to make us miss our dinner cruise."

"This is important to you, too." He practically pulled my arm off, dragging me across the store.

"If you say so."

"I do."

Before I knew it, we were standing in front of the card aisle. "Did I miss someone's birthday? I thought you said your mom's was next month."

"You didn't miss anyone's birthday." His eyes were dancing.

"Sooo...what are we doing?"

"You forgot something."

I tilted my head. "I did?"

"Right there." He pointed to a hot pink envelope with my name on it, smack dab in the middle of the card section.

"What are you up to you?" I yanked on his tie, pulling him in for a kiss.

"Hopefully more of that. Go get your card."

He didn't need to tell me twice. This time I pulled him along. I only let go of his hand to pluck my card out. I carefully opened it and pulled out the sparkly card.

The outside read, *If I Haven't Told You Lately*... I opened it up, smiling to myself. The inside was also filled with sparkly gold letters that read, *I Love You*. As much as I loved when he said those three huge words—and loved saying them in return, because I loved him with a love that I didn't know was possible—I was anxious to see what he had to say. In Reed fashion, there was his numbered list of ten.

1. Everything

2. I

3. Do

4. I

5. *Do*

6. *It*

7. *For*

8. *You*

9. *I love you.*

10. *Look down.*

I dropped the card and looked down to see Reed on one knee, ring box in hand. My hand covered my mouth. Happy tears popped up in my eyes.

"Samantha Decker, I love you and Cody. I want to be wherever you both are, whether it's on the sidelines or on the field. You just tell me, and I'll follow you wherever you want to go." He opened the small black velvet box to reveal a stunning, round-cut diamond solitaire ring. "Marry me?"

Happiness filled me to the point I couldn't speak. I nodded and nodded some more. "Yes! Yes! Yes!"

He slid the ring on my finger before standing and wrapping me up in his arms. "You just made me the happiest man in this grocery store."

I laughed into his chest. "I love you."

He pressed a kiss to the side of my head. "I love you more."

I believed him.

I know you've been eagerly awaiting my list of "must haves" for my next husband. Well, I finally know exactly what I want. Here's my list in no particular order:

1. Spine-tingling kisses. (Okay, this is pretty top of the list for me.)

2. Knows how to put the toilet seat down and does. Every time.

3. Younger than me.

4. He must love my son like his own. No exceptions.

5. He absolutely must love Autumn Moone books and be willing to read them to me out loud.

6. Sense of humor is a necessity. He'll need it to survive my family.

7. An outdoor enthusiast is a plus, especially if he loves long bike rides.

8. His thighs must be bigger than mine. I can't handle that kind of pressure.

9. *He must sign all my legal documentation, see much earlier post about NDAs.*

10. *Last, but certainly not least, he must love me. And not just any kind of love. But the kind of love that needs no words. The kind that comes from acting.*

I should probably mention I've been lucky to find a man that meets all the requirements and more. You might be asking yourself, "Is she getting back into the game?" The answer is, no. I found a man that loves the sidelines. So I'll still be the Sidelined Wife, but I'll be more than a wife. I'll be a partner. If you have the chance to find one, hold on tight. Life is better on the sidelines with someone who's willing to walk beside you every step of the way.

Yours Truly,

The Sidelined Wife in Chief

P.S. Look for my new cookbook, Glorified Cookie Recipes and More, *in a store near you or online.*

THE SECRETIVE WIFE

More Than a Wife Series: Book Two

I have big news for you.

You're pregnant?

I sighed, holding back the tears. That put a damper on the actual surprise. *I wouldn't tell you that in a text.*

My phone immediately rang.

"I'm sorry. I know that. What's your news?"

"Now I feel like I'm going to disappoint you."

"I'm sorry, Delanie. Tell me, please?"

I stared at my large monitor. That monitor and I spent a lot of time together. Sometimes it was my only connection to the outside world when I was under a deadline. We had a love-hate relationship for that reason. But there on the large screen, my name—or should I say, my other name—and latest book cover sat near the number one spot on the *New York Times* Best Seller list in the eBook and paperback category. It wasn't the first time, but it never got old seeing my baby there.

"*Black Day Dawning* hit number one." I couldn't say it without smiling.

"I'm so proud of you, Autumn Moone." Only he could call me that.

I tensed. "I hope you're not around anyone."

"I'm in the truck all by myself."

"You could come home for lunch." Our private lunch hours were my favorite.

He groaned. "I want to more than anything, but we have to finish up the Finley job before tomorrow. They're having a huge summer bash this weekend. But how about I take you to dinner tonight to celebrate?"

"I'd like that."

"Think of where you want to go, and I'll be home as soon as I can."

"Hurry."

"Delanie?"

"Yes."

"I'm sorry about earlier. You know I love you more than anything, and whether we have a baby or not isn't going to change that."

I sighed. "I know."

"I'll see you soon."

I leaned back in my office chair and stretched my neck. I loved this space, and the man that built it for me. My secret hiding place. When we had the house built, Peter insisted that he finish the attic for me. There was no one more thoughtful than him. I only had to look at every aspect of my office, from the countertops that lined one side of the room, lending me a huge desk. I loved that I could spread out on it when I researched each project and book. The built-in shelves were filled with not only the books I'd written, but the books I loved, like *To Kill a Mockingbird*, or *Jane Eyre*. The most thoughtful items were all the framed posters of each one of my books that hit the *New York Times* Best Seller list. He would get an actual copy of the paper, blow it up, and frame it. There were five on the wall now. Soon, I knew there would be six.

I swiveled in my chair, stopping to run my fingers across my old, red manual typewriter. I thought my parents were so weird when they gave that to me for my tenth birthday. My parents were weird, or at least different than most. When Cat and Ron—my parents, who insisted on being called by their first names (long story)—presented me with the typewriter instead of the computer I asked for, they changed my life, though I thought they had ruined it. I wrote my first novel with it when I was twelve. *If I Lived on the Moon*. It inspired my pen name and the moon tattoo hidden where only Peter could see it.

I also wrote the book that launched my career on the old thing. I missed the sound of the keys and the typebars making contact with the ribbon and paper. I never intended to write romance, but I found I had a penchant for it. I blamed it on the built up sexual tension from being in love with a man I thought could never be mine. A priest.

I never wanted anything or anyone more in my life. Hunter Black came to life because of it all. Every one of Peter's qualities were poured into him. Laine, his true love that he could never have, was me. I cried into the typewriter many a night, trying to purge myself of Peter. It didn't work; if anything, I wanted him more.

I was supposed to be writing gritty, raw, real-life pieces that changed lives. Instead, I was fueling fantasies, mine the most. Now that I was living out my fantasy with my priest, it didn't make me feel so guilty.

... That wasn't as awful as it sounded.

ABOUT THE AUTHOR

JENNIFER PEEL IS THE AWARD-WINNING, BESTSELLING AUTHOR OF THE Dating by Design and Women of Merryton series, as well as several other contemporary romances. Though she lives and breathes writing, her first love is her family. She is the mother of three amazing kiddos and has recently added the title of mother-in-law, with the addition of two terrific sons-in-law. She's been married to her best friend and partner in crime for a lot longer than seems possible. Some of her favorite things are late-night talks, beach vacations, the mountains, pink bubble gum ice cream, tours of model homes, and Southern living. She can frequently be found with her laptop on, fingers typing away, indulging in chocolate milk, and writing out the stories that are constantly swirling through her head. To learn more about Jennifer and her books, visit her website at www.jenniferpeel.com.

If you enjoyed this book, please rate and review it on
Amazon & Goodreads

You can also connect with Jennifer on
Facebook & Twitter (@jpeel_author)

Other books by Jennifer Peel:
Other Side of the Wall
The Girl in Seat 24B
Professional Boundaries
House Divided
Trouble in Loveland
More Trouble in Loveland
How to Get Over Your Ex in Ninety Days
Paige's Turn
Hit and Run Love: A Magnolia and Moonshine Novella
Sweet Regrets
Honeymoon for One in Christmas Falls

The Women of Merryton Series:
Jessie Belle — Book One
Taylor Lynne — Book Two
Rachel Laine — Book Three
Cheyenne — Book Four

The Dating by Design Series:
His Personal Relationship Manager — Book One
Statistically Improbable — Book Two
Narcissistic Tendencies —Book Three (Coming Soon)

The Piano and Promises Series:
Christopher and Jaime—Book One
Beck and Call—Book Two
Cole and Jillian—Book Three

More Than a Wife Series
The Sidelined Wife — Book One
The Secretive Wife — Book Two (Coming Soon)
The Dear Wife — Book Three (Coming Soon)

Made in the USA
Coppell, TX
18 November 2020